STEPHEN FLORIDA

STEPHEN FLORIDA

Gabe Habash

THE BOROUGH PRESS

The Borough Press
An imprint of HarperCollins*Publishers*
1 London Bridge Street
London SE1 9GF
www.harpercollins.co.uk

Published by HarperCollins*Publishers* 2017
1

A catalogue record for this book
is available from the British Library

ISBN HB: 978-0-00-826509-0
ISBN TPB: 978-0-00-826510-6

Set in Adobe Jensen Pro by Palimpsest Book Production Limited,
Falkirk, Stirlingshire

Printed and bound in Great Britain by
CPI Group (UK) Ltd, Croydon, CR0 4YY

MIX
Paper from
responsible sources
FSC C007454

This book is produced from independently certified FSC™ paper
to ensure responsible forest management.

For more information visit: www.harpercollins.co.uk/green

To Julie

The mind is the limit.

—ARNOLD SCHWARZENEGGER

STEPHEN FLORIDA

MY MOTHER HAD TWO PLACENTAS and I was living off both of them. I was supposed to have a twin. When the doctor yanked me out, he said, "There's a good chance this child will be quite strong." This is the story my parents always told me, but I never really believed it.

In a moment, after I refasten the Velcro over my laces, I will stand up out of this folding chair. I will square my bulge in my singlet and good-luck tug each shoulder strap. And after I've counted the spectators in the bleachers (seventeen), I will ask Coach Hargraves to box my headgear. He will oblige. Then I will walk onto the maroon mat, enter the white circle, shake this Poor Richard's hand, and when the referee lets me go, I will come after him with everything I have. Noise. And in the second it takes for me to hold the pin, I will hear something snap in his arm. This is like breathing.

You haven't spent any time in North Dakota, but if you had, you'd know this time of year is useful for airing out your head. I will use three minutes outside in the parking lot to stand by a snow clump, watching for birds and settling down, thinking how it's finally November and the season won't be over until March, thinking about my weak, sweaty good-bye to the whole thing before it gets sucked inside me for good.

I once read about the idea of internal age in my Teams & Group Dynamics class. I got a C+ in that. Imagine: there's a tight little peach-pit core inside you with a number carved into it, and that number is the age of your best self. Most of the time people whine about not being at or being past their internal age. Not me. I'm in my golden age.

I believe in wrestling, and I believe in the United States of America.

I am a motherfucking astronaut.

MY NAME IS STEPHEN FLORIDA and I'm going to win the Division IV NCAA Championship in the 133 weight class.

That's it. Do you believe me when I say I think about it every day, every hour, at least twenty times an hour? That there isn't much in the way of detail? I'm telling the truth. I can lie, but I wouldn't lie about this. When you want something bad enough to starve for it, it's not clear what it'll look like until it finally happens. I know that there's a white pedestal with eight steps and that you pose for the photographers with your wooden trophy, which is the exact same size as a nice desk clock. This happens in a place called Kenosha Arena in Kenosha, Wisconsin, where there are six mats of all different colors and the seats are blue and all two thousand are filled up with people. Below the arena is a basement with old lights and enough space for each of the wrestlers, winners and losers, to find his own shadowy corner to cry in because he's happy or because his season's over. It's where everyone goes when it's over. It's tradition. But that's not for a while, and I'm not there yet.

Can you believe I used to share this with people when I was a dumb freshman and thought I'd pull the sword right from the stone? Now I keep things to myself. I edit and develop in my own mind. If someone wanted to know about it, I figure they'd ask, but I have a shaved head and a face that appears mean in repose and I'm quick to anger, which is something I got from my dad, which helps me out in wrestling but not in interpersonal communications. I took a class on that, too.

I don't get ahead of myself now. It's something I've been working on. But I still think about the arena, the mats, the pedestal. I can't help it. I have ecstatic visions of climbing down into the basement. I think about them when I'm riding in the team van, when I fold my laundry, when I tear off my scabs, when I take a shit, when I'm sitting through a lecture in an overheated classroom, pretending I'm looking down at my textbook, but really have my eyes closed in a low-level doze of distant concentration.

I'm thinking about them right now. One day, everyone will know who I am.

Why, if I pull this off, they could tell my story in the *New York Times*!

Whenever I'm not thinking about them, I think about how to get them. Ideas are just neurons in your brain squirting chemicals at other neurons. Do you have dreams of arm bars and front headlocks? The special squeaks and thumps heard in practice, which is the sound of your own flesh's wet exertion? Have you looked for a long moment at a splotch of sweat on the mat and decided to lick it up, only because it came from inside you? Do you practice your stances, hobbling around like a Quasimodo by yourself, until your knees lock up? Do you think of hair as a vanity? Do you fucking distract yourself with a five-hundred-page *Barron's SAT Vocabulary* book, guaranteed to boost your Verbal score one hundred points on test day?

But, as I said, it's important not to get ahead of oneself, and so I grip down on my bench in the locker room and screw my eyes to my surroundings, because life is only the present. The red lockers and the two dozen guys in here, the coaches standing around with their arms folded, that's the present. The red walls, the bench sticking to my skin, that's the present. The fifty years of dead and alive men that have been in this locker room, they're the past. They each had a moment to matter, but they don't anymore. What matters is that smell of a bunch of derma oxidizing, that smell like a line of wet aluminum bleachers, that's also the present.

"Stephen gets an extra piece of chicken at dinner for breaking that kid's arm."

Coach Hargraves is a nice man but I don't listen to him. The year my coach told me to "envision the perfect match, and then strive to materialize it," I lost more matches than any other year. Now I conserve the energy I'd use listening, save it for myself, while in front of me Hargraves's glottal hum hits around my ears and my brain skitters down. Simpleminded thoughts stand up in my head, like flowers, like individual top-heavy sunflowers that bow and slump over when they can no longer take the weight. Next to Hargraves are the assistants. Eerik, Fink, Whiting, Farrow, and Lee. I don't really distinguish between them until one occasionally separates from the others. They stand in a line in their white shirts with the little red George Washington head on their breasts, "Presidents Assistant Coach." Can anyone imagine them going home to their children? Having private hopes? Crying at classical music? I can't.

"Florida?"

"Mm?"

"I just said, any words of encouragement? For the young guys?"

I shake my head, shrug, keep shaking my head.

On the big chalkboard, Coach made us all write our classes down. I don't know why. One of the coaches, I don't know which one, gave us all cassette tapes with mood sounds we're meant to listen to in our sleep. They all keep talking about "community accountability," which is the theory that you are more likely to be true to yourself and reach higher if you don't want to let your herd down (animal comparisons are often made around here). This is to scare wrestlers into not being the weak link, but I'm not the weak link, I'm not a part of the herd at all, I look out for myself and that takes all my effort and all my time. Inside the locker next to mine (now Ellis's), it says in very old writing *Who wants to see my pentis.* The locker four down once belonged to Mycah something, we only had one year overlap, and the whole time, he was about to quit because he couldn't bear his mat herpes. They badgered and guilted him into staying. The locker two down (now Sherman's) was Flores's last year and for the three years before, the whole span during which he kept growing, a Mexican farmboy from Illinois who kept growing and measuring his height in rising marker lines on the inside of his locker. He went from 133 to 157 during his time at Oregsburg. I haven't heard from him since May. No one has. Flores, who had small feet and bad teeth and apologized beforehand for his halitosis, who gave ojo to at least three of his teachers, who went back to Illinois and just got swallowed up forever.

Quietly, something is being passed around the room.

There's a problem where I always want to put my fingers in my mouth, especially if I have to sit still in one place. Rolling the ridges of your knuckles over your slightly parted jaws is a sensory pleasure you can get anytime you like. It's good sometimes to have your face against something harder than itself. That way you're never surprised by how hard contact is. If you believe the universe is a place of hitting, where one thing collides with another, the pattern repeating all over, your arms turn to cradles and you begin to want something to root you to your senses. I'm not saying it always has to be violent. My grandma had a tabby cat named Poker she found as a stray, and he liked getting in my lap and I was always giving him the ear pets he liked.

"We're going to Miles City in just three days," Hargraves says.

Miles City is a place of buildings and people. It's in Montana. There will be a quad where I have to wrestle three times in four hours. It helps to tell yourself these basic things because it establishes a mind-set for completing them. The fastest pin in history is nine seconds. I rub the divots of old scars on my forehead, the place between my eyes where I felt a tiny painful pebble under my skin two years ago and was afraid I had a very problematic neurological growth, a tumor or stroke pebble that would kill me before I had a chance to get to Kenosha. I went to the student health center to prevent a tragedy and when I expressed my situation, I was told it was a pimple.

Linus drapes a towel over his head. He rolls a lacrosse ball around under his left foot for his plantar fasciitis, which he got in high school from cross-country and bad shoes, which everyone knows never fully goes away. He won his match today. He's thinking about going home to read. To read! I'm thinking about that one field east of Dickinson on the way to Miles City where you see a red-winged blackbird on each and every post.

Fink or Farrow adds something to what Hargraves just finished saying.

Coach Whiting notices the object being passed by the wrestlers but pretends not to. Some of them are looking at it for longer than others. It's coming around the room toward me.

It's very difficult not to think about the banana sitting in my locker behind me! I need something for my mouth. I promise myself the banana later. I've never made a promise I didn't keep, I've made the promise to myself and to my grandma to win my championship. Up in an armpit of the United States, where no one can see me, I change shapes and become something slobbering and furious in order to get what I want.

I've been jogging my leg this whole fucking time. I sit still to end the attention I'm drawing.

I live in the luckiest place on earth. The papers have called it that. It's true. The only thing that's expected of me is the only thing I want to do. That is called luck. Luck is to own a thicker meaning of existence, a place inside you shelled off from flabby friends and exhaustion without purpose: I'm on a one-lane road in a thick metaphorical forest with no distractions. Everything I do is intentional. To arrive at the end of the road is to know Glory in the biblical sense, to put your paternity in Glory. I walk around, putting my paternity on things. I haven't studied much on the saints, but it sounds exactly like what their lives were like. At the end of his good works St. Bartholomew was misunderstood and skinned alive. Up to the present they've hung on to bits of his bones and skin in basilicas, and his arm is in a cathedral. With all of the saints, you see their cartoons smudged on papyrus with all kinds of bright colors shooting out of nowhere around them, and sometimes I believe that if you look hard enough, you can see those colors in the real world.

I don't have any secrets. I'm not hiding anything. My parents both died in a car crash when I was fourteen, and I went to live with my grandma. She died of heart disease. I told her when she was dying that I was going to Oregsburg, that I was going to wrestle, and she put all her money with my parents' policy, and Rudy Unger, the estate lawyer my parents set me up with, holds on to it and tells me what to do with it.

The note's at Sherman now. He glances at it, then passes it to Ucher.

My grandma didn't care much about wrestling, but she knew

what it meant to me and so it made her happy. I told her I was going to break off a piece of my championship trophy and bury it next to her. By the end, she was barely giving a shit about any goddamn thing, but she was a good Christian and could appreciate the Old Testament ceremony of it, so I guess it made her happy.

And if we're on the topic of confessions, I might as well: I have been here three years and failed. I don't like to use the words "last chance," but I'm not delusional. This is my last chance to do what I promised. It's been so long since I've felt it that I've forgotten what choice feels like. There are scientists in the polar circles and missionaries in Micronesia, these people choose to be put in foreign, forgotten places for science or God service, and they can lean over the rim of renounced free will, they kneel down in the church and say, "I'm ready to hear about what God has in mind for me!" and get the water sprinkled on their heads. I am in North Dakota, in a town called Aiken, which you have never heard of, and I am only here for myself. Even an idiot knows you can't accomplish anything meaningful without the possibility of failure. My three-year failure will be totally forgotten in the face of a fourth-year success, which is always, always what gets remembered.

Ucher hands it to me. I cross my legs and look down at it in the hidden bowl of my lap. It's a white napkin that says in black ink: *Something needs to be done about Louise.* I don't pass it on, which would be to Linus, I crumple it up and drop it on the floor, under the bench.

Choice is a perfect gift, and in modern times more people have it. They teach you all that shit in class. Because there are more options nowadays, someone can *walk away* from what troubles them. But not me. I'm locked into myself, I'm locked into my five months, I've been locked in, waiting for them my whole life. I want the trouble. It's what I promised. I promised my grandma. I wouldn't wish this on anyone nor would I want anything different.

Hargraves says, "Kill the head and the body will die."

THEY CALL ME and Linus faggots jokingly to our faces and less jokingly behind our backs. They call us that because we skip out early from the chicken dinner (each wrestler takes a single chicken breast—Fat Henry gets two—some vegetables, yogurt, an apple, and maximum twenty ounces of water), which is prepared for the team by Eerik's wife and Lee's wife, two coaches' wives who like to cook our primitive meals for us together, but they don't call those nice ladies faggots. Faggots don't give birth to quarter-Arikara children in Eerik's case, white children in Lee's, cook for their husbands' team and feel good about it in their straight hearts. Only the two best wrestlers on the team, which we are, get called faggots.

I leave after eating, quickly, because I really hate eating in front of other people. I'd rather be alone, and being with Linus is the same as being alone but also a fix for loneliness, a positive solitude. Linus leaves with me because he's my friend.

Linus is five four with thin eyebrows and acne. I met him when he was trying to take the 125 spot from Slim John Carpenter, which he did, quite quickly. A lot of times you see young guys come in and not really work too hard, not really know what it takes to get what you want—they don't realize it until later, or not at all. Not Linus. He took 125 from Carpenter, rolled him over, cradled him in the first week of practice. He's a freshman, the only weight class smaller than me, the only person on the team where being with him makes me forget to wonder what being lifeless would be like. He knew what he wanted as soon as he came through the door, and rapidly made them all look lazy. I tell him he's too wise for his own good. I tease him for his vanity because he gets his ears drained by Fink after his matches, something he insists on despite the fact his nose is bent to the right from a bike accident. "Everyone loves my face *and* my personality," he brags. He has a room down the hall, but he likes to sit in the chair in mine, leaning back on two legs and squeaking it, just to make himself feel less homesick.

On the main path, he walks backwards next to me and whistles, unmindful of the ice patches. He's too young to be afraid of getting hurt, there's a flock of hummingbirds in his head. "I forgot what ice cream tastes like," he says. Linus pinches his fingers in front of his lips, pretends to inhale, and blows the breath out like smoke.

I don't really miss anything anymore, but I know he's like everyone else and falls for life's left-behinds. Everyone's unfortunately born with a memory. But this is what I tell him if I sense he's sick over it: if you turn your thoughts over to the nothingness of what's here, nothing land, nothing people, nothing houses, nothing lakes, nothing cold in nothing bones, you can squeeze your happiness to a pinpoint—you are here to wrestle other men like your oldest enemies, leave them damaged or worse on the mat, until you're by yourself. I'm not one for bringing up memories. Whatever part of the brain that's in charge of memories, it's probably somewhat retarded in mine. Yet if you pay attention to the simplicity of your ritual, like stooped men praying in lightless pagan hovels, you can live without your memory. It's surplus.

I'll tell you what else I know: that the buildings of Oregsburg are nothing but shadows in the week after daylight savings, but I can find mine by scent and pattern, like a dog. That the Frogman, who has straight antlers and is silently giggling at me, is behind one of the walls. That Linus is walking faster because he wants to get back to *The Shining*. (He gets mad at me when I rub my dick on his books. It's only through the pants, anyway.) That there's absolutely no noise at eight o'clock at night, no one outside walking, and it creates the illusion that you're alone. That it feels good to be close to your building, to know that your bed is inside and you will sleep in it soon, before you wake up tomorrow and follow a schedule more rigid than what most people can put up with, but that most of all, approaching your bed is a pacifier-level comfort because you don't know what would happen if you had your purpose taken away from you.

I guess I should describe myself.

No, I don't want to do that. But in the interest of keeping any potential listener on my side, I suppose I can share something personal. It's that my name isn't really what everyone thinks it is. In the third week of my senior year in high school, when I was living in Hillsboro with my grandma, I sat down at my lab table for first-period physics, the study of the world's rulebook. It was a Tuesday. Mrs. Cosgrove came into the classroom and handed me an envelope with a red seal in the upper-left corner that said OREGSBURG COLLEGE. I thought I'd heard of the place, though maybe I'm making that up now. On the outside, it said my real name but on the inside, in the letter from Coach Hargraves, it was addressed to Stephen Florida. It was an invitation to come wrestle for them, on a full ride. But because Division IV is forbidden to give athletic scholarships, they'd combined a favorable need-based financial package (all grant, no loan) with the Harriet Howard Leadership Scholarship. I got that because of "exceptional displays of leadership and commitment, and the capacity for setting a model example for peers at Hillsboro High School." When someone puffs you up with this kind of language, you believe it. It was written on a piece of good paper that's now in a box in my closet. According to this official stationery, the only requirement for the scholarship was that I "give a presentation on an unspecified topic in March of the graduating year." It was the only real college offer I got. Before the letter was handed to me, I was looking at a few community colleges nearby. My grandma was sick at the time, otherwise I would've gone right away to meet Coach Hargraves and to see the school. I don't mean to give the impression that I was making up my mind. I knew right then I had my chance and I was going to take it. On a Monday in September, I didn't know what I'd do after high school. On Tuesday, just like that, I had a piece of paper promising me four more years of wrestling. I called them during my third-period break and they sent me the application materials. It happened very quickly. They said things like they could make my SAT score work, that everything was taken care of, and they were still calling me Stephen Florida. Grandma, who promised she was in very little suffering and indeed possessed an air of total resignment as the clock wound down, reading and rereading the first chapter of Thomas Mann's *The Magic Mountain*, died at the end of November with the book in her lap and took all the white lights with her.

I got the acceptance letter in the first week of December and that weekend took the Greyhound three hours west on ND-200 to Aiken, a town even smaller than Hillsboro. I met Coach Hargraves. He shook my hand and said, "This is Stephen Florida. The man who's going to help build Oregsburg wrestling." I liked the sound of that, it made me feel good. He called me "a corner brick." He was an old coach but this was a new school for him, and the program itself was just starting back up after being cut because of Title IX years ago. I didn't think much about how or why they found me. I didn't care. He dropped me off at the admissions department, where I got signed up for my classes way in advance. It was there, in the admissions office, that I figured out why my name had changed. Behind the desk, there was a nice old lady holding a piece of paper two inches from her nose. Her name was Ms. Rutledge, and when she lowered the paper she looked brittle enough to be broken by anyone older than twelve and she had, no kidding, the thickest glasses I have ever seen. They extended from her face like telescopes. They were foggy and yellow. What happened, I knew, was a letter of interest was to be sent to Steven Forster at Hillsboro High School. This woman, Ms. Rutledge, had misread my name. "Hello, young man," she said. "How can I help you?" I signed it, I signed it all *Stephen Florida.*

What did I have to wait around for? Nothing. I got to Oregsburg as soon as I could, on the bus the day after graduation. It was June. There was no one there. In my new room in McCloskey Hall, the one I'd have for all four years, I unpacked my clothes and put my nice shirts on hangers. I wanted to get started. I put on sweats and ran outside. It was not as hot as I'd wanted it to be, maybe upper seventies, but it was so bright, light shining off everything, that I had to squint to run. I passed a Christmas tree patch, the trees so small they looked like large broccoli. A few cars went by. I was running on roads I'd never seen before, everything was strange to me. I was sweating through my clothes on new roads and looking up with my eyes shut. I felt like I'd come somewhere that had no one else in it, or no one else had really been there before me, but more than that, I'd picked it. It was my choice, it was intentional. I stopped running, miles from school and in a place I didn't recognize but was somehow familiar, like a distorted vision of the past, fields in every direction. One tiny red crop duster was buzzing over a field, and then another very far in the distance. In one of the fields off the road, I saw a tremendous metal arm hundreds of feet long spraying water over acres of corn. It seemed like a process of the ice age. Hundreds more center pivots were all over, spaced far apart, churning all around, and standing still I could sense the movement on all sides, and though I have never been in an airplane I knew that when you flew over and looked down, there were massive green circles all over the earth. I began to love Oregsburg very early.

I took three years of my life and sacrificed them like pretty virgins thrown in a volcano. And I don't want to lie, so I won't say I didn't expect to have a championship by now. It was never going to be easy. That's something you pigheadedly learn in hindsight. I pigheadedly wrestled and wrestled, playing wiggledick for three years, during which time I finally figured out that the trophy was never going to be handed to me because I *deserved* it, during which time I was often so tired I wanted to throw up, so unhappy I wanted to throw up. But I guess all along I've been waiting to see what happens in my fourth year, the very last year of my life, which feels long and formidable like a pregnancy or a North Pole trip, and because it's so long, parts of it I spend clipping my toenails on my bed while Linus reads Stephen King in my desk chair. Parts of it I dwell on what it'd be like if people from the sticks of North Dakota descended on the places where I wrestle, the poorly ventilated heat boxes that mostly smell like cleaning spray and concrete, if even a few of them knew who I was by sight and waited for my match, if a widow who nevertheless still had the zest of life saw me from behind and said, "Hey, it's Stephen, look at that tight butt," or maybe children shouting for a memento, and I'd toss my headgear to one and I'd hand my shoes to a little girl, who'd try them on and smile because they'd still be sweaty. I could give intimate souvenirs to fans after every match.

"I'd like to go to Maine," Linus says. "Small towns creep me out."

None of this will ever happen. There's no money for extra headgear and shoes, this is all a flight of fancy. There are no children looking for heroes in tiny gyms, no horndog housewives. I keep my bullshit to myself, and I always try not to believe other bullshit.

On the side of the big toe is a blister I clip open and fluid comes out of it that smells. I tell myself that I'm not a goddamn coward.

"Man," Linus says. "You are really going to town on those nails."

Five months, a winter, can be an oppressive and long thing to people other than just the drinkers. You can look out the window, miles and miles of land designed to demonstrate emptiness, pump sites, mud, rigs covered in rust, fields where durum and flax and canola used to be. A hole of a well: that's what winter looks like. Food processors, water haulers, and rich roughnecks driving their cars through it and walking and sleeping in houses in it, and every time you look out the window, it's pressed right up against the glass like a goblin waiting for you to notice so it has permission to leap in your face.

"What's that smell?" Linus says. Without looking up from the book, he lifts his leg, releases a trumpetous fart, and laughs a little.

Here's what I regret: that I didn't win every time I wrestled, that too many losses have already happened, that I didn't pledge to wrestling earlier in life, that I'll never know how much better and faster I could have been, that I never had any brothers or sisters, that I won't ever be as strong going right as I am going left, that I wasted so much time wrestling not to lose, that I was too eager and fell right into Derrick Ebersole's duck, that at regionals

I shouldn't have tried to grab Chris Gomez's right ankle and I let him out and I couldn't get him back down and that was it, that my grandma had the stroke, that I couldn't do better on my SAT, that I've forgotten sometimes how to be mean, that I couldn't hold the near-side bar, that I don't remember what my grandpa looked like without the help of a picture, that years ago the ice was where it was and the road curved where it did and the other car was where it was and that the other driver had to go, too, and also that I sent that kid to the hospital by himself, that his parents hadn't ridden in the back of the ambulance and there was no audience to cry over him.

"I don't think a serial killer would ever come to North Dakota," Linus says. "Maybe Sioux Falls. He'd kill one person and then get bored and probably go find more interesting people to kill in Minneapolis."

There is a hidden growing torment in me. I keep myself occupied and try to forget it, but in moments when I can't lie, I know that I'm susceptible to it more and more, that the misery is digging itself out.

The Frogman moves in the corner. I don't look.

Linus says, "What's the difference between a bug bite and a rash, because I have this one by my neck."

But I also know I can have wild swings in my thoughts. I've gotten used to this over the three seasons at Oregsburg. I think of this discrete period of my life as a room, and these are simply the dirty problems I find inside with me to take care of. I keep everything clean around here, the Frogman is always in the room with me, he came along sometime after the accident but I try to keep him in the corners, try not to look, because if he's let out and gets his way something might happen.

Linus is where he was before. This is my room. I'm not ready to go yet. As it always does, the purpose returns, it comes around the corner at the last minute.

The two best reasons to do anything are

1. To prove to yourself you can do it
2. To prove to everyone else you can do it

And I will put my head down, remembering that I've been afforded these five months. They are mine to take, and this is my entire life. I am a good donkey.

Linus says, "Your feet have a tremendous amount of dead skin on them. I'm just pointing it out."

What I'm thankful for: this season, drive, motivation, success lust, that I'm not fat, that I'm not a handicapped, that I don't have fucking spina bifida, that no one can hear my thoughts except me, that activeness forestalls the sludge of the cosmos, that my hands are big for my size, Linus, Oregsburg, that my great-grandpas put it in my great-grandmas and that my grandpas put it in my grandmas and that my dad put it in my mom, that I wasn't born in King Leopold's Congo or Siberia, that my sinuses are a high mountain cave and there is a little grendel in there tending her mushrooms, that I'll never have too much time on my hands, that there are other wrestlers out there waiting for me to come tear them down, my grandma, that I have a job to do.

"God, Stephen, the fire hose just tried to attack Danny." Linus closes the book, but not before reading the first lines of the next chapter. I've noticed that when he gets really fixated, books or wrestling usually being the cause, he develops a kind of general wetness around his lips and spends a lot of time wiping it off with the back of his hand. "I'm going to go to sleep now. Six thirty, then?"

I nod. I thank God I'm a modern orphan, given a chance instead of singing for my supper, covered in chimney dust.

"You know I haven't heard you say anything in two days?"

I hear that male's arm snap again and again. "Mm."

He's by my window, book tucked under his arm. On the sill, he looks at the picture of my parents holding me as a baby on the couch in my living room, which I never remember until someone else is looking at it, but he doesn't say anything. Instead he wipes a finger across the sill next to the picture and says, "Your room is so clean. It's almost abnormal how clean it is."

"Clean, clean, clean, clean, clean, clean, clean, clean."

"Tell me what happens at Miles City."

"You're going to wrestle three times, win three times, and have a 4–0 record at 125."

"No, I mean, like, in—what happens if I lose?"

"Well, in a tournament there's something called a wrestle-back, but this is just four schools—"

"I know what a wrestle-back is. I'm just thinking about what's going to happen."

"Start telling yourself facts. Here we go, I'll start. You are Linus Arrington. You are sitting in a chair in my dorm room, which is . . . five doors down from your own dorm room. It is November. November is one of the cold months. Stalin was a weatherman and his left arm was way shorter than his right because of a carriage accident. You wrestle for Oregsburg College at 125 pounds. You won your match today. You are from Bellevue, Nebraska."

"My father's name is Dale, my mother's name is Tina. Milk is white. I have wrestled since I was seven, and I won my first college match. In three days, I will be in Montana, wrestling in Miles City."

"The Miles City gym smells like every other gym. You have won your first match of your career here. You are 1–0 as a President."

"If I'm aggressive I will win."

"You are going to win three matches in a row in the Miles City gym because you are a heinous 125-pound barbarian and they are all cheesecakes."

"I'm a heinous barbarian and I will perform evil on their heads."

There's a certain way Linus's face looks when he believes something. I feel like I've known him a long time when he does that, like I lost my milk teeth with him biting into corncobs in Nebraska, like I had a different babyhood, like I'm a whole different person.

Linus says, "Do you ever think about what life would've been like if you were born a girl? Or if you had a clubfoot? Or were Asian? Or in New Mexico?"

"If I had a clubfoot I'd kill myself."

"Me, too, I think." Sometimes I worry that Linus has difficulty grasping abstract concepts.

"A different life . . . doesn't seem like a different pencil to write with," I say. "I have all my legs and feet. You do, too. I'm good at wrestling and so are you. Those are the circumstances. Point is. That's the pencil I was given. You got the same pencil."

"All right."

"Put your forehead against mine. Stable as a table?"

"Stable as a table."

"Let's go, sweet child. I'll tuck you in."

"Can I use your toothpaste? My mom didn't put any in the package this time."

After he shuts his door, I turn down the hallway, empty except for the cleaning lady at the far end scrubbing the vomit off the trash chute. The floor runs in a square, rooms on the outside, communal bathroom in the center, which I head into. A freshman named Perry, who will live to be ninety or die next summer, who knows, leaves a stink in the stall he exits. He nods, I nod, I don't know his last name.

I turn the sink on. In the mirror, I check for signs of impetigo, herpes, ringworm. I turn the razor on. I run it over the buds on my pate, mowing down the little guys before they can grow big. Insect teeth on the top of my head. A peeler for the potato.

I read about flensing in my Culture of Global Capitalism course. I sat up in my seat and imagined three hundred years ago. I saw a massive, ugly whale shored up on a beach, grinning dumbly with its big mouth and its small eyes while fishermen tromped along its back in their boots, stabbing and hacking with knives and hooks in straight lines to make panels of blubber to be peeled, just like wallpaper, the wet sucking noises as they're pulled off a red-white underflesh. And the fisherman yanked harder at the pieces that wouldn't come off the fascia, tearing until they separated from the connective tissue. The mess in the sand. And when all the blubber was flensed, the fishermen walked away with it, leaving the stupid peeled whale there on the beach, bloody and white, a muscle skeleton, eyes bulging and mouth open, still smiling, the sun setting over the waves.

There is no ceremony. These are simply the things I do in between. I leave the shower, walk down the hallway back to my room. For a second, a cloud can pass in front of the moon. I do math in my newly shorn potato. I will wrestle something like twenty-four times this season if everything goes how it's supposed to, and round it off to seven minutes per match, giving a total of, what's that, 168 minutes total. Less than three hours—168 minutes—that's what will be put down in the records, to be permanently studied by the world's progeny, tracing the table's lines with their fat fingers. The 168 minutes that matter. The rest, what won't be recorded, is clipping toenails, dead whale thoughts, toweling off your human skinfolds, breaking scentless wind on boiled chicken breasts and oil-free vegetables, fondling your belly button, jumping off your bed to touch the ceiling, reaching in your desk down below your collection of help line and faith pamphlets and pulling out your *Barron's,* turning to the "350 Most Common Words" page. *Impecunious. Inane. Incontrovertible. Infamy. Inimical.* The rest is maneuvering your mind away from the wrong things, more than keeping to the right things.

I'll tell a secret: think about what connects the rest to the 168 minutes. That's it. Everything else is flensing. The past is flensing. Losing is flensing.

I do push-ups. My towel falls off at twenty. One two three four five six seven eight nine ten eleven twelve thirteen fourteen fifteen sixteen seventeen eighteen nineteen twenty twenty-one twenty-two twenty-three twenty-four twenty-five twenty-six twenty-seven twenty-eight twenty-nine thirty thirty-one thirty-two thirty-three thirty-four thirty-five thirty-six thirty-seven thirty-eight thirty-nine forty forty-one forty-two forty-three forty-four forty-five forty-six forty-seven forty-eight forty-nine fifty. Wormhole, black hole. Invisible far-off radio frequency. Unknown bloop from the hadal deep. I'm trying to push into a deeper place.

PRACTICE IS ONLY AS BORING and difficult as it looks. And it looks something like an active prison playground: two dozen wrestlers puttering around, their goals hidden in the silence of their heads, Led Zeppelin and Cream at seven thirty in the morning, sounds of slapping. The dry winter gym heating inside your mouth and hair. I believe that the more time you spend thinking about what the fuck you're doing here is in direct proportion to your worseness. If you just buy into the craziness, you're a lot better off. Did you know that in the Roman Empire, a doctor, upon consulting a woman overrun by hysteria, would instruct his assistant to make loud noises and release bad smells into the room to scare the womb back into position, and that the assistant wouldn't think twice? That's why the Roman Empire lasted fifteen hundred years. I bought in a long time ago.

To keep on task mentally takes practice, just like practicing switches or cradles, but my personal choice is, for instance, to picture the Subway turkey, six-inch, wheat, no cheese, no mayo I'll permit myself afterwards, the roughly 280 calories I'll get back, the chemicals released in the brain upon smelling the steam of Subway bread. I like to think about what's in front of me, the two dozen matches spread out over long days, and how these sloppy practices are the means in between. I don't need food anyway, I fill my guts with this.

I'm paired up with Whitey Williams, who looks like a ghoul because of a propane tank incident when he was thirteen. His face is both the color and texture of uncooked ground beef. He's 141 and he likes to go with me in practice because he's bigger but I'm faster. I don't mind, but he has this rare disorder where there are these outgrown nubby flaps of skin all down his spine. I've told him, "Your back looks like a fucking stegosaurus." At least seven times since I've been here, I've seen Whitey get an early first-period takedown in matches because his opponent will touch the stegosaurus back and get creeped right out of his zone before realizing that he's going to lose if he doesn't stop screwing around and touch the nubs.

He goes outside single, but I bear down and turn over to grab on to his back but he's up before then so we're just hitting at each other. He's telling me about this girl named Lauren who he caught staring at him in the library. He went over and asked, why are you staring? And she said, because you have the most beautiful face I've ever seen. And so Whitey said, wait until you see my back. And when he lifted his shirt up right there in the library and presented her the nubs, she basically shit her pants and dragged him back to her dorm room saying, I must paint you, I must paint you right now. But when they got back to the room there was no sign of the painting materials anywhere, Whitey said, and before he knew it she had pushed him on the bed and he realized she was only trying to get his shoes and socks off. Interested to see where this was going, he watched as she got his feet naked.

He gets a hand on my scalp and pulls. "Shrimping. Are you familiar with it? It is the meeting of toes and the suck function of the mouth in the name of sexual pleasure."

I flip his arms outside and get him tied up from the inside. Knowing Whitey's a liar and also because it's gross, I just say, "Well."

"It was something completely out of right field."

"Left."

"What left?"

"It's left. Left field."

"Oh, fuck you."

This is all at half speed, fireman's carries at half speed, duck-unders and takedowns and rides at half speed. Coach Hargraves blows the whistle and people move to different places. I'm on my back and Coach Whiting has his hands on my forehead and I'm lifting against him pushing down, I'm doing army crawls across the length of the gym, I'm jumping rope, I'm doing the pegboard, I'm doing pencil rolls, I'm doing the stairs and holding on to my vomit until I get to the trash can, I'm wrestling Simon Fjelstad and Harry Pfaff and Paul Kryger, who is my weight and wants to be better than me, but he will never be better than me. All is necessary and intentional, the way I like it. If one thing slips a screw, I screw it back in until it's sound again. One of the coaches walks around saying, "Miles City, Miles City." I take a breath and blow snot on my sleeve. If you're doing it right, it feels like getting caught in a small room with a bleach scent. I've learned thirstiness is a temporary matter, it'll just go away if you wait long enough. I get a short break and stare up past the wall mats and the empty spots where banners are supposed to hang. The sharp white lights turn the skin both pasty and clear, sweat looks messier, and I'm conditioned to pay attention to what I'm seeing, not unlike how operation room lights make you pay attention. I never stop paying attention. I pay attention to Linus doing twenty pull-ups and then waiting to do twenty more. Pete Crest jumps off the mat, where he's been near-fighting with Clark Lowe, he takes off his shirt and ties it around his head to catch the sweat, and for a second I think he's going to take his shorts off, but instead he dives at Clark for real, trying to actually fight him until they're separated. I pay real attention and can hear the other part of the team slamming weights over in the weight room down the hall.

Paul Kryger is an antagonistic Dutch lunatic, but he doesn't see what I'm doing, he's too busy trying to beat me. No one likes to do live-gos with him because at least half the team's had his fingers up their asses—he's basically set the world record for checking the oil. Some have gotten used to it. He's checked my oil in the past and still tries to sometimes, but he's not good enough for it to be a nagging problem. During our live-go he's expected to come at me and does. Spit from his mouth lands in mine when he tries to pull behind me, saying, "Fuck you, Florida, fuck you." The coaches are yelling at him to shrug. But I wait for things to go my way. He can't shrug past my right side because I push down on his head with my right arm and twist him like a scarf in my lap. He's muttering, "Fuck you, Florida, you fancyboy, you pussy shit," and jamming his elbow into my ribs, hard, because he wants to take the 133 spot from me. He stabs the point of his elbow between two of my lower ribs. "Hey," someone says, "hey." But if I have bruises on my ribcage, where would I be without them? I would not be myself if I didn't have bruises on my ribcage. And though Paul Kryger wishes me to die, wishes me to leave Oregsburg and never come back so he can be the 133, he'll never get it because he doesn't want it as bad as me, and all I would like to tell him is he would be better if he wasn't so angry, that is, if he wasn't so stupid on top of being so angry, but I don't tell him this. I don't tell him anything. I feel no pity for Paul Kryger or Paul Kryger's future bride and unborn grandchildren, who surely will be bastards, who are all going to be denied the story that Paul Kryger was the 133. I will make sure that story never exists. I will take something away from him so that he'll never have it. And while he's calling me a bitch pussy and banging my ribs I kneel down and get him onto my shoulders like a baby lamb, he's a baby lamb now. He is guided by my arms to the mat, and thereupon he finds his disappointment.

I'm told by Coach Farrow, "Jesus, Florida, you can't slam him like that or they'll see it in the match," but I know he doesn't mean it. Kryger, holding his hand, has to be taken to the training room by Fink, but I'll give him credit because he doesn't whine or anything.

Suicide sprints, jump rope, rope climbing, five times, arms only. Two and a half hours after I've started, I've finished. I go to the showers and get dressed. I brush the vomit out of my teeth and get my backpack.

STUDENTS TEACHERS DESKS PENCILS PAPERS. They're on the other side of the wall, I'm in my garden knocking over and smashing the flowers.

I took extra classes my first couple years so I could take fewer classes my last couple semesters. This fall I'm doing Drawing II, Meteorology I, Basic News Writing, and What Is Nothing? I worked ahead and I use the extra time for practice. It's not that I don't want to get my education, I just have to save my energy for the right things. In another life, if I wasn't so good with my body, who knows, maybe I could've been on the cum laude list instead of doing half measures to ride out a 2.6. Outside of wrestling, I've always taken what I could get. They offer tutorship but I don't partake. It'd just be one more person you'd have an obligation to, and anyway, I've realized you can get by just by picking out a few specific things you like for papers and memorizing for tests. For example, in my Politics of Therapy class, I ignored all the other thinkers once I heard about Wilhelm Fliess, who talked about how the nose is tied to your privates in the 1800s and it'll sometimes bulb up during screwing and a lot of times people will sneeze over and over during (he even came up with a surgical procedure to cut that tie), and I knew I was going to write about it. I got a B- and the paper was titled "Looking to Our Past for Our Future." Also for example, I could draw and explain the AD–AS model like the back of my hand. College is easier than high school.

I go to the rooms I'm supposed to on time and keep my head above water. Probably I could've gotten more out of my classes. I like to understand things. I like to spot problems and try to figure them out, which is all wrestling really is. When education is practical, I'm in favor of it: for example, the first time I visited a library resulted in the high school sophomore fistfight with the boy named Maxime, a tall French boy who liked to skateboard. He and I did not get along, he had a habit of zigging in front of my path as I walked into school, and when one day I told him he'd better find a new place to skateboard, he said some French words to me that went by too fast but I caught *salaud*. I wrote it down on a piece of paper. That afternoon, I went to the library and took a French-to-English dictionary from the shelf. I found the class Maxime was going to come out of, and when he came out that was that. The result of all this was three days' suspension and two weeks' detention, which I spent on cheap daydreams about being on the deck of a boat where the wind was so strong it blew off my cap! It was hard for me to doubt the practical value of books after that.

I leave Meteorology, where I got a C- on the midterm because I messed up the sizes and temperatures of the atmosphere layers and because I forgot the chemistry compositions—the argons mixed up with the neons and that kind of thing. But in the long run, I still think it's a good class for me because there's a lot of matching, a lot of if-it's-not-this-it's-that. This type of thing is like a mental trip to the fishing lake. It's relaxing to think that Leon Battista Alberti invented the anemometer in 1450, which can measure wind speed and wind pressure.

These facts move to a light place somewhere toward the back of my brain. Food is an afterthought, class is an afterthought, people relationships are an afterthought, hydration is an afterthought, sleep is an afterthought.

I cut through the brown grass on my way to Drawing in the McKnight Studio, which is by a parking lot and the road bordering campus. I pass some dead landscaping with nylon tape stuck in the branches. From under some bare plants, a male finds a splotch of snow, balls it up with a few mulch sticks poking out, and fires it harder than he needs to at a female, who screams in shock when it hits her shoulder. When the laughing male tries to come up and apologize, she takes a mulch bit out of her hair and tries to stab his ear with it. The two of them go running right past Kyle Glanville, who's a nice kid with a skully face. I met him three years ago in my orientation group and, as it turned out, he's one of sixteen or so black students out of the eleven hundred total enrollment.

"Hey, Stephen, what's up?"

"Hey, Kyle. Where you headed?"

"I put off fucking math until I couldn't anymore. Geometry. Sucks."

"I took that two years ago. You got, um, what's her name, Corrigan?"

I can see from his face that we've talked about this exact thing before. "Yeah. I'm with all freshmen and sophomores. They think I'm special needs and I hate it."

"Secants. Descants. I can't remember any of that. I just remember there was a parabola on the final problem and she gave me quarter credit for putting the vertex and the, what do you call it, in the right place on the graph."

"Shit. The final has parabolas on it?"

"Yeah." Because I don't know what else to do, I look up at the top of the clock tower.

"What's that there?"

"My spit cup. Got a match soon."

"Oh cool."

"Water weight."

"Yeah."

"So." When I try to inch away, he doesn't move. His hands are holding his backpack straps, and I don't know if he's lonely or if people are racist to him or just uninterested. If he thinks we were supposed to be friends because we were in the same orientation group.

He says, "Hey, you wanna hang out sometime?" Kyle Glanville is a person who could've been a more important thing in my life, I think, just like how sleeping in or camping could've been a more important thing.

"I can't," I say, and he understands, I think, and when he says "See you around," I get that he doesn't mean it. His tone shuts the door.

I have five minutes until class, so as cars fly by at fifty on the road posted twenty, I wait in the parking lot outside McKnight, which is basically a big shed. Drawing II! Oregsburg College has hidden me under the umbrella of its bachelor of arts in liberal studies degree. That is superior intellectual padding. I was told I could "design" my curriculum! Well, I did: I've taken classes called Crisis Communication, Debating Human Rights in China, Mass Atrocities, Food Chain Physics, and Theories of Leadership. Before I stopped trying so hard at school, history used to be my favorite subject, especially bad history, because knowing about the worst things that had happened was somehow the only way to make them any less horrific. I don't remember one thing from Chemistry of Life, or even the name of the professor who taught it, only that she was a woman. I got a C in that. There are text-books for these classes. I couldn't believe it! Can I be expected to buy all of them, let alone read all of them? Class is a hobby. They cut you all this slack, they keep cutting it year after year. This walking back and forth to buildings, remembering facts and opinions temporarily just to spit them back out and forget forever, it's what passes for occupation until a match.

During the first week or so I met Linus, he said, "Don't you feel like it's . . . a little bit weird here?"

I remember looking down at the legs of my chair, which Linus was bending back. They were cracking. "I don't know," I said, which was true. I didn't know, because it'd never occurred to me to notice whether the school was weird, or ordinary, or whether it was something in between. I was using Oregsburg for a different purpose than every other student around me, including Linus. I remember thinking at the time that nothing would be any different for me if the school had one hundred thousand students or one. And what I said next was, "You've never been to this part of the country before. Probably you're just used to where you're from and need to get used to around here," which was maybe a little true, but anyway was good enough because he nodded.

And still, these silly classes I took make up what turns out to be my higher education. It will always be a part of what I am, things happen and then fall away, it's no less permanent than what happens in a match. I have to live with all of it. And lately, twenty-one years of living with things has begun to wear thin. Eighteen years of living with it, then graduating to three more years of living with it, where all you do is live with it. I'm up to my neck in it, I'm stuck with all this history and it never leaves me alone. It's enough to make you imagine what could've been different, to make you turn over small thoughts about whether what you are is what you should be, whether you've made the correct choice. I just need one thing to live with that I want to live with. That'll be enough.

And what am I going to do with myself, with a degree in liberal studies? To which I answer: Have you even been listening?

There's a girl standing next to me in the parking lot.

"Hello," she says. I know her.

"Hi. I know you."

"Mary Beth," she says. "I was in your Drawing I class. Last fall."

"You're a better drawer than me."

"You wrestle?" Her breath fog is close enough to nearly reach my face when she talks.

"You remember?"

"Not really, maybe a little. You got the ears, the puffy," she says. "What's so good about wrestling?"

Wrestling is a series of momentary ejaculations, passions that originate and evolve based on their relationship to another's passions. Wrestling is, at its core, one passion set against another passion for the purpose of determining which is stronger. "I always liked it," I say.

"You any good?"

"Yes."

"Did you do the homework?"

"Yeah, I sat in that parking lot over there last week and did the gestures of the people going into the stores." I point to the buildings across the road, the Pharmart and the twenty-four-hour diner, Allnighter.

"Can I see? Are they good?"

"No. Are yours good?"

"I went to the nursing home, you know, Early Sunshine? I got some of the old people sitting on the porch and watching TV and stuff. I think they're all right."

She gets out her pad and shows me, her fingers touching mine for a moment. Her drawings are really good. There's one of a woman in a wheelchair pointing right at me. I don't know how she got the perspective right.

"Do you have a match this weekend?"

"A quad. Three matches. In Montana."

"How are you going to do the assignment? For next class?"

"I'm not sure. Other classes I can do in the van but not drawing."

"Right."

"The car shaking and all, you know?"

"Well, I hope you win your matches."

"Thank you."

She puts her pad back in her backpack. "Are there any women wrestlers?"

"Probably, somewhere," I say, and then add unhelpfully: "If I were born a woman and all other circumstances were the same, I'd be a wrestler."

"Tell me your name again."

"Stephen."

"I think we're late, Stephen."

ON THE NIGHT WE'RE SUPPOSED TO LEAVE for Miles City, a reported snowstorm on the Montana border pushes the departure to the next morning. I can't sleep, so I put on my sweatshirt and go outside.

I take the usual route, around the Finch Building and past the Memorial Classroom Building, where during Shakespeare and our out-loud reading, I read as Malvolio (I could act all right) and talked about the yellow garters, rooms where there are ghosts of my flatulence, ghosts of my fingertip dust, hair ghosts, ghosts of my presentation on China's treatment of farm workers that I got a C on because the professor told me I both completely skipped over the Big Jump Forward and said the words "not good" too much. In the underpass where the science labs run above, there's a clump of both sexes, their chatter echoing off the tunnel walls. One female says an economics professor has been fired ("banned for life from setting foot on Oregsburg's campus" is the exact wording) for punching a boy in the mouth during his class because he wouldn't stop whistling. Then another female asks her friend how she got so skinny and the other female says she tricked herself into believing toothpaste is a dessert. Now she brushes her teeth five times a day. Then a male says to the group, "What the fuck is a 401(k)?" There are so many people at Oregsburg I dimly recognize, a foggy family a thousand children big put together for four years, small enough that you keep running across the same people who end up meaning nothing to you, the same way they don't recognize me, don't know that I wrestle every day for the school like a servant.

Near the clock tower I go around pulling up the decorative winter cabbages they've just planted.

I walk into the student union. A vending machine, a TV, some chairs and couches. On the other side of the building, where you can't see, there's the cafeteria full of things I can't have. All-purpose tile, all-purpose carpet, big windows, bathrooms down a little hallway. No one is around, so I sit on the couch. Idle time is not my friend. Someone's left behind a novel about knights, which I read for thirty seconds before boredom falls on me like a collapsed tent. Sometimes I wonder, if I were a character in a book, would I be sympathetic? Would I make a good good guy? On TV, there's video footage of a four-story building in Philadelphia that's fallen in on itself. The bottom of the screen says people are inside, trapped or worse. But no one is watching. No one is in the room.

A moment later, the door opens again, and a cleaning lady enters in her blue uniform and her yellow rubber gloves with her wheely trash can. I'm sitting there, by myself, rubbing my head on the couch.

"Hello," she says.

"Hello," I say. "That accent is familiar. I want to say Italian?"

"I am from Russia." She picks up a smaller trash can and dumps it into the larger trash can. There are old muscles in her arms. Her name tag says "Masha."

"Which part?" I ask, and she says an unspellable word that I guess goes with a place.

"Is there a college in that place you said?"

"Yes, there is a college. And there is a park with a lake and the big bus that will take you and fifty more and buildings that are bigger than any buildings in this part of America." I ignore her civilized picture of her hometown. Instead I imagine girl Masha playing in the dirt with roosters and hens, and there's a sky that's not nice to look at, Masha pairing up the right rooster for the right hen, rubbing her muddy hands on the eggs that come back from her matchmaking.

"Is America strange?"

"Not so strange."

I like to imagine why she came here, but only if it stays vague and safe and I don't have to think too deeply about it. I like to think it was a specific moment that disrupted her life and birthed out who she'd become, the one doing a circle around the student union and taking out all the trash.

"You clean the floor where I live. McCloskey. I've seen you using the utility closet. It's right near my room." If you go into the bathroom a little after midnight, sometimes you'll hear Masha sheepishly call out from the doorway, "Hello, may I enter?"

"Yes." She has frazzled reddish hair. "I am very tired. Very tired all the time. All the time I work five to one. I clean one out of four parts of the college, there are three other cleaning women who do what I do, but the other parts of the college. Sometimes I see them when I go between the buildings, and they are very tired. But what do I say? It is quiet. It is all the time quiet."

"That's true."

"So I just go to work. Monday, Tuesday, Wednesday, Thursday, Friday, Saturday, Sunday. It is Friday, you know?"

"Yes," I say, though I don't know what exactly I'm agreeing with.

"And you? You study at the college to be doctor?"

"No, not a doctor."

"Oh." She has begun spraying blue cleaning fluid on the

windows. It runs down and she catches it with a rag. "You are coming to the college to do something different?"

"Yes."

"Your family is happy."

"Yes." At some point, I've stood up from the couch, but I don't know when. "And what about your family? Are they here?"

"My husband go when we come to here. He go with my daughter and he go with her. I do not hear from them."

"I'm really sorry."

"Ah, it is O.K. I just work, you know?"

"Yes."

"Your mother and father, they must be proud to send you to the college." She has finished with the windows, doing a not very good job, leaving loopy streaks all over. "I am proud of my daughter. I have not seen her for seven years."

"I'm so sorry."

"Ah, it is O.K." She pushes her trash can up to the side of the couches a couple of feet from me. There's some kind of stain on the carpet. Kneeling down next to it and taking a bottle of carpet cleaner from the little rack attached to her can, she sprays seven or eight times and the white foam curls over the spot. "See, it is O.K." She reaches out her rubber glove and puts it on my tennis shoe. I get the sick, gross feeling of excitement at the bottom of my stomach. She puts her other hand on my shin and rubs it. Her glove leaves a wet handprint on my sweatpants. We get to the place we're trying to go, which is her standing next to me and us touching each other. Her gloves have come off. The erection returns compulsorily, which is a word in the *Barron's*. Is it O.K. that the first reason I like that this is happening is because she's just so nice? And that the second reason is because I'm lonely? God, I love a challenge but sometimes I can't take the withdrawal! Her fingers warm up. There is no kissing. My eyes close, I hope hers do, too.

"You are smart young man," says Masha. "You would like to occupy me a tergo?"

"I don't know what you're saying."

While I likewise touch her through her official blue pants, I am aware that she is Masha, the one and only Masha. I take my nonbusy hand to the top of her polyester pantyhose and leave it there, fisted up in the seam. Her unsentimental jerking finger motions are good in a final, definite way. She is a woman who's had sadness and means business. The woman on TV says a man in South Dakota is causing nervousness among residents in his town because he is carrying a hammer around everywhere. It's been going on for two weeks. He hasn't done anything yet, but he's frightening the neighbors, who are calling it "menacing." But the police can't do anything, there's no law against carrying hammers.

It is difficult to stop her before the orgasm shows up, but I do. There are many monk qualities in me.

"I have matches in nine hours. I wrestle. I have to keep my competitive, you know, intacted."

She nods. "You are the smart young man. Always thinking."

I say, "Can I ask how old you are?"

"I am fifty-three."

"Jeez. Well. I have to go now. Thank you for making me feel better."

"You are a young man with the beautiful haircut." She taps my face not super gently, and pushes the trash can out the door.

The TV woman reports that North America is experiencing irregular weather patterns.

I pull the drawstring tight and reiterate I haven't broken any rules.

And then the news ends. That's when the TV goes black and the place is quiet for a moment, and I see the men's bathroom door slowly close. It's down a hall in the corner, thirty feet, next to the women's and a door that opens to who-the-fuck-knows.

"Masha?"

I can't tell if I'm alone. A weird silence fills the room like a gas. Nothing happens that doesn't really happen. This is what I keep telling myself. The Frogman is the thing under the drain.

I push open door number three and end up outside by the Finch classrooms. I run back to McCloskey fast. I run on the main path, no one around. I'm not fast enough, something is behind me. But I get to the lobby, sprint through it, where the two students working the front desk cheer at me, tell me to go faster. I hurry to my room and slam the door. I have either been gone twenty minutes or two hours.

One night when I was nine or ten, I noticed the water was draining slower in our shower. So I finished showering and, still naked, I kneeled and lifted up the drain. The last of the water gurgled down. The way our shower was, the drain had this silver disc at the top. I pulled on that. There was a bending metal stake attached to the end that was supposed to reach down the pipe. Wrapped around the stake was a huge glob of hair, but it wasn't just hair. It was fingernail bits, what looked like skin, and white and green globes or eggs stuck in it. It was this bulbous, furry wet mass that was clinging to the bottom of my drain, where I stood every night, sitting under there all along.

There's something I'm scared of.

A note slides under my door. I sit still waiting to hear whoever left it move away. Five minutes pass. Nothing. I quietly move toward the note and pick it up.

I SEE YOU

I turn it over, with the feeling I always get when the Frogman's nearby.

COME BACK FROM MILES CITY WITHOUT LOSING
OR I WON'T GO AWAY

I DON'T HAVE THE PATIENCE FOR THIS. Steele looks like Sterling looks like Richardton looks like Dickinson looks like Belfield looks like Wibaux looks like Glendive looks like shut in the van for six hours with a lot to think about, looks like a big straight line with a million fence posts, looks like something stuck in your teeth. And when you want out of your skin so you can rush somebody and just get your match started already, and when you get out of the van six hours later, the same things are still there to think about because you haven't made any headway into finishing them off—that won't happen until the referee lets you go with his fucking whistle. I walk into the gym faster than the rest of them, I'm the first one to the locker room and pick the one in the corner.

I do my weigh-in. Fiddle-fit.

Pedialyte. Yogurt and half a bagel.

What will make my thoughts less ugly while I wait for my turn? I live in these little chambers of dissatisfaction like a frustrated prince. I'm constantly reminded that I'm not owed anything.

Look at the ceiling. Stands ten rows high, half empty, half the people in them other wrestlers from the three other schools waiting for their turn. Twelve, thirteen . . . fourteen total women. Two black mats, two matches going at once. A man in a sweatshirt with a camera. Two boys with ammonia spray and a towel. No windows. Subduing your gross need to gag. Forgetting the human body has bleed and tear and break functions, never mind that there are small squares of your head designed just to inform you about fear and misgivings. Forgetting all that and replacing it with What You Have Convinced Yourself Is True. There. That's what it looks like. Now you can take a test where they ask you what a match in Montana looks like and pass that shit.

Some of the famous wrestlers throughout history include George Washington, Abraham Lincoln, Benjamin Franklin. In seventh grade, to get you interested they tell you this, but I didn't need any extra interest and I would've stuck any of those assholes.

Take notes, here comes the routine. Fifteen minutes before the first match I walk out of the spectating area and exit the gym altogether. A parking lot, a basement, a bathroom, any of them will do, the only thing that matters is that no one is around. I am by myself. For a full twelve minutes, what happens is brainstorm time. This looks like my warm-ups coming off, taking shots at an imaginary opponent, jumping rope quick enough that it whistles. In my private corner, I spit on the ground. I tell myself I will come back to that thing I've left—that spit—in fewer than ten minutes, and I will have won. I've done this so many times that I know when twelve minutes are up, I'm on a schedule, I'm a creature of habit and something clicks, and then I go from privacy into the gym and to the edge of the mat and wait for my opponent, I'm skin and gristle and little water, Stephen Florida without end Amen.

As a rule, I study up on the first opponent, which I know beforehand, and then take things as they come and do my scouting on the rest between matches. For the last three days, I have reserved lurid visions of my match with Brett Espino, a junior from McNaire College who likes to bait. This is an apprentice tactic, I've spent the span of time in which I slide into night sleep thinking about Brett's visage in sharp discomfort, his teammates forced to watch, the purple that comes to his cheeks as the inevitability mounts, shame, purple shame for everyone, and in my dorm bed the thoughts of all these things give me a clenched nutsack and a moderate boner. I am ready for you, Mr. Espino.

Spit on the ground. Cue the villain music.

On the place where the floor changes to mat, Linus puts his forehead on mine. Stable as a table. Coach Hargraves smacks my headgear. Good-luck tug. I stand in the middle of the circle and wait as he comes up to me. I look right into Brett Espino's face. If there was a Nobel Prize for wrestling I'd win that shit every year.

Before the referee can speak, I say, "I'm going to have fun eating you, Brett."

"Cut that out, red," the ref says, "or I'm killing this before it starts."

Tasks of repetition. Times of perfect fulfillment. You're only who you really are when you're doing what you really want. I am so much myself, I could never be anyone else. I keep up the task of finding out how the world works, locating its pulley systems, and placing myself in the center. Facts: A human thighbone is stronger than concrete. The stuff in a camel's hump comes out green. I didn't learn these things without falling off the horse. Get back on the horse. That's a fucking saying you'll have to get used to if you're going to find your center. Inherent in it is how fucking repetitive getting back on the fucking horse is. Get back on it. Get back on it. Tell yourself you're not a wastrel, you're not carrying on for nothing. Drink your green camel-hump juice and say to yourself you're not a wastrel. Find your center and fuck it until it's pregnant with your little babies so they can come out and find more centers to fuck.

From the whistle, like I knew he would, he tries to bait me. He won't let me tie him up. He keeps moving away. I keep trying.

He's watching my belly button. I'm watching his face. He's moving clockwise around the circle. What is so strange about this is that I'm on a road I'm going to be on exactly once, I'm never going to be here again. I'm never coming back. He smacks my hands away. He wants me to go low. Half the period's passed with me trying to cuff him. A surge of impatience goes up my back and into my hair, and I try to go low, which is a mistake because it turns out he's one of those extra-physical types and he clubs his hands down on the back of my head, and after I'm on the ground his right knee bangs the side of my head, and then he's on top and gets control just long enough for the two points, but the thing about the extra-physical types is it's usually a cover for a lack of skill, and you learn how to deal with it just like anything else, so I push, shoulders against his thighs for leverage, and my knees are off the ground while he digs his hard parts into my soft spots. He's scrambling to get behind me, but I'm standing by now and batting his hand away from my stomach. I'm away from him for my one point. Whistle.

And then I have one of those sudden bad little moments when I'm not being challenged, which is when I question the whole thing. Why did I latch on to this? I'm going to be let out in six months. With nowhere to go, what am I supposed to do? When did the future become as unfaithful as the past? When I was a kid, I was always afraid of how heaven never ended, and one night trying to fall asleep, I just couldn't take it, it really got into me, I threw off the covers and ran down the hallway hyperventilating, and my mom found me gagging into the toilet. After I die, no one's going to be there to check my tombstone for typos.

Some of these saplings I can sedate with one-third of my mind, but because I have nothing else I put my whole self into it, which is why I sometimes get away from myself.

The referee flips the disc and I pick top. There's not going to be a third period.

Brett Espino's mentality is simple: he doesn't like to be bottom. Because one cannot bait from the bottom, he does not like the bottom, even if he's up 2–1. When I kneel down beside him, through my fingers I can sense in his skin his anxiousness to get out so he can ride a 3–1 lead and resume the fishing game we just spent a period playing. There's something like sympathy in taking my position behind him, placing my right hand on his right elbow and my left hand seatbelting his stomach while he looks straight ahead, letting me. I place my ear on Brett's back and hear his heart. "Oh, Brett, I told you I was going to eat you," I whisper to him. Something like sympathy, I could fall asleep if we stayed here long enough.

But the universe shakes its rainstick, and the course of history follows the only path it was ever going to, and I imagine there is a sadness in seeing, from the bleachers, the exact steps Brett takes in the exact spots he's supposed to, exposing himself to the conclusion, which is my forearm against his nose and his weak, frenzied exhales before he stops struggling and I push him down like a planting root, like burying a secret, and pin him. There are a few handclaps when my arm is lifted, and I walk back to my corner of spit down the hall and spout nonsense I'll never remember. This feeling, which lasts about one minute and then it's gone, is completely round and full and soggy, and it lifts me out of everything bad. I'm completely mad with it.

I go to the bathroom, roll my singlet all the way down my body so I'm shitting naked, except for the banded red wad on my knees. A lot of people will tell you the middle part of a quad or a bigger tournament is the worst: when there are still more matches to wrestle than have been wrestled. Erasmus first posited the idea, which everyone now knows, that the worst enemy of the utopia is boredom. But I like the challenge of getting through it, of cutting through the boredom fat, I like the part where you're stewing in your juices because it opens up new causeways of thought, strange new ones you never saw coming. Part of the fun is batting away thoughts you shouldn't be having at this time—what's going to be on midterms, Mary Beth's neck, which I can look at by picking the right seat in Drawing. Even better: twice I caught her looking at me. This is all very exciting.

I count two smallish stools, a good number. The timing is also fortunate: a clean colon can sometimes give you a little boost, the impression that you're as fresh as you were before your first match.

Some feet go by under the stall and stop at a urinal. It's Sherman. "Hey, Stephen, is that you? I shouldn't tell you this, but a few people are whispering about whether Linus could beat you. There are whisperings."

I wipe. Sherman's already lost twice this year. In fact, only me, Linus, and Fat Henry are undefeated. Oregsburg, as a team, we aren't very good and we've never had anyone win a championship.

In the top corner of the stands, I watch Linus win his match like I knew he would. I eat a banana. I watch the next opponent, a person named Damon Kennedy, scratch out an 11–5 decision.

A little boy sucking at a Capri Sun sack climbs up to my corner of the stands. He sits down next to me. There's a Band-Aid over his left eyebrow and his hair sticks up all over. I guess he's been following the bracket sheet because he says, "You're Stephen Florida. I like Florida. If the United States was a man Florida would be his penis."

I admit to him that it's true.

"You could be my favorite wrestler. I'm going to root for you."

"Thank you. What do you think of him right there?" I point at Kryger, who's sulking on the side of the mat.

"I think he's a dumbbutt."

"Me, too. What's your name?"

"Dylan."

"What happened right there above your eye, Dylan?"

"It was a bike chain."

"Ouch," I say. "See this tooth? The front one here? Half of it's fake because I ran into a fence chasing down a Frisbee."

"Who threw the Frisbee? Were you mad at the person who threw the Frisbee?"

"My dad? No, I guess I never thought to be mad at him for it."

"Can I touch it?"

After I let him pull on my fake tooth, I sign his match info pamphlet.

And then it's twelve minutes until curtain, so the pattern repeats itself.

Spit. Walk. Crowd. Stable as a table. Headgear smack. Tug. Hello.

A middle-aged woman on her hands and knees is patting around the rim of the mat. She touches my shoe and my organ flutters, reminded of my Masha.

"Can you help me locate my contact lens?" She squints up at me.

"I can't help you right now."

Close your eyes. None of this, indeed very little of life at all, comes from divine inspiration, but what little makes it through, never more than an instant, shows itself in wrestling. The rest is stubborn, repetitious work. I go out to my fields and do my job. If it's boring, it's because you don't understand the peace of mind that habitual hard work grants. Open your eyes.

When Kennedy ties me up, he smells like what I figure my brother would've smelled like, if I ever had one. He fidgets with me like how we would've messed around in the yard, knocking each other into a pile of leaves and smashing them on each other's heads. His arm is inside my arm. At one point, I bite his hair. I need to stop pretending people are people who should care about me. He keeps pushing me back but I stay lower than him. We go outside the circle and return to the middle. He holds my hand and pulls me down. I push him away and we detach. He puts his palm on my forehead and pushes. With his other hand, he grabs the back of my neck. We rub our heads together.

I'm holding on to all this for later, I'm cataloging to remember. He keeps pulling on my neck, trying to open me up. I'm not going to let him open me up. He keeps putting his right hand on my forehead. It's not unpleasant. Kennedy has a 3.89 in criminology at Wright College, where he goes, it says so in the program. He's a good wrestler. You start to lose track of time, to forget. The whistle blows. I move down to the bottom for the second period and Kennedy gets on top. He gets a caution. We reset. The good stuff won't come until later, I'm mainly in the time of cheesecakes, which are the rung below parsons, but I'll remember beating them anyway, I'll remember all of it. He pushes and we tip forward and my face hits the mat, I don't know how bad, but his right arm is off my right elbow, and so he's trying to hug me now around my neck. But just then, the whistle blows. The match is stopped because of the blood coming out of my nose.

I go over to where my team is. Fink jams paper up the slot. His fingers dig in my nostrils, pulling the skin. This is fun.

Hargraves is in my face. "Stop fucking smiling, Florida. Put your fucking Manson face on and go snap that fucker's dick off like the fucking chimp you are!"

I return to the center and crouch down for bottom. On the whistle, I turn with my knees on the mat, but he has me in a tight hold so we just end up face-to-face. I can't get my arm up, and where my hand ends up is trapped right against his crotch, palm out, and I'm unable to release it. The opportunity presents itself to give the nuts a squeeze, to give Kennedy the five-on-two. A brief and sharp squeeze, which no one sees, but causes Kennedy to pop off me and let go before immediately trying to punch my face and choke me. They've got him off me in no time flat, he's disqualified, and I lie there cowering like a butterball for dramatic effect.

"Is it over?" I whimper. The referee helps me up and raises my hand while Kennedy's pained cries of "Fucker! You fucker!" fade away and he's dragged out of the gym. I haven't given anyone the five-on-two since seventh grade. I got caught that time.

When I'm walking off the mat, I can tell by Linus's face he saw the squeeze. Fink stops me to cut the nosebleeding, which has started back up again. "Goddamnit, Florida, goddamnit," Hargraves gleefully barks, hitting my scalp like he's nailing down a railroad spike, which feels good. There's a copper taste in my head.

I walk down the length of the hallway outside the gym, step my shoe in the spit I've left under the water fountain. From now on, the people I face should be given whatever the opposite of the benefit of the doubt is. Unmindful of time, I reach the end of the hallway, lean for a second against the frosted window plates that twinkle with streetlights, not real sunlight, and for a moment I remember that there is something outside of this going on. Sometimes I get so close that I forget.

I say appropriate words to Linus after he wins his second match, then I sit in the bleachers next to him. Two matches won. I keep my foot down on Miles City, I won't let up until I'm asleep tonight in my locked room with the lights off. For fear that the long span of a quad might dull your edge, it's useful to remind yourself about the big picture. Three wins this season, zero losses. A few struts, a rebar cage for the thing I'm building. Progress. I eat an apple.

Linus says, "This is easier than I thought it would be." I wipe my eyes. Then Linus says, "Neither of us are going to lose, you know."

The scenes this season are what will be in my biography, a photo taken of my face right now next to Linus is what will be on the cover. I look at him and realize he looks just like me. There's a towel on his shoulders, he's grinning and he doesn't even know it. He's living in the funhouse, too talented for anyone else to have any of the fun, he uses it all up, and he's always had it coming. He just takes what he deserves.

"I know," I say.

I saw Poynter wrestle earlier. I always used to remember their first names, but my focus is tightening and something has to go. He beat a good wrestler named Pike in the quarters and then the four-seed Osse in the semis because you can tell it matters to Poynter—it's why he's won two matches today. Like a pious pilgrim, walking around the New World rattling the less devout, staying up late and gazing into his hut's fire, blasting away more wild turkeys than the other pilgrims—that's what I think of when I see him bring down Osse in November like it's March. Osse is only a sophomore, Poynter is a senior, like me, and he is aware of his own dependency on every match. Every match will put you one iota closer to proper, safe seeding at postseason tournaments, and proper, safe seeding can be the difference between losing and winning. He's not scared of anyone, and he will not be scared of me, but he's scared of himself if he loses.

I wait on the side for the last matches to wrap up. Fat Henry loses. By then, Poynter is on the other side of the mat. He's tired with worry, you can see it from forty feet away. Hargraves, Linus, Sherman, Simon, assistants, other fucking people are talking to me. I rub the sore spot on my ribs that Kryger gave me. Hopping in place, maintaining his heart rate, Poynter is a weary totem, and I tell myself I won't be like him. I'm going to kill the Frogman.

Poynter is standing lower than me in the circle's center. If I believe I am Stephen Florida I am Stephen Florida and he will keep breathing. I hear an air-raid siren somewhere far away. You broke a human arm. You are going to win this match.

Right before the whistle goes, Poynter says, "If you try to squeeze my shit, I'll kill you in the parking lot." The match starts and Poynter crawls around on his hands and knees. I crawl with him. We stand. We tie up. We break. Poynter's fingertips touch the mat. I dive forward at his right leg. After a few seconds, I have his ankles. Like a small livestock, a slimy thing you're tasked with bludgeoning for the sake of the farm, because you have two sisters and your dad says you're the oldest, I have his ankles. He falls and I scramble up his body and hold on, unsure whether I've been rewarded for the takedown. I am lost for a moment while trying to turn him and my hands lock around his torso and the whistle blows. "Locked hands, one point, green," the ref says, just as we're stumbling out of bounds.

I check the board and see I got my takedown points. We return to the center. I recognize that he's the first parson of the season. I get on top of him. The whistle blows and he struggles. He keeps rebuilding his base. I keep tearing it down. Poynter hasn't lost this season, but I'm going to change that. It's my job to make other people upset and sad. I squat on him. He shows his shell to me, I'm trying to turn him over and get to that sweet underbelly, where the meat is. Two minutes into the first I have 1:33 riding time.

I keep trying to pry him open. Every now and then he brings an arm up near my shoulders, and I bend his fingers back. At the end of the first I have 2:33 riding time.

I choose bottom and get out. He lets me go but is after me as soon as I get the point. He quickly pushes my arms to where I can't use them, and it's my fault, he gets behind me, and all the losses I've taken over the years, all the way back to when my mom and dad were still here and I was not fully grown or sure of myself, they put on the stirrups and ride through my mind. But I'm not weak willed anymore, I have little respect for doubt and I always do what I tell myself I'm going to do. I'm better now. Look at all the holes in this cage, I can escape through any of them.

From the side I dimly hear Hargraves yelling, "Kill him! Kill!"

Granby roll. I put the textbook and all the rest in my head. I do it and just like that he's under me, I'm his overweight father and he doesn't want to play anymore. For many seconds, I crank on his neck, staring at his scalp. He's blessed with a small head. His head skin crinkles on my arm, and I wonder how thankful his mother was when she pushed out a baby that had such a small head. The whistle blows.

He picks bottom. And the reality is that he's a good wrestler, good enough that I can't pin him, but not as good as I am, and this becomes a fact. Wrestling is unprejudiced and open minded, and it's impossible to argue with. It always tells the truth, and that's why so many men love it. The truth is I've been the one ridden for a period straight. I've been the one who's good enough to not be pinned but not good enough to get the guy off my back. When someone is riding you for two whole minutes it's enough to turn you back into yourself as a baby, as your most frustrated self, running into things all the time that aren't what you want them to be. Poynter is a medium-level wrestler, a minor talent, good enough to get a takedown on me, but not good enough to be remembered after his last match. Men made of mesh, men made of tinsel, paper, dust. I was one for the seasons before this one. I was an infant with no good pictures, with an asymmetrical face, but now I am squatting on Poynter's body, turning off his water, riding him until the end of the match. How many things in the world must get worse before they get better? My grandma said I should have choices so I own two nice pairs of pants, two button-down shirts, and two ties. I put my shit in the Miles City toilet and my spit is dry in the hall by now. Fewer and fewer questions need to be asked about what's going to happen. I'm answering them. Look. There are things that can be expressed only by wrestling. I'm showing you. This is what it's like to stick your whole hand in the nest.

Dylan is standing in the bleachers with a sign that says STEVIN FLORDA FOR THE MAYOR. Men with cauliflower ears are clapping for me.

Linus wins his last match.

4–0.

It's dark. We head out to the vans. I'm going to study meteorology, I have my flashlight. In the parking lot, Whitey sneezes ten feet away at the same time a breeze comes through and I get wet spackle in my mouth.

WE FIND A BAG OF ORANGES. From Linus's window, we fling them across the path at a botany classroom (there are tall plants in the windows). The oranges smack against the glass, scaring them in the middle of their leaves lesson. The professor comes all the way out of the building and stands on the snowy grass, staring at the face of our dorm and trying to figure out which window we're in. "Security's coming," he yells, hands on his hips. Another orange makes its debut, hitting his shoe on the second bounce.

The junior who lives next to Linus, Brandon, buys his first-ever skateboard and tries it out in the hall. On the maiden trip, his head hits my door frame and he walks a few steps before easing himself to the ground. For ten minutes, he incorrectly answers basic questions. Then, all at once, he smiles and says, "Ha-ha. I remember now."

A red squirrel gets stuck in the stairway and for a while we keep it on the floor, letting it run around wherever it likes. It gets in Perry's pillowcase, and when he lies down for sleep, none the wiser, it bites his eyebrow. There's poop everywhere. We feed it nuts taken from the cafeteria salad bar and after two weeks it's noticeably obese. We feel bad and let it go.

I make myself smarter with books. Every day, when I come home from practice, I read the scholarly text-based articles for my What Is Nothing? class or bone up on the synoptic scale. When I've had enough, when the fizz gets too high, I do something to sweat it away. Then I come back and sit down at the desk again.

There's always noise outside my door but I don't bother with any of it. A sentence I encountered one night for homework said, "(A proposition can, indeed, be an incomplete picture of a certain state of affairs, but it is always *a* complete picture.)" It also said, "It is clear that there are no grounds for believing that the simplest course of events will really happen."

Where I run into trouble is the little cracks of time that won't be filled by wrestling or studying. One week after Miles City, just before Thanksgiving, I sit in the chair at midnight in my room, trying out blind contours on things out my window. There have been no more notes put under my door. I sketch the tree, whatever varietal tree that is, in the ghoul light from the path's walking lamps. My drawing looks like something a dumb person forced to draw would've drawn. I have a complete, unbidden erection in my sweatpants. I haven't had an orgasm since after my last match last season. From what I remember it feels like a doorknob turning open. In high school, I got two handjobs from a small girl the year above me named Tiffany. And if Tiffany sounds like the name of a girl who would give you exactly two handjobs, then let it be known she preferred to be called Tiff, and though I was 122 pounds at the time, I would've broken the jaw of any dingfuck who touched her. I liked her O.K. but her hand could've been anyone's hand, I didn't need hers, in particular, really.

At Oregsburg, I haven't had anything last past three or four days since they usually move on when they realize I don't have any time. A summary of my romantic encounters:

1. Three years ago, they had a cotillion in the gym for freshman athletes. They put up red and white streamers and dimmed the lights and played bad music. It was meant to foster fraternal feelings between the males and females.

The central activity was they gave you a frilly card with the name of an opposite-sex athlete and their sport, and the game was to find that person. I got a card that said "Megan Volleyball." I walked to the other side of the gym holding my card, where a cluster of the volleyball team was sitting on the bleachers. I asked one after the other. "Are you Megan?" Eventually, I found her. "Are you Megan?" She was way taller than me, I could tell even sitting down that she was.

"Yes," she said.

"Who's on your card?" I said.

She opened her card, clearly for the first time. "Well, aren't you Stephen?"

I said, "My name is on your card?"

And when she squinted at me, I recognized I hadn't fully grasped the style of the game. I looked around the gym, the other males were not bluntly questioning the females, in fact, no one even had their cards out. Many were dancing to the outrageous music. The cards were a pretense to get us all talking, frippery and a last resort, and no one needed them. I had thought they wanted me to be Megan's swain.

2. A nameless sophomore who when we kissed said, "What do you think?" and I scared away by saying, "Time to fucking circle the wagons."
3. A volleyball captain (who didn't remember Megan, who had by then transferred, I heard, because of family issues), who I thought might work out since love is just finding someone exactly as crazy as you are. The captain used her teeth quite freely. We made each other feel special for a little while.
4. The last time I was intimate was fourteen months ago

when a junior named Meredith smashed me against a wall and worked me around a bit.

5. Various other minor physical frictions and affectionate transactions.

But that's all water under the bridge. I believe I've matured. For instance, after my last match freshman season, I came back to my room and in an extended spell of frustration masturbated seven times, I wanted it all out of me, until I couldn't anymore and it started to feel needless. But I don't do that anymore, I've grown up from all that.

I get up, put my sweatshirt and Ponies on.

An ongoing problem is this: What can I do with myself when I can't make myself better? A jog is always a sensible choice, so I head outside into the dark. It's a Saturday, bass from stereos coming through walls and windows along with occasional laughing. My next match isn't until December 7. It will be against Joseph Carver, the 133 Konstantin College will trot out, and I haven't even seen a picture of him but the excessive waiting time guarantees a valuable meeting experience. The two weeks until then pass in stupid, small doses. I'm running faster, and it's not for any other reason than it's something I have control over so I want to use it. I am running fast enough that I can outrun my spit. I wonder what Mary Beth's contours are of. The erection tries to return, but I'm running and it loses.

Small dots of light in windows are the only signs of life, and I'm thankful I have the main path to myself, thinning to a single presence in sweatpants, jogging out frustration, as though on the moon, the oval-shaped campus and the roads on the fringes where the grass and dirt stop and cars do not slow down. My blue and white and yellow and green existence.

The student union is empty, the TV is on. I'm not asshole enough to pretend I didn't come by on the off chance Masha is doing the trash. Maybe next time, I guess.

I cover the left nostril and blow out the right. I lick my teeth. If I had hair the wind would be blowing it around right now. A bunch of loops, a bunch of practice grab-ass for incremental progress, days upon days of small progress, days of my body becoming more and more alive. All the days with the leash off, I make something of every one of them. I'll never quit, sweat blotching my sweatshirt, lung burn, chest burn, leg burn.

Memorial's rooms run in a straight line, two floors that look like a long prison row, classroom doors exposed to the elements and a rail on the upper floor. I hit the stairs and head up to the second floor and, because I have to go, decide the first bench is as good a spot as any to whiz from. My stream can take a little bit of time to start. And it is in that waiting time that I hear voices somewhere below. For the same reason I do everything, which is to see what'll happen, I turn myself toward the rail and lean on tiptoes to fit my twiglet over the top, and the modest tide that emerges results not in the sound of whiz hitting pavement but of whiz hitting top of head, and the voices stop. When I do something particularly bad, like this, it feels like more than just one person is looking down on me.

While I finish up, there's what I take to be shocked silence. Like a cartoon, I imagine a line of steam rising up from below. Then a male voice screams, "Some pervert is peeing on us! Get him!" Fast footsteps as I flop it back inside the sweatpants and decamp.

I experience no remorse for what I've just done, which is a pattern, because I can't remember the last time I did something bad enough to inspire real, actual *remorse*.

It's good to run for a reason and being chased is one of the best. I do a full sprint around the upper rim of the college, and when I'm sure I've lost them I stop in a slim gap of Rainbow Building's northern wall, where a pillar hides me from everything. I had my Greeks & Romans class here, on the other side of this curved wall, I was eighteen and sucking on the sour end of the carrot stick. My breath extends beyond the pillar, like air bubbles from a nasty lake predator popping on the surface. I hear more voices. Both sexes. A different group than the pursuers. Leaning forward, I put my open mouth on the pillar, moving my lips on the freezing stone circumference, and as the voices come closer, thinking of nice students unaware of what's hiding up around the bend, I derive indescribable pleasure from mouthing a piece of architecture.

When they pass, I fall in behind. There are six of them, all carrying six packs or wine bottles. We go around the curve of Rainbow, the girls wearing nice shoes, and I infer that we are on our way to a party. Because I'm quiet and they're loud they don't hear me coming up behind them. At least two are wearing perfume or cologne.

There's a little stretch of hedges on the path between Rainbow and Mooney Dormitory, and that's where they turn. The last one, a male, holds the door for me. "Thank you," I say. We cross the lobby. At the far end the elevator doors begin closing, but they see me coming and hold it open. I crowd in.

"Thank you," I say.

"Who do you know up there?" a female says.

"I'm in class with Mary Beth," I say.

"Oh! I'm in Tuesday-Thursday Ethics with her. You're not in that one, right?"

"No, I'm in Drawing."

"Are you an art student?"

"No, I wrestle."

"What's your name?"

"Stephen Florida."

By this time I'm already in the apartment, which is big and full of people and loud. These cotillions are what I've been missing every night around the place. I'm being taken by this girl, who has her hand around my bicep in a familiar fashion that brings about the return of the boner, through all these people until she stops me and tells this other girl, who's name comes at the front end of the sentence and is blared out by the music, "—Stephen Florida. He's the one in Emmy's art class, the wrestler. Look at him."

Whereas the first girl, who has now disappeared, was pretty with darker hair, this one is pretty with lighter hair. "So you're the wrestler," she says. And before I can ask why she said "the" instead of "a," she says, "You want to take your hat off? Your sweatshirt?"

"Yeah." Both come off.

"Do you want me to put them someplace, wrestler?"

"No, thanks. I'll hold them."

"Suit yourself." She points to the other end of the apartment, across all the people. "Emmy's that way, in her room. She crashed pretty early."

I go into the party room. Something smells like body and feet. I realize it's me. It's about then that I notice sundry narcotics paraphernalia. Pills and powders on the counters and tables.

Probably because of my smell, the partiers make room for me and the trip through the party room is easy. A male has found a lampshade somewhere and has it on his head. Someone hands me a beer, a green bottle, and the mind will play strange games with you—from holding a bottle, you will remember the running adolescent scheme you had collecting glass around your town in order to save up for a transistor radio, you will hear your mother saying no broken glass, and you will remember the feeling of ignoring her command, of discarding it away. I watch them dance and hold conversations at the same time. It feels like everyone in here hasn't washed their hands.

I pass my beer to the nearest male. "Here."

"Hey, man," he yells above the music. "Did you drink any of this?"

"No."

"You didn't pee in it or anything, right?"

"What?"

"Why not? Ha. I'm just yanking on you." He makes a crass hand gesture, then puts the same hand on my shoulder. I wait for him to swallow half the beer using his anonymous face. "Tell me something. Do we know each other, because I feel like we know each other." In his other hand is a doobie, which he catches me staring at.

"Want a suck?"

"No."

"Why?"

"I don't. Get involved."

"Why?"

"I don't know."

"Too bad." He sucks on it once. "Do you know why I do?"

"No."

"It makes things interesting. It makes everything more interesting."

I look down at my shoes.

"Hey, man, you are very sweaty. Are you all right?"

I'm not doing anything, it seems to me, to provoke this question, but I've been making people uncomfortable my whole life without meaning to, so I'm used to it, I'm used to hearing this same question.

"I'm fine."

Over the male's shoulder, Kyle Glanville walks by. We make eye contact. A thing like disgust shows up on his face, then he turns away. I miss Linus. He's at the freshman mixer meeting people the normal way, not lurking around parties and urinating on people. Potentially, probably, I could, I realize, feel remorse if something bad happened to Linus or Mary Beth, on account of me.

The male has finished the beer. Then the previous song ends and "Jesus Is Just Alright" comes on and he says, "God is a woman." The first person who said this idea to me was my best friend Bird, and years later this party boy with no face is acting like he's the first to come up with God is a woman.

Despite the many scraps of conversation going on around my head, I hear at least three separate ones from various sides including "balcony" and "peed" and "pervert" and "cut his throat." On the dance floor, the sides these are coming from seem to keep changing, giving the feeling of being enclosed by my accusers. As part of math's consequence at a thousand-person school, where there are only so many parties, the chances of ending up at the same one as my victim are not so low. "Let me get you another," I say to the male, grabbing his bottle and moving deeper into the crowd.

At the far end of the apartment, I open the first door I come to and close it behind me.

Drawing II is Tuesday-Thursday. In the week since I came back from Miles City, Mary Beth's been sitting next to me and I've been walking her to her next class, Renaissance & Its Discontents. Luckily, it's in Rainbow, which gives us a ten-minute walk from the drawing studio. I always go to my next class, Basic News Writing, and sit in the back, unbending paper clips and thinking about her. She seems to carefully reveal more and more things to me, and whether it's her intention or not, she becomes a more and more permanent thing, wedges herself gently into my life. She grew up in Thief River Falls, a town in northern Minnesota known for cemetery desecration and bull riding. She's doing eighteen credits, the maximum allowed, and when I asked her three times if she'd like to do something sometime, she said she's busy, "But not 'busy' like I'm blowing you off. Because I'm not. I'm actually busy." She's doing a work-study twenty hours a week at the mediocre art museum next to the student union. She wants to be a gallery director, maybe work for a museum one day. She tells me about how the job always changes, how she can travel and work closely with painters, sculptors, photographers. She likes how she doesn't know where she'll end up. I ask if she's tried showing her stuff to someone somewhere. She gets mumbly and says she's not good enough, it's just something she does on the side.

I look at the walls of her bedroom, which are covered with sketches and prints and tiny paintings, and I see that she wasn't lying about being busy. There must be sixty or seventy taped up, including a few on the window. One in particular. It's tiny, a five-by-eight, and it's of a male, though the lines are so scraggly and rough it almost looks abstract. Maybe fifteen different colors are in it, but the primaries are blue, green, and yellow. The figure, made jagged by the strokes, is sitting in a chair in an empty room, it looks like. Because of the sharp lines he looks both at rest and agitated. Or maybe the best way to say it is the agitation is in the room with him.

"Stephen, is that you?" She moves in her bed. Her eyes are very dark brown, though she hasn't opened them.

"Yeah."

She reaches up and pats the front of my shirt. "You're sweating."

"Yes," I say. "Sorry about that."

"It's O.K. Can you put your hand right here?" She takes my hand and places it on the side of her face. I brush her hair behind her ears. She pulls me and I kneel at the side of her bed. Down, down, down. I put my ear against her temple and can hear the hum of her thinking, like a hidden underground power plant by the side of the road.

"Will you come to my next match?"

"Yes."

When she asked me what I wanted to do after I graduate, I told her I hadn't thought that far ahead.

MARY BETH STANDS AND PEDALS while I sit on the seat like an oblivious princess. "What's the most you ever weighed?" she says. It's barely snowing.

"I hit 145 two Marches ago. It was after the season and I got lax with the intake." A bus blows past the opposite way, south and toward school, wobbling the bike. "Don't go so fast, I'm gonna fall off."

She swerves in an S pattern up Prairie View Road to screw with me, and I have to clamp down my grip. I would get more sensory pleasure from holding her shoulders if she wasn't going so fast.

On the way north, by the Pharmart roadside, there's a homeless man shaking a paper cup. She slows down and I give him the change in my wallet. Bending his scoliosis back even farther, he thanks me four times and compliments me on the prettiness of my girlfriend. After we pedal away, she says nothing, no sign of being impressed.

Mary Beth is taking us farther from Oregsburg than I'm used to. Farther than the Honky Tonky, north of the Haldon quarry they abandoned because of the granite radiation, all the areas where I run with Linus. The time between cars keeps growing. Yellow weeds that apparently don't die in winter. The same things over and over. She makes some turns, and houses are fewer and fewer. We go so far that anything man-made becomes noticeable, a rusted gardening can filled to the brim with snow, mailboxes, boards about fruit for sale with painted white arrows. In one of the fields, there's a horse backbone sticking out of the snow. It thins out to just telephone poles. Wind blows. The snow comes off the roads like old-woman hair, then disappears completely.

I speak selectively, afraid I'm going to topple the thing Mary Beth is allowing to happen between us, which so far has included mouth affection and body caresses on top of her comforter. We're still in the phase where you try to make the other person think you don't have flaws or take dumps. The telephone wires strung up on the roadside keep leading like bread crumbs.

"What are your parents like?" she says.

"I'm sure probably a lot like your parents. What are your parents like?"

"My mom and dad had me when they were super young, so I think I ruined their fun a little bit. We always had dogs because of my dad. The one that I remember best we named Pierre. You know how the pet you remember best is the one that was there when you changed the most? That's why I remember him. I got my belly button pierced when he was around and my dad had him come in the car when he got his first kidney stones. In the middle of the night he was in the backseat hugging Pierre while he was yelling at my mom to run the red lights." She turns her head. "Are your parents coming to any of the matches this season?"

"I think so, yeah. They need to see when they can make the drive. It's far for them."

"Yeah."

Out of the snow, far off and at the end of the field, a small white house appears. She turns onto a small dirt path on the left. I guess this means we've arrived.

There's a little hill, between us and the house in the distance. "Last stop," she says. We get off under a tree, and she turns to face me. For the first time off of a mat, I'm thankful for something before it's done happening. Her hair is up. I think she is wearing eye makeup. I'm bad at describing faces, they are what they are and Mary Beth's is about as nice as they can get, which is fun to look at and great to think about touching. She has on a green mackinaw. She puts things in my head without trying, I obsessively catalog her gestures and the way her lips move and memorize the painters she names, and I calm down because I'm so busy concentrating on her. She's a marker on the map to consider in six months, when OC time runs out. The fact that I don't know what we're doing right now is a large part of what makes it so exciting. Maybe she plans to take me somewhere to resume our passions.

She covers up the bike with a shaggy tree branch and pulls me up the little path that leads to the top of the hill. Even through gloves, holding her hand makes me nervous, and so for no reason, I ask the first question that I can think of.

"What's the worst thing that ever happened to you?"

It takes her a moment to answer, which I take to mean there are choices to pick from. What are we doing? "I went out in the snow when I was seven and got gangrene, I lost three of my toes."

"Jesus. How?"

"I got lost in the woods. Do you want to see my toes?"

"I do, if you want to show me."

"Dummy, I'm kidding. I broke my arm. But I got ambidextrous from that." She looks at me and her left ear screens the sun. It turns bright red. All the blood vessels running along the inside part of her ear. "What's the worst thing that's happened to you?"

In these types of situations, where I don't want to say anything about myself, I typically ask the other person more questions. I'm not used to spending this much time with another person. I clear my throat and point to the green pickup truck moving down the road. "Is that why we came out here?" I say.

"Oh shit, get down," she says, and yanks me so we're both belly-down on top of the hill. She removes binoculars from her mackinaw! She points them at the truck, which turns into the driveway of the house. A man gets out. "That's him, all right."

"Why do you have binoculars?"

But she doesn't seem to hear. She sighs and mutters, "I hate it here."

"Mary Beth?"

She hands the binoculars to me. On the near side of the house, there's a door with two steps that the man clears of snow by sliding his foot across. I can't see his face, but I do see that his hair is in a ponytail. There's a black case in his hand. He unlocks the door and goes inside.

"That's Professor Silas, Levi Silas, music department. He's my Intro to Jazz teacher."

"Why are we spying on his house?"

"Because his wife died four years ago. He was there, it was the bathroom of that house. Look at the window." I aim them there, but we're too far away to see. There's absolutely nothing between us and the house, nothing really on any side, making a sneak-up impossible. A strange, dark splotch is on the side of the house, a cloud around the window.

"What happened?"

"I'll tell you what happened. There was a 911 call in the middle of the night. It's five seconds or so long: Silas is on the phone saying there's a fire, come right away. You know where the closest fire station is? Down past the mount and near the creek? By the time they got the fire trucks out here he was standing out in the road, and the fire was coming out the side of the house. They put it out. They found her naked and burned up in the bathroom. The door was closed."

"Why was she in the bathroom?"

"That's the problem. They brought in all these fire investigators with dogs. They found a candle in the bathroom, next to the wife. That spot on the house is the leftover fire damage. Looks like he painted over it."

"What did he say happened?"

"He said his wife liked taking midnight baths. With the lights off and smelly candles and rag over the face and everything. Or that's what I heard. He said it wasn't unordinary for her to get up when she couldn't sleep and take a long bath. He said he woke up, went over to the bathroom to call his wife back to bed, it was late. Saw the light from the fire under the door and opened it, grabbed her hand and thought she was right behind him, she was yelling to him that she was going to put it out, and so he made the phone call and ran out of the house. Her old friends won't talk to him, won't have anything to do with him. From what I heard, they questioned him and questioned him and questioned him. But he never got arrested. I think they tried to get him to slip up on his story, to crack him on why his dead wife was in the room where the fire started with the door shut, but he wouldn't do it. What else can you do? He said the door must've been knocked closed as she tried to put out the fire, and no one else was around to say anything different."

"Let me summarize. You're saying that he's saying that in her franticality, she knocks shut with her foot or elbow the bathroom door, in effect sealing her own tomb."

"Yes, that's exactly what I'm saying he's saying."

"Why would he kill his wife?"

"Why does anyone kill anyone?" she says crazily.

Because there's no answer to that, I ask, "How do you know so much about this?"

"I hadn't heard when I signed up for Jazz this semester but when I showed up on the first day, there were only four other people in there."

"So?"

"Stephen, it's an *intro* to *jazz* class. It's in Opal Hall, one of those huge rooms. Every single one of those seats should be full. There should be a waiting list. The final exam is he plays you songs and you have to say whether it's Jelly Roll Morton or Bill Evans. So I started asking around."

"He hasn't hurt you, has he?"

"No, Stephen."

"It's not funny," I say. "Threatened you?"

"No."

"Are you sure?"

"Yes. Relax, he's completely normal in the class. That's what makes it even weirder."

"Was the class good?"

"Yeah. I asked for some of the records he played for Christmas."

"Why is he still teaching if he's a murderer?"

"When I asked my roommates they said he's friends with Lee James."

"Who's him?"

"'Who's him?' Is that what you said?"

"Yeah."

"Oregsburg's president, dum-dum." She scootches closer until the side of her butt is touching my side and I do not object. "They have their own jazz trio. I heard they practice on weekends in the music building. That's probably what he's coming back home from. The case he was carrying was his trumpet."

I stare at the house, like some meaning will appear. "I guess the next question is why did you bring me out here?"

"I've been out here five or six times by myself. I don't know why I keep coming. Every time I look at the house it like . . . fucking distorts into some symbol of what's wrong with Oregsburg for me. And I wanted you to see it. This person just gets to live in a small nice house in a field north of school. This is where he lives. Shit. He keeps getting to live here, he murdered his wife and he still goes on every Sunday playing the trumpet, then he gets to go back to his house and makes tea and showers in the room where she burned to death and then goes to sleep in their bed. Is it just going to stay like this forever? Until he dies of old age in his sleep?"

At some point, the binoculars have been forgotten. Her ice-cold hand is under my clothes, squeezing and pinching my back. She looks at me with the womanly intent.

"I think under people's skin there's good and bad," she says. "With a lot of people it could go either way. This place, it's like an experiment, it's like a test for the people who live here."

"I'm not sure I understand."

"Yes, you do. You know exactly what I'm talking about. It takes a certain kind of person to live here. A lot of people, the cold, the separateness, it doesn't affect them. But some people, it does something to their brain. It's floating around here."

"Does what to the brain?"

"I've only taken one psychology class—"

"Have you heard of Wilhe—"

"But there are a million ways the brain can screw up. There are more variables of disorder for the brain than any other part of the body. Dyslexia, aneurysms, multiple sclerosis, Parkinson's, a stroke. A kneecap, that can only break, can only break or fracture or pop. A brain, the number of ways it can go wrong, it's frightening."

A car goes by on the road at the bottom of the hill.

"What do you want?" she says.

"I want to win the championship."

"Not that. I knew that already. Why do you want that? What's behind that?"

"I want to become my full self before I die."

"Why do you want that so badly?"

"Because I'll have years and years of happiness and fulfillment. Isn't that what I'm supposed to say? Something like that?"

"Don't talk down to me. Let me get this straight. You win the championship in Kenosha in March, and for the rest of your life you're happy. You don't win—"

"I'm going to win."

"You don't win in Kenosha in March and you're unhappy for the rest of your life?"

"Yes."

"How does that work? How can your entire life be determined by one ten-minute period?"

"You've never wrestled before. And it's seven minutes."

"Did you ever do sets in math?"

"Yeah, probably."

"It's where you group a bunch of related things together in the little brackets. You should know what a bracket is."

"Don't talk down to *me*."

"But yours is like a bracket with one thing in it. It's a one-thing set."

"Why else does the world exist than to test you and see if you're good enough to pass the test? I've been preparing for this since I started wrestling. When I was eleven. Everything outside of wrestling is devoid of mystery and deep faith. If this isn't my test, what is?"

"I don't know, Stephen, but you don't, either. That's the point. You're not going to turn into a fireball in Kenosha in March and extinguish from the world. Life is long. Possible future tests? O.K. How about being a parent? Moving to another country or doing something that helps someone else? What's the point of living the rest of your life if the high point happens when you're twenty-two?"

"The point is to put the rest of my life on the right track with what I do when I'm twenty-two. To affect the next fifty years with something good. Then I die at seventy-two, wrinkled like a turtle and peeing in a bag, but that's fine. Because I set things in order when I had no wrinkles and could control my body and used it as a tool to stomp down all these other doofuses. Or, on the other hand of the coin, a bus comes out of nowhere and kills me next year. You'd say, 'What a waste!' But it's not a waste. I'm dead, but look what I've done. It doesn't even matter that I'm dead. It's about taking control of your life, about nothing ever telling you what you're incapable of."

"You're putting all your eggs in one basket. You have no fall-back plan. You only care about one thing."

"That's right. Caring about the one thing makes it what it is."

"No. You can choose to care about other things. It's not healthy."

"You don't understand. I don't feel like I have a choice."

"No one's questioning you doing this. I'm talking about your mind-set, your way of thinking."

"But the way of thinking is part of it," I say. "It's necessary. The act and the goal wouldn't be what they are without the way of thinking."

"What are you doing for others?" she says with a fierceness that she thinks closes the door on our talk. But I don't let her get the last word, I don't let her think I'm sensitive.

I say, "I'm setting an example."

A light has gone on in the house. It's gotten darker.

"I'm sorry."

"Me, too."

She is quiet for a second, her mind unmixing her moods. I barely have differences in moods, so I wait for her to tell me what she wants me to do. If she tells me to sprint over the hill and run into the house and kill Silas, I will do it. It would surprise her how fast I would do it.

She says, "Why do you like me?"

"Because I've never met anyone who thinks the way you do. You work harder than anyone else. You're always busy because you're working. I can't even guess what you're thinking most of the time. It seems like you can turn things into what you want them to be. I like the way your lips are. You showed me this house. Is that what you meant?"

She seems to be searching my face for something, and after a while says, "If we got married I'd be Mary Beth Florida. Isn't that weird?" She turns me over onto my back, takes her glove off by biting the fingertip and pulling, saying, "You're very cold. Let's help you out with that." In my sweatpants, she uses a different technique than Masha. First of all she starts slow, setting the scene so to speak, in a way that I find a lot more romantic. I can't decide whether she wants me to look at her or close my eyes. "Like this?"

"I'm not allowed to finish, that's the only rule, I think."

"That's weird."

"I'm sorry. You're doing a really good job."

"Thank you."

She loops the drawstring of my sweatpants in an intricate way around my parts. I don't know what to do with my brain or my eyes. I squeeze the cold dirt on top of the hill. I say, "Tell me something about your life."

"Anything?"

"Yes."

"I'll just keep doing this while I talk. Is that all right with you?"

"Yes."

"When I was a kid, there was a rash of dead goats across Minnesota. The towns by me. They couldn't figure out what was going onto these farms, into the livestock pens, and pulling out the guts of the goats. It started in the town just south of me, Red Lake Falls. At first, they thought it was a neighborhood dog, and so they rounded up a bunch of unclaimed dogs and shot them. But then in my town, some goats started turning up with their bellies open. And by then it had stopped in Red Lake. So then people started suspecting a pack of wolves or coyotes migrating north. But then everyone realized that couldn't be right: If it were wolves or coyotes, why were they just killing goats? Why weren't we finding other animals?" She stops at points in the story to lean down and kiss me, which is aggressive and nice. "By then they were putting a daily count, a little red box in the top corner of the paper every morning, it got to be a thing you'd check when you woke up, to see how much higher it'd gone. It kept going up, twenty-seven one day, then twenty-nine, then thirty-four. It went on for about two weeks, up to thirty-nine. And then for a few days it would still be thirty-nine, and after a few days, they took the box out of the paper, and the next week we heard about dead goats up in Hallock, right by the Canadian border. At the time it seemed like a pretty big story, but then you find out something that everyone around can't stop talking about is only being talked about by the people around you. When I think about it now, I just picture this abstract thing, like a cloud or shadow, moving north when no one's looking. The weirdest thing about it was that the goats' intestines were just pulled out, not eaten or messed with, it was like something just took them out to look at. And the whole time it was happening, I was staying up really late with one little light on in my room. I was on the first floor and there was a big open field out my window. Pierre was sleeping on the floor. I couldn't remember why I was forcing myself to stay up. I think I thought whatever was killing the goats would show up if I did. It would be three in the morning, and I'd listen and look at the window, looking for something I would only recognize the moment I saw it at my window, trying to get in."

"I think you should probably stop."

She brings my hand over to herself, lies down on her back, positions me so I'm straddling her. "I have no dumb rule against finishing." I use my concentration very strongly. She comments on the largeness of my hands. What are you doing for others? She closes her eyes and tips her head back. Snow gets in her hair. Her moans, which I don't care for a second if they are for my benefit, I commit to auditory memory. She obviously doesn't care who hears. They spring from her throat louder and louder so I keep an eye on the Silas house while she lets me finish her off.

When she's done, she holds my acting hand and puts the fingers in her mouth. "You bite your fingernails, huh?" she says. Her eyes do that dreamy woman thing that you see a few times in your life if you're lucky, and for a moment I think she will fall asleep on the hill. "Aren't you ever tired? Don't you ever want to rest?"

There have been ten billion women in the world, stretching, speaking, itching, laughing, eating, burping, and none of them have made the impression Mary Beth has made. Every step of her life dents the earth harder, like she's sucking up more air than everyone else. She's more destructive, taking it all up, like in my middle school acting class where the teacher screamed at you to use the whole stage. *Mind your own business* is the standard of North Dakota, but she ignores all that.

From my mouth, where I don't have time to carefully stack the words up to make these thoughts, I say, "You smell good."

"I like how you smell, too."

"You're a lot smarter and better looking than me. You must know that."

"Flattery!" she says. "I like talking to you. And I like looking at you."

"Nah," I say. "I got these ears."

She rubs my head and her fingers gently move down to my ears, the space behind. "I know."

IN THE LOCKER ROOM AFTER PRACTICE, Linus shows me a note from his mom. It's a tear sheet from a pad you stick on your refrigerator.

Dear Linus,

Terry and Lynn are doing good. Terry spends weekends shooting his potato gun and Lynn runs out into the fields with Dad's surveyor wheel to measure. He keeps tinkering with it, he's trying to beat his record, which is 120 meters. Dad is talking about you a lot, he likes to talk to Bill and Jenny and Curtis about you. How are your classes? Seems like every year there's more to do, I'm vacuuming nearly every day! Give your deodorant stick to Stephen if he needs some. We have extra sticks here and can send more because the Right Shop had them three for two.

Dad and Mom.

He says, "My parents say they'll come to the championship if I make it. In Kenosha."

"You're going to make it to Kenosha."

"They want to meet you. It'll make my mom feel good to send you the deodorant."

I give him the note back. "Tell her thank you." I have this quick, exciting vision of Masha sensuously rubbing up on her vacuum cleaner. Then in jumps Mary Beth, replacing Masha and putting the vacuum to venereal use.

In the hallway, Linus puts his hand on my elbow to get my real attention, and says, "Stephen. Can I ask you a question?"

"Yeah."

"It's sort of a weird question."

"O.K."

"You're going to think I'm stupid. It's really stupid."

"Ask it."

"You have to promise not to laugh."

"O.K."

"I'm serious. Promise."

"I promise."

"O.K. Do girls pee out of their butts?"

The first week of practice a few months ago, on a furlough night, we found *Jaws* on in the student union. It ended at two in the morning and we walked the ten minutes back to McCloskey yelling "Farewell and Adieu to You, Fair Spanish Ladies," which we didn't really know the words to.

We join the rest of the team for Thanksgiving in the conference room, down the hall from the locker room. It's been snowing all day, but there are no windows in here. It smells like poor food and is filled with hot air. Eerik's wife and Lee's wife stand off to the side with their arms crossed and mumbling to each other, possibly taking erotic pleasure from watching us put their food in our mouths. The two long tables are covered with big disposable plastic sheets, which are festive orange. Some of us are still sweating from practice, and we're all tired.

Nine days until Joseph Carver. In my pocket, I have a folded-up paper about him. He wrestles for Konstantin, he's 3–1. This isn't much to go on, but it's a start. My imagination figures up his family, his dinner table, his dog begging for scraps. Has he forgotten about me? I'm biting my turkey meat, just gnawing around on it. I am something that's always there but you forget. Like eyelids.

"Dude, if you ever wanna see what you'd look like fat just go like this." Ellis hunches his whole body forward and smushes his chin to his chest.

Sherman, next to him, says, "Dude, it doesn't really work for you. You have no jaw."

"Yeah, I have a small jawline."

"What's a jawline?"

"It's, you know, your jaw," Ellis says. "Show them what fat looks like, Fenry." Down at the end of the table, Fat Henry puts part of a roll into his mouth, squishes his chin down, and both tables cheer.

The coaches have their own table in the corner. They get sirloin. Later, they get to go home to houses where their children and wives are waiting to be with them, because our meal is in the early afternoon and so it's mainly a solidarity thing for our sake. I haven't ever made a point of sorting out their family situations, which ones are happy and how much. How I am has made them back off. For the rest of the team, they are there mostly to keep you committed and to make you inconsiderably better, maybe adding a win or two to their totals. I don't need them for that anymore. I just need them to medically clear me (Fink's job) and count my reps in practice (Whiting) and drive me to my matches (Eerik's job). That kind of thing.

There's a pitiful cornucopia on each table. Nate keeps doing lewd things with a gourd and laughing about it.

My boredom gets thicker. I don't want to be here. I pick a

booger out and wipe it on Whitey's nub. "What are you touching on me for, Florida?" He suspiciously rubs his back. I take the last broccoli stalk from my plate and put it into my mouth. I wash it down with one of my two allotted cups of skim milk, thinking of the tits on the cow it came from, a cow kept alive for its useful tits. Big meaty thick ones. Flapping around in the breeze.

Lyle says, "I saw this show where all these young people were riding polo ponies around and playing."

"They could do that?" Sherman says.

"Could do what? Who?"

"Be ridden. The horses."

"What the hell are you talking about, Sherman, that's what polo is."

"I thought that's what fucks your legs up."

"You are retarded because that's polio."

"Oh yeah."

Across the table, Kryger is glaring at me. I wait for him to say something. I'm thankful for any excitement.

The girl, the painter, is still with Whitey, and he shares their games with the table. "She had me play this intimate game. She stood on the other side of the door, I could hear her taking her clothes off, and she said, 'Guess which part of my body I'm smacking.' It was so erotic."

One of the least palatable aspects of wrestling is the pace. It begins in November and ends in March, and you're wrestling twenty or so times a season. You get roughly four matches a month, but that's not even really true because you get these unbearable breaks for Christmas and around postseason. Much of the season is a waiting room, pining over your schedule, dictated by faceless schedule-makers who sit around fatly and decide to make me wait, the gunk accumulating in my organs.

The gunk is like an egg that needs to be laid regularly, I don't know what to do with it all. The secret of wrestling is that it's really about self-management.

Every day, I look forward to practice, to the miniature fights they give me like conjugal visits, where I'm temporarily allowed to release myself until I'm told to ease up, lay off, cool it. I breathe faster for the entire practice, and for the half hours before and after. But it's not enough, it's never enough. And just like that, when I'm putting my clothes on after the shower, I begin measuring the time to the next time, because my gunk begins molding up faster than anyone else's. If I had my way I'd wrestle every day and the season would be four hundred matches long.

Linus, who's next to me, keeps lifting open *The Stand* in his lap and sneaking sentences.

Two pairs have been lumped together permanently on the team: the Raiskin brothers, Jerry and Tom, who clearly have at least one parent who enjoys making a joke of things, and William Belcher and William van Ness, who have no blood relation and don't even look similar, but one looks really old and the other doesn't, so they're called Young William and Elder William. The four of them are sitting together at the end of my table, and Ellis, noticing, points and asks if they've ever felt compelled to play doubles tennis, or ride two-seater bikes or teeter-totters for amusement or use one of those long saws that requires two people to cut down big trees.

I bite off the strip of skin that folds along the nail on my left middle finger. It takes about thirty seconds for the blood to trace an outline of the nail. I put it in my mouth and suck the jam out, but it keeps coming back. It won't stop bleeding, so I let it get deeper around the rim, and when it's finally sticky enough it stops.

"It's like, have you noticed that the number seven looks like a question mark?" Reuben says to Lowe, who nods.

I look at Simon licking his dinner roll before taking a bite out of it. I think he's majoring in accounting. He licks all the way around the roll, really luxuriating in it. I have nothing against him, but his life is not mine, it's a fart of a life. I couldn't be trained to care about someone else's money. That is Simon Fjelstad's unremarkable life, four decades of reading what comes up on a number machine, a grain thresher at the end summoning you through it.

Finally, Kryger says what he's going to say, which is, "Fuck you, Florida! You dislocated my finger!" Because the finger in question is his pointer, he is able to use it to accuse me. There's a black splint taped on, like a resting caterpillar.

"Dessert now, boys!" The wives walk trays around. Everyone gets a half cup of pineapple.

"I didn't dislocate your finger," I say, sucking the last of my mashed potatoes into my body.

"Then who the fuck did, fancyboy?"

Linus is wiping his mouth over and over.

"Don't get, what do you call it, contentious." I smack my lips. "If you want to be technical about it, what happened was your finger got between your body and the mat. So if you want to take it up with someone, I'd blame your own torso. Or go talk to the mat. Or your finger for desiring to bend the wrong way. In logic, the last person to blame would be me." I taste one pineapple, which is neither pinecone nor apple but is delicious and sweet and cold. "All I did was show everyone who you are. Which is a lazy loser. You're a lazy loser that I'll always beat. Next time I'll break your other fucking finger."

Suddenly, Kryger's attention shifts to my left, to Linus. "You going to just sit there and read, faggot?" Kryger throws a piece of broccoli and it hits Linus in the face. He picks up another piece, looks at me, and says, "Fuck your dead mother, and fuck your faggot boyfriend."

It's like there's no table between us, it's like there's no one else in the room. That's how quickly I'm on him. How quickly his chair is knocked over and my right hand is prying open his big mouth. That's how quickly I get my half cup of pineapple rammed into his mouth, the rim of the cheap plastic cup cutting his lips, which are chapped and ready for bleeding nice. Snot comes out of my nose. "I insist," I say. "I insist." He puts his hands up while I hit his face. He makes a noise. That is that. That is that. They get to me about then, but not before I get a wad of spit into his eye.

I'm dragged outside, and when I can see straight again, I'm in the hallway with Coach Fink grabbing my sweatshirt. The door opens and Linus pokes his head out, but Fink says, "Go back inside," which Linus does.

When we're all the way down by the inoperative water fountain, he says, "Florida, what big teeth you have." His idea appears to be to hold on to me like a leashed dog until it's clear I've settled down.

"When did your hands get so strong, Coach?" I say. "Put me down."

"Are you calm?"

"Yes."

He lets go but correctly intuits that he needs to stand between me and the room that has Kryger in it, because newly freed I have another sudden longing to rush back in and further deface his head.

Fink says, "You've got some like crying there in your eye."

"I'm not upset," I say. He laughs. His laugh is just awful. I wonder if he spent his whole life making it so awful.

"What's wrong with you?"

"Nothing." I realize that though I'm a good liar with my mouth, I'm a bad liar with my face, which can't hide a thing. There's a steady, insistent drip of water coming from somewhere nearby.

"You're angry, Florida. Not just now. In practice, in matches, after matches, during team dinners. Last year I saw you kick the handle off a faucet in the St. Gregory bathroom."

"Because that was after the fucking Frazier match."

"I saw you, same location, rip out one of the van's seatbelts."

"I had him. If the period was fifteen seconds longer, I had him."

Drip. "I know."

"So what if I'm fucking angry? I'm the best wrestler Oregsburg's ever had."

Drip. "You and Linus, yes, maybe." The dripping becomes a predictable noise, which I begin to identify with the face of Fink, which I find unpleasant.

"*Maybe?*"

"I know you're very ambitious. I know you've done a lot with a little."

"Do you even know anything about me? You don't give a shit. I had no other scholarships. I'm the only one left besides Linus that hasn't lost this season. No one's had 133 but me for three years. I built my fucking house on 133."

"There are ways to shape your inside problems so they may benefit you," Fink says.

"I don't know what you're talking about."

"For instance, the monastics, the Buddhists, they'll take a vow of silence."

"You can do that? Why?"

"A lot of reasons. It's a spiritual thing."

"What's the longest vow of silence ever?"

"I don't know, smart-ass." Increasingly, I know that his position as my coach is preventing something malicious on his part from entering this conversation. A snap character judgment is that Fink is bad at keeping the real Fink side turned facedown. So, of course, I will keep pushing. "Some people go more than ten years. There are vows of celibacy, vows of poverty, vows of obedience."

"I'm already doing those. I didn't know there was a name for them. I don't think I need any more ideas, thank you."

"Keep your fucking head on, Florida. That's all I'm saying."

"Where else would I keep it?"

"You should refresh that noggin of yours. The mind is the fruit." Here, in a vulgar gesture, he makes his hairy square middle finger stick out and pokes my temple hard, twice. Old-man strength, which is really just the fibrous iron strength of the fingers, is a result of lifelong handgrip use and masturbation. "Kicking apart bathrooms and attacking your teammates isn't sustainable. And that's only what I've seen, who knows what debauched shit you do unsupervised. It's probably disgusting. You're lucky you're talented enough to still win while on the side you veer off and do all this negligent, perverted nonsense. I've seen your type before. I can tell you how it ends. You're going to flame out. Or get caught. You're going to do something you regret."

"I don't regret anything that gets me what I want."

"I guarantee, if you keep up like this, you're going to lose."

"At the end of the year, when I win at Kenosha, I'm going to remind you you said that."

"You're living in laws made up in your own head. You're by far the biggest deviant I've ever coached." He's making no effort to soften the spray of spit on his consonants, much of which lands on my face and neck. "You have no attention for what's outside yourself. There are laws, and you're never going to get 'what you want' unless you stop being a solipsistic mess. Let me give you an example. To draw the man on the bench, first you must draw the empty bench."

"What is that? Some Zen parable?"

"Why do you speak in such short, autistic sentences?" I've never met someone who talks so easily. If you really pay attention, you can see that he takes a small breath before starting up, but other than that, it's like there's no trying, like he's unrolling a roll of toilet paper out of his mouth, along the floor. "Let me tell you a story. Where I grew up in Idaho, there was a prehistoric animal and cryptozoology park. For the kids. It was called Big Scary Monster World. You'd see little boys in their shorts climbing into the open mouths of huge fake crocodiles, playing with the hard rubber teeth—"

But before he can launch into whatever lesson that was going to turn into, I yawn aggressively. "That's nice," I say. I wonder how much of Mary Beth I can fit in my mouth. "What is the main take-away of this hallway encounter, would you say?"

"You don't listen very well."

"Look, Coach. Let's finish this up like friends. I appreciate you checking our physical charts, supplying finger splints for teammates who think they can beat me, that kind of thing. I'm calm now. Your parables did the trick. Can I go?"

Drip. "I think you should stay away from the rest of the team for today." Drip.

"Was going to anyway."

"See you for drills, Florida."

"Keep up the good work, Coach."

When I get away from him, I wipe off the globs of his spit from my face.

It's fucking snowing outside. It covers everything, the roofs, the cars, the bushes, the sidewalks, the dirt, the lightposts, steadily and thoroughly, like the smothering pillow over a deathbedder's face. Students skate a few feet for fun on the ice, some fall, it gets on their hats and shoulders and they don't wipe it off.

There's no one in the student union, but through the plate glass the TV goes, something on the other side, activated, a fish-tank spookiness. No one at the career center, no one in the health center, no one in Grunwald Auditorium. I'm going to make it nine days to my next match without saying one more word. Vow of silence, vow of doubtlessness. Vow of poking Fink's eyeballs out, knocking them against each other like big wet cherries. There's no one in the pointless Petrusse Art Museum, where Mary Beth works the front desk, where she's told me they make up those little backstory cards, the ones they put next to the art telling you conception nuggets. She told me she extemporized one that read: "The 'monk' seen pensively walking the dunes in Caspar David Friedrich's *The Monk by the Sea* (left, in oil-on-canvas reprint) is actually no monk at all! He is Noel Friedrich, the bastard agnostic brother of Caspar. Friedrich often took his younger brother Noel out for air along the cliffs at Rügen between 1804 and 1808, until Noel himself died in the very same deep depicted in the painting, drowned when he mistook the waters for the town square. It is thought that *The Monk by the Sea* is the most personal of Friedrich's paintings for this reason." That one was my favorite.

I'm not going to go to Mary Beth's apartment. She's not there, she told me she was going home, and though I've considered getting inside and sleeping there alone, I won't. We've spent the last three nights together, twice in my room and once in her's, where she stayed up late reading while I slept, and then she woke me up to take my clothes off and kept finding ways to prolong our fooling around like letting me suck the mole on her upper back, and afterwards I fell asleep again with her rubbing my head. "You're a physical person," she said. She applies this cheap lip balm and when she's close by I get full whiffs of it, which now drives me crazy. She's one of two alive people who can make me feel less alone, but I'm not going to go find her, not even if it was realistic.

My dorm comes up out of the snow suddenly, at the end of the path. Fourteen total lights on. Snow mounding up at the bottom of the front door. In the summer between my freshman and sophomore years, they redid the steps in the main staircase. When I started my second year, my muscle memory told me to pick my feet up at the former step level. But they redid them to be slightly taller, and I kept kicking my toes against them. I tripped up the steps for almost a week before I got them right. Why do I remember this and not my mom's cigarette brand?

I cling to the one-percent chance she's sitting against my door, waiting for me to come back.

But of course she's not, the space in front of my door is empty, the entire floor is empty, she's back with her family in Thief River Falls. Last year after Thanksgiving I did a thousand crunches and consumed a mild laxative, but this year feels different. The whole year feels like the end of the world.

The floor phone rings down the hallway, around the corner. My soaking shoes squeak on the tiles. I check Masha's utility closet, but it's locked.

I am more enthusiasm than talent, so what happens if my enthusiasm is taken away? I guess I could triple my weight and go to Japan and become a sumo. I could be fat in Tokyo, though I promised myself I'd never be fat.

I'm on my bed, and I've reopened the fingernail. Blood's halfway down my finger. Rudy Unger dangles somewhere far away, dangling like a spider with his many bug arms wrapped around my money. Maybe I'll get a place in a place with jobs and look for a job. Maybe I'll ask him to give me all of it at once, I probably have enough to put it together for a flight and food for a few months. I am not poor or rich, at the moment I am afinancial. But I will not be rich when I graduate, though I could get on a plane for the first time and fly to a place where no one knows me, where I can make money off my body. I can sell my blood and semen. All the little countries in the big continents. I need to buy a map first, I'll read up on which cultures really value things that look good, what jobs can be had for having a great body. I'm not above showing it for money. I'm not really above anything. I've heard there are sex shows all over now, including the Netherlands, which would suit me fine since they accept suicide there, so if I ever got tired of playing with myself in front of a crowd I could just be done with the whole thing.

I stare at the far wall, the far wall of the room I've lived in for four years. Small gut smudges are all over it from where I've mushed the bugs. No one else knows how full of gnats the building gets in the summer when I'm the only one here, under practice regimen while everyone else is away, and the school years come around again and the building fills, but they all still come and go, and I stay the same. What am I going to do? Less than six months until I have no plan left.

A knock on my door. "Hey, Stephen, you in there?"

I go to the door and open it. "Perry, what are you doing here?"

"I live here, jackass."

"It's Thanksgiving."

"I know what day it is," he says. "The phone's for you."

"Who is it?"

"I don't know, it's a woman."

"A woman?"

"She's been calling back every hour. She told me to pick up when you came back. I heard the door and figured it was you."

I jog down the hall, hearing Mary Beth's voice already, thinking that if she asked me to come to Thief River Falls by foot, I would do it.

I put the phone to my ear. "Hello?"

"Honey, this is your Aunt Lorraine."

It isn't Mary Beth's voice. It's a woman's voice, but it's not Mary Beth's or anyone else's. It's older, calling from somewhere much farther away than Minnesota. Something I don't have a name for gums up in my chest.

I say, "Can I help you?"

"Hello? Can you hear me, honey?"

I have given no special thoughts to my Aunt Lorraine. I have not thought of her since I got to Oregsburg. Standing in my hallway, it's impossible for me to imagine her walking around and living in the world except as unrelated to me, the same as I'd imagine a stranger in Brazil or Madagascar. With some work, I bring up her face. She has just now appeared, stepping back into her skin and blood, resuming a placeholder, as if suddenly popping up found after being missing, Amelia Earhart swimming out of the ocean and waving her arms, "Here I am!" upping the planet's population by one. Attached earlobes, I somehow remember that. Hair that didn't get to her shoulders. I guess she has the same eyes as her brother, my dad, my dad's eyes were probably the same as hers. She moved all the time, cutting up her life into bits like food for a child, stopping by once or twice a year to sleep on the couch, snoring with a sleep mask. Until she flew out of America, and then she stopped passing through. And that was that. She never had a husband, I don't think she wanted one. That was her.

"Are you there?"

"Who is this?"

"It's your Aunt Lorraine."

To my surprise, I discover I'm already prepared to make anything up that I need to. What do I have to lose? I listen to her voice, and though the tentacles connecting her life to mine were always weak, her voice drops pieces of familiarity through the phone and into my ear, pieces that hollow out my head and remind me that I'm inside a very big building and that the world is very large.

I say, "How do you spell my first name?"

"With a *v*, Steven, honey, a *v*."

"What's my last name? My real last name?"

"Forster, dear, same as mine."

"What's my name?"

"What? Steven Forster. Honey, why—"

"Do you have identification?"

When they told me my parents were dead, I screamed for ten minutes. There was no one left for me to say I'm sorry to, to take the apology that I needed to give.

"Steven, listen to me. I know you have a lot of questions, I wa—"

"Why didn't you come to the funeral?"

"I was in Australia. I live here."

"Not good enough. You're still there?"

"That's what I wanted to talk to you about," she says. "That's why I called."

I'm hitting the phone against the wall. Please tell me what I'm supposed to do with all this? I try to hold on and catch up. I went to their co-funeral without any interest, I already knew how those things went. I noted without interest who was there and who wasn't.

Sensing what's on the other end, she says, "I'm sorry." I don't answer, and I think she clears her throat. At some point I've started squatting at the foot of the phone. Time passes, and it becomes clear that one *I'm sorry* is all I get.

One time, I waited in a car with an adult woman who was not my mom. Rain all over. I was in the passenger seat. The wipers weren't going and I was watching the mess the rain was making on the windshield. The radio was on, a man's voice on talk radio, his words just vowel sounds now in memory, but I remember the voice sounding like a phone voice, like it was talking straight to me and the woman I can't remember who was next to me. We were waiting in the rain for whatever we were waiting for and I think that was Aunt Lorraine. My mom and dad didn't have any other siblings. And then all these years later, on Thanksgiving night, the phone rings in my dorm, and it could've been anyone but it was my Aunt Lorraine.

"It's all right," I say. I wrap the coils of the phone cord twice around my hand. The one time I went into Aunt Lorraine's apartment, she had a few items of food in her fridge, but nothing to drink, and I asked her what she drank, and she said water from the tap, except for when they're doing building work and the water's rusty, and I said, then what happens? and she said I don't know. Aunt Lorraine didn't have enough furniture in her very clean apartment, but when I opened her closet it was stuffed to the ceiling. My mom said she was "the type of person who throws out a towel after one use." How could I refuse a phone call from my aunt? How could I not listen to what she has to say? I'm prepared to accept these terms.

"I made a mistake with you. I'm a terrible person and there's no reason why you should ever want to speak to me again," she says. "But I'm your aunt. Nothing that's happened and no stupid thing I've done can change that. I'm the only one who knew your dad when he was a baby. I saw him when your mom was pregnant with you. I never saw him happier. He was always next to your mom, asking if she needed anything. He must've asked her a million times a day. I remember how much wrestling meant to you. You must've been ten or eleven the last time I saw you wrestle. I'm sure you're on the team at your school?"

"Yeah."

"Good. You used to wear your headgear to the table. You wouldn't take it off." She laughs. "You'll have to forgive me if I sound nervous! I have butterflies. I've been thinking about this phone call for a long time."

"How long?"

"Longer than you think," she says.

I haven't heard her voice in ten years, so I have nothing to recognize. I say, "You don't have an Australian accent."

"Of course not, honey, I'm American."

"Yes but don't people who go to foreign countries for a long time start having that country's accent?"

"Sometimes, yes. But not me."

"Why are you calling now?"

"Steven, listen. When's your next match?"

"My next match is in nine days."

"Next Saturday?"

"Yeah."

"I'm going to come to it."

"You're going to leave Australia and come to North Dakota? In a week?"

"Yes." She is talking fast, and how am I supposed to not get more and more excited as she goes? "I quit my job. Well, I'm going to relocate. I'm going to try to wrap some things up. I think I have a connection there. In Carrington, you know where that is? It's an hour drive away, but I'm going to get a house with a bedroom in it that I'm going to keep for you. I'll come pick you up. I'll see you whenever you like. You'll have a place to stay. We can spend Christmas together."

"You're going to come to my match? Next weekend?"

"I'm going to come to all of your matches. You can come for the weekends. Bring a bag of your clothes and I'll do your laundry at the house," she says. "Isn't that what college kids are supposed to do?"

The sister of my dad, seeing the place where I live and sleep, positively crying her eyes out at this small room. Buying new shoes for me, trips to the dentist, sending me back to school for the week with leftovers in Tupperware. The logistical specifics become runny and surreal. It's difficult to imagine them, but that doesn't mean I haven't already accepted them. The imagination is allowed to fail once in a while.

"Steven?"

Maybe she drives me to Fort Mandan, Fort Union Trading Post, the aquarium. Maybe she meets Linus and Mary Beth, maybe she's there in the bleachers.

"Have you talked to Rudy?" I say.

"Rudy?"

"The estate lawyer."

"Oh, him. No, I haven't. Steven, I think there's plenty of time for all that. I want to meet your friends, hear about your classes, hear about your life. I want to help give you a normal life. But first I want to watch you wrestle next Saturday. How does that sound?"

"It sounds good."

"Oh, I can't wait to see you! Tell me about yourself."

It takes considerable effort not to spit it all out: Linus, Mary

Beth, that I haven't lost yet, the Frogman letter, the remote house on fire, the murderer living inside it, Kryger, Fink, how different I feel now compared to how I felt one minute before the phone rang. But I don't. I just say, "I've gotten a few A's here. A-minuses, I mean. Intro to Religious Studies and also Arthurian Romance."

"I'm really very impressed."

"Next week I have my final in Meteorology. That's probably going to be my hardest. The week after, after you're here, I have What Is Nothing? and Basic News Writing, but those shouldn't be too bad."

"Good. That makes me happy. That would've made your dad and mom happy, to know how hard you're working. I'm going to be there in nine days. Would it be all right if I called you one more time? Wednesday? I just want to be able to talk to you one more time before I get on the plane."

"Yes."

"I've been alone, too. I've made a mess of a lot of things in my life. But I'm not going to do that anymore. You and I don't have to be alone anymore. I'm going to go now, but I'll call you on Wednesday. O.K.?"

"O.K., Aunt Lorraine."

"I'm going to hang up now. I love you."

The vortex is both inside and outside myself.

"I'll need you to tell me you love me, Steven." Her voice is suddenly aggressive. "I'll need to hear it."

"I love you."

"Great, I love you, too. Good-bye, Steven."

"Good-bye."

I AM IN THE GYMNASIUM. This is true. I haven't put anything in my body since Thursday, I haven't needed to. I came here three hours before the start, two hours before the rest of the team. All true. I knocked on Linus's door this morning and he came with me. We walked down the main path, no birds making any noise, our feet crackling on the ice. We did crunches with four layers on and sat in adjacent stalls of the bathroom with our hoods up, barely talking, because the bathroom gets a direct feed from the boiler room. On the other side of the divider, spitting and panting, he said, "Are you O.K.?" And I said, "Someone's coming to watch me."

Weigh-in has already happened. I was lower than I've ever been, 130.3, and got some looks until I told them I wasn't trying to cut down a class. They've disinfected the mats, the bleachers are as full as they will be. Mary Beth sits at the end of the first row, she told me she wants to hear all the noises that I make. For ten minutes, I sat next to her and she held my hand, she asked me how the Meteorology test went, and it was the first time I felt like someone other than Linus wanted me to win. When I came back to the team at the side of the mats, Linus was wiggling his eyebrows at me.

Joseph Carver and I have seen each other. Normally, there's a feeling of reality becoming reality, of actualization, when you see your person beforehand. It's a feeling of ownership and responsibility. I try to work up my standard feelings, ignoring this time's obvious differences because I'm good at being blind to the facts, and I start by picturing what Joseph Carver slept in, how good he slept. This is a conference dual, against nearby Konstantin College, so I picture the twenty minutes it took him to get from there to OC on the highway. Even though I was out of my room by the time it happened, I like to imagine my window, and in the distance his vehicle going by, coming closer. I see in the program that he's 4–1, that he majors in art therapy, and I feel high fondness for him.

But as the first match starts and mine gets nearer, and I don't see Aunt Lorraine anywhere, I hear what she said on the second phone call over and over. I was sitting down in the hallway next to the phone and it was the following night in Australia, very late. She was different the second time from the first. It sounded like she was in a quieter room, and she talked a lot softer and slower, almost like she was lying down. Whatever butterflies she had the first time were gone.

"I get so lonely out here, Steven."

She told me she would recognize me, that it hasn't been so long that I won't recognize my aunt. After a series of transfers, her plane was supposed to land in the late morning, about the time I was sweating in the bathroom. She promised me she'd be here by the time my match started.

I keep watching the bleachers, and then I sense Mary Beth looking back at me, and so I move my eyes to her, make her think I was looking at her all along. It is in the nature of the stupid young man to think he is contributing to the conversation on mortality, or identity, or anything, but he is not. This is something he realizes long after the fact, if he is lucky.

My draw comes second to last. Linus gets third to last. Sherman wins. Whitey loses. Harry squeezes a cup of applesauce into his mouth. Kryger and Fink seem to be talking about something. My match is going to start in fifteen minutes. I make eye contact with Joseph Carver one last time before leaving the gym, and he smiles.

I choose the most private spot, the weight room, a tiled hallway and then a perpendicular second tiled hallway away from the gym. The backup lights are on, the ones that go when no one's inside. Mirrors are everywhere in here, I can see my butt simultaneous as my chest without craning my neck or anything. My head shines. I spit on the rubber floor. I love this time of year. I've got to cut this short, I've got to be out there for Linus. Got to be out there for the matches! I hold Joseph Carver's face in my head. For God's sake, please challenge me. I force myself to remember the puffy palm skin of Mary Beth's right hand, how she let me compare it to her left hand, and how she pinched the tiny barbell calluses at the bottoms of all my eight non-thumb fingers. "This little Florida went to Oregsburg... this little Florida loved going to Drawing... this little Florida loved listening to Mary Beth pretend his fingers were all Floridas . . . this little Florida knew in its little Florida heart that Mary Beth could pin him, pin him down if she really wanted to."

I tug up the shoulder straps of my singlet. I tug them up over my head so they X across my neck, and then I pull. I pull until my head turns red in the bad light of the room and my sweat shines, and, as though a slide is inserted over my eyes, I don't know how long it takes me to realize that I'm making noise, forcing all the blood out of my head until I'm just a white pusticle on top. I'm inside something deep, scooping through the lowest guts of the whale.

I jog back to the gym, just in time to see Linus. He lets the kid dance a bit before engaging him and switching him around. Hargraves is hopping up and down. I try to focus on Linus without looking at the bleachers, but I can't. Planes land all the time. I keep looking for her, and then I see Mary Beth, and she screams, and I know to look back at Linus because he's won in the first period. And I start clapping but Linus is already running right toward me, he's already ready for his next match, he's doing this huffing, panting thing to psyche himself down or sideways or whichever, and he's banging his headgear against mine, yelling, "I'm better than him! I'm better than him!" The crowd claps. Hargraves is staring at Linus like he's in love, like he's never seen anything like Linus before. It takes him a full half minute of hammering heads with me before he comes back to the world, and for the first time, I realize Linus is not only very good at this, he's unbeatable, he's never going to lose. And then, like a coin turned over, he's back to a normal animus and smiling, saying, "What's this singlet trick here? You gonna teach me it?" He unties my head from the knot.

The loudspeaker says, "One hundred thirty-three. Florida, Oregsburg, Carver, Konstantin."

"You don't look so great," he says.

"I'm fine."

"Stable as a table?"

"Stable as a table," I say, and he slams his head against mine.

I walk to the middle of the mat. Mary Beth is watching me. I try to get one last glance at the bleachers, but I have to search too quickly, and any of these faces could be her.

December 7 will be history. I keep making history like it's my job to manufacture it. The traffic on the nearby roads, the color of the tickets ripped at the entrance, the total money collected. How many people were actually here in person to see what happens between me and Joseph Carver? No one will ever know. I love this time of year. So much has become clear to me recently! Most eye-opening of all is that wrestling is not the only thing in life preordained. Everything is preordained—what happens outside the mat circle is as preordained as what happens inside. This modern destiny is not determined by God, but what can you do? That's the joke, nothing is determining everything, and there's nothing you can do about it. Laugh at the joke of it, at how hard it is to understand, at how hard you try to understand it anyway, and maybe for a moment you do, it's right there, you have it, and then your mind slips and the thing crawls back under the furniture. Ha ha ha ha ha ha ha ha ha ha ha ha ha ha ha ha ha ha ha ha ha ha ha ha ha ha ha ha ha ha ha ha ha ha ha ha ha ha ha ha ha ha ha ha ha ha ha ha ha ha ha ha ha ha ha ha. The tickets were always blue and the money was put in an envelope inside a desk while outside the roads were empty. All this is true: I was born slippery: they told me to pull up the curtains on the class play: Silas burned his wife down: I never once saw my dad without a beard on: all this was always so. Just like how I was always going to end up in this circle with Joseph Carver on December 7, with nearly one hundred people paying one dollar each to watch. Mary Beth was always going to be in Drawing, Linus was always going to be in my path, Masha was always going to be cleaning the student union, my Aunt Lorraine was always going to be on the other end of the ringing phone on the second floor of McCloskey on Thanksgiving, and so on and so on. I love this time of year. But only you have the privilege of seeing how your preordained life finally plays out. Oh, that's how that was always going to happen, you think, the moment after the letter from the Oregsburg Admissions Department lands on your lab desk, the moment the Frogman begins undoing the lock on your door. The sarcastic thing is that you're still surprised when it happens. You're slapped in the face over and over like a hysterical maid, no less surprised the last time than the first time, that is the sarcastic joke after all, you could not help it, you could not ever not be surprised.

Let the record show that Joseph Carver gets my left leg, he is fast, two points for him, and he rolls around on top of me until we leave the circle and have to reset in the center, where I quickly get the escape point back. Let the record show that spit comes out of my mouth when Joseph Carver mashes his palm to my visage, that Joseph Carver makes a deep sideways scratch on my head, let this silly record show that a jury of faces watches this gross public act, watch as I make bricks out of mud. Pay attention. I can't lose. I can't lose. What are you doing for others? They force me to express myself. Relentless cleverness! Unflappable confidence! You know how when you live in a room for a long time and you make the room smell like you? That's what I'm doing with the world. I'm alive! I am showing them. No one is a fraud who entirely commits to the mission. My body was preordained to weigh 133 pounds. There are too many people in the world to care about more than a few. I worked harder than everyone I ever met until I met Mary Beth. What is Mary Beth's last name? "If we got married I'd be Mary Beth Florida." Listen to these work sounds, look at what I'm making. I can't turn my gift off, I become smarter, I am a smart young man and I bring good into the world. What are you doing for others? I give birth to Swiss Army knives. I'm making loud noises and scaring wombs back into place. What happens if you take Stephen Florida out of this place? Everything starts to fall apart and then comes crashing down. I lead life to a bright warm corner with a blanket and a rocking chair, where it can look out the window at the bluebirds until life pulls the curtain down. I can't stop, I can't lose. Let the record. Have I contradicted myself? The Frogman is behind a woman in the fourth row. What are you doing for others? Hello Joseph Carver hello. How much time is left is it too late? Steven over here Steven look I made it! Steven listen that sound came from you when Joseph Carver went for your left leg like you knew he would one thousand times before and it came from your knee. The pain is telling you something Steven your mouth is telling you something it is telling you to say good-bye to the next five months help good-bye to everything say good-bye say your last words good-bye.

A TIME BEGINS I'D RATHER SKIP OVER. Let's get it over with.

Linus and Mary Beth are looking at me, and before I can ask what's happened a doctor walks into the room.

"Hello, son, I'm Dr. Moon." He leans on the bedrail, tie dangling, a bald old white man with a face that's a pouch of sweat. "I like your hair, it's almost shorter than mine!"

"What hospital is this?"

"St. Brigid's."

I throw off the sheet, see that I'm wearing one of those butt-apparent smocks.

"Listen to me, son. When's the last time you had some food?"

"Thursday."

"Water?"

"Thursday."

The doctor nods at the tubes running their mouths into me. "Those are fluids. You came in severely dehydrated. In fact, you passed out from it. Furthermore. The only reason you're not in a great deal more pain is because the nurse came in and put some morphine into the IV."

"Is it still Saturday? What time is it?"

"Look at me, son. You've torn your medial meniscus. That's your knee, the left one, but I bet I didn't need to tell you that. What it looks like in your knee right now is the ligament, that's bone to bone, is like a piece of torn clothing. Like this. If you look under the sheet, you'll see swelling, a soft and quasi-mushy encasing around the joint making it quite large. It's called an effusion. The good news is that there are far worse injuries for an athlete like yourself to sustain. The other good news is you have two options." The doctor's gold watch catches the overhead light. Does anyone with a gold watch have any morality? "The first option is a complete heal, a total repair, suture your ligament back into place, and you're looking at six to eight months' recovery." Mary Beth and Linus are watching me and I wish they weren't. "The second option is a much shorter timeline. We go in there and snip away the dead tissue to allow it to repair, it's not a complete repair, you'll never have a perfect knee again, but you're looking at four to six weeks."

"Do the snip."

"The snip?"

"The second one, the shorter one."

"Right. I see from your paperwork that you're on Oregsburg College's plan, but—"

"Call Rudy Unger. Give me a piece of paper and I'll write it down. He has all my money."

"I have to ask this, Stephen. You're sure about this?"

"Yes."

"All right, son, good enough for me. We're going to run your paperwork and get this all in order. We're going to keep you here overnight and do the procedure first thing in the morning. You'll be able to go home tomorrow afternoon. The nurses will give you more instructions, but you'll have crutches for two weeks. After a few days, you can start physical activity, light weight training, stationary bike. I would recommend swimming as part of the rehab."

"Where is there to swim?"

He stands up straight and points out the window. "If you go northwest on 52, like you're going to Anamoose, on the way you'll find a swimming club. Used to be a member myself, no time anymore, though. See this pudge? I didn't have it when I was younger, but it happens to the best of us. I'll give them a call, tell them you'll be stopping by. I'll tell them it's part of the rehab. They'll let you in."

✦

At some point, Moon leaves, and I'm left answering delicate inquiries from the only two people I care about, inquiries I answer politely even though I'm so embarrassed I could throw up, and between their asking there are long spaces of no talking, spaces where you can hear medical beeping and Christmas music from the hall. What can I possibly tell them? I have no questions, no opinions, nothing to say. I want them to go but I don't want them to leave. 4–1. With my top teeth, I scrape my tongue and spit in the bedpan. I have a loss, the familiar feeling of carrying a loss is back this year.

How could I have been so fucking stupid? I never asked her any questions, I didn't know where in Australia she was, I never asked what her job was, I never asked for details about my parents. So fucking stupid. I try to forget it like a ring of old keys, like the rest of it. It's not important anymore who it was. I give up.

✦

Later, Hargraves shows up. He puts his hand on my shoulder like I'm a legless Purple Heart. "Tough break, kid, tough break." He's an astoundingly old man, how did I never see it before? He's one of those people who holds on to his job for too long, so that after he finally decides to retire, his body will give out, the distraction finally gone, and it will remember it's time to decline, basically the same principle as how when one old person dies, their spouse dies soon after—you lose the last support and hit the freefall. "I myself have had thirteen operations. Shit, two hip replacements. My knees still bother me most days. Keep your head on right. That's important." He tells me what I already know, which is that he believes in me at 133 and as long as I can prove myself by season's end, he'll enter me into the regional tournament. He takes a calendar pinned to the wall and flips to February, puts his finger down. "Our last regular season dual, right here, February 5, Garnes College. That's your shot. I'm not gonna put you out there injured, but if you get ready for February 5, you beat Kryger in practice that week to stake 133 again, you go against the 133 for Garnes and show me you're back, I'll make sure you're at the regionals, and you'll get a damn good-ass shot." He shakes my hand. "Rest up, Florida. You get your meanness back and get fixed up with Fink. He'll get you cleared and ready. He knows other people's bodies better than they do. You'll be goddamn pillaging again in no time flat."

✦

I reach over and pull the curtain aside but there is no one in the other bed. I swear I heard something. My brain is tugging me in one false direction after another.

Sometimes I think about what my life would be like without wrestling, without the constant nagging presence of it, which on certain days can feel like a giant house with a very low ceiling and no doors. But who am I kidding, the question always ends up turning itself around on me: How has my life turned out with it?

✦

Linus and Mary Beth stay, visiting hours wrapping up, but they don't know what's going on. They can't see it from the outside. They can't see that I'm not even in the bed anymore, I've already pulled the mask down.

Linus announces he's going to the vending machine, a flimsy excuse to let me alone with Mary Beth because vending machines are taboo to the wrestler, and as soon as he leaves she sits on the bed. She holds my hand and instinctually does that gesture where you push someone's hair to the side, someone who's lower than you in the world, but I have no hair so her fingers just skim my hairline. She lifts the sheet. My joint has become enlarged and monstrous. She doesn't make any sign that she's upset. I find that the sicker I feel inside the prettier she looks. She puts her head on my shoulder and tells me she can hide in the bathroom when they come by to end visiting hours, and then stay the night with me. She says we can ride the bus back. But because all I want is to be left alone I tell her that I'll see her in Drawing on Tuesday as always, the comfort of our new pattern, and as she holds my head and kisses my cheek, it's almost enough to change my stupid mind, which is bright enough to realize how lucky I got with her. Linus comes back, then she's gone. It's amazing how fast she's gone.

In his lap, Linus has a new Stephen King book called *Rage*. There's a page dog-eared near the end.

"What's that one about?"

"A crazy person."

"Crazy how?"

"You want me to ruin it?"

"I don't read books."

"This high schooler named Charlie attacks his teacher with a wrench, then after getting expelled he gets a gun from his locker and shoots another teacher before holding a class full of kids hostage. The kids all start to sympathize with him."

"Why does he kill people?"

"I told you, he's a crazy person."

"Yeah, but he has to give a reason."

"He says he doesn't know."

"How's your fasciitis?" I'm on a morphine loop but my love for him is not contaminated, or it can continue to exist despite the contamination, it froths up in my throat like an elemental part of my physiognomy, and I know that whatever happens I'm never going to forget him.

It is my understanding that most people of moderate or greater intelligence possess a mix of believing they can do something better than anyone else and also fear that they are core frauds and are terrified of being found out. Let's call these two states, which often alternate, unflappable confidence and crippling fear. The average person will possess an animus that alternates between the two opposite states largely evenly, fifty-fifty. But I'm of the opinion that the top of our species, the ones who do not necessarily do something great but are capable of something great, possess a balance heavily weighted toward unflappable confidence, to the point that those most likely to do something great barely notice the crippling fear. It's like a whisper on the other side of the room. That whisper is human hesitation, that whisper is the consideration of consequences, and it's poisonous. In one of my first few days with Linus, when it was already clear that he was someone special to me, I asked him. He was reading a book. "Do you ever feel fear? Like really great fear?" I saw his eyes run to the end of the sentence, and he put his thumb down on the page to keep from losing his place. He looked up at me. "You mean about wrestling? No." And that is why, every time he beats somebody, I'm not surprised.

The nurse sticks her head in the room and says visiting hours are up.

Linus says to me, "Do you want me to pick you up tomorrow?"

"No." In five minutes, when he's gone, I'll want to have apologized for being like this, for pushing him off the dock, but I can't get myself to say it now. "I'll see you tomorrow at the dorm."

"Are you sure?"

"Yes, it's late, thank you for coming, good-night."

"Want me to leave the book in case you can't sleep?"

I shake my head, he says good-night, and probably when he's at the elevator I feel the fucking apology want to come out of my mouth.

✦

Hospitals at night are very quiet.

✦

A different nurse from the previous nurse comes in with a syringe and asks if I want more morphine and I say yes please.

I wait until she leaves me and then I lift my useless body up to use the bathroom. I put no weight on the left leg, and the medical cords flobble as I hop my way over there. They told me to call the nurse if I had to go but I didn't do that, no stranger's going to assist my bathrooms.

✦

The attending nurse is a tall black woman who looks like she never has time for makeup. She brings in the food tray and I stop her before she departs.

"Can I ask you a question, miss?"

"I have a million—"

"Please?"

"I have like two minutes."

"I got a few phone calls from my aunt, someone saying they're my aunt. They said they wanted to come visit me, I haven't seen them since I was a kid." I pat the Salisbury steak dry of gravy and eat part of it. Midway through I come across some funny resilient gristle, so I bite that for a while for fun. "I don't have any family. My parents are dead. What should I do?"

"What should you do what?"

"Should I track this person down? Phone records? How do I even do that?"

"You want to know if you should leave off this secret person, who's probably lying, or try and find her."

"Yes."

For the first time, her face clears of stress in favor of something like explicit nurse concern. "You don't have anyone else?"

"That's right."

"I don't know, family is important. But this sounds like bad news. I think you should forget it."

✦

The TV keeps me company. *Rawhide* is on, then *Bonanza,* then *Gunsmoke.* Chester and Matt first have an argument about drinking hot tea when it's hot outside, but then young Timmy shows up saying he's been seeing all types of bizarre shit at night, a man and woman robbing and killing people and then going back to their weird shed outside town. Matt is doubtful because Timmy likes to make shit up but he goes with him anyway because he's Matt. And sure enough the man and woman come back to their weird shed and count their robbed money in front of the hidden, watching Matt and he jumps out and shoots all the crazies to death in their chests. The moral starts as don't lie but ends up being tell the truth.

✦

They take pity on me and let me wheel down to the end of the hall. It's a busy hour, so I push my limit a little and go around the corner, where I discover the hospital chapel. There's a rectangular yellowish window behind the altar. I roll up and put my palm on it. It's not outside light coming through. Some kind of fake yellow bulb's behind the surface. On a side table, there's a statuette of a particularly pretty Virgin Mary, the prettiest Virgin Mary I've ever seen. I roll up to her. She has the baby Jesus cradled against her torso, looking down at him with an enraptured visage, and I sort of have to reach around his head to touch the bumps under her garment. While I yank myself I experience eternal, depthless frustration, frustration that someone might walk in at any minute so I'll have to stop soon, and for all the other obvious reasons.

✦

At some point, I guess between the second and third morphine refill, I start to measure time by the rate that the metronome effusion pain in my knee rises.

✦

If I can be honest with myself, one of my big problems is not facing things head-on. Non-wrestling things, I mean. For instance, if I had told Mary Beth and Linus about Aunt Lorraine, or Mary Beth about my parents, or Linus about Mary Beth, now I could talk to them about it and disperse the pressure. But I never disperse the pressure. I keep it all to myself like the exit's connected by tube back to the entrance, it's all doing laps, and now I'll never let it out. It's my own show.

✦

I'll never tell Mary Beth about Masha. Sometimes I think I can be honest with her but whenever she's with me I clam up like a real coward, as if I don't want to ask for help on the test. Something about the way she looks at me. I've twisted up too many things I'm ashamed of to be able to know which string to pull first.

✦

I'm not sure I see much difference between the past and the future, they're both featureless pasteboard, but the present is a hospital room and a knee full of dirty bugs.

✦

I remember the names of the ninety-nine wrestlers I've ever lost to: 1. Ben Davis. 2. Jeremiah Gross. 3. Patrick Young. 4. Mike Fett. 5. Terry Blalock. 6. Mike Hunter. 7. David Silva. 8. Andre Rasmussen. 9. Charles Powell. 10. John Orlov. 11. Lewiss Tong. 12. Kevin Cunningham. 13. Jaimie Whitehouse. 14. Edward Kittle. 15. Abram Boone. 16. Andrew Wright. 17. Greg Knox. 18. Adam Kirchner. 19. Dan Acee. 20. Lester Whaley. 21. Theo Jernigan. 22. Justin Maine-Hershey. 23. Fred Husbands. 24. Sean Harris. 25. Tom Neufeldt. 26. Myer Hayes. 27. Martin Whitten. 28. Will Springer. 29. John Daniel Hoy. 30. Bernard Hafrey. 31. Kyle Maclean. 32. Elliott van Zwet. 33. John Kot. 34. Mike Mehl. 35. John Tobias. 36. Brian Nesci. 37. Wayne Sullivan. 38. John Henry Rees. 39. Ben Demeke. 40. Zach Coe. 41. Robby Hughes. 42. Jon Pruitt. 43. Francis Melliar-Smith. 44. Pat Hasko. 45. Laurence Rzepka. 46. Tom Nawn.

47. Kip Auerbach. 48. Andrew Shipp. 49. Jess Nardell. 50. Marsh Margolin. 51. James Davis. 52. Mill Hamm. 53. Evan Sanders. 54. Myer McDermott. 55. Curtis Woll. 56. Nikola Glenn. 57. Ross Wagner. 58. Stanley Sutton. 59. Ellary Carter. 60. Norman Seeger. 61. Clay Goodchild. 62. Jacob Niedewski. 63. Corbin Kendrick. 64. Ivan French. 65. Robb Penman. 66. Marco Russell. 67. Adam Gansheroff. 68. Grant Weber. 69. Isaac Chasson. 70. Benjamin Crouse. 71. Patrick Seber. 72. Jason Lane. 73. James McDonald. 74. Brian Leape. 75. Scott McKee. 76. Ryan Campbell. 77. Todd Smith. 78. Josh DeWitt. 79. Alex Thompson. 80. Bill Fisher. 81. Ian Seaver. 82. Tony Burden. 83. Alan Jones. 84. Mark Broadfoot. 85. Kyle Brown. 86. Albert Perry. 87. Nick Grant. 88. Terner Reid. 89. Jose Yandell. 90. Tom Schneider. 91. Rudy Banks. 92. Caleb Karns. 93. Chris Gomez. 94. Ben Brown. 95. Derrick Ebersole. 96. Dan Vernon. 97. Jeff Riddell. 98. Bart Frazier. 99. Joseph Carver.

I had them written down in a notebook I kept until high school when I got them all memorized. They all have a number that orders them in time with when they came into my life. When I get access to the press sheets, the tournament brackets, it's the first thing I do: check for a name I recognize. I tracked all this info down. Seventy-seven of them don't appear anywhere in the materials, meaning, I have to assume, that they're not wrestling anymore. Cross off the names, you have twenty-two left. Eight of those wrestle in the other divisions. Cross them out, you have fourteen left. Wrestlers in my division, my weight. I'd like to start with those fourteen. I would do anything for another chance. How wonderful it would be to carry that notebook around, if I still had it, finding all ninety-nine of them, getting to compete against them again, to redo it and spend the next few years working back through my past, wiping clean the record one by one, crossing the names off until I got to Ben Davis, who was a thirteen-year-old with red hair and braces when he got a 4–3 decision on me in Oakes in front of my fucking parents.

✦

"Mr. Florida, you should get some sleep. You have a big day tomorrow."

More morphine for me! Yum-yum morphine! Put it in myself good!

✦

February 5 is my birthday.

✦

Who was that on the phone anyway?

✦

I think about them getting in the car. They were going to see a movie, I don't remember what one, something my mom wanted to see and my dad was going to make her happy. I hate the commonness of how they died, the predictability of the death of one's parents in a car accident. I get tired of retelling the same story. The details never change. I don't want to tell it anymore.

✦

There's a rotting smell in the room like it was just here next to the bed but ran out into the hall when I woke up. I grab my fluids pole and hop to the door. I look down the hall. "Who is it? Who's there?" At the end of the hall, a nurse gets up from her station and starts coming toward me. I duck back into my room and shut the door. The smell is coming from the bathroom. The door is cracked. The light is on in there. I hobble over and pull it open. The seat is up. I go over and look inside, and it's full of vomit.

✦

The nurse, a different one, wakes me up and tells me it's time for the surgery. She waits outside while I go to the bathroom, which is clean, and then wheelchairs me to the operating room, where there are more people and Dr. Moon.

Well, they give me the gas and out I go.

✦

I wake up and within seconds, like they know, a nurse walks through the door.

"One to ten, please quantify your pain."

"Three," I say.

She makes some scribbles on her clipboard. Teeth or horns grow out of her red face, which is the red face of the devil. "Thank you, Mr. Florida. There were no complications."

✦

Later, I wake up in my hospital room. I pick up the buzzer and the nurse comes in.

"I'm ready to leave now."

✦

I take the bus home and crutch up to my room. My only instructions are to go to the student health center in a week to get my stitches out and to rest in the meantime. I haven't had this little to do in years. In a normal week, I hover between 133 and 136 and leading up to weigh-in I like to feel the weight come out of my body, I like to feel it vanish. Work pain success.

I used to think the best thing in the world would be if a camera crew followed me around and documented everything, but now I can't think of anything worse.

For a very long time, I look at the stitches.

✦

I go to class, take my final in What Is Nothing? The whole exam is a single sheet of paper with only one question at the top: "What is nothing?" I don't know how to start, so for the first half hour I draw pizza slices in the margins, then I write all that I know until I don't want to write about it anymore and I hand it in. Afterwards, I shut my door and get into bed. Someone knocks. "Hello? Stephen? I have to talk to you about something." It's the voice of Linus but I don't make any noise, I pretend I'm not there, and he goes away.

✦

I have figured out that a good way to make time pass faster is to sleep a lot.

✦

I wait until I'm least likely to run into other people to leave my room. I shower with my leg outside the curtain. When someone spots me in the hallway and asks what happened, I just mumble, "Nothing serious," and they leave me alone. At the cafeteria, I scrape some peanut butter into a cup. I take some fruit and put some celery and two eggs in my pocket and bring it all back to my room. I do dips and use the resistance band under my bed. I scoop out the peanut butter with my hand and spread it on my face.

✦

At one point, though I don't very much care anymore, I look over my definitions for Basic News Writing in my bed. I go to class and take the test. Because I came to every single class and put my name on the sign-in sheet passed around the room, I'm given the preferential final, which is one hundred definitions. This was the deal Mr. Mills offered on the first day of class and I took it. My test in part looks like this:

18. __________, also called lower thirds, are electronically generated captions superimposed on a screen.
19. ______________________ is what we call interviews with members of the general public.
20. A ________ is a short name for an in-production article.

I grab my bag and take the test up to Mr. Mills at the front of the lecture room, leaving while the slack-ass kids taking the nonpreferential test start their essays. I'll never see any of them again.

✦

"Are you in there? You should have some help with your knee. If you're in there make a noise or something."

✦

A few nights and days stocking up on sleep makes you restless.

✦

I was hoping to avoid Mary Beth after our last day of Drawing, but of course that doesn't happen. After I hand in my sketchbook to Mrs. Caple, which contains a blow-up sketch of my stitches, autographed, I find Mary Beth waiting outside the studio.

"Are you all right?"

"Yes."

"Do you want me to carry your bag?"

"No, thank you."

"Where are you going?"

"Nowhere," I say. "Are you going to Renaissance?"

"Yeah, have my final. Want to walk with me?"

"O.K., I can do that." My mouth remains shut because of extreme embarrassment. I try to smile. We're at the central part of campus where everyone else needs to walk to get where they're going, a hundred different directions, and they all make way for the cripple and his partner. Mary Beth is the hardest person to be around because she amplifies my embarrassment to the highest level. So, more than anyone, I've been avoiding her, but perversely I don't want anyone else's help but hers. I can't picture anyone else doing it.

I just need to tell her I need some time to figure this out. First I need to get my stitches out and start rehabbing, then get back into the routine and shit on Kryger and come back and get to regionals, then get to the championship. It sounds so easy when put in logical order. One night's homework reading said, "In a certain sense we cannot make mistakes in logic." I can tell her to just wait a few weeks and be patient, when she comes back from the holiday break, I'll be fine. I start small.

"Is the final going to be hard?"

"No," she says. "I have to tell you something." That same homework said, "In logic process and result are equivalent. (Therefore no surprises.)"

"Tell me what, Mary Beth?"

"That I think if I had met you before all of this started, I wouldn't have let it start. But I didn't, and so it did."

"What do you mean?"

"When I met you, I was sending out letters to museums and galleries in Minnesota, Wisconsin, Michigan, Illinois, anything I could find. I was doing it since September. I stopped sending them a week after I met you. And then we started talking, and this whole time I've been hoping that none of them would write back, that I wouldn't have to make this fucking decision. But one did write back, it's from a gallery in Birmingham. In Michigan. It's just an assistant position, but . . ."

She hands me the letter and I hold it in front of my face but I do not read the words.

"How are you going to finish school?" I say, which means we've already moved on to the formalities. I kept waiting for the consequences and now here they come.

"I only have two electives left, they're going to let me take them in Birmingham."

"Oh, that's good." I give her the letter back without looking at her.

"I have to go, Stephen. When I got here three years ago, it took me about three weeks to get sick of it. I don't like it here, I never liked it here, really, until I met you. Oregsburg isn't a good school. I only came here in the first place because they gave me the best scholarship. I told myself I'd never set foot in North Dakota after I finished school, and I only stuck it out because I thought it gave me the best chance to go somewhere else and move on. This is what I've been killing myself for, you of all people should know what that means. Do you understand?"

"Yes, I understand."

"Look at me. Do you?"

"Yes." She's crying, but I start crutching toward her class. "You're going to be late for the final."

"Goddamnit, this is so stupid," she says. "I'm leaving tomorrow morning. I wanted to get dinner with you tonight. So I'd like to do that before I leave, if that's all right."

"O.K."

"Good, I'll come to McCloskey at seven. I'll wait outside for you. At Allnighter?"

"Yes, that sounds good."

"Are you sure you can find something? I'm not sure they have anything you can eat."

"Don't worry, I can find something."

We're at Rainbow. "I wish I could just skip this test because I think there are things we should really talk about. So don't be late, O.K.?"

"Yes."

"Thank you for walking with me," she says. And then kisses my cheek and goes inside.

I stare through the glass doors of Rainbow, which strangely do not reflect back at all. All you can see are the people inside.

✦

Later, I'm convinced that something has gotten under my brace and so I keep undoing the straps to get it open right there on my bed but when I do there's nothing, of course there's nothing. And so I refasten everything back up but then I swear something's there, I can feel it touching me, and I quickly undo it all over again.

✦

"Stephen, I'm going to go to the Subway, do you want me to bring you something back? You don't need to talk or open the door, I'll wait here a minute, you can write down what you want on a paper and slide it under the door, O.K.?"

✦

In the night, when no one else is awake, I leave my room to shave my head. The tip of my crutch stabs the cold sandwich left at my door. I shake it off and lettuce scatters in the hallway.

I encounter no one and stand in the communal bathroom, waiting for the sounds of people. When I'm convinced I'm alone, I do a quick loop past the mirrors and showers just to be sure, and then I head to the sixth stall (there are ten altogether), close the door, and set my crutches against the divider. It is mildly humiliating, even with no audience, to hoist myself with one good leg onto the toilet. I commence shaving my head, head shaving as meditation. The old sensation of the clippers is a pleasure that never diminishes, the buzz is dulling and senseless in my ears. My little hairs drift down to the mouth of the toilet and start forming like rare algae on the surface. I'm going over my crown when I think I hear a door. I shut off the razor. I breathe through my nose. Footsteps. Quickly, I snatch up the crutches from the ground and hold them just as the bathroom door opens. The footsteps start down the row of toilets. Someone stops right outside my stall. "Stephen? Are you in here? Did you get my sandwich?" My messed-up leg twitches, fighting against the rest of my body trying to hold still. Sometimes lying is your greatest weapon. I'm full of lies like bees. "Shit, I guess he's not in here." As the footsteps go away, I let myself down and exit the other door.

I'm ten feet from my room when I hear again, "Stephen? Goddamnit, let me talk to you." And he's going to come around the corner right now, directly between me and my room, so I quickly open the utility closet door and close it quietly behind me. I don't want to be anywhere that freak can find me.

The closet is big enough for four people but it's all mine. All mine. There's rusted metal shelving against the one wall, bottles of bright liquids, duct tape, a wrench. A drain in the center of the floor. It's uncommonly hot, at least fifteen degrees above room temperature. The gigantic water heater takes up half the space, radiating waves of heat. There's a mop bucket and a broom. On the eye-level shelf, there's also a lipstick tube, nail polish, and a hand mirror propped against a white paint can. The handle is chipped. It's showing me my face, but what I picture is Masha hiding in here, making sure she looks nice for her cleaning route, an old vain Russian woman snapping on her yellow gloves and going to work. I fully extend my arms and touch both walls, listen to the submarine noises of the large building I'm inside. I feel very safe, like if a bomb went off outside, I'd be safe in here, like no one could ever find me if I didn't want them to, a needle in the haystack.

What are you doing for others?

✦

I wake up in the closet. My shirt is soaked through with sweat.

I dump a bag of nuts into my mouth and walk out.

In front of Petrusse, I don't see him coming until it's too late, Kryger kicks my crutch out from under me. It's my fault, I should've been paying attention. A few of the other wrestlers are with him, it doesn't matter who.

"Fucking crippled-ass fancyboy, you're never getting 133 back from me. You should go put a gun in your fucking mouth. Hey, Hoss, you hear what I said to him?"

"I laughed," the other says, "didn't you hear me laugh?"

He mashes my nose with the finger I dislocated, which will heal in time for his next match, which should be mine, in January. Everything in time. When I get cleared to wrestle again, I'm going to break his ribs and put him out for good. Logic must take care of itself. They're laughing behind me. I pick up the crutch and keep going.

✦

There's a note waiting under my door. I pick it up and lock myself inside. I try to see without opening it up, convinced it's the Frogman, he was just biding his time.

Stephen,

Sorry I didn't get to see you before I had to go. Look I know your going through some shit and are sad and don't want to talk to anyone but it is only a knee tear. You will be back in no time and I know you will keep winning. I am your friend and I am telling you this.

Did you talk to Mary Beth since the hospital? We were talking when you were unconscious and she told me she basically loves you. I made sure to remember the exact words and that is what she said. You should talk to her about this stuff she is really super fine and I don't think she would lie about that.

I will miss you but I'll be back soon.

Linus

I go out into the hallway, but I have a surprise: Linus is lurking at the end of the hall.

"Why are you avoiding me?"

"I thought you were gone."

"Why?"

"I'm sorry."

"Did you eat the sandwich I got you?"

"No."

"You are really bad with other people's feelings."

"I know, I'm sorry."

"What does that mean?"

"It means that I'm sorry, but also that I avoided you and didn't want your sandwich."

"I expected you to apologize, but this is weird." He looks at the paper crumpled in my fist. "When I wrote that note I was really upset but now I'm upset about something else, what you're doing right now. I don't like this. This is fucking weird. I don't think I mean much of that note anymore."

"Then I'll just throw it away."

"Did you ever think that wrestling was maybe mostly luck? That you can work hard and give yourself a really good chance to win, but it's still mostly luck?"

"You don't know anything. You're a goddamn kid."

"I'm glad I'm leaving. I need to get away from you."

"I'm glad you're leaving, too."

He kicks my crutch out from under me and I need to use the wall to keep my balance up. The door slams very loudly in the hallway.

I do what I intended to do before I was interrupted, which is drop the note down the trash chute. At the bottom, I hear the whirr of the compactor. I take my time getting down to the front entrance. I stand in the cold and watch the school thin out, watch as it gets darker and the males and females carry their bags away, drive off in their cars. They're all leaving.

Free of anyone who knows of my existence, I feel free to wander, to see what I can find by exploring at night.

✦

At least one-fourth of what I'm about to say is untrue.

✦

Just kidding.

✦

I start by crutching my night route. I do it very slowly, I suppose to make myself feel like old times but it doesn't work. I hate the clicking sound the crutches make when they hit the ground, the predictable two-second space between clicks while my body swings forward and I reset them. I hate how at first I had to consciously keep my left leg curled up, but now it's second nature to have it curled up. I hate my sore armpits, I hate how sweaty the handgrips get.

I hear them before I see them, the six males barking up the path toward me. I stop right under a lightpost where they can see me and let them approach. They must be some of the last remaining students, having male fun on the empty campus. When they come up, I hold out my crutch and trip one of them.

"Watch it, gimp."

"Fuck you."

"What'd you say?" He comes up very close, close enough to smell the alcohol on his breath. "You got something to say?" He is the closest but the other five are circling around me. All this attention.

"No, nothing to say."

"What the fuck did you say a second ago? You wanna say it

again, gimp?" In his defense, he's being very fair and patient with me.

"No, I didn't say anything."

"That's what I thought."

Before he can turn away I ram the crutch up between his legs, hard. His knees buckle and he screams, and then my face is being hit and I'm being kicked in the neck and ribs and it probably would've gotten a lot worse if the fair-haired leader didn't yell at everyone to stop. He comes over and kneels across my chest. "Hey, I'm not trying to fuck up no gimp." One of the others says, "Just knock his teeth in and leave him, let's get out of here." And for the first time I look, really look, at the others, and I see Kyle Glanville standing there just before it hits my mouth and I taste sour. I get kicked in the head and in the void, which is red and not black as they'll have you believe, I jump from thought to thought like they were all lily pads, from my commitment's false bottom to the furl of Mary Beth's eyebrows and when I am all done with that I come home to the night sky and my mouth's blood and drool. I lie there for a while. I reach out my arm and check that all the straps on my brace are still intact. Then I turn my head and open my mouth and more blood falls out.

✦

Back in the closet.

✦

I've been wondering if there isn't a differing value of life experience, whether there's no such thing as case-by-case. Whether love is the same no matter what, suffering is the same no matter what, and the idea of "everyone's different" is just a sentiment created to help explain the failure of people who don't get to the standard.

When I was a little kid I saw a boy in my class named Gary break his foot when he tried to show everyone on the playground how far he could punt a chunk of ice. I felt sympathy when two of the larger kids carried him away crying.

✦

I find out the full routes of the NDTA buses. There are two: the single route that comes through north-south (called the Black Line), and the single route that comes through east-west (called the White Line). I take one and then the other, and I find out that at the end of them the driver is supposed to ask you to pay a new fifty-cent fare before turning around and starting the route back over, but the driver will not ask for your money if you have an upsetting swollen face and spend your time leaning your forehead against your crutches, head pointed at the floor, he will just let you ride in the back row for as long as you want. People will not sit next to you until they have to. On the return ride, a father with a backpack sits with his red-haired son right behind me and lectures him about the importance of eye contact. I pretend to snore loudly to shorten the lesson.

✦

The library is empty, the cafeteria is empty, I eat yogurt mixed with fruit by myself, my floor on McCloskey is empty.

✦

Two of my teeth are loose. It's the important ones in front.

✦

I find a crossword puzzle book someone's left behind in the laundry room and immediately tell myself I'm going to complete the whole thing, that I'll be really talented at crosswords by the time I'm done with the book, which has five hundred puzzles, each one harder than the last. I sit down right there between some baskets but quit after two.

✦

Nothing is the absence of consciousness, when oxygen stops being pumped into the brain. Most people would probably argue that there's no such thing as nothing. But I, personally, would say there is. I've been heading toward it for some time now.

✦

It's snowing again. It started when I wasn't looking.

✦

It's in the corner of my eye but whenever I try to get a look it runs away, and I feel like it's always going to be there and I'm never going to know what it is.

✦

I hear the gentleman whose job it is to shovel snow off the paths scraping around outside. I put on my sweatshirt.

"Hi."

"Hello."

"Do you know Masha?"

"Who that is?"

"Masha. Nice tall lady from Russia."

"No, not who that is."

✦

I have this game I play where I go outside and lie down and wait as long as it takes for my body to get covered in snow. No one's looking. I can do whatever I want.

I don't feel so good.

✦

At the student health center, a man I never see without a surgical mask is the one who takes out my stitches. Over his shoulder is a woman also wearing a mask. She hands him the tools and cotton balls. After they're done, he asks how I'm doing. I say I'm O.K., and he says, are you sure? and I say yes. Then he asks me if I'd like to talk to someone, and I say yes.

On my way out, I grab a pamphlet that says *Am I Suffering From Depression?* It's twice as thick as the others on the rack and has a racially ambiguous girl looking out a rainy window on the front. In my room, I start on the quiz, but it starts to seem like they're asking the same question in different words and so I stop after question twenty. The quiz is 150 questions long.

For a long time afterwards on my bed, I stare at the scar on my knee, which looks like a flatworm. There are no noteworthy thoughts or conclusions during this time.

✦

I go to the training room for my first meeting with Fink, who makes it clear he doesn't want to be there. I get up on the table and wait as he pretends to write something down in his green notebook. Either he started hating me first and I started hating him because I sensed that, or I started hating him first and he started hating me because I started hating him, our hatred wrapped up in each other, or our hating started separately, each deciding independently to hate the other.

"Show me," he says.

I roll my pants up and show him my new flatworm.

"Have you been getting enough magnesium? A deficiency can cause some pretty erratic behavior, and I know you're susceptible to that."

I don't answer.

"Good, great, rest some more," he says. "As for rehab, do what you feel is right."

"I will."

He points at my face with his pen. "I see you've had a busy couple days. Something happen?"

"Nothing happened."

"Ah, 'I fell down some stairs.' Say no more. You don't have to tell me, just doing my job as your trainer! So. Plans this holiday break? Family? It's always good to spend the holidays with your family."

I think about how human conversation is mainly about what's not spoken, what's between the lines subtextually, and I think maybe we are setting some sort of record.

"No, I'm going to stay here. Get better while everyone else is away."

"That's good. It's good to get better. I think it's important for you to get better." And then he puts his hand on my knee, sort of wraps it around the spot. He starts with a little pressure, but then his hand tightens. I stare at him and he looks back at me, squeezing harder and harder and though it hurts I don't intend on ever giving him satisfaction, and at the same time I can feel a hot animal substance gathering behind my eyes.

"Are you going to take your hand off my knee?"

He removes his hand, puts the cap on his pen, and closes his notebook. "Yes, I think we're all done here. Going to go home and see my family."

"What'd you write in that notebook?"

"Merry Christmas, Florida."

He zips his coat and leaves me alone in the training room. With my leg stuck out on the table, I wait and listen to his snow boots squeak down the hallway, farther and farther, until the door opens and closes. I lift my poor ass off the table and open the drawer, study the organized medical supplies and liniments, full of Fink's nasty fingerprints. On my way out, I pass by the door with the frosted window that says COACH OFFICE. It's installed for Hargraves and the head coaches of the other sports, but Hargraves doesn't ever use it. Through the window, on the worn desk, there's a jar of Ben-Gay. This feels like some kind of test, but I go inside anyway. And just as I'm turning around, I hear a shifting sound and notice the dark lump up in the corner of the ceiling. The lights are off, but I can tell it's a bat, and I eye it for a while to see if it moves, because I don't want it flying down into my hair when I turn my back. I grab the Ben-Gay and shut the door.

✦

I do little test runs without the crutches, from one wall to the other in my room, then ramp up to laps around the floor. Eventually I do sit-ups, push-ups, stationary bike at the gym. The crutches go under the bed. I had forgotten what it feels like to get better. All around me I can feel everyone staying the same while I get better, a cloud lifting or just plain tuckering itself out.

It says Ben-Gay will stop your neuralgia whatever that is so I rub that shit all over my left leg. Then, for Christmas, I buy a high-priced pillow. It's a gift for myself.

It's hard to figure out when I'm ready or not ready for food because I don't feel hungry. So I take guesses and force things down when it seems O.K.

✦

I go into the closet. For many hours, I meditate on failure.

✦

Every night, after locking my door, I can hear a muffled thump coming from what sounds like the bathroom. It always begins at one in the morning and always stops four minutes after it starts.

The handle on the paper towel dispenser comes off and Masha has no interest in fixing it or notifying someone else, so there are no more paper towels.

I take an unhelped walk down the main path in the afternoon, it's snowing and no one else is around. I go to the center of campus, under the clock tower, and walk circles around it.

One female trudges up to the Petrusse doors, tries them, then peers through the glass, and walks away.

✦

I open my desk drawers and take my textbooks, the three years' worth I've been saving, and carry them to the bookstore. I sell them and use the money to buy a ratty copy of *The Magic Mountain*, then I go to the thrift shop next to the Pharmart and buy an old CB radio. I also buy a rubber Halloween gorilla mask that's on clearance.

I put the radio on the floor of my room. I listen. They're mostly truckers passing by on 52 or 3, almost all of them make note of the snow. They all have the chains on their tires, and they point out stalled cars east of here and patches of black ice. The snow keeps coming down out my window, and I put my head down on the floor next to the radio and drift off. These puffs of air pass through my skull like dreams from fifty years ago. A conversation goes on in the room while I slip away, the same voices as before, the same old voices. Radio voices, phone voices. Am I dreaming that it is so quiet in the room that I can hear the soft pushing of the snow on the window, am I making it up that way out there something happens with the sunspots' movement and down here the radio pitch switches? There are quiet breaths, a sudden faraway noise repeating, and it's coming from the radio.

The breaths stop and then a voice says, "I'm sorry, I'm very shy."

I sit up. The breaths come back.

I look at the speaker holes, waiting for what's going to come out to come out.

"Please don't get mad at me," the voice says.

I stare at the radio, the device that let this thing into my room.

"I am going to go away if I don't know you're there. Please talk."

I pick up the handset. "Who is this?"

"I have different names."

"Is one of them Frogman?" Breathing, then something that sounds like lips smacking. "Aunt Lorraine?"

"Be careful, if you frighten me I will go away. I told you I'm shy."

"Where are you?"

"Where are you?"

"I'm not going to tell you that," I say.

"That hurts my feelings. I was going to tell you something."

"What? What were you going to tell me?"

"My feelings are hurt. Please say you're sorry."

"What were you going to say?"

"Please apologize."

"I'm sorry I hurt your feelings."

"I think I'm going to tell you a secret. Can I trust you?"

"Yes."

"Do you trust yourself?"

"Yes."

"Do you want to know the secret?"

"Yes."

"What I'm about to say has really happened!" There's giggling through the radio.

"What happened?"

"I like the idea of going somewhere where no one knows who I am, coming into a little town where no one knows me, wearing nice clothes no one's seen before, and I go down the street until I find a quiet house where the lights are on and through the window I can see the woman who lives there by herself, she is in the kitchen washing dishes, and I look at her through her window and can see what her head would look like without hair, and she can't hear me as I enter her house through the back door and quietly come up to her because her house is very quiet and I don't want to disturb that and I stand right behind her and she doesn't know I'm right there, she doesn't know what's coming next. I reach down—"

There's a loud sound like electronic bending and the radio goes back to the old voices. "There's some orange barrels tipped over the line, by . . . uh . . . where the fuck am I anyway . . . Fessenden . . . little past the grade school there . . . going east." I've moved to my bed, farther away from the radio on the floor, but I don't know when this happened.

✦

I've started locking myself in my room before dark, storing up snacks from the cafeteria and working up a sweat. I take out the *Barron's* intending to do the vocab exercises but instead I draw diagrams of whales and then some wolves on the blank pages.

✦

The snow keeps coming down until the power blinks before going out completely, and then the building goes silent. I sit on my bed, waiting for the PA system to tell me what's going on, but after I think fifteen minutes of nothing but the wind outside, it's clear there's no one else in the building to get on the PA, that I'm stuck by myself in the dark with the thing in the bathroom. The school has fully cleared out, who knows how close the nearest help is? Under my door, I can see the flicker of the backup lights.

I take out the plastic bag of roasted zucchini and squash, now obviously cold, and pour a butterscotch pudding cup down my throat. I lick the inside of the container. This is my midnight snack.

I have to pee but I don't dare open the door, so I open the window and climb up on the ledge and let loose into the blizzard.

I have no access to a scale here and I feel like I'm gaining too much weight.

In the dark, I find my laxatives box under the pamphlets and this leads to me shitting out the window.

I put on my wool hat and three sweatpants and three sweatshirts and my brown coat. One-legged jump-roping, the rope scraping the ceiling, and push-ups and sit-ups and one-leg scrambles, and then I try doing some running in place but I don't push my knee too hard. No water's in the room so I collect some snow in the empty vegetable bag and consume that.

I measure time by how many bathrooms I do and so far it's four.

♦

This isn't so bad. Nothing can get me in here. I can't even see myself. I once read that humans stuck in total darkness for three days can become completely blind, due to eye atrophy. In my room, drenching my layers, I drown out the noises outside my door with the medicine ball, I throw it down over and over and over. What does North Dakota mean to me? In seventh grade, I was 13–8. In eighth grade, I was 10–10. In ninth grade, I was 11–14, no postseason. In tenth grade, I was 16–13, sectional qualifier. In eleventh grade, I was 23–11, district qualifier. In twelfth grade, I was 24–8, state qualifier. At Oregsburg, in my freshman season, I was 21–13, eighth place in regional, not good enough for an invite to the Division IV championship. In my sophomore season, I was 23–11, fourth place in the regional, not good enough for an invite to the Division IV championship. In my junior season, I was 25–10, fourth place in the regional, not good enough for an invite to the Division IV championship. It wasn't until college when I jammed enough histories into my skull that I began to feel them rattle inside, clinking like glass and importance, the palsy of history. They matter more and more and I wrestle harder and harder. I wish I had ropes to do pummels. I keep going, I'm trying to outlast the snow. More sit-ups. More bag water. I eat two graham crackers.

Here's a math question: During the course of a life, do most people in the world experience more happiness or more suffering?

♦

I'm very sticky now. Appetite! Slime, slime! I rub it on myself. I outpace any suffering with my appetite, I lick my arms and bang my head against the wall three hundred times, I can't get enough. I'm ready to be let out now.

✦

You lock yourselves in the room where you sleep with the person you love. This is the most intimate thing you can do with this person. I've locked myself in two different rooms with Mary Beth and at the time I couldn't believe my luck.

✦

I'm trying to remember when it was I first heard about tubal ligation. Top five extra organs, kidneys, spleen, gonads, colon, appendix, piling up in a big old dumpster. Back in health class, black-haired Ms. Garrett, who just totally excreted the loneliness smell, had part of her jaw removed for her mouth cancer and she kept telling us she was cancer free, cancer free! She taught us that poor people get pregnant more easily and would sneak in racist shit like how most diseases came from China. It must feel so good to get the bad part of your body cut out.

An experiment for the human being with a vibrant breed of loneliness is to self-insert the middle finger of the writing hand into the anus.

I have considered masturbation but I've convinced myself that whatever it is I'm holding on to in there is worth holding on to.

I open the window and wipe off the snow and see that the weather's stopped and that there's some decent daylight in between the frost fog. The snow is at least four feet deep. I get into bed and go back to sleep and wait for them to come get me.

Attention.

The PA system crackles and through the fuzz, I hear a man clearing his throat. "Hello. We are here. We are here to help you out. We will fix the lights in a moment. Please stay where you are."

I open my door. I have put the gorilla mask on. The hallway is lit by small bulbs stuck in the four corners of the floor so that it's bright at the ends and darker as you near the middle. Distant electric fizzes. The place is trying to come back alive. I head forward into the darkness. "Please give me two more minutes. We are coming." The backup lights in the bathroom strobe with no pattern. When I turn the handle, no water comes out of the sink. I try flushing a toilet. Nothing. I walk down the line of stalls, every single door open. The lights tick and flicker. I turn the other corner, making my circle, and stop at the row of shower cells. There are eight. The curtains of the first seven are open. The eighth has been drawn shut, and it is moving.

"We are here."

Two campus security men are in the hall and I run past them. "Hey, are you O.K.?" My knee is fine now, I realize, I can take the stairs at full practice speed. This is no problem. Outside, there are people starting to shovel the snow.

✦

Without a direction in mind, I jog around areas with the least snow, move from overhang to overhang, all the dark groins of the college.

Linus is in Nebraska and I'm glad he's gone. Boy am I glad I don't have plantar fasciitis! I hope something bad happens to him. He doesn't understand anything, he's just a kid. He doesn't understand me anymore, and I don't understand myself in relation to him. When he comes back, I have to keep his mouth away from my prestige.

Around the corner of Opal Hall, I spot a rattly snowplow burring past some pine trees, shooting snow off the highway, clearing a direct path of habitation east. Toward Konstantin College.

Ice. I don't need anybody. I don't need anybody. I can pass around here undetected, I can do whatever I want. I'm the one in control. Ice. Cold.

I stomp behind the plow that's pushing aside the snow with its face. Snow gets through my socks. The clouds from my breath go away. The temperature rises so quickly that I can feel it.

When I get about eight miles outside of Oregsburg, there's much less snow. You can see dirt everywhere, as if it hasn't snowed on the highway in a week, as if the clouds didn't move west to east but squatted on Oregsburg, did their work, and then disappeared.

I start running. I have a plan.

All this time to myself. I have time to take stock of the big picture. What do I think about? Does it count as considering mortality if, passing a scraggled bunch of roadside trees, I imagine death as a black stump you continually bump up against? If I cross over to thoughts of God, a wild man who is sitting up in the clouds playing with his crayons? And what does it mean if they fall out of my head ten seconds after I have them, gone for good, how much validity can they possibly have?

Most of life is adulthood, mostly husbands who are prosecutors coming home with liquor buzzes and hard-ons from doing justice, ready to hide it inside their wives who are mostly in missionary, staring at ceilings, life is mostly wet stone buildings, collars, rain, snow.

A single car drives by, heading back toward Oregsburg. Inside, they might've heard for an instant my voice singing through the lips-hole of my mask, "Farewell and adieu to you, fair Spanish ladies, farewell and adieu to you, ladies of Spain."

There is a story I read in the suicide pamphlet about a woman from Jamestown who had such bad headaches that she drove the hour and a half to Bismarck in order to take the elevator to the nineteenth floor of the capitol building, the tallest building in the area, and jump out of an open window. Did she check below beforehand to see what she'd besmatter? But what I kept getting hung up on was how much time she had to think about it. She had the whole car ride and elevator ride up to think about it.

I pass a pile of rusted iron girders at the edge of some tall grass leading to woods. A mother possum emerges huffing from the pile and trudges toward me, her pregnancy dragging on the ground. She begins hissing and chases me off.

Under some distant fog, you can see the small cluster of Konstantin buildings. But on this side, there are little farmhouses dropped in scattered locations, divided by enormous brown fields. Skiffington is more spread out than Aiken.

The temperature is over fifty. It must be late afternoon. I stalk around the houses. This is what happens when my discipline doesn't know where to go. Taking off the mask, I go up to a house that looks like it contains nice people. I knock. A middle-old lady comes to the door. Wives who smell like their husbands and children.

"Well, you're a long drink of water!"

"Hi, ma'am, I'm visiting from Yankton and seem to have gotten turned around. I was hoping you could direct me to my cousin's house. The Carvers?"

She eyes my sweatpants. "Yankton! Long way from home, aren't you, cowboy?" I think right now she is recording a lasting mental image of my bulge. "You certainly do look like a Carver, however." Her look moves to my face for the first time. "I see the resemblance, even with that fight-swelling there."

"Yes, ma'am. We all look alike."

"Two farms down, Mr. Carver. Red roof, surprised you didn't remember that! Tell them I say hi, and you should be wearing warmer clothes than that. It's going to storm."

"Thank you, ma'am."

I put the mask back on, go down a main Skiffington thoroughfare until I come to a side road on the left, where way at the end of it, I see a red roof. If the Carvers happened to be looking out of their windows, they would have plenty of time to see me coming up their front drive, marching between their silos and barn. But I get all the way up to the house, have time to walk around it. What do you even do on a farm? I cannot shake images of dinner triangles, rose-colored sunsets, old man Carver braining the hogs. A big window on the side is open and from inside, I hear a woman's voice on the radio. I approach the window, stick my head in. It's the kitchen. Something smells like smoke. "Nearby residents are seeing a record snowfall, leading to widespread power outages and road blockage, while close-by areas are puzzlingly clear. More after this." The inside of the house is brighter and warmer than the outside. While observing the Carvers' clean and inviting house, I get the sour sense of being very far from my home, which itself is not a real place as it should be with furniture and cared-for floors, it's only a dense feeling inside my whatever, a feeling of familiarity.

Someone's coming, so I duck down and make my way crouchwise to the front door, shoving the mask down my pants. The doorbell is cheerful.

The person that comes to the door is the mother. This is how I know: she has the distinct look of a woman who has given birth, which is lifelong and both tired and satisfied.

"Jesus, son. What happened to your face?"

"Good evening or afternoon, Mrs. Carver. My name is Stephen Florida. I attend the nearby college Oregsburg. A few weeks ago—"

"I know who you are. Why don't you come inside."

"That's really all right. I was actually hoping—"

But she's leading me by the shoulders toward the kitchen where I just stuck my head. She sits me in a wicker chair with a strong weave that crackles comfortingly when I put myself down on it.

"Can I make you some eggs? I'm sure you're like Joey and don't eat anything. He'll eat eggs sometimes, though."

"No, thank you, ma'am. Really I just—"

"What can I get you for the problems you're having with your face? We have iodine and bandages in the bathroom there, if you'd like."

"No, thank you, could I—"

"You need to eat. When's the last time you ate?"

"Recently."

"I'll make you some eggs."

So Mrs. Carver makes me eggs while I sit and wait in her kitchen, at the table where Joseph Carver eats. I compliment her on her red sweater. She puts the eggs in front of me. They're scrambled. "That's only two. Under two hundred calories total. No salt, no butter. Olive oil. You eat that."

So I chew with my back teeth. The digestive feel is one of tossing an egg in a large hole, and there is more upset than pleasure in choking down Mrs. Carver's eggs. But I'm not trying to upset anyone so I get them down for her benefit. She stands by the window where my head was, watching to make sure it all goes in. Her slacks are midway up her stomach, a menopausal bump pushes out the zipper area. She takes out a cigarette and lights it.

"We were all sorry about the match," she says. "I was very sorry."

"Thank you."

"Joey was very sorry." She looks right at me. "What was it he said? He kept saying it. Oh right. 'If we wrestled one hundred times he would've won fifty.'" She angles her breath out the window and taps the cigarette. "You came over from Oregsburg?"

"Yes."

"It's bad over there?"

"Pretty bad."

"Mm," she says, then looks out the window, in the direction of the college.

"Is Mr. Carver home?"

"Mr. Carver is no longer in our lives." If the first instinct is to think he's dead, it's certainly replaced by the thought that he's run away and deserted them, and I believe this because of the way she says it.

"Well, thank you for the eggs, ma'am."

"You're welcome."

"Is Joseph home?"

"No, sorry, he's not."

"Where is he?"

She sucks the cigarette hard, the ash end crawls toward her mouth. "I don't think that's any of your business."

"Is he on the property? I could go find him. If I could just have a word. Won't take long."

"I'm afraid he's not here."

I stare at Mrs. Carver's old wrinkled face, the source of these lies, I pick her eggs out of my teeth and understand that no amount of talking will get her to change her lies.

From the upstairs, a floorboard creaks.

I knock the chair over, Mrs. Carver running behind me, yelling, "Stop, stop! Please!" But I've already found their stairs, I'm up them two at a time. At the top, there are three doors. One is closed. All I want is to wrestle him again, my knee is better now and I'm ready to throw in again, I'm going to get him in a cross-face cradle in his own bedroom, I'm owed another shot since my knee cut things short before, it's the fair thing. I throw open the door and it is a very small room with a bed and at the window there is a wheelchair and a girl with a blanket over her knees and she turns her head and looks at me, her face and head disfigured, she looks happy to see me, her arms crooked and her hands in twisted fists, her mouth wide open and drooling.

"Get out. Right now," says Mrs. Carver from right behind me.

On the driveway, it begins to rain. I put the mask on. There is a fable about rain in December. When it happens, it is a sign of error and depravity in the people it falls on, and the harder and more prolonged it falls, the worse the human offense, which is why the residents of Sodom and Gomorrah could never stay dry. The rain spatters the pavement, soaking the dirt, and it begins to fall harder.

And maybe I would've just gone home and things probably would've been just a little different if I hadn't heard the goat. But I did, I heard the goat.

The Carvers' barn has a whole bunch of animals around it. The pigs and the cows don't mind the rain, but the chickens step around under the roof in the shadows, they are too stupid to clean themselves. But what I am interested in is the billy goat. I confess I never used to try anything like this but then a ways back my brain snapped in half. His big bell rattles around on his neck as he chases the fillies around, and they pretend like they don't like his attention and bombast. He lets out the goat noise. He's very good about letting everyone know he's there. He trots out into the rain and over to the fence to get closer to me. He puts his front hooves on the fence and looks at me by turning his head to the side. He has a long curled beard.

I hurdle the fence, my feet sucking into the pen's mud. He tries to get away from me but I have his back leg, his nice coarse fur, dingleberries on the lower long furs, great unhappy noises as he tries to free himself, but I have him. They've disbudded his horns and they are only modest nubs. I grab his other leg, saying, "Here, billy," and yank him close. I'm going to cradle this fucker. The goat kicks my face, knocks the mask off. I dive into the mud. Skiffington mud has a mustardy tang. He shakes his leg out and runs away, his bell clanging, making a shrill ruckus that warns the others to stay away from me. But then I see what he's really doing: he's not running away, he's only making a wide loop of the pen to build up a head of steam, and he's making the turn and galloping back toward me, kicking up mud everywhere, his bell flailing, lowering his head, and I stand up to welcome him. I catch his hard skull in my stomach and he knocks me back into the fence, which snaps easily. I land on my back and he keeps going, veering crazily around in the adjacent pasture, waggling his head around and bucking. On my back in the rain, I hear a woman crying, a sound coming from Mrs. Carver, who is standing ten feet away, dripping wet in her fine red sweater, a sad and sorry sight indeed, telling me she's called the police.

While running zigzags between the islands of shrubbery around Skiffington, avoiding the authorities, I have time to reflect on my choices. I touch the spot of the kick. My hands are wet from the rain and mud and blood. When I think I see a patrol car through the fog, I dart off the road into a field, kicking the chins of the furrows, a potato field with no potatoes to speak of, fields like dead overturned horses. I find a particularly nice hole and kneel down so no one can see me.

On the ground in the neighboring furrow, there's a closed foam container. It contains a large portion of sweet-and-sour pork, only a few bites taken. For the first time in a long time, I feel hungry, childishly, uncontrollably hungry. I dig the plastic fork out of the rice and begin eating. I swallow it down, all of it, I push it in without any breaks. None of this extracurricular activity that happens outside of the mat will be recorded. I close my mouth and run my tongue around inside, tasting the last bits of pork and sauce that didn't make it down to my stomach yet. I lick the container. The permanent record will contain only numbers, wins and losses, time of match, and decision. Everything else will remain unknown. I stick my finger down my throat and throw it up, all of it, bent over with my hands on my knees. It takes a few minutes to get it all back out.

Am I who I said I was? Am I a wrestler? If I jump off the top of the capitol building and my spirit escapes, does my spirit upon entering another body turn again into a wrestler? Does it resume all this? Or is the link so weak that wrestling ends along with the body? Does the entire feeling end just like that? This center inside me, encoded with tilts and cradles, could go up in smoke at any moment without a body willing to do its dirty work. You grow up fearing what you don't understand, but by the time you're older, it becomes far more complicated than that. The difference between children and adults is: adults have lots of problems and the young have one big problem.

After kicking the girders and making sure the mother possum is out running her errands, I relieve myself on her nest.

I would trade my family and Linus and Mary Beth and all the

kid friends I had growing up that I can't remember anymore for a championship in Kenosha. I would trade slightly less for the chance to wrestle until my body quit on me.

For the first time in a long time, I admit to myself, out loud as if to another person, that I let Mary Beth go. Without an idea of what Birmingham looks like, it remains a hazy optimistic cloud that contains her laugh and a bunch of strangers listening, which raises my jealousy all the way up, jealousy for people I can't even picture. Once or twice already, I've taken out maps of the northern U.S. states and calculated with a ruler the distance to Birmingham. It looks like about a sixteen-hour drive.

✦

The next morning, first thing, I head up the stairs with the CB, to the door that leads onto the roof, which is locked. There's a little electrical box on the adjoining wall, and resting on top is where I find the key. It's still basically night. Empty alcohol bottles are piled and stacked in elaborate ways around the roof, so many that the more recent ones seem to be in honor of the older ones, a hidden museum that's always been right above me. I go to the edge and lean over to make sure no one's goofing around down there, then I drop the radio sixty or seventy feet below, which isn't enough to destroy it to full symbolic satisfaction but it's good enough. Then I walk back downstairs and sleep for a while.

✦

I can't believe I used to be scared of dying. What a relief that will be.

✦

Was last night New Year's? Practice is starting back up in two days if that's true.

✦

I open my desk drawer and reach inside, taking out a handful of sundry pamphlets. *Alcoholism: The Family Disease, Why Am I Always Hungry?, What You Should Know If You're Arrested.* A few long hairs are tangled around the pamphlets, and they belong to Mary Beth. I put it all back in the drawer and close it shut.

✦

What I'd really like is to see if Mary Beth's left anything in her room, to get a more exact idea of my emotional location by standing in her empty room, then sitting down in the center to know what I'm up against in the long run. But I don't have access to Mooney, so I go to the second-best option, which is looking in Linus's room for an object to rekindle my fraternal feeling for him, a photograph, his Neosporin tube, anything. I'm feeling forgiving. I can't tell if I miss him or not, so I don't know whether to feel guilty. And it doesn't matter anyway because his door is locked, of course it's locked.

✦

I take the stairs down to the lobby, and I'm on my way out the door when someone yells.

"Hey!"

I turn around. It's the male front-desk attendant.

"You're Stephen Florida, right?"

He tells me they have a package for me that is taking up too much room. He leads me behind the desk and points to a tremendous box. I carry it up the stairs, banging into walls on the turns.

It weighs practically nothing. There's no return address, just my name, Stephen Florida. I cut the tape with a pen. Inside are thousands of peanuts. If the Frogman has sent this, I concede it's a pretty funny joke and so I plunge my hand in there, I'm going to get what's coming to me as fast as I can. But all I get are more peanuts, which in the box ecosystem function as water, my hand going through them, peanuts spilling onto my carpet, the mess I'm making, I'm up to my shoulder in it, and that's when my hand gets ahold of the paper. An envelope. I open it up, take the white card out.

> *The "monk" seen pensively walking the dunes in Caspar David Friedrich's* The Monk by the Sea *(left, in oil-on-canvas reprint) is actually no monk at all! He is Noel Friedrich, the bastard agnosic brother of Caspar. Friedrich often took his younger brother Noel out for air along the cliffs at Rügen between 1804 and 1808, until Noel himself died in the very same deep depicted in the painting, drowned when he mistook the waters for the town square. It is thought that* The Monk by the Sea *is the most personal of Friedrich's paintings for this reason.*

I rub the knob on the rear of my head. On the back of the card is Mary Beth's address and a phone number. I fold it up and put it inside my shoe.

✦

Early on, maybe when we were going to Silas's hill, I think she knew that I didn't want to talk about myself, about the past, and so these long stretches of not talking would take place, time in which we would've been shoring up the basics of myself, but it was nicer just to have the quiet.

◆

First thing in the morning, I sit at my desk in my boxers and my skin turns very cold as I write a letter to Mary Beth, a whole page of paper. When I'm getting dressed, I feel another set of things to say come up, and so I sit back down, open the letter, and write a second page to her, front and back, then I put them in an envelope and seal it up. On my way across campus, I mail it.

I head to the training room for my second meeting with Fink. I wait for fifteen minutes before it becomes clear he's not coming.

On the posting board under the clock tower, there's a police sketch of someone who looks nothing like me.

◆

I take the White Line west, and I'm the only one who gets off at my stop. As I walk across the parking lot to the swimming club, I realize for some reason that I am clenching my asshole very tight.

I climb up on the lane-eight diving block and gracelessly leap off because I haven't been swimming in ten years. I wash the goat mud off until I am clean again. I swim the pool back and forth forty times. Wrestling. I'm going to wrestle again soon. The exhaustion that comes over me is nothing like what I've been feeling lately, it's earned and honest and not perversely soiled. I push harder to bring it on quicker, to have it more. I get out of the pool and find the trash can, and though a flavor hint of the sweet-and-sour pork comes into my mouth when I burp, there's nothing in there to vomit up.

On the bus back to Oregsburg, there's a book on the seat in front of me, a paperback mystery with a yellow cover. It's set in an Italian seaside town, and the first clue is a dead man with a petunia pinned to his chest. But then I recognize that I don't care who the killer is, that finding out seems like an outstanding effort, so I put the book back. And then sleep comes down on me like an elevator and I'm at the bottom of the shaft.

✦

One day I told myself I'd wake up and see my normal face in the bathroom mirror, all healed. That day is today.

It's only been one night but I can't help it, I've been checking every few hours if she's sent a letter. This morning I ask and when the male goes back to check the stacks of sorted incoming mail, he comes back with a single envelope.

But it's not from her. It's from the office for the Harriet Howard Leadership Scholarship, informing me that my presentation time is set for the first week of March, right before Kenosha, which at the moment feels far away but only because so much will be decided by then. In real life, March is not far away at all.

✦

The trip to the gym in the morning, still way before sunrise, is an irrationally sentimental experience that I extend by walking very slowly.

Fink lounges on the bleachers, picking his teeth with his car keys. The next thing I notice, though I don't mean to, is that Linus is missing. Everyone else is here. I stand off to the side, pace around the outside of the gym away from them so they don't talk to me, and wait until Hargraves comes in, which is last. He blows his whistle and they start jogging. I go up to Hargraves.

"All right, good to see you, Florida. How's the knee?"

"It's doing really a lot better. I'm ahead of schedule. I think I could do some drills, some live-gos."

"Great to hear, Florida," he says. "I talked to Fink about this, he thinks—and I agree with him—that you should take it easy. It's only natural that you already feel ready to get back in there. But we don't want to make it worse."

"You talked to Fink about this? What did he say?"

"We think you should bike this week. Next week we'll see, take it from there."

"Bike?"

"The first thing that goes is the endurance. Have to keep that up."

"But I have been. I can run. I can at least do the bleachers."

He puts his hand on my shoulder. "I know it's hard as hell, son. But you don't want to damage what's trying to get better."

I walk away and he shouts, "You've still got time!" or something like that.

They stretch and I bike. Lee and Whiting take half to the weight room for legs. The rest stay. They do reaction drills and I bike. They do bridges and wall arches and cross bars, they do situations and I bike. At different points during practice, one of them will glance in my direction, trying to see what I'm thinking by my face. "Explode on the whistle! Explode on the whistle! Explode on the whistle!" Hargraves yells until the meaning gets knocked out of it, until it sounds like a different language. During live-gos, Kryger locks up Simon and then hits a cement mixer, whipping Simon's neck. "Who's gonna be the bully today, huh?" Hargraves yells. "Ass dragging doesn't happen anymore. This is January. Ass dragging is some fucking December shit." Simon keeps getting up and trying again, but he's too eager, Kryger keeps putting him down, whipping his neck, more and more aggressively. Two minutes in, Kryger whips Simon so hard that Simon yelps. From across the gym, Fink looks up from the mat, right at me.

He smiles. These are unique challenges that are being given to me! I remember Fink's smile. I remember Kryger's taunts. I snip them like newspaper photos to save for later.

A bunch of whistles blow and everyone quits and sits down while Hargraves talks. He tells a story about the man in the glass, everyone is quiet except the swishing my wheels make. "I notice some of you are a little bit slow today. That's O.K. You've been away for a little bit. But we're gonna keep taking it to you, it's gonna keep ramping up the next two months. You knew we were gonna be hard on you. This is what you signed up for." Then he lets them go. I wait for fifteen minutes in the empty gym so I don't have to speak with any of them in the locker room. There's a puddle of myself underneath me.

I grab my towel from my locker and walk straight to the showers. Only Carpenter and Nate are in there. They ask questions immediately. I rub suds into my ears and face and try to listen to the crackle of the water against the tile rather than their voices.

"How's the knee, Florida?"

"Feeling good."

"You gonna be back before regionals?"

"Feeling good about it."

"They got you on the bike?"

"Bike, yeah."

And then they talk to each other about the girls they fucked over Christmas, and for a moment I wonder if I'm a different species. For maybe the hundredth time since I received the box of peanuts, I think about Mary Beth, who's the only reason any of this is palatable. They talk about the Rose Bowl, wanting to have kids, a person called Jack Careowhack, their fears about getting jobs after college, shoplifting Schlitz six packs and balloons, using the balloons for whippets, pot. I shut off the water and get out.

I sit on the bench in front of my locker with the towel over my head.

"Man, I'm fucking going places, bro."

"Shut the fuck up, you're not going anywhere."

"Yeah? Watch me. I'm going to graduate school. Health science. Start calling me Doctor."

"Yeah? You're gonna write your dissertation?"

"Dissertation on that sideways vagina."

I stare into the fuzzy pink cotton, inhaling my own hot air while the locker room clears out around me. Lockers slam, zippers go up, laughing, burping. I'm afraid things are going to get worse before they get better. Ignorance changes into fear. Fear turns into distrust, then violence, which changes into dirt and then dread and then a disease of the mouth and then hydrogen and then stars and then a chemical accident and then brightness.

I take the towel off my head. The locker room is empty, all the lockers are shut. A fly buzzes around, bumping against walls and the lockers. Historically, the salt smell of a locker room creates nervousness in people who are bad at their sport, but in the talented it creates nothing, no feeling, it's part of your job. I used to feel the first and now I feel the second. On the chalkboard, Hargraves wrote:

WAYS TO BREAK YOUR OPPONENT

1. *Set a fast physical pace.*
2. *Hustle back to the center.*
3. *Attack immediately after a takedown.*
4. *Release him and attack immediately.*

5. *Continue to wrestle in all situations.*
6. *Don't let his actions positive or negative faze you.*

I go to the bathroom. Sherman's in there, a towel around his waist, combing his hair very carefully in the mirror. "Greetings."

I go to the sink next to Sherman and put my mouth under the faucet. He's still parting his hair, one strand at a time. He's doing a pretty good job.

"How long you been doing that?" I say.

"While," he says. "How's the knee?"

"Feeling good."

"You talked to Linus at all?"

"No."

"Really? Thought you were friends." He finishes and heads around the corner into the empty locker room, where he goes to his bag, three down from my locker.

"We are," I say. "What happened?"

He grabs a deodorant stick, looks at me as he wipes. "Oh right, you weren't there. Fink told us before practice." He puts his shirt on, pulling the head hole extra wide so his hair fits through without touching. "Linus's grandma died. He's gonna be back in a couple of days. Maybe a week." He starts rolling his socks on. His toenails are long, which somehow contradicts his neat hair. "She went in with sudden chest pains and was gone by the next morning." I don't say anything, but get dressed at my locker. "Can't believe you didn't talk to him." I'm looking down at my feet, tying the laces of my left shoe, but can tell he's staring at me from the corner of my eye. "What were you up to for the break?" He's still staring, the same way the rest of them were staring when I was on the bike. "What's up with you, why are you being so fucking weird about everything? Don't you ever think about what you look like to other people?" I don't answer. "Hello? You're like a big fucking grump." I take my shoe, the right one, and get up and begin hitting Sherman with it. "What the fuck?" he yells, but I keep smacking him in the head with it, messing up his arranged hair. "What the fuck?" he keeps saying, and it takes him fifteen seconds of me not stopping to realize he needs to get out, which he does, grabbing his bag and shielding himself, leaving me alone in the locker room, which I guess is what I wanted all along. I grab my backpack from the bottom of my locker. Underneath, there's a snapped wishbone and a note that says *Happy Holidays*.

✦

I register for spring classes. I'm taking Nonfiction Film, Unusual Disorders, Geography I, and Introduction to Jazz. On my way out, Ms. Rutledge hands me an envelope with my fall grades.

Before going home, I sit on a concrete bench and watch students walk by the posting board. Most of them just glance at the police sketch in passing, until an honest-faced male stops in his tracks and stares. Then he looks over at me, then back at the sketch, and once more at me, like I'm a horse in a dog costume. We're at least twenty feet apart. "Hello!" I say, and he puts his head down and leaves.

I open the envelope. Drawing (B), Basic News Writing (C+), What Is Nothing? (C+), Meteorology (C-).

✦

Back in McCloskey, I stare at Mary Beth's phone number and after a long time work up the nerve to call, but Brandon's using the phone, so I head back inside. I pluck out each of the hairs that grows on my shoulders.

I dream that I'm outside Linus's door yipping like a dog.

Sometime in the middle of the night, I give in and call Mary Beth's number. It rings and rings but no one picks up because superstition is the belief in the causal nexus.

✦

The difference between how I miss Linus and how I miss Mary Beth is that I don't ever really hope to see him again. With Linus, it's like something's already run out, like the hope is beside the point.

✦

I catch myself whimpering I want to get back on the mat so bad. They all look alike, hitting the mats, grabbing each other around the neck, pulling. This is for them somewhere between a hobby and a habit. Something they can put on a key chain or tell their wives about after sighing. But Fink and Kryger, the proud worm, are different. Am I the only one who notices it? Seeing both of them in one place creates a strange effect. Kryger does the drills, making a show of doing them hardest or fastest, Fink watches, puts his whistle in his mouth from time to time and leaves it there, but never blows it.

I also wonder if to work for something very hard necessarily requires pushing other people enormous distances away from you.

For the whole practice, Hargraves is unhappy. He blows his whistle disgustedly, he keeps stopping drills. No one is working hard enough. This is "not what he likes to be seeing." No one is ready. What no one says is that no one, since Linus isn't here and I'm on the bike, is good enough to win anything at regionals anyway. It all looks sort of like an elementary school play. The other coaches watch as he flogs Reuben with his whistle's string for "lollyassing." Finally, he gets so fed up he untucks his shirt and ends practice, telling everyone there is no practice tomorrow because no one deserves it, telling everyone they better use their day off to get their heads on straight.

Some of them get ice packs afterwards, knees and shoulders, and I miss and envy the ice packs. A few of them stop by my locker and ask about my health, Fat Henry and Whitey and Harry slap my shoulder. Weeds grow out of my mouth, hang down on my chin and flop around when I speak.

✦

I try calling again. Without any expectation that this is real, or that it will amount to nothing all over again, I'm overtaken by something yellow and delirious when I hear the phone pick up, and I'm about to say something but she says something first.

"Fuck you."

"Mary Beth?"

The phone line cuts out. "Hello?" I say.

I dial up the number again, and she picks up right away. "Do you know how long I sat in that fucking diner waiting for you? Do you know that I put a dress on for you and it was zero degrees? I don't know if you know this but I don't have time to recline and eat bonbons. Do you know how bored I got?"

"I—"

"I had four Cokes. I hate Coke but it's all they had. As soon as I figured out you weren't coming I left. When I got home I threw my earrings out the window. I don't know why. Do you know how boring that was?"

"I'm sorry."

"I hate being bored. You made me really bored."

"I'm sorry."

"What were you even doing when I was sitting there?"

"I don't remember. It's been an unmemorable month."

"Is that self-pity? Shouldn't that've dried up a few weeks ago?"

"What's going on?"

"I think that's obvious. I feel like there's an emotional and also spatial dental dam between us."

"What were your hairs doing in my drawer?"

"I was looking in it, stupid."

"Yes, well, why?"

"Because I knew you had them, the pamphlets, in there. When you went to use the bathroom or something I looked through all your stuff."

"Well . . ."

"Well, what?"

"Didn't you think something about them?"

"Are you embarrassed?"

"I'm not embarrassed."

"I thought you might be suicidal at first but then I figured out you weren't pretty quickly. But that's doesn't mean I don't worry and I think you would've figured out by now that it's part of why we're talking on the phone now, isn't it?"

"Yes," I say, just to say something, trying to keep up.

"Listen, I'm not going to make this into a big thing, and I'm not expecting it to be some turning point where we both say we're both sad and you apologize and we make up just like that, and you say to yourself, 'That's it, no more messing around, I'm going to be a big boy and quit moping and that's that,' and I come to your match in Wisconsin and you win 133. I have my own life here. I'm happy. I don't think I can flip the switch for you right now. I miss you terribly, a lot of the time I can't sleep. But I've already booked two exhibitions here, and I'm doing it because I barely go to bed, and some of that is because I miss you, but most of it's because I'm hustling my ass off. I hope you're not wandering off into that swamp pit of yours, because I know what you're like when you get like that. You're like me. You have to keep the blinders on, you have to stay exhausted, it's how you know you're doing it right. I promised myself I'd never set foot in North Dakota again and I still mean it. I don't miss that hole one bit, so I guess don't get your hopes up or whatever is what I'm saying. I have to go, I have too many things to do right now. Don't get too much sleep. I miss you."

I hang up the phone, and though I know she's not calling back, I stand there for a minute just to make sure.

✦

One day in December outside the Drawing shed, Mary Beth grabbed my arm and asked me, "When are you going to take me on a date?"

At the time, I remember thinking she was clutching me like the cosseted duchess we all read about, but I also remember something in her face, her eyes, which I hadn't seen before, which now strikes me as fear, a fear of sadness, because I think she already knew what was going to happen.

"O.K. What about tonight? What do you want to do?" I was nervous, because there was nothing to do around here.

"Oh, I'm sure you'll figure it out," she said, and the thing in her face was gone.

And I will make this short because I didn't come up with the world's most original lineup, we watched a weak December sunset at three thirty over some buildings, and then I took her to a female movie, and though I was worried about my unoriginal decision she watched the whole thing with insane intent, like it was going to have some big secret ending, but it didn't, the farmer and the schoolteacher just made out like crazy at the end after some obstacles were cleared, and she wouldn't let us leave until after the credits were over, as though she wanted to pay her thanks to all of the makers by sitting through the scroll. We were the last ones in the theater. Then I took her to a bar with loud music and nursed a cup of water all night and she ordered a basket of fries, which I tried to dissuade her from, saying I had a reservation for two at the good German restaurant, but she said, and I remember this very clearly, that she was too happy to go to the good German restaurant, and she ate the bad fries and I made a fool of myself dancing for her enjoyment, which I didn't mind, and I shouted over the music, "I'm a big fool for you!" and we were dehydrated and sweating, and who knows what time it was when we walked home, with her hanging on my neck, looking down at her feet and the snow and smiling like a delirious person.

We went through the lobby and up the elevator and to her room without talking, and I remember feeling more and more excited with each new door we were passing through, like I was heading toward a tiny center that only I was told the location of, and after she'd locked her door behind us and turned the lights off I realized the center wasn't tiny at all, it could be large and anything.

She had my shirt off and I had her pants at her ankles, and I said, "Is this our second date?"

"Does the time I jerked you off on the hill count as a date?"

"I jerked you off more than you jerked me off."

"I'm really glad you're not wearing sweatpants," she said, and then she raked her nails down my sternum.

Her eyes were brown and I'm not trying to be an uppity poet when I say that the world shortly became more than a freezing ice ball, which is what I always thought it was, and so I said, "Wow."

"Did you say 'wow'?"

"Yes."

And I could hear her start to say something just as I started to explain, but in the end neither of us said these statements, because she had put her hand over my mouth.

✦

The next morning, I take a stealthy trip to the gym because obviously "no practice" means you're still supposed to come to practice, just that the coaches won't be there. I want to see who correctly read between the lines. I peek through the small window of the gym door. Doing the bleachers is Kryger in front, behind him Lyle, Ellis, Nate, Carpenter, Harry, Whitey, Fat Henry. "Pigeons mate for life!" Kryger yells, which isn't true, if you've ever seen a pigeon you know that's not true, but that makes me think of the opposite of that, which is lions, who fuck for fun, and then humans, who fuck for a lot more complicated reasons.

I leave and take a run south. The route I always do, all the same scenery. Quonsets, a white water tower. The route ends with my favorite tree, the one that I passed for the first time four years ago, one that got sick from the inside and died a long time ago, a tremendous goiter bulging out of its trunk. Now I always run by to see how much worse it's gotten. One time with Linus, I said, "I'll pay you five dollars to lick the goiter," and he said, "I'll do it! I'll do anything for five dollars!"

I get finished just as the bus is getting to the stop. I ride it to the pool, do forty trips.

✦

I crack open a new sketch pad and try to draw what I think Levi Silas looks like. Over the next three nights, I keep doing sketches and taping them up above my desk, beside the best sentence I ever wrote. Two years ago, I got a C+ on my Debating Human Rights in China paper after I spent fifteen minutes straight, a personal record, sitting at my desk and doing nothing other than creating this sentence, the last one of the paper: "This persistence of the Chinese's indefatigable will, even in centuries, will still be remembered." I believe that this sentence is the best sentence I've ever written. I believe it raised the paper from a C single-handedly, and so I cut the sentence out of the paper and taped it up over my desk. The wind flutters it when I have the window open, it likes to draw attention to itself. And now alongside it, there's a row of seven different Silas sketches, but they all ominously resemble a different person.

✦

In the grass field west of town, two cows run into each other like rams. They hand out neon flyers telling everyone to stay away from the cows.

✦

One week when I was nine or ten, my mom tried to quit. She didn't buy any cartons for seven whole days, and you'd see her walking around the house with a toothbrush in her mouth, chewing up the bristles.

✦

A little bit after it happened, I sat with my grandma in Rudy Unger's office, rolling and unrolling my blue tie as he called a bureaucrat who carefully explained over speakerphone why only a percentage of my parents' pensions would be transferred to me.

✦

My mom had more friends than my dad. She would carefully drive a carful out to Kraft Lake, Mrs. Venders and Mrs. Tomasi and also sometimes the awfully attractive and childless Mrs. Blankenship, whose image I experimented with in the first days of my own personal masturbation, and they'd all sit in the car and drink out of a big silver flask that she didn't want us to know about even though we did. "Do you think George could kill someone?" "Yes. I could never marry a man who couldn't kill someone." "Oh, for Christ's sake, shut up about all the husbands all the time and pass that shit." My dad didn't have friends, he had my mom. In high school he had a public urination charge and a disturbing the peace charge, separately but within a week of each other, the first from a long night at a dance hall, and my mom told me it was a direct result of her challenging him to drink ten Sankas, which he did of course to impress her, and she knew the whole time that the men's room was out of order, and the second charge at the same dance hall when he started a fight with other local toughs over of course my mom, defending her honor or whatever. He didn't deny any of this when I asked him.

One of the last things I can remember about my dad was he started to tell me about the time in college when he woke up without his shoes, but my mom quickly interrupted and told him to stop.

✦

Since I have the time, I ask Farrow after practice if he can help me out with scouting Garnes's 133. He says he'll see what he can do. Three days later, he hands me a sealed envelope with my name written on it. I tell him thank you and put it in my bag. I carry it back to my room, feeling the thrill of having something of great value in my possession, and lock the door. A single typed page. Everything there is to know about Jan Gehring.

Gehring does a lot of hand fighting. Will bait wrists. Steps back and shoots low. Constant movement. Very patient and waits for his spots. Prefers to let opponent make mistake than force them. Record: 8–2.

And just like that, Jan Gehring becomes a fateful person to me. The way the season works, there's nearly a month between the end of the regular season and regionals. I treat him like a final I need to study for. He'll be the only person I get for keeps until March.

What I have done is add to my game every year. Because if you don't learn something new, if you don't keep learning, you're fucked. Anyone will tell you that. In the last year of high school, I was working on the Granby series. By my first year at Oregsburg, I was drilling my switch and my Peterson roll. I spent my entire sophomore year pounding and pounding away at the outside sweep single, I did it so many times it started the pain in my knees, I did it so many times I would begin the move before I realized I was doing it. What you do in the summer is build off what you already have offensively. So after working on the outside sweep single, I worked on my shrug from the same tie up, then I worked on my double for when guys want to keep me from tying up. Last year, I started doing spladles, which I haven't been able to use since last November. This year, I've been working and working on my cheap tilt, then adding a ball and chain tilt for when I've got the guy's wrist trapped. I learned how to see things slower, slow enough that I can move when I need to move. While everyone else was studying, I was hitting the dummy in the gym, and I knew no one would come find me. Most of the time you go to these tournaments, you're all standing around, you hear someone go, "Hey, watch out for his cradle" or "Watch out for his arm bar," because they know that the best wrestlers have their go-to move that they're going to turn all their opponents on. I don't have one, I don't think that way.

I'm pleased Jan Gehring is not some snail cephalopod and is good enough to help ready me for regionals. Mainly, though, I'm thinking about Mary Beth and, to a lesser extent, Linus, and what I'm supposed to do about them.

A day or two after our big date, I asked her, "Why do you hate North Dakota so much?"

"I don't know," she said. "It's a representation. It's the biggest representation I've ever seen."

"A representation."

"I didn't learn anything I didn't want to learn. It was a reality I wasn't surprised by. When I met you I felt like someone was trying to make it up to me."

And I imagine Mary Beth taking a long road trip from Michigan to come see me. She takes various highways, which connect and funnel her farther and farther west, Wisconsin and finally Minnesota, but when she approaches the North Dakota state line, which is a dotted line drawn in the dirt as though for surgery prospecting, she paces back and forth, unable to cross, and when it's clear that there's no other option, she turns around the way she came.

✦

At Thursday practice, the first time I see Linus again, I remember that he is only a seventeen-year-old. Seeing him again is like walking into my room except all my clothes in the closet have been rearranged. He has a fragmentary beard. And then whatever the feeling is, it's gone.

The whole rest of practice, he's showing up everyone else, including Kryger. If they give him any extracurricular sympathy, I don't see it. After twenty minutes, Hargraves stops practice to tell everyone to be more like Linus, which causes an involuntarily yowl on my part because I was mistakenly under the impression that this would all be very straightforward. I just have to get through another week of this. That's what I keep telling myself.

When practice is finished, out of the corner of my eye I watch them file out, dallying around on the bike, taking a theatrically long time to towel off, hoping he doesn't hang around and wait for me. He spends a minute talking to Fink, who says something I can't hear but that clearly interests Linus, who looks intently at the shitman. Then Linus walks out without saying anything else to anyone. I quickly scramble off the bike and grab the last person to leave, Whitey, and ask him to do live-gos with me. I need the practice. Need it like a fucking transfusion. He tells me he doesn't want to hurt me. I tell him, plead with him, that my knee is fine, nothing's wrong. He tells me again that he doesn't want to hurt me. He leaves me alone in the gym, the lights buzzing and the family of six dummies sagging against the far wall without expression or opinion, free of fault. I walk over and briefly take my frustration out on them.

In the locker room I shower, clean up, get ready, with the understanding that Linus is coming. The chalkboard says: *The virtue of wrestling is to be a spectacle of excess. —Barthes.* You can tell when Fink is the one supplying the chalkboard material.

"Hey, Stephen."

He has his bag over his shoulder. He's ready to leave. It seems I am to be leaving with him.

"Hey."

"You going to McCloskey?"

"Yeah."

"Want to walk together?"

"Yeah."

Exiting the gym, we go up the main path toward the dorm. Empty sentences, totally empty sentences, are said. "Labile" is a word I found in the *Barron's* for a test I've already taken and done poorly on.

"How were your grades?" I force myself to ask. His try at a beard is upsetting for all possible reasons.

"Pretty good. 3.6-something. I have to get above a 3.2 to keep my scholarship." I listen to this lazy genius toss out his accomplishments. "How were yours?"

"Really good, actually. I didn't calculate the, you know, three-point value, but all Bs, definitely. Needless to say."

"That's good."

This is the only place in the area where you can feel crowded by buildings: you're in between Memorial and Finch, the student union and the clock tower and the cafeteria and the health center and Petrusse and the career center and Grunwald. I don't have any reason to say anything, I'm going to wait to see what he has to say.

I have little psychic room for Linus's grandmother, I can't imagine her dying of anything other or less than heart problems, of a massive heart attack, a tidal force of pressure that knocked her onto the ground and swiftly pushed her life out from her body like an unwelcome tenant. Why should it be any less painful than that? Why should he have to suffer less?

Back in October or November, when we were leaving the cafeteria, Linus said to me, "Most people aren't good at doing what they say they'll do. I've met a lot of people like that. But you're not like that."

Now, in McCloskey's afternoon shadow, he says, "Wouldn't it be funny if I woke up one day, like two weeks from now, and felt different, and felt like my body naturally wanted to be bigger? Like it was the natural thing to put on three or four pounds? And then I told Hargraves I wanted to wrestle 133 now? And we had to wrestle off for 133? Wouldn't that be funny?"

I say yes or something. My kneecap tingles, warbles up like a nose just before the sneeze arrives.

He holds the door for me. "How's your family?" I say.

"O.K. You know?" he says.

I nod, go ahead of him up the stairs. Our footsteps make noise. I hold the door for him.

"Hold on one second," he says. "I have something I want to show you."

"O.K."

I follow him down to the end of the hallway to his room. He opens his door and goes inside, but he only leaves the door open a little bit. It's wide enough that I can see the lights are off, but I can't see what he's doing. No noise comes out, no rustling. Thirty seconds pass this way. I'm about to ask him what's going on when his face appears in the dark door crack and he says, "Never mind," and I reach out my hand. "Hey—" but he's closing the door, hard, and it slams right on my middle finger. I don't scream or at least I don't remember or think I do. Linus says, "Are you all right?" and I hold my hand to my chest and walk bent over toward the bathroom, where I stumble into one of the stalls and shut the door. Blood feels like it's spraying out of the end of my finger. I'm making this coping hissing sound through my teeth. I ride the waves of pain for however long it takes. Pretty soon I'm able to have thoughts. If there is a heaven, would my grandma look up from Thomas Mann to find his grandma standing there, to talk over our differences while looking down on us from the clouds, or would they purposely avoid each other? On the toilet I can't tell if I hate Linus or if he's fucking with me. He might've turned eighteen over Christmas. At first I worry that he's going to come find me, and then it becomes clear he's not and that seems strange until I understand that it's not strange anymore. I get up and lock myself in my room.

I hope for the odd circumstances to align so that I will need to wrestle Linus. I don't care if he's beating people in practice two weight classes up. I don't care. I'm hoping for an excuse to take my good shot at him.

✦

I wake up, find a folded piece of paper under my door. It says:

I think we have some things we should talk about don't you think so? If your not ready to talk about them I understand but I'll be on the couches around 2 or something if your ready to talk about shit.

Everyone gets to take it easy since there's the double dual tomorrow. There's a lot of talking and listening. "Wrestle for each other! You're wrestling not just for yourself, but for every other guy in this room!" I keep biking, try to prevent Mary Beth's theoretical disapproval, which is the best I've got for now, so I keep the blinders on.

✦

At two thirty I go to my meeting with Mrs. Caple at McKnight. I sit down on the other side of her desk, which has scrambled papers and a mug of tea. The lights are off, except for a dusty lamp that gives off yellow light. I smile at her and she smiles back with her fifty percent smile. We try anyway.

"How's your break been?"

"It's been good, thank you. How's yours?"

"Very nice. Have you been keeping up practice?"

I don't tell her about the Silas sketches, but I say, "Yes."

"Good. I have your portfolio here." She hands it to me across the desk, looks at me through some mysterious prism, possibly pitying. I set it down next to her mug. "When I was first taking art classes," she says, "I had a sketchbook just like that one there. Then one night I spilled pizza sauce all over it. I'm not sure I really ever got over that. So take good care of it!"

I can tell she's waiting for me to request an assessment of my drawings, but I'm not going to do that. It's clear we're reaching the end of what we have to talk about together.

"How did you like the class?" she says. She takes a drink of tea.

"I feel like I understand art pretty good now. Like I can really see it."

"That's wonderful, Stephen," she says. "Do you see the art in what you've done here?" She pats the pad with her fingers, but I don't need to look, I know what they are.

"No, there isn't any art in those."

She winces.

"Mrs. Caple, can I ask you a question?"

"O.K."

"The student of yours, Mary Beth, what do you think of her artwork?"

You can tell you're dealing with a bona fide adult because they don't look away when you put them on the spot. Mrs. Caple probably would've been a good wrestler, because she stares right back at me. "Why are you asking me that?"

"Surely we both know the answer to this question."

There's only one moment of hesitation, as if the weighing of honesty had an exact time measurement. "I thought she was promising last semester. Is. Is promising. I was excited for her to take the class again, but her work this semester stalled out. I'm not sure why. Sometimes that type of thing can happen, you know. You burn out, get tired, anything. Sometimes it just happens like that, and sometimes it doesn't matter anyway for the students with talent." She tips the mug back, finishes the tea. "I have to go. I have to meet my husband."

I take my portfolio. "Thank you, Mrs. Caple. I'm glad I took your class. Both semesters."

"I looked at those drawings a lot." She points to the portfolio under my arm. "I'm not exactly sure why."

I start to say thank you, "Th—," but don't, because I'm not sure what she means.

"I think maybe because . . . I felt like there's sort of a significant amount of effort in those. You did a great job trying."

I nod my head like a Depression-era gentleman and take my B portfolio out the door with me.

✦

I head around the side of Mooney and figure out where the earrings likely landed out her window, digging my hands into the snow. It doesn't take too long to find them.

✦

I wake up in the middle of the night. It's impossible to get a full night's sleep before a meet, even if you're not wrestling. You can't untrain yourself, the body will kick you out of your dreams. Two more hours until we have to be at the vans. My boner stands straight up like a flagpole saluting the president. With no hands, with only the power of my mind, I wiggle it like a TV antenna.

✦

In regard to the fingernail it becomes a question of whether the fingernail will fall off or not.

✦

Early in the morning, I dial her number. She picks up before the second ring.

"Hello."

"Did I wake you up?" I say stupidly.

"Couldn't sleep."

"Me neither. You must think I'm desperate."

"I think you are and aren't."

"What do you mean?"

"I know you miss me, I know you're lonely. That's what this is about, isn't it? I knew it as soon as the phone rang. That's why I picked up. The phone's on my desk. But I also know if I didn't pick up, it wouldn't make much difference in the long run."

I don't say anything.

"Would it?"

"Well."

"You'd still go right on at practices and matches and Kenosha and so on." And so on. Before Mary Beth, there was no *and so on*.

"It's way more complicated than that. I'm rehabbing every day. Fink is cockblocking me . . . I can't get anyone . . . to listen." I sputter out, leaving out the earrings, leaving out so much. Talking to Mary Beth has a way of making clear what's unimportant. "How are you so sure?"

"I don't know. It just seems like nothing gets too disrupted. Nothing big gets disrupted much. If you want it bad enough." The thing about her is there's sadness, except it's only nearby in the same woods as her, she never lets it get too close.

"You mean like everything works out in the end?"

"Yeah, a lot of things do work out."

I try my luck. "What about us?"

She's silent for a long time. I can hear some sort of scratching coming through the phone, in the room with her, on her desk, under her lamp, under her hand. "Do you know how many times I've thought about coming back there?"

"Ten?"

"How many times have you thought about coming here?"

"More than ten."

"That's a lot. Is it as many as Kenosha?"

"It's hard not to think about you when I think about Kenosha."

"I know you're bad at lying, but are you lying?"

"No."

The scratching stops. "I knew you weren't."

"I'm going to miss the vans if I don't go. I think we should meet."

"You shouldn't miss the vans."

"I said I think we should meet."

"I heard you. Do you think that's a good idea?"

"Don't you?"

"It's a sixteen-hour drive between us."

"Yes, it is."

"I'm busy all the time. I barely have time to think. You have practice."

"Doesn't matter."

"We knew each other for a few weeks and had one or maybe two dates. Probably one real one."

"I will get there so fast. Whenever you want me to get there, I will get there."

Her pause indicates that the logistics and whether it's a good idea are both beside the point. "On my drive here I stopped at a diner just past Winona. Route 61. It'll take you a little more than eight hours. Do you have a car?"

"I can get a car. I'll be there."

"It's called Two Spoons."

"I'll be there."

✦

I get to the vans an hour early and walk around the parking lot, thinking of this season as a glass bottle, a discrete object stuck in my hands. Petrusse's oldest exhibit was a permanent installation from a Romanian who placed bottles on thirty-foot-tall pedestals, where nothing was really stopping them from falling off, and it was Mary Beth's least favorite in the museum. I'm watching the brief shapes my breath fumes make.

✦

Crookston, Minnesota, is three hours east, and only about four hundred miles from Winona. Far past Konstantin and Johnson

Lake, I look out the window for the northernmost barn I stripped paint from for money. Outside Northwood, I spot it in the distance. I did it with Morris, the neighbor boy my grandma pitied, who was at least twenty-three. I remember Morris driving us the hour north in his truck, talking to me about battles of the French Revolution. We got to the place and he took his shirt off and lay in the grass, taking huffs of paint thinner while I did the job, scraping to the bottom of ten layers applied on an eighty-year-old barn. The barn is red now. There are at least fifty more that have had my hands on them, but this is the farthest one up.

When we cross the Minnesota state line, we drive by a bowling alley called The Icon that promises it's the only bowling alley in the USA that straddles two states.

I am the last person out of the van. They don't even let me carry any bags. We are not far from Winona. All you'd have to do is follow the highway down. That's all you'd have to do.

A talk is had in the visitors' locker room, where I stand at the periphery with my hands in my pockets and have a daydream that goes like this: I become a Man of the River, a Riverman, pulling out walleyes from the waters with some fucking straw in my mouth, telling the Minnesota kids ghost stories in exchange for their moms' cherry pies. How long would the river be able to bear my shame, and so forth?

I make the hallway's acquaintance. I drag my face along its windows, which provide a direct view of the Long John Silver's on the other side of the road. Three cars wait in the drive-thru. I reach the end of the one hallway, so I turn a corner and there's a man and woman talking there. "Meetin' in the hallway!" I shout to them, and they immediately stop speaking.

With my middle finger off the ground, I do so many push-ups

that I end up facedown on the floor of the locker room, panting and going down the road to sleep. At the end of this road, I find vole skulls in pulled-apart owl pellets, I find the secret of the experiment. I wake up six centuries later with a checkerboard smushed on my cheek, but I am still the same person. They all come in, one by one. The person most identifiable as a bucket of fish chum is Sherman Moody. The person most like a sad detective is Slim John Carpenter. The person most like a ditch digger in the Old West is Clark Lowe. The person most like someone else you've met, many times before, is Reuben Crest. The person most likely to die of ass cancer is Coach Eerik. The person most identifiable as a run-over stray cat is Coach Lee. The person most likely to be sucked into the quicksand of rubbing and rerubbing his eyes is Tom Raiskin. The person most likely to stop and watch a parade is Jerry Raiskin. The person most likely to die because of thrombosis is Coach Whiting. The person most identifiable as a bird that flies away when you get close rather than a bird that opens its mouth meanly is Ellis Pendergraph. The person most identifiable as the moss on a rock is Coach Farrow. The person most likely to offend women, over and over his whole life, by asking them how long until the baby is due is Whitey Williams. The person most identifiable as a madman barely held within his sanity as if in a leaking cage and liable to split free and head out over the enlightened terrain in a bursting fever is Paul Kryger. The person most likely to fall down an open manhole is Young William. The person most identifiable as something in a lab dish you know you shouldn't look at is Lyle Gervin. The person most likely to be happy is Ucher. The person least likely to kill his father is Harry Pfaff. The person most likely to stop trying, to quit altogether when it stops making sense is Coach Hargraves. The person most like a monument the marauders would destroy first is Linus Arrington. The person most likely to keep one vow but break another is Stephen Florida. The person most likely to get a rare disease native to the jungles of Brazil is Elder William. The person most likely to eat with dirty utensils is Simon Fjelstad. The person most likely to particularly enjoy the taste of an animal with multiple stomachs is Coach Fink. The person most liable to panic about the phone call with the blood-test results is Fat Henry. The one most likely to write poems to a person who doesn't exist is Nate Mayfield.

If I had legal access to a car, I would leave right now and drive to Winona. I don't care that I'd be a day early. The only thing stopping me from doing it is the law . . . then I get an idea, a wonderful idea, which I stow away in my mind's pocket, to think about later.

While admiring the smudges left on the window from my visage, I spot a cat in the Long John Silver's parking lot. I head outside, cross the street. The cat hides in the bushes as I put my hood up and enter the restaurant. Inside, the counter girl watches me pick through the trash. "Hey," she says sadly. "Hey, come on, please." I get a barely touched fish breast out of there and start peeling off the bread. The cat is suspicious. It's some kind of black-and-white mutt cat with a tumorous body. I sit down in the parking lot and coax it out by putting some fish on the ground. It doesn't eat too fast, it lets me sit there and watch it. "That's a nice friend." Cars go by in the drive-thru while I break the whole fish up. For years, I would see my grandma's cat and wonder how it was able to stand all these days with nothing to do. Eventually I realized, while watching the cat turn its ears and listen and watch out the window and clean itself five times a day, that attention was its own kind of existence. The cat knew everything that was going on in my grandma's house. The rest of the time it spent mashing its forehead into plastic bags and sleeping.

✦

I'm starting to think that I haven't missed the lesson but that there never was a lesson to begin with.

✦

Late that night, I walk up to Silas's house and find that the idiot left the keys in the ignition. I enter the vehicle and violate the sixth amendment and gas it out of his driveway before he emerges from his house and sees that it's me behind the wheel. I don't have time to rethink anything. It's only after I'm nearing the state border three hours later that I remember Silas never ran out bleary-eyed in his long johns, how strange it is that I got away so easily.

There is little traffic until the sun starts to fluff the sky. Spiders hang above me and I have to glance off the road every few minutes to make sure they don't descend and succeed. Would I jeopardize my reinstatement for a chance to rendezvous with Mary Beth? Yes, the answer is I would. One time when she was at class and I did the laundry, I saw our underwear touching in the hamper and I got a boner just seeing that. And I remember I would've done anything to make it work with Tiff, to prolong her affections, and I specifically remember losing to Ben Demeke because I closed my eyes on a lazy shot while thinking about her, because I couldn't think of anything else, her face was like a goddamn blindfold. I make great time, and it is to my great pleasure that there is one other car in the Two Spoons lot. I know it's hers before I even cut the engine. I look in the rearview and tuck in my nose hairs.

She's at a booth, facing the door. She watches me walk toward her, and the second I see the mechanics of her eyes, her fingers holding the handle of her white mug, she ceases being the key to my moral emancipation and becomes Mary Beth.

I pause at the booth, unsure how the greeting is supposed to happen. There's no one else in the diner. "Hello," I say, and lean down and kiss the top of her head, the smell of which unwraps my loins. It's unclear whether I'm supposed to sit on the opposite side or next to her, but she takes my hand and sort of guides me across the table. Her fingers find my weight calluses.

"Just like how Allnighter was supposed to be," she says, and I see I'm to push us through the early weeds.

"How long have you been here? Did you wait long? How are your classes?"

"I'm doing them accelerated. In March, about the time Kenosha is starting up, I'll be done."

"Great!"

"Stephen, this—"

"You said you had people interested in your work? Tell me about that."

"Stephen."

"And your own work? It's going well. I mean, it's going well?" I feel like a doll who's quip cord is being yanked over and over. "Why won't you tell me about it?"

"I did. I did tell you about it."

"It seems like you're speaking somewhat metaphorically around the bush."

She blinks and turns her mug around in a circle on the table, which is very sticky with something. "You know something? I haven't masturbated since I left. I've been tired, but that's only part of it. Instead, a lot of the time I'll just stand at my window and watch people drop off their laundry across the street. It's almost as fun and illicit as masturbating. I'll admit I got excited when I first got in the car, but it went away by the time I got to Wisconsin, before that. You won't even come."

"As soon as the season's—"

"No—"

"I'll come right now if you want me to. Right now, on this table."

"Will you? Will you come right now?"

Her smile is the same, the exact same, individual strands of hair and how her face hasn't changed. One morning, I woke up and she was asleep next to me, and her hand was covering my eyes. "I missed you."

"I missed you, too, but I'm not sure this was a good idea."

"But you agreed to it."

"Did I have a choice?"

"Why isn't it a good idea?" Suddenly, I'm aware that there is no waitstaff, there's only a distant clanging noise in the kitchen. I get out of the booth and stand by the cash register, knocking on the counter. "Service, please, for the lady?" My nose is running and I'm also crying and so I take a napkin from the dispenser, which distorts my face and fingers. I clean myself up with my back to her, then put the napkin away in my pocket. I sit back down in the booth. "Why isn't it a good idea?"

"Here, have some."

She hands me her tea, and I drink the rest of it. My intent is unintelligible. "Is there someone else? Is there another man?"

"No, there's not."

Then what's the problem? Why isn't this working? Why can't I make things agreeable for once? Why is what I want an expense? Why is she letting me hold her hand and rendezvous if her intention is not the same as mine? "Then what's the problem?"

"I told you. I have a different life now. I explained all this on the phone. What did you think was going to happen?"

"What did you think was going to happen?"

"Basically what is." Just for one moment, I have the notion that I'm reenacting a trauma, my trauma masterpiece, and I'm in the wrong place, that I messed up the directions and came to the wrong diner. But then how do you explain her being here?

"You aren't answering me."

"Why are you talking with, like, air coming out lispy? Open your mouth, let me see your teeth."

"You aren't answering me."

"Are you o.k.?" She spits in a napkin and dabs some recent dirt mark I didn't know was there. Only once did I call Dakota Grid, the local electric company, after I figured out their phone number routed to an answering service that spawned a stream of safety tips in a pleasant faceless female voice, such as be mindful of snow buildup, while promising me an employee would be on the line shortly. I called at three in the morning, when I had no chance of getting someone real, when I could just listen to the cycle.

Sometimes you need to tell a story about something that happened to you, ten times or a hundred, only to get it off your back, to clear it out. But this particular story I needed to tell just once, because when I told it to Mary Beth, she just nodded and forgot it, which is why I told her. To her, it was just something that had happened. A few minutes later, I heard her laugh and my stomach fell open. Like that.

"I really miss you."

"Did it ever occur to you to think about why I liked being with you?"

"Oh."

"I'm glad to see you. But did you ever think that maybe neither or both of us weren't ready for this? To meet in a highway diner halfway between? I'm not the jewel in your story, I don't just go along with your story as, like, a prize. You don't look well. Are you O.K.?"

"I'm wonderful."

"How much thought did you really give this?"

"All the thought in the world."

"What did you think about on the drive here?"

"Your face, which is pretty enough to be put on the silver dollar."

She sighs and says, "I'm sorry I left you behind like that," which I take to be my cue for the big reveal. I hold her hand.

"Look out there. See anything unusual about it?"

She sees that I've really done it, then says, "Are you stupid?"

"It's Silas's truck. I took it! It's a gesture."

She pulls her hand out of mine, still looking at the truck, not at me, which is where I thought she'd be looking by now. "Why, Stephen?"

I had eight hours sitting behind the wheel to reconsider, but not once, not until I made it to Winona, looking at Mary Beth's lovely, lovely face, did it occur to me.

"Shit." There must be police out all over looking for me. "There must be police looking all over for me. Are you excited?"

"You need to get that back right now. Now."

"But I got the asshole's truck for a reason. A real reason. I brought it here for you. So we could . . ."

"So we could what?"

"So . . . we could get intimate in it."

"What?"

"As in, defiling his memory. Together."

"Stephen, go home right now. Put the car where Silas can find it but not see you. Or you will be arrested. Go home, and pretend like this terrible idea never happened. Any of it." She floats the word "arrested" out above the table like a theoretical precept, like a big bubble from the soap bottle. Theory, theory, theory, the air between us seems to be made of different nitrogen levels, and the difference is vast, vast enough that I could never get her to interpret my gesture the way I'd wanted. "I can't believe we both drove eight hours for this. This is fucking crazy."

"I'm sorry," I say, and something about saying these same old words, for the sixtieth or sixty-first time, brings about my realization that Mary Beth is the only real component of this whole symbolic gesture, which has fallen apart, as if I had shown up at the doorstep with dead daisies.

I pay and hold the door for her. In the parking lot, she kisses my cheek in the disinterested European manner. "For Christ's sake, take care of yourself." And it's only after she's gotten into her car and disappeared that I remember her earrings glittering on the dashboard.

Well, I have eight hours to think things over but I don't use them, just like that woman who was determined to use the state house for her headache cure. I drive excessively fast to get back to where I came from, without ever really coming to a conclusion why. I leave the truck teetering over a ditch just down the road from Silas's house and then take a circuitous route home, where everything is just as I'd left it, as though I'd never really been away.

✦

I try Mary Beth's number again, and as it's ringing I tell myself not to be surprised when she doesn't pick up. That's not how this works.

But when I replace the phone, still in my fingers, it rings again.

"Steven, honey, don't hang up. Just listen." The voice comes so quickly that it's a moment before I realize it's not Mary Beth, it's Aunt Lorraine. "Don't hang up. Don't. I couldn't come, I can't come, because I got fired. I fucked up again, I've really made shit of my life this time."

"What did you do?"

"I made a lot of bad decisions, Steven. I can't." She's crying.

I have no experience with a crying woman, so I keep my mouth closed, full of patience for the opportunity to right our toppled relations, listening to her monologue of tribulations, increasingly aware, as it winds toward its finish, that this will be quite easy, after all, to fix.

"I owe a lot of different people a lot of money. I feel really bad I did this to you."

"How much money do you need?"

✦

The fire alarm wakes everyone up in the middle of the night. We go out and stand in the snow for half an hour. The problem turns out to be that someone set a bag of hair on fire.

✦

Well, the last semester of classes! Time to get to work and finish up my education! Honest to goodness, I didn't know if this day would finally be here, but hello, here it is!

Mr Gorman is the fat Geography teacher. I start sliding, attention-wise, during attendance.

"Mango?"

"It's Margo," a female voice says from the back.

"Says here 'Mango.'"

By the time we're a few paragraphs into the syllabus, I know

Geography will be a class I sleepwalk through, to be forgotten by summer in the white void. To most people, college is for growing your concepts, such as the location of Lebanon, such as what "ethos" means, such as what exactly the United Nations does. But sometimes I regret that I'll never have the intensity of feeling I had growing up, you never do, emotion like pins and thorns, intense happiness, intense dismay, missing my parents, blindly pining over Tiff, crying over blowing it in the match against Clay Goodchild, or James Davis, or Andrew Shipp. When you're younger, and for me it stopped when I finally got tired of being angry after they died, you walk around hating everything and loving everything equally. I guess when you're at the tail end of growing up you're susceptible to thoughts of your growing up, but that doesn't make them interesting or useful. Sadness for the past is sadness for circumstances that no longer exist.

While the teacher summarizes the overarching important shit to know, I look around at all the other students. Taking in information. Human husks, husks of humans. It becomes an all-day job not turning into everyone else, keeping myself from old, tired dreams.

◆

Jazz is no regular-sized classroom, it's a big goddamn room in Opal Hall, hundreds of seats, all of them empty. I'm the first one there. I'm paying attention to every detail as though I'm an investigative reporter for Mary Beth, and though I hope to talk about all this with her, this year has finally taught me not to expect anything I hope for to come my way. And so I just scrape the sleep gunk from my eyes and blink, content to watch. With strategic care, I pick my chair, most of the way toward the front, dead center. Before long, two students come in, then two more.

One of them is male. They pick out seats the farthest away from anyone else, so that when we're all situated, the five of us cover the room like a life-sized graph of inner desolation.

I reach down my sweatpants to unstick my sex from my right thigh and at that moment, a brown-haired female enters the front of the room and sees me doing the feature presentation. Eye contact happens. Her expression shows disappointment, though we've never met, and by way of explanation what I come up with is: "Sorry." When she finally chooses a desk in the farthest back corner, I try three different times to get her attention and convey that my sorriness is true, but she pretends to be looking for something in her bag for five full minutes.

It's past start time. At the front of the giant room, before the chalkboard, there's a table with one of those music players, the kind with the horn, like the big colorful bell flowers in the jungle that lure in bugs.

Levi Silas opens the door and comes in. Something mystical or tectonic happens.

I am repulsed and fascinated by the secret things he's done, repulsed and fascinated the whole time he talks. He politely and briefly introduces himself and then gets us to admit we're not in the wrong room.

He does attendance. As there are six of us, this takes fifteen seconds. When he calls my name, there's no hitch to indicate he knows I'm the car thief. The last name he calls is "Pervis Robinson."

I turn around, all the way, because I refuse to believe there's a person with this name. Eight or nine rows back and off to the left is the only other male, Pervis.

Silas digs through his black leather satchel. He extracts a stack of papers and sets them down on the table. Then he pulls out a big black record and tinkers with it on the player.

"Grab a syllabus on the way out. That's it."

Music starts playing. He doesn't identify the song. In fact, he takes his bag and goes out the door! Is he coming back? I turn around with my eyebrows up as though to say "What gives?" to the five of them behind me, but already two of the girls plus Pervis are descending the aisles. They each take a paper and leave. The song continues. The two other girls chat as they head up to the front and take a paper, leaving me listening to a weird song in a cavernous room by myself. I first double-check that I'm alone, but I don't feel safe so I go all the way up to the last row just to make sure Silas hasn't snuck in and started watching, or that he hasn't voodoo-sprinkled his wife's burned hairs in the aisles. I look down at the whole room, almost the size of the gym, while the illogic of the situation crashes down on my brain. And as I listen to numerous instruments blat around the musical scales, which sounds like it was recorded during the fucking Civil War, I realize Silas is beginning his routine, the same routine he's had for years, this song has been played on the first day of every single Intro to Jazz class since the start, since before Mrs. Silas was dead. I'm surprised then not surprised that he's treating this time like all the previous times. But then I'm happy that I get to show him why this time will be different. I'm the one he can't fool.

✦

First thing Tuesday, I wait for Hargraves. He doesn't come. After they get everyone going on the drills, I go up to Fink, who is saying something to Linus, but quickly dismisses him when he sees me coming.

"Where's Coach?"

"Not feeling well." He has one hand in his shorts pocket and uses the other one to hold his whistle up to his mouth, tilted ninety degrees, so he can tongue the tiny ball inside.

"O.K.," I say, turning to join the jogging line.

"Where are you going?"

"Drills."

"No drills. Bike."

"I did the bike last week."

"So?"

"The plan was to do the bike for a week. Today's Tuesday. It's been a week."

He glances down at my knee. Licks the ball. "You been taking care of yourself?"

"Yes."

"Bike today. We'll talk to Coach when he's back."

I bite down so hard on my teeth they split like cracked nuts. "When's he back?"

The world's slowest shrug. "Maybe tomorrow."

It takes all my moral energy to turn away from him, and I yell into the gym, "Something's fucking fishy here!"

In a position of extreme disadvantage, I decide it's best to let whatever's happening play out, at least for another day or two. And so I let my head loose like an untied balloon, fill it and fill it with hot air.

I shower and sit in the locker room with the rest of them because I don't want them to think I'm flustered. I listen to see if anyone mentions Hargraves.

Kryger has stopped calling me fancyboy. He's stopped acknowledging me altogether, he's wrapped up in his new place on the team, winning his first two 133 matches, handily, a surprise to everyone including himself, though he pretends it's not, pretends it's natural and expected, stomping around the locker room, shouting louder than anyone else. He thinks I'm no longer a threat to him.

Linus doesn't wait for me to walk with him. He just leaves.

✦

Rudy Unger's office is across the highway on the nice side of town. I walk in, tracking mud and snow onto his entrance rug like it's rayon. My distaste for this place and for Rudy is nothing he could've prevented, he reminds me of my parents, specifically the fact that they're dead.

His secretary buzzes me into his mahogany office. He sighs and stops writing in the ledger on his desk or whatever it is.

"Sorry about the rug. I need some money."

"O.K."

"I want you to send it to here." I put the paper scrap in front of him, on top of his significant documents.

"Who's this?"

"Aunt Lorraine."

"How much?"

"Two thousand dollars."

He's of the age where he looks over the top of his reading glasses at all distant objects. Everything is skeptical to him, being skeptical's what got him all this mahogany. "You know, I've met Lorraine. She's an irresponsible person. The car she used to drive had one green door and three brown ones. She carries things in plastic bags. Always has been, always will be." He touches the paper with his pen. "This money is likely never getting returned to you."

"I know," I lie, but then I see he's right, and then I'm mad, but then I realize I don't care, I don't care about money flushed down the toilet, I don't care about money in flames.

"How's the season going?"

"Couldn't be better."

On my way out, I take five pillow mints from the secretary's desk and suck them into oblivion and, relieved to finally have one thing settled, forget Aunt Lorraine, who's probably covered in lies.

✦

The two other classes happen but I wasn't paying attention. I skip one to swim.

✦

I'm going to miss the next two duals and a double. Four matches down the drain. I'm attempting to reset my mind-set, reset my thinking toward the match after them, because there are only five left after this block I'm missing, five total matches until post-season. This is what I get for thinking I could cut the corner on all this, have the 133 handed back to me. But the difficulty of this test is not something to grieve about, it's something to be thankful for.

✦

I walk into the student union just in time to catch the last ten minutes of *Old Yeller.*

✦

I watch two sparrows hop around a parking lot trying to have sex.

✦

I smear myself all over the inside of my room.

✦

They scheduled the Sheridan-Huron meet in the middle of the afternoon. On my way out, the familiar female at the front desk hands me a letter on official Oregsburg letterhead. I thank the female, who has been at the desk for at least two years and obviously knows my identity. They make you sign in and out at the front desk if it's after midnight. I've been writing Steven Forster in there for all four years just to see if they'd say something but they haven't.

The letter says I have a meeting with a doctor, a therapist doctor, on February 15. The words "as requested by you" are in there. At the end, the letter apologizes for taking so long to schedule an appointment, and then it's signed by Dr. Cynthia Barnes.

No days off. So before anyone arrives, I go into the weight room for an hour and then I go back home. I shower for a preposterous period of time. A team meeting is scheduled for 1:00 p.m. and I take my time walking to the gym, very slowly, with the goal being to get there with my eyes shut. It's not like it's hard, it's a straight line. About halfway, I hear a female crying so I open my eyes. She's near the bottom of Finch's steps, repeatedly attempting to pull an aluminum handcart stacked high with boxes up the flight. She's on the second step. Her kind of crying is the mouth-open kind. When the top box slides off and bangs to the ground, whatever's inside breaks. She wails, looks around for help, but there's only me. She watches me expectantly, sniffles, and blinks. I start walking again toward the gym with a limping leg. I point in the direction I'm going, which is away from her. "Sorry, doctor's orders," I say.

I pace around the locker room. I can see myself, as if from afar, as if I was a nasty fly on the wall, waiting for the coaches. When they all come in, I put on a big show of being involved, nodding and laughing at things I don't even hear, jumping in place. Fink tells everyone that Hargraves isn't going to make it. While he's talking, I make sure to stand right in his line of vision, front and center. I get in the middle of the huddle and bark and shout with the rest of them, louder, pushing and punching, part of the team. I run out with them, I clap and scream myself hoarse for every one of their matches, even Linus's, even Kryger's, give them towels and do push-ups with them to get their heartbeats up. I stand right next to Fink the whole meet, degrading myself for my need but I don't mind because need is always degrading.

Afterwards, back in the locker room, Fink gives a short speech saying that even though Linus and Kryger and Harry were the only ones that won their matches, he liked the heart they all showed. During the speech, I say things out loud like "that's right" and "next time" and "yep." Fink lets them all go, and I hang around while he talks with Eerik and Farrow, pretending to tie my shoes. He writes something in the green notebook he's always carrying around, then puts it into his gym bag, slinging the bag over his shoulder and heading out into the hallway. I'm right behind.

"Coach, wait up."

"Florida. You were very helpful today."

"I just had the mentality that, if I'm going to sit out, I can help my team in other ways." Like a chimp, I grin when anxious.

He puts a Twins hat on. He's looking through his bag. "Glad to hear you're enjoying your new role."

"Coach, with all due respect—"

"Damn it, where are my keys?"

"With all respect—"

"Look, Florida. I know what you're doing. It's high up on the pathetic scale and really, I'm a little embarrassed. I swear I put them in the front—"

"With all the respect in the world—"

"Hargraves and the rest of us have been all on the same page with regard to your injured status. Which is wait and see. So let's wait and see."

We're at the end of the hallway. He's putting his gloves on. "With all due respect, what the fuck do you think you're doing?"

Fink stops, looks right at me. "Take your hand off my arm. Right now." I do, thinking it'll finally give me an answer. But he just does that mouth-clicking thing, the one mothers do when they're disappointed in the youth, and zips up his coat. "You're the most tone-deaf person I've ever met."

He pushes open the door, makes prints in the parking lot snow. I'm learning that Hargraves listens to Fink. I'm learning that Fink will be head coach of Oregsburg when Hargraves hangs it up. I'm learning that Fink is smart.

✦

Watch me put all this shit back together.

✦

I stop by Finch to get any notes I missed from Geography, and Mr. Gorman tells me to "just read the first half of chapter one and you'll be fine." At the music department, they tell me that Silas doesn't have an office.

At the library I check out two books: *The Encyclopedia of Jazz* and a giant book on crime.

I head back to McCloskey, through the lobby and up the stairs, and before I know what I'm doing I'm walking down the hall to Linus's door and I knock, or maybe I don't, but I definitely try the doorknob. It's locked. While standing there breathing on the door

I swear that I hear someone shushing and someone laughing. I don't try my luck, I've run clean out of luck to try.

✦

At Oakes Elementary, I tortured myself getting other kids' attention, pulling the fire alarm and running away, holding down the flusher on the toilet until it overflowed, wasting most of a roll of paper towels by stuffing them into my shirt to imitate a pregnant woman, and for this and generally clowning around with equipment like markers and glitter, I would get kicked out into the hall two or three times a week, and I would walk the hallways whistling like a vagrant. I think my mom was especially worried about me, but the truth is someone always wanted to tell me about my attitude. Mostly I remember being bored, being disturbed by boredom, and I would do anything to get out of sitting where I was told to sit. Mostly, I remember wanting to get outside to play with Bird.

I was friends for the first five years of school with Frank K. Bird. He was my best friend, the tallest kid in our class, a Sisseton-Wahpeton Sioux (he made me write it over and over until I figured out how to spell it) who needed glasses at five, who found out he needed glasses because he one day told his mom the colors on *The Jetsons* were bleedy.

Do people remember how friendships as old as kindergarten begin? I don't. I only remember jumping off the high metal bars with Bird, acting like I smashed my head against the loud aluminum slide and throwing mulch at kids to make Bird laugh, Bird sighing all the time and wiping his glasses on his shirt, I had the applesauce brains of a child but no one could make me laugh like Bird did, he would call anyone "Triar Fuck" and got sent home at least twice for it, at lunch he sculpted boobs with mashed potatoes and two wrinkled peas as the nipples, when we were on the same team in dodgeball he'd guard my side and I would run at them because I could throw harder than anyone else and was full of directionless anger, Bird got sent to the principal's office when his project for the imaginary plant project was a Penis Plant, I remember taking the bus to school hoping he wasn't sick, I didn't care if any of the other kids were there except him. We put M-80s in buckets of water and then did a few mailboxes and learned the valuable lesson of quitting while you're ahead. We'd throw things on roofs and beat the hell out of each other until one of our noses bled, we'd have gibberish conversations that we said were Italian, we'd break windows with sticks, this was in the time when I always needed Band-Aids, we chewed a few sacks of gum and crammed the whole yellow gob into a drainpipe behind the post office, his mom tried to teach us Mille Bornes but we didn't want to learn how to play Mille Bornes, we cut open a pillow, we'd have Jujubes-eating contests, we'd watch *The Smurfs* and *Touché Turtle and Dum Dum* and *Yogi Bear* and *Deputy Dawg* for hours and press our wide-open eyeballs against the colors of the television to see what would happen and eat Kraft and drink grape and orange soda mixed together, we called it "a cocktail" and pretended we were drunk and high society and had big, sad problems, we'd yell cusses into echoing empty halls, Bird's dad stopped us when we tried to put their unused Twister mat in the oven, we'd find empty bottles by the road and smash them against rocks, we'd slap each other in the face with our gloves and say "I challenge you to a duel," we found a bunch of discarded termited wood and placed it against the side of Bird's barn and shot it a thousand times with pellet guns, we took apart an Etch-a-Sketch and when we saw its secret we were disappointed and shook all the powder out and broke the frame, I had to get in a fight with a boy named Grady because he called me "Dickstein Perez," and when he was on the ground Bird kicked him and I punched his head (do you know that when you hit someone hard enough in the head their hands will open, as if letting go?), and for this we both got suspended, three days for me and two for him, and during the whole first two days we leaned sticks together in the woods and played Fort Sumter, and on the third day I went back by myself and tried to play again but it wasn't the same. I remember Bird sighing a lot, sighing all the time, asking him if something was wrong, him shaking his head, me learning to just sit there with him and stop asking stupid questions that had no answers.

When we were nine, we made an official pact, contract handwriting on paper and everything. The pact was this: when he turned fifty, I would travel to wherever he lived and kill him. He didn't want to live to be older than that. When you're nine, fifty seems like a long time away, and he could see no point in living past that, that was enough. I remember being sure I understood why he felt this way, but I probably didn't, I was nine, and he was only four weeks older than me but he would go into these long silences and just put his head down. We decided on a gun, that I'd ring his doorbell and put the gun right to his forehead and end it for him for good, because that would be quickest. I remember him making me feel like I was agreeing to do him the deepest kindness, that he wouldn't think about asking anyone else to do this for him, that only I understood. I tried very hard to imagine his reasons, to figure out his reasons. And I remember thinking that if he asked me if I wanted him to do the same, even though that was impossible, I would've said yes. But he didn't.

Of course this was never going to happen, I would've gone away for murder if I did what I'd promised. This was not a time of logic, no friendship worth anything is logical to the outside world, plus I was only nine and Bird was in pain.

And then a few months later, during the summer, he was gone. Something happened with Bird, but I didn't know what. His dad wanted to move them closer to the reservation, the one Bird had shown me that looked like a shark tooth in the extreme top right of the South Dakota map. It happened so fast I didn't think to get an address to write him. You don't think about things like that when you're nine. I hung on to the contract for a while, then threw it away because I couldn't read it without crying. And so I returned to the normal state of not having any friends. A few years after Bird left, I got bored of running around by myself, and I became a wrestler. There was nothing else to do, so I became a wrestler.

And I guess for a while I was like the other young males until I wasn't. After Bird left, I quit all that. The time between his leaving and when I started wrestling is a total blank. Like I said, I have problems with my memory. But after that, once I'd moved in with Grandma in Hillsboro, I stopped stupidly veering around so much. "You are being too stern, you're too stern for a boy your age," she said over and over when I got through dinner without speaking. I didn't like to talk anymore, every time I had to give a school presentation, I was corrected and told to look up when speaking, being serious was the only way I could see to handle it.

I kept wrestling. And then I got older. Over the summers in high school, I would lift and practice with some other kids on the team and jog around town at night. During the days, I worked for the husband of my mom's friend Mrs. Tomasi. He ran a pesticide company, a white warehouse that had a permanent chemical stench that got inside your nose as you drove up the gravel drive, and I spent my days loading his red pickup full of pesticides, drums and jugs of it, and after I got my license, I'd drive them out to farmers and gardeners. Abamectin was for the potato psyllid and you couldn't let livestock anywhere near it, we stocked imidacloprid and dinotefuran, which were disguised in big white bottles under names like Cavalry and AntiTidal, we had different poisons for the aphids and the cutworms. I'd map my routes and it'd take all day, and I'd drive back with the windows down, the sweat stuck on my face, and I'd get paid in cash. At night, when I practiced, even after changing clothes, I could still smell the chemicals. The other kids on the team would make me wash my hands twice, they didn't want my dirty hands touching them. And even after we were done and I'd finally had a chance to shower, I'd get under the covers, the lights off, and I'd still feel like there were chemicals on my skin, like I'd dragged them into bed with me. Then I'd fall asleep and do it all over again.

What are my reasons? Bird had his reasons, everyone has to have their reasons. I have my reasons. Until Mary Beth, no one ever asked me to explain myself.

✦

Orange vans containing Aberdeen College wrestlers drive into the gym parking lot and let them out. They have orange singlets and orange headgear, and some bit of time later, I watch Linus start his second period on top and immediately, robotically, put one of them through a suffocating crossface and pin him for good. I eat more dirt. I keep eating the dirt. I imagine getting Joseph Carver on his back and straddling his face-up body and gripping my left hand to the horseshoe of his jaw and yanking it open like a cash register. I am not sleeping when I have this thought, but it feels as if I must be.

✦

I dream that I was forced to dance with Linus at the fiesta. In this dance, I was the woman.

✦

I drag myself out of bed. I drag my dread around with me everywhere like a dog on a leash. She tried to tell me when we were on the hill spying on the wife-arsonist that I shouldn't put all my eggs in one basket. It's a lesson I should've learned a long time ago, that I'm trying to learn, and that I think I'm finally, after all, figuring out.

Now I take my lessons to heart and with that in mind, I go right up to Hargraves, who finally has returned to practice and is the person I need to talk to to iron this whole misunderstanding out.

"What did Fink say?" Hargraves says.

"He said to ask you."

Hargraves looks at me, which I interpret as a prompt for elaboration.

"Because you're the coach," I say. "You're the one in charge."

"When's the last time he looked at your knee?"

"A month ago," I say with too much excitement, but he doesn't seem to hear.

"Have him take a good, close look at it. I gotta start this fucking bitch." And then he puts the whistle in his mouth and practice begins.

Fink is supine on the bleachers with an apple. He doesn't stop eating it when I approach.

"Coach Fink, what is your first name?" I would like to fling a harmful powder in his eyes.

"You know what my first name is, Stephen. It's Roland."

"That is a terrible name. Roland Fink, I'm going to need you to stop fucking things up and just generally shitting all over the place." He smiles, and the rage becomes more red, or redder, a full-blown outrageous negative emotion, and he waits for me to say it, to say what I'm going to say, and I say, "I hope you choke to death in front of your kids and your wife tries to stop you from dying in front of your kids but you die anyway."

Fink's smile, if it's possible, gets larger, gets circus large, gets larger than his face. "Bike, Florida."

I'm profoundly confused!

Hargraves whistles practice dead in the middle of the live-gos and stalks straight through the bodies to Ucher. He stands over him, breathing hard through his nose, his dewlap shaking with fury. Ucher's weight fluctuates like an insecure teenager's based on what Hargraves needs, in his five years he's wrestled at 157 and 197 and the classes in between. A plaything for Hargraves's whims, I've seen him choke down fourteen pounds in two weeks and lose double that a month later. Ucher has a wife and a kid, he likes to hunt and fish when he wants to, a lot of the time at the cost of practicing, at the cost of getting better, which Hargraves definitely knows. He already has a foot out the door, if he ever had one in. Everyone likes Ucher, he doesn't bother anyone. He's only a year older than me but he feels like the whole team's relaxed older brother, one of those people that makes everyone in a room more comfortable just by being in it.

"I wish just one week would pass without having to see you do that turtle lock-up thing you do. I swear to God, you've done it so many times it's like you're practicing it, like it's your trademark or some fuckshit. When's the last time you didn't do that in a match?" He kicks Ucher, who's on his back but has his hands up. "I asked you a question."

"I don't know."

"You don't know. You don't know! When your opponent's on top of you, he's trying to push you forward. That means what? What does it mean?"

"I don't know."

"It means you get up. You explode on the whistle and get up, motherfucker. Get in bottom position. Get in bottom right now." Ucher rolls over and does so. Hargraves gets on top of him. He blows the whistle. Ucher tries to stand, but Hargraves shoves down on him and Ucher hits the mat face-first. "This is exactly why you're never going to be anything but what you were. You're as good as you were when you were in high school. You're locking up against freshmen. You're no better. How does it feel? I liked you better when you were fat, then I knew why you didn't work hard. Again." They get back in position, the whistle blows. Hargraves, wheezing, can barely keep Ucher from getting out, he's locking his hands around Ucher but Ucher says nothing. "Show me you can work hard one time before you leave. Show me right now!" Ucher turns and smashes the bulb of his elbow into Hargraves's mouth, producing a deep, thick thud. "Again!" They get back in position, Hargraves puts his ear against Ucher's shoulder blade and when he blows the whistle, blood sprinkles out onto Ucher's shirt. Ucher waits for Hargraves to get tired, and again turns and elbows Hargraves in the mouth. "Again!" He spits and they reset. Blood gets on the front of Hargraves's shirt and the mat. Ucher elbows him in his mouth again, harder than the other times, and when he does, Hargraves stumbles back, sways on his feet. Then, slowly, he lifts his hand and points to the corner of the gym, at the mop and the white jug of disinfectant. "Clean the mats," he says, turning to everyone else, "practice is over." Then he walks out of the gym. No one leaves for a few minutes, and I don't even bother chasing after him to further explain the Fink situation, I just finish my interval, staring down at my black and purple and red and blue finger.

None of the coaches are in the locker room. Only the rest of the team, Lyle spitting his muck in the trash can, ice bags on his shoulders, pretending to listen to Clark, who's attempting to explain the concept of either epistemology or eschatology, Ellis eating a banana extremely slowly, Whitey with his shirt off picking his back nubs, making the same gonorrhea joke he always makes.

As a last-ditch effort to find a coach to whine to, I stop by the training room. The window shade is down on the COACH OFFICE door that is, upon testing, locked. I give up for the day.

Parked in the lot, its nose aimed at the gym door, is Ucher's red truck. Snow meanders down, and the wipers are on the lowest pace. Ucher's sitting inside, and he's looking right at me. I figure it's not possible to pretend I haven't seen him, so I start over there. It's only when I'm alongside that I realize he's staring straight ahead, into what the behavioral scientists proclaim *the middle distance*. I knock.

He rolls down his window. "Hi, Florida." There's a beer in a cozy in his lap.

"Hi. How's your elbow?"

He flicks the headlights on and off. "Why don't you get in? Got something to tell you."

I go around the other side, shut the door behind me.

"Heidi's pregnant again. That's not what I wanted to tell you."

"Well, congratulations."

"She's coming soon. A summer baby." Ucher has careless long hair that he scratches often. "We found out the sex. Girl again."

Ucher tells me a story from before any of us were here. "I don't know why I waited so long to tell you this, and what's weird is I probably never would've told you if you hadn't knocked on my window. Life's funny. My first year here, which would've been the year before you got here, I had a pretty rough go of it. Which is why, what happened in there? Doesn't mean a thing. Not a goddamn thing. I was already working at Briscoe, doing the service rounds, what I mean is I was filling up the vending machines all over this part of town. Driving all over.

"The point is, I say all this to say that in that year's December Hargraves found out he had lung cancer. It was going to kill him in six months, or it was supposed to but it didn't. Because he got the lobectomy? He got the lobectomy in time. They cut his chest open and cut out the cancer part in his lung. The doctors x-rayed him again but lost it. They weren't sure they got it. All this happened over about a month, him finding out and then getting the surgery and then finding out they couldn't find it. They thought they got it out, but they were saying, basically, we're not sure, we can't ever be sure. Anyway." He flicks the can top, flicks it three times, which generates the distinct metal twang. "Anyway, that weekend we had a dual. And so the day before, Hargraves gathers us all in the locker room to tell us a big secret he has. We're all dead from practice. He takes a piece of yellow chalk and draws a spiral on the board. And then what happens is he gets to talking about all types of bizarre shit, I'm talking Kabbalah, I'm talking different ideas on morality, I remember he kept saying 'prehistoric' over and over. And then I think about, ah, ten minutes later, he finally arrives at his main point, which at this part he pulls out a marker from his pocket and then started drawing all kinds of circles and spirals on his face, his whole face. Which I suppose was to illustrate that he's going to have the whole team hypnotized so we can focus better. He was going to bring in a hypnotizing doctor. That was it."

"And did he?"

"Hypnotize us? No, no one ever mentioned that again. He never called any doctor. There was no goddamn doctor. By all appearances he goes back to being himself after that. But every now and then something like this happens." He gestures toward the gym with the can. "Like this elbow shit. Crazed things come out of a crazed factory. Someone living with something that can kill you. Whenever it feels like. Maybe. You never know."

Come to think of it, I recall the time two seasons ago when we were all in the locker room smelling something weird and in trying to find the source, Flores found a dead, wet lobster in Hargraves's gym bag, under his clothes. At a match last year in Montana, I went into a stall after him and there was urine just all over the seat. And then, while Ucher finishes his beer, I remember the first time I felt something was wrong, my first season here. Hargraves doesn't do this anymore, he's gone bowlegged like an old dog, but the one time in practice, four years ago, when he showed me just how hard I have to wrestle if I want to dominate, I felt deep dismay in his bones. And I saw as if through different eyes Hargraves's old-man skeleton, devoid of cartilage, covered with calcium clusters.

"You want a ride home? I gotta get going."

"It's O.K., I'll walk."

"Too late, I'm going. Which place's yours?"

"McCloskey."

He drives without turn signals. The snow is coming down hard enough that I worry about how fast he's driving, but he has two children, so I say nothing. Last year, when without warning Sawicki quit the team, leaving a blank at 165, Hargraves had no better option than to command Ucher to quit eating and slip down a class to fill the spot. Which Ucher did, though he did not excel in his new place. But it never ended up mattering, no one expected anything else, who even had their head turned in the right direction?

"You're gonna be all set for postseason?"

"Don't really know."

"I hope so. You take this too seriously for it to not work out."

✦

January is for two-a-days. So I make a habit of doing a real practice after my sham practice, after everyone's left I come out from my hiding place in the bathroom and do it for real.

✦

Under the snow in the Honky Tonky parking lot, I find a card for a phone number called 1-900-AZZ-TITZ. I get a woman named Topaz on the phone who tells me to have my credit card and my dick ready. I hang up.

✦

The whole ride to LaMoure I lie down on top of the bags in the back of the van instead of like an upright normal person. No one comments, I just flop around back there whenever the suspension shifts. I gargle discontent. I pretend I've been shot in the head. As we're walking out of the locker room to enter the gym, I tell Ucher to tell them that I'm going to the bathroom. I don't know why I bother.

I head outside and run for a very long time. So long that I lose track of time, so long that I realize I might not make it back to the gym in time for the vans, so long that it gets dark again and I hope they leave without me, that I'll have an excuse to be stuck here, long enough that the anger I started with comes out of my body, and I run slower, not thinking anything in particular, taking unplanned turns, not thinking anything at all.

I get back to the parking lot as they're shoving their bags in the vans, and I pretend like I've been there the whole time but clearly no one buys it.

✦

In my bedroom that night I have to masturbate because I keep hearing the sexuality of Topaz's voice in my ears, I flog myself until I get the shame out of my system. I barely get an erection. And then while trying to fall asleep, in the distrustful middle consciousness, I imagine that at Fink's house he invites my enemies over for dinner. A real fucking feast. Because I don't know where Fink lives or what his house looks like, it somehow becomes more believable and frightening. He stands at his door and hands a plate to Kryger, Frogman, my aunt, Levi Silas as they come in. They're eating the goat. It's on his table. They break off the legs and get goat slime on their faces.

✦

I still have such brilliant dreams of her, of Mary Beth, but I try not to dwell, I try to save their chemical radiation for times when I really need it.

✦

Stephen Florida is losing it.

✦

I go into the dark gym and by the light from the hallway I drag the tire from the corner into a place I can see and take the sledgehammer and do hammer throws, making the only sound for miles away, throwing them normal and then harder and harder, pretending I'm at the Big Strength Tester at night with all the lights and everything and trying to hit the bell at the top of the thermometer to win a stuffed animal for Mary Beth, a toad or a ladybug, something nice at least.

At some point I sense something like meaning creeping up behind my shoulders, hanging around behind my neck, but whatever it is, it shyly goes away.

I jump rope and hold one hundred Supermans for thirty seconds each and get to the top of the pegboard and do all the ladder shit and shoot the expressionless dummy three hundred and fifty times and do one hundred v-ups and hold a plank for seven minutes or what I count as seven minutes, four hundred and twenty seconds.

The workout yields a drenched shirt. I reach the end of the hallway to discover a locked door. Locked! I attempt a spit but it's so thick it doesn't go out all the way, it just rappels down and smacks my belly. There's a scruff of stagnant sweat around my eyes. I walk back up the hallway, hearing the water-fountain drip they'll never fix, walk to the other side of the building, to the other door that is surely locked, and is locked.

✦

I pull the materials out of my face to make all these little crazies, pounded and shaped from the clay and meat of my worries and thoughts, and then I send them off. One by one. Off you go! Someday the figurines'll come back and I'll cry for them because I won't recognize them.

✦

I do every drill in the book for an excessive number of reps and throw up a miniature amount twice and drink some water from the dripping fountain and find some stale opened granola in the training room, which is the location I end up sleeping in, on my stomach on the exam table with the lights on.

Only I don't fall asleep for good. I get up in the night, and as I'm heading to the fountain so I can rip a piss in it, I see something between the medicine cabinet and the wall.

This is one of the moments where one's fortune shifts, I already know it, it comes abruptly and certainly, that's how luck works, it suddenly gets on top of you like a screaming fat woman.

Crumbs fall off my chest as I crouch to pick it up. I knew it. I knew it.

The green notebook, the same one Fink wrote in, the one he always writes in. Like a collector, I open the cover. In the upper-right corner of the first page is the neat signature *R. Fink.* In my hands there is a document of true evil.

The first pages, I count five of them, are entirely filled up with the letter S. Like this:

SSSSSSSSSSSSSSSSSSSSSSSSSSSSSSSSSSSSSSSSSSSSSSSSS
SSSSSSSSSSSSSSSSSSSSSSSSSSSSSSSSSSSSSSSSSSSSSSSSS
SSSSSSSSSSSSSSSSSSSSSSSSSSSSSSSSSSSSSSSSSSSSSSSSS
SSSSSSSSSSSSSSSSSSSSSSSSSSSSSSSSSSSSSSSSSSSSSSSSS
SSSSSSSSSSSSSSSSSSSSSSSSSSSSSSSSSSSSSSSSSSSSSSSSS
SSSSSSSSSSSSSSSSSSSSSSSSSS

Then there's a gap of blank pages, five also, and then, on the next few pages, all over the place, are miscellaneous drawings and figures, large and small. A compass. The sun with a face in it. A mushroom cloud spinning out of a yellow stain on the paper. Some long division. A thoroughly detailed pagoda that takes up most of one page. Some phone numbers. What looks like a desert island full of crabs, so many crabs they're on top of each other and buried. A cowboy boot with a spur. Then the drawings stop. The last part of the notebook has very small writing, spaced apart. What it says, in part:

scapulae

Maybe Ill get the kid to help

I wonder how long it took the other cow to bleed out.

I have been back to the same place now for three weeks. Feels like Darwin on the Beagle, feels like never left. The erection begins in car, by time I pass that droning silver generator on the roadside. Maybe I should be more careful but I don't care. After I get there and turn the lights off.

During those years he met his seminars,
went & lectured & read, talked with human beings,
paid insurance & taxes;
but his mind was not on it. His mind was elsewheres
in an area where the soul not talks but sings
& where foes are attacked with axes.

After Louise goes to sleep I get out of bed and go up to the attic. I know I've kept telling myself I'm not ready but I can do it

The giant pipe organ installed in church in the German countryside playing one long note scheduled to play for 675 years finish some time in 2600s Weights hold down keys Tourists walk into church and look at organ which behind a cube of acrylic glass to reduce volume.

One Sister have I in our house,
And one, a hedge away.
There's only one recorded,
But both belong to me.

Another Reminder of Michael, his Shoshone face in between coughing and spitting, Reminder of the hospital, Remember the cf that killed him, Remember the year before or after Mrs. Wagons used to shut door in bathroom and untuck the nice white shirt and untuck your shirt and tuck it back in over and over and reach down inside and twist, but that wasn't so bad was it? Remember always thinking but then once asking him Are You Lonely, He looks up into the corner of the ceiling. What does he see? An angel hanging upside down with ruined wings and dirty robes? I don't ask him. He wrote the poem for me and the poem was The man who has dreams without words never talks in his sleep.

Dead man dead

Leopards break into the temple and drink all the sacrificial vessels dry; it keeps happening; in the end, it can be calculated in advance and is incorporated into the ritual.

I think the easiest is to turn the gas and

As if a snake could love an eel?

133 is ok but lets see where this goes if hes held out

I turn my eyes to the Schools and Universities of Europe
And there behold the Loom of Locke, whose Woof rages dire,
Wash'd by the Water-wheels of Newton: black the cloth
In heavy wreaths folds over every Nation: cruel Works
Of many Wheels I view, wheel without wheel, with cogs tyrannic
Moving by compulsion each other, not as those in Eden, which,
Wheel within wheel, in freedom revolve in harmony and peace.

A funny feeling skitters up and down my backbone. I read it on the table, over and over, deciding Fink is also the person with something behind his back. Then I fall asleep.

✦

I wake up to humans walking around in the hallway. I hide behind the table until there's no more noise, and then I run down the hallway and escape outside.

I walk home, across the school, a place where news doesn't get out or does but no one listens. No one knows what I have. Hargraves is the one I have to show the notebook to, no one else will believe me.

✦

When I'm shaving my head at the sink in the bathroom, Linus walks by behind me. I look at him in the mirror. I think his mouth moves but I can't hear over the clippers. When I'm done I hear a shower going, but I do not pursue the line of inquiry. Yes, I do. I go right up to the curtain and annunciate above the running water, "Do you know when I first met you I worried that you didn't understand abstract concepts? Like you were a simple dyslexic. Now I know once and for all you're a whorish slave just like me."

And then: back in my room, the tremendous vertical heat pipe in the corner makes a ticking, increasing like a starting train, like the Frogman tapping with long fingers to let me know it's not going to leave me alone that easy. A piece of paint falls off. It clicks faster and faster until it slows down and stops. In the hallway, a door slams.

✦

Wrestling has kept me busy for about ten years but I've been worrying more and more that it'll do nothing for me once it's over.

✦

Monday morning, I get dressed and slip the green notebook inside my backpack.

After taking my usual seat (the other five do, too) I screw my attention tight for the whole Jazz class and concentrate on Silas's face.

"I'm going to play 'Caravan' by Thelonious Monk. His middle name's Sphere. Remember that for the test." I underline *Thalonius Sphere Monk* in my notebook. In the margin of the same page, I do an A/B comparison, with the A row being Silas and the B row being Fink and the comparison being Evil. "Caravan" elapses, and once I ensure Silas is doing his standard eyes-closed, arms-crossed pose during the song, I complete the chart. The comparison is decided in a best of three categories:

1. Is there a logical explanation for why he is so evil?
2. What does he do at night?
3. What is the worst thing he's ever done?

It looks like this:

	1	**2**	**3**
Silas	none	plays his trumpet/ rubs hands together	wife-killing
Fink	potentially abused	home with family, driving past generator, up to no good	?

Category 1 goes to Silas but Categories 2 and 3 are won by Fink. But remember this is only a preliminary chart.

After the song finishes, Silas leans forward in the chair and puts another record on. He says, "One more song. This one is called "Round Midnight' and it's the most recorded jazz standard. Who knows what a jazz standard is?"

A total of five seconds pass.

"It's a composition held in ongoing esteem that is often used by many musicians as the foundation of jazz arrangements or improvisations."

A male voice, the voice of Pervis, asks from very far away for Silas to repeat the definition.

"A composition held in ongoing esteem that is often used by many musicians as the foundation of jazz arrangements or improvisations." He puts the needle on. "Pay attention to this version. Because later we're going to hear Miles Davis's version and you'll need to be able to differentiate between the two."

The song starts, and it sounds the goddamn same. I write *piano bingle* next to *Thalonius Sphere Monk.*

Silas writes *Thelonious Monk* on the board. I make the spelling correction in my notes. I turn around to see what exactly is going on back there, just as one girl chucks a crumpled ball of paper at another girl. The paper bounces off her head. She uncrumples it, looks at whatever's on it, recrumples it, and drops it below the desk, by her feet.

After the song, he gives us some biography bits. Monk didn't finish high school, was an evangelist and played the organ in church, got his start with Coleman Hawkins. Blah blah blah. Silas could not sound less interested in relaying the information. I circle *Coleman Hawkins* because "Body and Soul" will be on the listening test, too. He puts on one last record, one he leaves on the player. "'So What' by Miles Davis, from *Kind of Blue,* a record of great significance to me, and to music as a whole." He says, "See you Wednesday," and leaves the room.

By pretending to finish up some notes, I'm the last one in there. The song plays for no one else as I walk up to the back corner and scoop up the paper ball and hide it in my pocket. Halfway across campus, when I'm sure no one from the class is around, I open it up. What this appears to be, though I can't be sure, is a drawing of the male-female act of penetration. The female side of things is crude but all-right accurate. But instead of the male part of the bargain, it looks like it's a ponytail doing the job.

I'm collecting data on him. Soon enough I'm going to figure this entire goddamn puzzle out.

✦

During practice, I keep my mouth shut. I observe all of it, observe most closely Fink for signs of agitation, but get nothing. I hold on to my knowledge, I don't want to blow my whole load before I know what to do with it.

And anyway, I forget all about the green notebook in the locker room when Hargraves stops everyone and says he needs silence. Then he takes out *Amateur Wrestling News,* the new issue, and turns to the rankings. He tears out the page and holds it up importantly like the Ninety-Five Theses. "This latest ranking for the Division IV 125 weight class has Linus Arrington of Oregsburg College ranked number one." Above the shouting and the clapping, he yells, "This is the first time in the program's history we've had a number one," and after Crest and Clark and Ucher and Lyle and the others are done shoving him and shouting, during which he looks like a young pharaoh, Linus lifts his arms and makes a *V* sign on each hand like Richard Nixon, shouting, "I'd like to thank the Academy!"

Hargraves tapes the page on the chalkboard. The noise takes some time to die down, there has not been an actual reason to celebrate in the locker room since we qualified for the conference championship, which was four years ago, which was before most of them were around. I walk up to the board. 11–0. The glaring realization of Linus's ownership, something he went out and took, something he deserves.

I will admit, I have no delusions at this point in time, it's from a place of woeful envy that I wait for all the coaches to clear out and then I aim my shoe and throw it across the room at Linus and it strikes the side of his face. "Get out of my goddamn locker room." I keep my reasons straight! What everyone else interprets as smallness is really me letting Linus know that I'm still here. That I'm not going away. That I'm going to allow the rest of them to tackle me, the back of my skull nicking the chalkboard, call me asshole, call me piece of shit, mush my face to the cheap scratchy carpeting that smells of decades of old water and chemical cleaner, but I feel like I'm floating, like I'm the gas thief who's broken into the dentist's and found the good stuff. Linus grabs his bag and leaves without saying anything, which is how I know I've gotten to him. I start laughing. "Let me have my shoe." One of them behind me with his knee on my neck says, "Linus isn't your scrapegoat." Because I've figured out that anger is best used when rolled into the greater part of determination, or commitment, or whatever. And I've already maxed out the anger quota. I don't have bad judgment. I have no judgment left at all. Kryger walks up slow and comfortable in his new place, and kneels down. He looks at me closely, like he's never seen me before, or has, but not in the way he should've, as if now he wants to get it right.

"Calm down," he says. "Sit still until you're calmed down."

"You sound like Fink." I let them keep my head on the floor with all their distasteful hands because I have the key, I have the green notebook. And though I don't know what exactly its significance is, when I hold it in my hands it throbs and spittles, slavering to spill the beans. And so I slacken. Close my eyes. Deep breath. Patience.

✦

My asshole is the dark zero.

✦

Like a baby, I try Mary Beth's number, but she won't help me get out of this, it's my own fucking problem.

✦

No one is out on my night walk to the gym. As I turn off the main path and cross the grass, I see a car in the parking lot. It's parked in the fringe of the lot, out of the reach of the floodlights, with the headlights off. I step back into the shadow and pull my hood over my head, squatting in the grass. I watch. On the random days where Hargraves calls for a second practice, I have had to readjust and come later than normal, but this is the only time I've seen someone in the lot this late. After a minute or two, when nothing happens, it's clear whoever's inside hasn't seen me. Then the passenger door opens and someone gets out. It's Linus. He walks in the opposite direction, away from the campus's middle. I can't get closer without stepping into the light. Then I hear the gear shifting and the headlights turn on. The car pulls onto the road and drives away. I never get a good look inside.

✦

After my second season, after I lost eleven matches, I went back to Oakes to look at my house. I just stood there in the road, staring at the front door. I must've been looking for some time, but when I heard a car coming down the street, I turned and ran.

✦

There's a surprise waiting for me at practice, first that Hargraves isn't there to show the notebook to and that he won't be coming to Watertown later. The whole plan's fucked. I try to get information out of one of them but nothing comes of it because of the second surprise, which is a black-and-gray-haired woman in some sort of expensive blouse-skirt combo, doing the rounds and talking to the team, making most of them puff out and peacock around. She carries a notepad. She's a reporter with the *Wells Register.*

It's obvious why she's here. I just resume my place on the bike. After removing Mary Beth's card from my shoe so I don't soak it, I do my fucking prescription. I have to keep reminding myself I have the green notebook, but I can't get Hargraves alone, I don't know where he is. All my sweat falls off my face and swamps under the bike. During drills, the reporter buzzes around Linus, mooning over him. Kryger tries to get her attention until he realizes she's not biting. She writes down stray things they spit out, things that, sucked free of circumstance, may appear wise or perceptive but really are just pulled from the mouths of buttholes.

Because the coaches insist on talking to her in my vicinity, I hear more than I'd like.

Fink: "What Linus is doing here, it's extraordinary. No one's talking about it. It's like, 'Oh, some kid is up there in one of the Dakotas winning a few matches, that's nice.' But that's not what's happening. If you've seen him wrestle, he's not just winning, he's destroying his opponent. There are three or four times during a match, he's doing things no one else can do. He's just demolishing these kids. I've been around the sport for a long time. He's the best wrestler I've ever coached, and he's only wrestled, what? Twelve, thirteen times at this level? He has no ceiling. I mean, the sky's the limit. Soon people are going to see what this kid's capable of, and it's going to be something else."

Another one I can't remember the name of: "I don't know why schools weren't tripping over each other to hand him a scholarship, hand him the keys to the program. But their loss is our gain. We're lucky to have him. I think he takes pride, you know, in proving everyone wrong."

I find out her name is Patsy Pierce, this when she jumps in my way as I'm heading for the exit.

"Mr. Florida?"

"Hello."

"Can I ask you a few questions?"

"Why?"

"Well, I'm here doing a story on Linus Arrington. How he's the first Oregsburg wrestler to get ranked number one?"

"Yes, he is my son."

"Well, anyway, he told me you're his best friend."

"Is that what he said?"

"Or most trusted. No—closest. Actually, I don't know, I can't read my own writing! Isn't that funny? It's one or the other. Also called you his own personal role model. Is that true?"

Here he is, having fun with me through the media. We feed lies to each other. I don't mention my inner feeling about Linus, which is that Linus and me are having a deep disagreement, bordering on the philosophical. Once, I sat up late with him pondering balance, on how important balance is, and we looked out the window, as if true wrestling balance could be found in a tree like a nuthatch, or a rare drooling vulture.

"I've really got to get going. We're leaving—"

"Three questions. Then I'll let you go. Promise."

"O.K., go ahead with it."

"Question one. Tell me about yourself."

"I'm from Idaho," I say. "My parents love each other very much. As a child they took me to a prehistoric park where I was just fascinated by the animals that used to live. I have two sisters. Janice is in the navy and Gladys is a very successful insurance agent. I take studying very seriously. I get all A's."

"And how have you changed since Idaho?"

"You mean since coming here? To wrestle for Oregsburg?"

"Mm-hmm."

"I've been the same since I was born. I just had to wait for myself to grow into what I've become."

"And those scars—sorry, do you mind?"

"No, I don't mind."

"The scars on your forehead. From wrestling?"

All the scars take up residence in my forehead, it's the most popular block in the neighborhood. I had a little bit of acne in middle school, long enough to make a mark and then leave, and during my last season at Hillsboro in the weight room, the bar slipped out of my hand and crashed against my head. It took a week for the headache to die down. "Yes," I say.

"Question two. You've had some success here."

It does not sound like a question, so I just look at her.

She says, "What I mean is. Wrestling is about great sacrifice, isn't it?"

"For me, I haven't had to sacrifice that much."

"Does failure scare you?"

"No. Other things scare me."

"Question three. Everyone knows wrestling is a notoriously challenging sport. Can you give some idea of what it's like?"

"What what's like?"

"Everything. The season. Doing all this." She gestures at the gym, waits for my insight.

"Well . . . well, it's like catching liquid in your hands!"

An expression like she thinks I've recently lost my mind. She writes something in her notepad.

"Is that good?" I blurt out, bending over the pad to see what she's writing, because I don't want my stuff taken out of context.

"Very interesting. And how do you manage what that feels like? That feeling?"

"Sometimes I become the person I'm meant to be."

After she tells me thank you, she gets whether it's with a *ph* or a *v* and walks away.

✦

While waiting for them to pack the vans, Nate pretends to be holding a microphone in front of Linus's face while various members of the team laugh about it.

✦

On the drive to Watertown, I read Fink's notebook. I read it again and again, the bags rumbling underneath me the whole way, memorizing the words. I decide what makes him so evil is he has the capability to guess your insides. What I mean is that he's figured me out and is acting against what I want for an unclear reason.

One of them in the van tells a story. A girl, a sophomore or junior, started dumping gasoline all over herself in the middle of school, under the clock tower, but was tackled before she could get the match struck. Two different people say she was singing "Can I Get to Know You Better" by the Turtles while she was getting on with it.

Sometime later, someone else in the van says that Fink's wife is coming.

✦

We get to the Society Motel, which has a red neon sign and yellow safety lights that dredge it out of the dark. It's late enough that no one goes anywhere.

✦

I wake up screaming, sure a smiling man is pushing needles under my fingernails. "Shut up, Florida!" someone yells, and then I realize it's the middle of the night and my bed is scratchy and the sheet has four cigarette burn holes in it and I'm sleeping in someone else's mental stains and my roommate is Lyle.

✦

A long time later, the light is shining on my head through the window, through the flame-retardant curtains.

The parking lot is gravel with weeds turned to brown sticks. All the vans have gone. Cars pass infrequently.

I'll admit that I've thought about the last loss of last season every single day since it's happened. That's about eleven months now. I will admit that for a week or two last year, I'd get out of my bed and walk to the library and after a little searching I'd find some of the most popular suicide sites. I got paper cuts on two fingers turning the pages of the thousand-page *Historical and Statistical Manual of Depression and Suicide*. Nanjing Yangtze Bridge, Golden Gate Bridge, Prince Edward Viaduct, bridges bridges bridges. Bridges where they install phones with direct connections to suicide hotlines, bridges where they keep raising the rails. A suicide forest in Japan inspired by a book where people walk past signs letting them know their life is valuable and please don't throw it away. At the end of chapter seventeen, a note about pentobarbital, high doses of it, bought from pet shops in Mexico to induce painless death in pets that owners take home and swallow themselves. Suicide tourism, organized, thought-out trips to Cambodia, the Netherlands, Switzerland, places where euthanasia is legal. If I looked closely at my fingers, at the paper cuts, and squeezed, I could make them talk like little mouths. This felt good. Sitting at a shaky basement library table, looking this up, getting cuts from studying. But Mary Beth was right. I was never more than a casual suicide-thinker, gazing up at the rafters of the cafeteria and failing to imagine one of them holding my full weight, as though the body dangling up there was an actor, or a dummy in a wig stuffed with straw.

One of the white doors opens, number thirty, about halfway down the motel face on my right, and a woman with a baby comes out. I know, because fate insists, that this is Mrs. Fink. Mrs. Fink has a walking boot on. The right foot. She clumps it by me and goes to the office at the other end of the motel.

I have an idea.

In the office, the baby is hitting Mrs. Fink in the arm. Standing at the counter to the side of the desk, with her free arm she takes a foam cup and fills it with coffee. Then she sits on the couch against the wall. There's no one at the desk, no one else around. Events proceed quickly. I've put on Lyle's wool beanie to hide my identity and ears. I walk by and as I pass, the baby cries and Mrs. Fink swears and says, "Excuse me," saying it to me.

She points at the counter. "Can you hand me that ring rattle?" Next to the red stirrer straws is a transparent plastic ring with several colored balls settled inside it. I walk it over, sure the object's smothered with the saliva of the child, but she takes it, or rather he takes it and jams it into his mouth, as much as he can fit.

She doesn't say thank you, which I find interesting and chalk up to the state of motherhood, where you are no longer so full of gratitude all the time. "It's his favorite, it makes such an enormous racket," she says. "I just had to get some coffee, he's driving me up a wall."

She crazily pours half the cup down her throat. The baby bounces on her knee.

Opening up the sewer pipe, I say, "He's a cute little buster. You guys just passing through?"

She says, "I wish. We're with his daddy. He wanted us to come watch him work. Says he needed to see his daddy at work. Course that was before this fever hit, on the drive down. You hear that, squirt? The man says you're cute!"

Instinctively, I start putting together a cup of coffee for myself. She says, "And you? Passing through?" I mimic the steps she took, mixing sugar and two creamer thimbles in there.

"Yeah. My wife and I seem to always be doing something like that. She's in a family way. We're gonna have a girl."

"Now you tell me right now that coffee isn't for her!"

"Course not! More for me, heh."

The baby coughs twice on the ring rattle.

"You know something?" she says. "You look somewhat familiar to me."

"Is that so?"

"Yes. Have I met you somewhere?"

I force the cup to my lips but I don't drink and the liquid just wets my mouth. "Wow! Isn't it funny? A chance meeting in a transition place, a person you may or may not know. It sounds like the making of a short story!"

She takes down the rest of her coffee, looks at me brightly. "I guess you're right! It is funny."

The notebook is just a few doors down, inside room fourteen, inside my backpack, tucked under some clothes. I could recite the relevant passages for her first, and then show her the original scripture.

"This goddamn kid," she says. The baby's asleep with his face down on her shoulder. She talks quieter, with her face very close to her son's. "When he gets some sleep I can finally get some."

I turn to throw my empty sugar packets in the garbage under the counter. When I turn back around, her head is down and she's asleep.

I toss my coffee into the snow. I go down to room thirty, but not before tearing a sample page from the green notebook in my room. The little chain is caught in the Finks' door crack, and I go inside. All types of baby paraphernalia covers the room, the sheets are unmade, which I sniff. I slide the notebook page under the blanket. Three dollars are on the nightstand for the cleaning lady. In the bathroom, I wash the sickness of the baby off my hands. Next to the sink, inside a plastic bag, there are two toothbrushes, one green and one blue. I take the green one and then the blue one and scrape the bristles along the inside of the toilet. I put them back in the plastic bag. But on my way out, I have a sudden change of heart, and I take the page back out from the bed. I leave the room. What the fuck is wrong with me? If only he didn't have a kid this'd be a whole lot easier.

As I'm shutting the door behind me, a few doors down, the cleaning lady stops her cart and stares at me. I would not be telling the whole truth if I said that thoughts of Masha did not come flooding back. Needless to say, I'm not worried she'll tell on me, no one really wants to disturb the safety of their routine.

✦

I sneak into the gym and locate the faculty directory, but there's no address or phone number for Hargraves. I have no way of getting in touch with him until he comes back from his crazy island. I break some equipment.

✦

In Unusual Disorders, we talk about animal suicide and autothysis and traumatic insemination and self-cannibalism, observed in rats and octopuses.

One girl in the front says her brother used to squeeze her cat's belly until it yelped and would claw his arms up to get away but then would come back and sit in his lap like it never happened until it happened again. The point being animals have no memory so how can they commit suicide?

Another student interrupts and says but what about dogs that people beat the hell out of? "They do that for dogfighting, and other dogs they beat spend the rest of their lives with their tails tucked, afraid of loud noises, that kind of stuff. All I'm saying is they remember the pain."

When I was a little idiot I thought suicide was eating seven Flintstones vitamins.

And then a third student brings up a point and no one knows what the hell she's talking about, but this line of inquiry ends up in a parsing of autohaemorrhaging, which is the deliberate ejection of blood by animals as a defense mechanism.

"So," Mrs. Willard says, "how are you supposed to prove willfulness?"

✦

In Nonfiction Film, we watch a movie called *Komarov,* about the first fatality of outer space. Parts are so boring that I need to pinch my nipple to keep from giving in to the sweet sleep. Toward the end, there's a photo of three Soviet officers sternly looking down at a white table, upon which there's a gnarled black chunk of coral, and it turns out that's what's left of Komarov.

✦

Late at night, on my way home from my evening workout, I peer in some windows. Nothing special. But from the shrubs behind Leon, I swear I see Linus, taking his time on the main path. He's going in the direction of McCloskey. I begin following him, he looks over his shoulder like in the movies, so I act like I'm studying the posting board and duck behind trees when necessary. Eventually, my tail produces this surprise: he makes a pit stop at the student health center. He's in there for just about three minutes. While waiting, I'm in earshot of two females arguing by the front door about whether one of them is being rude. When Linus comes out, he heads straight back to McCloskey through the lobby and up to our floor, but I am disappointed to find he just goes to his room and locks the door. The slit under the door goes dark right away.

✦

I know I'm not the center of the universe but there's at least a forty percent chance Fink has mentioned to his wife what a degenerate I am. What I'm trying to figure out is how to balance the situation of what may be a potential family murderer versus ruining a family, but that family may be killed anyway, so that's what I need to figure out how to prevent, but if I don't say anything they might end up dead and I'll for certain be prevented from wrestling. So logically, the answer is the notebook must be shared, right?

✦

The first time I shaved my head, my mom standing behind me with the clippers in the bathroom mirror and me holding the waste basket under my head, I found birthmarks under my hair that I never knew were there.

✦

Where I end up on this Friday morning in late January is Allnighter. I walk past the booths and sit on a chrome barstool and order two eggs and a decaf tea. The smell of farts is not that different from the smell of hash browns. On the counter is today's *Wells Register.* The battle between my willpower and curiosity is not a fair fight and is over quickly, as right there on the bottom of the front page is the article in question.

THE FUTURE IS BRIGHT FOR OC'S ARRINGTON

One hundred and twenty-five pounds is the lowest weight class in men's collegiate wrestling, but at Oregsburg College's wrestling practices, the littlest guy on the mats may be the one you should most be afraid of: freshman Linus Arrington is the first wrestler in Oregsburg history to be ranked number one in his weight class.

But even in his short time pursuing perfection at Oregsburg, Arrington's faced adversity. On December 24, with Arrington 5–0 for the season and at the time home in Bellevue, Nebraska, to celebrate the holiday with his family, his grandmother, Lena, died at age eighty-eight of a stroke. An ordinary freshman may have used the obstacle as an excuse, but Arrington instead used it as motivation. Arrington refuses to make excuses, and he states he won't let his personal life and his personal tragedies define his career. "When my gramma died, yes, that was hard on me, hard on my parents," Arrington said. "But it really put perspective on my life and on my season. I'm thinking about her every day, I'm dedicating this season to her. Sometimes I can feel her helping me out from up there, like she's helping me turn the other kid."

The history of Oregsburg wrestling is a short and unremarkable one. The program has never had a wrestler ranked number one, has never even sent a wrestler to the national championship, held every March in Kenosha, Wisconsin. But with his undefeated record of 12–0 at press time, as well as the coveted number-one ranking, Arrington looks poised

I get fed up with it and try to read the item below. It's about a war hospital overseas where they're talking with the damaged soldiers. One of the quotes is "I feel lucky and unlucky at the same time," and I get fed up with that item, too.

The eggs arrive and I eat them while pondering the gruesomely flattering article I've just read. Sun comes in the window behind my back and lights up the metal gustatory instruments of the open kitchen. So much human innovation in the world. The tea mug, when held close to the face of Stephen Florida, inspires him to sweat, which is why he's holding it there in the first place.

✦

Whenever we'd go running and approach a group of trees, even a small group, Linus would shout, "Be careful of Lyme disease!"

✦

Late for practice because I lost track of time at Allnighter, I come down the gym hallway, my wet Ponies squeaking like alarms, and it's for sure whoever's in the locker room hears me coming. Nonetheless, I stop just outside the door in time to hear Fink tell the team that Hargraves had to go "out of town," that Hargraves assured him he's going to be back by Wednesday for the trip to Wyoming. I think about bursting in there, while there's an audience, and proclaiming like Paul Revere my fucking message concerning the green notebook, which I have on my person, which at all times I have on my person, but again I think of the kid and the wife, and I stop myself. Would he actually go through with it or am I overreacting? And if I am, how am I supposed to get reinstated? When the meeting is adjourned, I have to hastily crouch between the door and the wall as they all go by, some into the gymnasium itself and some down the hall to the weight room. And when I'm sure they're all gone, I slither into the locker room to find my bad suspicions come true: on the chalkboard they have taped up the *Register* article.

Hargraves is back Wednesday. That will do. Enough is enough.

I run, mumbling different variations of the Fink exposé speech, until I get caught up on the road by slow traffic, a whole line of vehicles trying to park in front of a blue-and-white-striped tent they set up in a field up 52. I slow to a walk.

The fuss is for a gun show. Though Mary Beth wouldn't approve, I fluff the snow out of my hair and eyebrows and go inside, I don't know why.

There's a whole side of the tent for the knives, but I have no interest in them.

I walk down all the aisles with unloaded guns pointed at me, up in the air, away from me, at the ground, at white men and skinny white men picking up guns and looking at them, aiming them, brainstorming about guns, fantasizing about guns, gun-related dreams, gun visions, and I am nervous. There's a sense that the people inside the tent are keeping a big secret from the people outside the tent.

In one of the corners is a table of war relics, a banner in black and white that says JACOB'S WAR RELIQUARY above a middle-aged man who says to me, "I'm Jacob," as soon as I make eye contact.

"How much of this stuff still works?" He catches me eyeballing a dirty old grenade, which looks like an exotic apple breed.

"This particular one is from the Japanese, World War II. But you'd likely have to stuff a dynamite stick right in there, right there, to get it to do its job. It's dead as a doornail."

"What about that ugly gun there?"

"FN Browning 1910, 7.65. The gun that started World War I. Dates are tough because records didn't make it through the wars, but I'd say between 1922 and 1924."

"Why is it so brown?"

"Unfortunately some poor storage there along the way. Doesn't really work anymore."

"How much does it cost?" The *F* and the *N* are engraved on top of each other on the handle.

"Oh, you don't want that one, I got a few more over here just like it, much better workable con—"

"This one, though, I could get at a discount?"

"Well, sure, if you wanted it more for show, that what you're saying?" I nod. "Would you like to see it first, at least?"

"Yes, I would."

It comes out of the case and into my hands. I hold it dishonestly.

He says, "How about a hundred?"

My wallet has eighty-four dollars in it. I hold out the four twenties.

✦

The pistol is under my mattress. I fall asleep.

✦

There's an accident just north of school. Four students, inebriated, were reported leaving the Honky Tonky, then creating enough of a scene at Allnighter to be thrown out. A few minutes later, their car collided head-on with a station wagon, killing three of the students and two of the three occupants of the other vehicle, including a twelve-year-old.

✦

For the sixteenth time this month, I run the same route, northwest on 52, but instead of going past the gun show tent, I take a detour. I end up in front of a record store I distantly remember seeing before.

It's someone's converted house. Boxes and crates and shelves full of records, all the way up the side of the stairs and in what used to be a kitchen, a green-tiled kitchen that gets plenty of sun, towers of records, no evidence of organization. Each room, and there are six including the bathroom, contains a record player muttering a different song. The man in charge is in the doorway of a former mud room, where the soundtrack for *Snow White and the Seven Dwarfs* is going. His bathrobe is blue.

"Do you have Miles Davis?"

"Which? You want *Sketches of Spain? Kind of Blue?*"

"*Kind of Blue.*"

"Follow me," he says, lighting a cigarette. He takes me to the living room, next to a big table that appears to be the cashier counter and has a lockbox and pad and paper on it, along with an open, facedown book called *The Freeing of the Dust.* He runs his fingers down the sides of a man-sized record stack, then lifts the top third and, like a magic deck of cards being cut, *Kind of Blue* is the record on top.

"You sell players?"

Still holding the stack, he nods at the record player on the table, playing some wailing opera. "You can buy that one."

Next to the exit, a sign says 99 CENTS above a couple of milk crates.

"That's the clearance stuff," the man says.

Flipping through, I find one that's called *Strength of Words*. The cover is a white background and a pair of black lips. At the bottom it says in black text "The New Language Society." I turn the record over: "The purpose of *Strength of Words* is to stimulate the language centers of the mind. It can be used by anyone who employs language as a tool in his everyday life: poets, speech-writers, doctors, lawyers. By the time you finish, you will strengthen your cogency through words."

I run home with the record player under my arm. Good workout. I put it on my desk and slip on the headphones and place the needle. It's a woman's voice, she speaks very slowly, without inflection, inserting two seconds between every single word.

> *Hello. Welcome to* Strength of Words. *In order to maximize the experience, please find a quiet place and limit the surrounding distractions. Please turn the volume up. Please close your eyes. Listen only to the words. Listen to nothing else. Let's begin.*
>
> *Hello.*
> *Limit.*
> *Crossword.*
> *Force field.*
> *Slide rule.*
> *Feldspar.*
> *Distance.*
> *Allergy.*
> *Kettle.*
> *Tire swing.*
> *Tamper.*
> *Hello.*
> *Donkey.*
> *Pregnant.*

Suck.
Cowardice.
Staple.
Cruelty.
Laughing.
Laughing.
Laughing.
Laughing.
Laughing.
Rope.
Hole.
Slippery.
Tickle.
Tongue.
Suck.
Smegma.
Choke.
Choke.
Disgust.
Infection.
Drowning.
Suck.
Suck.

I yank the headphones off my ears. I take the record off the player and go right out into the hallway and drop it down the trash chute, where it clatters and breaks and is gone.

◆

Sometime between Saturday and Sunday, I listen to "So What" 115 times in the dark and meanwhile can't stop imagining suicide statistics. They drop themselves at my feet like prizes.

✦

The reckoning is here, goddamnit, I have to squeeze my toes to confirm that this isn't a dream, and I didn't know that the reckoning would be a letter to Mrs. Fink until I sit down at my desk and begin writing it. Which I do, and it feels great.

✦

In the empty Pharmart, Glenn Miller plays for no one but me. I have the gun under my sweatshirt, in the elastic band. I try, I really try, to figure out if I ever really saw and seriously contemplated the edge. My mind is moving very fast now. I mean very slow. Something happens to me when I'm in the greeting cards. February 1, four days from now. It was always easy to remember my grandma's birthday. The first of the month. Four days before mine.

I buy her a pink card that has flowers on it, all kinds of watercolor flowers and a sentiment that makes me sad enough to quit any half-boiled robbery notions, sad enough to buy it with the gun tucked in my elastic sweatpants, pointing right at my dick, which is just as sad as the rest of me, as sad as my fingers and tonsils, sad enough that I throw the card away in the trash can in the parking lot. I have always been too stern for my age.

✦

I read the first chapter of Thomas Mann. Then I read it again.

✦

If I was a little smarter or not so sentimentally hesitant about his family, I probably would've figured my reinstatement problem out by now. I have a few days left to get cleared and then to beat Kryger for 133 in time for Garnes and Jan Gehring. Must consider all the angles: Fink is the crux of the mess, and I only have one chance to attack him, and he's such a pristine little shitman that I don't know how he'll play the green notebook once I put it out there. I am not in a position of advantage, but I have his incriminating wording to support me, and if I blindly swing in there, spraying all over the place like a zany fire hose, there's a chance at least one accusation will stick. I'm going to do it on Wednesday, I'll grab Hargraves in the parking lot as the vans are leaving for Wyoming and show him the green note-book. "This is your assistant coach!" By this time, the letter to Mrs. Fink will be waiting in her mailbox for her. "This is your husband!"

✦

A letter arrives from Mary Beth. In order to prolong the feeling, I put the envelope on my bed, lock the door behind me, and shower, the whole time thinking about what's inside, or not thinking about what's inside but just that I have something from her. The gun seems goofy and pointless when I think about her letter, and I start laughing in the shower. Back in my room, drip-ping wet in my towel, I start reading the note, which is scribbled on a small torn corner of sketchbook paper.

> *I started something and it ended up looking a little like you. It didn't start that way. I just wanted you to know. I'm not going to let you see it, I just wanted to let you know. It's really good.*

I want to tell her it's strange to be talking with someone like this. It's strange for me. My natural progression with people is to move further and further apart. So even this, whatever this is, is new for me. I reread the note, over and over.

✦

The picturesque thing to do would be to stand at the edge of Egg Lake and throw that tiny fucker as hard as I can, admiring my throw as it lands with a small splash and sinks somewhere in the middle. But the lake is frozen. So I step onto the ice and walk toward the center, where I spot a fresh ice-fishing hole. I drop in the gun and head back home in the dark.

✦

During Monday's Jazz class, I listen to Ornette Coleman and try to convince myself this isn't music's diarrhea. My distraction is thick enough that I can't give as much attention as I'd like to studying Silas, the flimflam man. *Melancholy* is a term I learned about in my reading and I've discovered it can be wildly addictive to nurse one's own melancholy, needless to say.

A wadded-up piece of paper hits my shoulder, bounces onto my notebook. I open it while Silas, his feet up on the desk, looks at the ceiling, Zenning the fuck out to the saxophone solo.

I swear to god this shit is so boring Im dying

And then a little below in a different handwriting:

1- Im so bored 2 did u see me picking my nose
2- Is it gross I want to fuck a murderer

So while the saxophone continues to burp and toot, I think up something to add to the paper. At last I write:

Ha me 2 my fingers up my butt

I crumple the paper back up and toss it over my shoulder, far toward the back of the room, putting my head down for the rest of the song to hide my laughing.

The song finishes and like always, Silas doesn't say anything for a full minute. I know it's a minute exactly because I've counted it and now I know he counts, too.

"John Coltrane died in 1967 on Long Island," he tells everyone. "Anyone know what he died of?"

Being closest to the front, I don't know if anyone's shaking their head or what, but he lets the silence last a while.

"Hepatitis. Anyone know how someone gets hepatitis?"

Another long silence, this time, one he doesn't finish. He just walks out. Puts his papers away and takes his bag and leaves. I'm zipping up my backpack when something bounces around my feet, rolls up under my desk. Another note. This time it's about me. What it says is:

That Stephen boy has a nice body but hes such a big weird freak

✦

Suicidal behavior has been observed more in female animals than male and in more vertebrates than invertebrates.

✦

Some kind of fair is in the student union on Tuesday afternoon. There are tables for the Army and the Merchant Marines and the Peace Corps and the Red Cross. I take their pamphlets, all of them. I look for sign-ups for human test subjects but there's nothing. I could join any one of these in a few months.

On the television, a Save the Children ad comes on and really gets me down about what I take for granted on a day-to-day basis. On the back of the blood-donation pamphlet, I write down the address they have on the screen, under the white woman and the phone number.

✦

Hours and hours of sitting in the library, sifting through the poetry section, I've figured out which is which, I've decoded the notebook. Thank God there are only two dozen poetry books in central North Dakota. I've figured out which is Dickinson, which is Berryman, which is Kafka, which is Blake. The remaining writings I am reasonably certain are Fink's, and I'm now sure he used these exact books for his notes: there's a sun with a face in the margin of the Berryman.

And it is with this scholarly burden on my mind that I travel from the library to the gym, so deep in thought, so pleasantly deep in thought, that I look forward to the workout as a means to stimulate the thoughts and turn up new angles on them, new considerations, which is after all what real thought is all about.

While walking down the gym's dark hallway I hear a noise in the back of the training room. Then, faintly, I hear "Scarborough Fair" playing from behind the door, inside the COACH OFFICE. Standing next to the exam table in the unlit room, I wait to be certain I'm not imagining the sounds, to make sure they don't go away. When they don't and I head toward the door, I have a vision of the great yarn ball untangling.

I open the door on Fink and Linus and see what I see. I shut the door on them. I run out of the room and down the hall and outside and don't stop until I'm up the stairs and in my room. I pace around. I sit down on the bed, and like a burning bush I see the secret, the biggest one yet, the soundless bottom of the well where concentration and certainty intersect, a place where the dodo and giant squid intersect.

The knock comes faster than expected.

"Can we talk?" Linus says. He has a bottle of water in one hand. In the other is a Stephen King book called *'Salem's Lot.*

I step aside as if to welcome him into the room he never visits anymore, the place where in September he sat at my desk and, though he is smart, smarter than me, he is shaky in English, so he said: "Roberts wants us to pick what we think is the most important line of poetry of the twentieth century and tell why," and I said: "'Do I contradict myself? Very well then I contradict myself.' Emerson," and he said, "From *Walden,* right?" and I said, "Right," and he said, "Great, let me write it here. O.K. What does it mean?"

But now in my doorway he says, "Someplace a little more neutral, I thought."

"Neutral such as?"

"What about that closet you use?"

He lets me open the door and enter first because in this situation, the leverage is mine.

"I was hoping to straighten up, but you just caught me at a busy time," I say, laughing at him, laughing right into his face. I feel like a king of infinite money.

Linus is cool like a lawyer, as if smothered by indifference and treating it as one of his weapons. "It's pretty simple." He takes a drink of water, prepares to offer me his bag of magic beans. "You forget the whole thing, Fink tells Hargraves you're healthy again."

"One hundred percent?"

"Yes."

He appears more vivid in the closet, releasing more odor and sweat than ever before, it all keeps increasing and increasing. Above his lip, there are pimples where the hair is struggling through. I cannot shake the feeling that he's the result of someone's careful long-ago idea, a grown weed.

While looking at his bent nose, it occurs to me: Louise is Fink's wife, the note in the locker room back in November was intended for Linus. *Something needs to be done about Louise.* I balled it up and dropped it on the ground. I thought nothing of it.

"There's something I've been meaning to ask," he says.

"What."

"Where's Mary Beth?"

It's all happening too fast. I slow events down with my thinking, the only way you can, I buy more time with a fake fit of coughing. I know what he is. I don't know his exact pathology, no one does, but I know it's a lot more complicated than the boy from Nebraska who went up to North Dakota and got gobbled up by evil. I know what I saw in that room, and I know he did not wrestle himself to 12–0 without something else inside him, anyone who has spent one minute watching him on a mat knows that.

"She had to go away." He nods, peeling my personality back with his stare. Only the people who really know you can find where the rind gives, and I look away, my eyes falling on his book. "How's that one?"

"Not far enough really to tell. Pretty good."

"What have you been doing at the health center?"

"I don't know what you're talking about."

"I'll squeal! Don't make me squeal!"

"Getting my anti-inflammatory."

"What for?"

"Tendinitis."

"Does Fink know?"

"Does Fink know? Of course Fink knows."

"Is it bad? How bad is it?"

"Manageable," he says. He puts on a big grin.

"Also, I want twenty dollars."

"What?"

"I just want it. Give it to me."

"I don't know if I have it."

"Go check your room. I'll wait here."

I wait in the closet, thinking it's time to forgive him. I've been trying to wedge him into the bottle, to repair things between us, but it hasn't worked and I don't know why. He is my fucking son. As he moves away, his lineage is somehow reinforced, his snipped relation to me. It will take a simultaneous, matching movement and we won't allow that to happen, never at the same time when it needs to. That I feel sympathy, that objectively he deserves my sympathy for what's happened to him, just makes our decomposing friendship even more frustrating. We'll never get it back. I turn to knock something off the shelf, but stop. All of Masha's vanity products have disappeared. There's no mirror, or lipstick, or nail polish, or anything.

Linus comes back, shutting the closet door behind him and dangling the bill. "Do you agree to the terms?" I try to snatch the money but he yanks it away, and so I put my hands on him and hold his wrist still with one hand and take the money with the other. He's laughing, he's all over the place, I try to hide my smiling from him. "Come on! Mend a fence. Bury a hatchet," he says, and then takes a white napkin out of his pocket, waves it around.

"You tell Fink that I'm not going with the team to Wyoming tomorrow."

"Tell him what?"

"Tell him I'm sick, tell him whatever you want, I don't care. You also tell him to relay to Hargraves that I'm going to wrestle Kryger for 133 at Friday's practice. Is that clear?"

"Yes." I push past him and open the door. "And you'll hold up your end of the bargain? I'll need a promise."

His hand is out. This is half penance, a half confession, like asking for forgiveness without saying what should be forgiven. I take it quickly, thinking about pulling it into the doorframe and slamming it closed, but I don't.

"Good-bye!" He follows me to my room and I shut the door in his face. I turn on my desk lamp and sit down to write two letters.

First I put Linus's money together with some of the money I have hidden under my papers and stuff the cash inside an envelope and make it out to Save the Children.

For the second, I don't think much about it, just Mrs. Fink going to the mailbox and seeing an envelope addressed to her. For the ninth or tenth time, but this time the final draft, I start writing:

Dear Mrs. Fink,

I'm sure you're a lovely woman. We've never had the pleasure of meeting. I have some I'm afraid rather troubling news regarding your husband Roland Fink and a student (or students) at Oregsburg College . . .

I seal them both up.

✦

But it turns out I have no cause to send the second one. I don't have to wait long at all to see how the situation resolves itself.

It's not ever clear if it's abuse or rape, whether it was wanted or unwanted, but Linus tells them it is. Of course, in the eyes of the law, this is only secondary to the fact that the act took place repeatedly when Linus was seventeen. And so the next morning, there are two police cars parked at the doors of the gym, and as I'm walking across the parking lot, two officers come out holding Fink's arms. A third one is behind, watching. They put him in the back of a car and drive off, lights flashing but no siren. Shortly thereafter, the whole team comes out of the gym, including Hargraves. I duck behind a tree but no one sees me. They load up the vans and then drive away. When they're gone, I go inside and do my business for three hours and at the end of it stand still under the exceedingly hot water in the shower.

I mail the other letter.

✦

While we're waiting for Silas to show up, a girl, a scatter of papers on her desk, turns around to ask the room, "Does anyone know what CEO stands for?"

I jump in and answer, "Chairman of the Entire Office," and would you believe it, no one corrects me!

Silas enters, eyeballs the five of us as a mental form of taking attendance. It's become custom not to expect Pervis.

He teaches us about Charlie Parker. He tells us his nickname was Bird. When he puts on "All the Things You Are," my eyes get wet and I put my hand over my face to keep anyone from seeing.

✦

In the afternoon, I go for a long run. Down at the end of a side road, where it turns into woods, there are two hunters without orange because it's off-season, stalking woodcocks or doves or sage grouse. In one of the fields, there are four hundred women crying facedown.

✦

A purple envelope with a hundred stamps on it arrives. The card inside says in blue bubble letters puffed out like balloons "Thank You" on the outside and "For Your Thoughtfulness" inside, and at the bottom it's signed *Love, Aunt Lorraine.*

✦

The news is on in the student union. A schoolteacher named Anna Michaels was shot in the face in the staircase of her apartment building. She survives. They find the man who did it just wandering around the building, a man with no connection to her at all, whose real name is Wilson Hyde, but he plays games with the police for a few hours, telling them his name is Joey Chandelier, and when he finally cooperates and they ask him for his statement about why he did it, there's a big deal made about whether they can legally include his shrug in the official paperwork. Four days later, while the paper runs a picture of Anna, her entire head a ball of bandages, the man kills himself in his cell by swallowing a bundle of wire that takes two days to do its job. A woman from the American Association of Suicidology stands in front of a bunch of microphones and calls the whole thing a tragedy. *Suicidology* is a real word and the American Association of Suicidology is a real organization. The weapon, the TV says, was purchased recently from a local gun show.

✦

That night, the phone rings. Someone picks it up, and a few seconds later there's a knock on my door. It's Perry.

"Phone."

"Who is it?"

"He says he's your coach."

"Tell him I'm not here."

"I'm not your goddamn secretary, tell him yourself."

I walk down the hall to the phone and gently hang it up.

✦

Bird and I called people we didn't like Stinky Pete. One day, for unclear reasons, we called a spindly boy in our class Stinky Pete until a girl told us to stop, at which point we rerouted the name to her, until we were sent to the principal's, who asked us if we'd lost our minds, and I remember this very distinctly, I pictured a basket being shaken so hard its apples tumbled out. And then Bird turned to me, nodded his head in the principal's direction, and said, "That's a grade-A Stinky Pete right there."

✦

I can see all the way to the end of the line. The path goes through Kryger, Jan Gehring, four matches at regionals (three if I can get a bye), four matches at the championship. I've got my mouth on the tailpipe of fate, sucking its incense. But one step at a time, as they say. I lick the salt off an unshelled sunflower seed from my spot in the middle of Unusual Disorders, the little bag open on my desk. I put the wet desalted shells back in the bag, sometimes cracking them when I visualize Kryger's enthusiasm, how his enthusiasm can be used against him. I can't help myself. Classwise, my attention wanes and falters, but in the last five minutes I run out of seeds and join the discourse, which is about a town in Colorado that established an anonymous public hotline where people could call in and they knew their calls would be recorded, and what they found when they played the tapes back were people either crying or stoic or nervous, confessing to all kinds of atrocious, unspeakable things they did in their pasts, things they couldn't before let out of their mouths.

✦

Life is mean and short, and I'm not letting go of the wind-up promise that I have access to the championship. I am not stupid, I'm not delusional, I'm aware of the smallness of the Division IV wrestling record book. But despite its smallness, it is still permanent, and I have in my hand the pen to sign my name into it. Right here. I'm not going to forget that. After I'm dead, from time to time, maybe someone will scan through the past results and come across my name.

✦

Another abominable glorious month! Happy birthday, Grandma.

✦

I get to the gym two hours ahead of time and sit at my old locker. Patience is in the room with me. Then they start to come in, smelling of Wyoming. It is not confidence, it's certainty. In high school, when I took biology I was on top of it, when I was doing chemistry I could scrape by, but when I got to physics I could not manage, I could not learn the trajectory formulas and gravity examples. The point being: all the time, people everywhere go further and further in their capabilities, until finally they butt up against their limit. I have reached many limits, but I have not reached my limit in wrestling, I know that for certain.

Hargraves, when he sees me, walks over and kneels like a father and quietly says, "I'm sorry."

"It's o.k."

Vindication after wrongful accusation is a satisfaction so instantaneous and profound it borders on the spiritual, and when they finally let me practice, something strange happens: I don't get tired. I do the drills I've done a thousand times before. I'm let loose to legally do all of it in the light of day. Enacting a pattern with your hands, something you know how to do right and well is a source of deep pleasure. I feel weaker and out of rhythm from being out so long, but the hours of biking and running make it impossible for me to be tired. I push ahead of everyone except Kryger, who then, too, falls behind. The degree of my exertion makes a big blue vein in my wrist stick out. It doesn't do anything. It just shows itself.

I've been on the bike for the better part of a month, sitting there and watching. I've seen Kryger's new tricks, I used all this time for scouting how he goes low single leg now and goes right away.

They all form a circle, gather around the mat in their soaking shirts, some of them with their arms crossed and their faces the tired faces you always see on wrestlers. Maybe because they have their whole lives ahead of them, I get the impression that they all could take or leave what happens between me and Kryger.

"Same as always," Hargraves says. "One match, that's it."

He blows the whistle.

No surprise, with Kryger there's no surprise. He doesn't even bother to engage high but instead immediately goes low, right for my infamous knee, but it's like I've seen it all coming, a shadow of clouds on the sea, I've seen his whole vindictive personality. I've known him for four years. He comes at me and I use him against himself by ducking him, my left arm grabs across and tugs on his right triceps. I am this way because I hate losing and winning is everything. I lock him up in a cradle, turn him, and pin him. I scream in his face, "Everything you heard about me is true!" They pull him away from me. "I thank God, every single day, that I don't have to rely on any of you! If you're waiting for someone to beat me, you're not going to get it. Have a nice evening!"

I walk out of the gym. Head straight for the shower. They're all coming in as I wrap up cleaning myself. On my way out, Kryger's going in and he grips the sides of my head like a clay water jug and my towel falls off and so does his but three or four of them tackle him and he slips on the tile and when his head smacks the drain, it makes a deep noise.

I dress in a hurry. Around the corner Kryger is yelling. When I'm jamming my feet into my shoes, I make the mistake of looking up and find that Linus is staring right at me. On the chalkboard next to him, someone wrote *I am what I am. —Jesus.* The book is folded open near the end in Linus's lap. Everyone seems to give him space, a parallel phenomenon occurred when I was pushed further and further from the team because of my knee. During practice, his face was flat, he was quiet the whole time, including when he threw up in the trash can, he didn't say one thing.

He says, "Do you know when you're thinking hard, you put your fingers on your front teeth and hold them? Like this?"

I shove my possessions into my backpack. As I'm trying to quickly get out of there, he says, "Is this about having the last laugh? Is that it? Because you know, the person who thinks they're getting the last laugh is never the one who gets it, is what happens."

✦

Through my time in the library, I've gotten a handle on some poetry basics, and on Friday night back in my room, I decide to use some of my work for good. I tear out a sheet from my notes where I copied down a poem because I liked it so much. I walk it down the hall and slide it under his door. I cannot help it if my sentimentality, even if I'm not good at acting on it, prevents me from giving up those I care about, especially those like Linus, who's pulling up the carpets of our friendship. Then I walk back to my room, lock the door, and at last, sleep comes to Stephen Florida, like a parcel of good news.

✦

First thing Saturday morning, I make an appointment at the career center. The earliest they can get me in isn't until February 16, the day after the mental doctor's appointment.

✦

As they're filing in for practice, I make sure to stand next to Linus so we're paired up for warm-ups. He knows what I'm doing but doesn't move away. When we start, I put my hands on him, stretch his arms for him, I'm close, hear his nose breathing near my ear, and it's there again, my attachment, like I knew it would be, it never really goes away because I have a weakness for him, my hands on his shoulders, he's been mine for a year, what's more is more, and when I take my palm away from his collar, it's covered in his sweat.

With Fink gone, small cracks of disarray begin. Hargraves brings his new adopted shelter schnauzer to practice. The whole time it barks and pisses in the corners, and then while Hargraves is making a speech, it walks over to Lee and begins fervently humping his leg, looking up into his eyes, as if asking him a question.

Hargraves stops practice right in the middle and demands a plank competition. The whole team is spread out over the mats, and Hargraves walks between the rows and occasionally kicks his foot underneath someone to see if there's enough space. One by one, they drop out. After seven minutes, it's just Linus, Kryger, Ucher, and Stephen Florida. Ucher drops out at eight minutes. Kryger drops out. Hargraves yells at me, "Florida, why you smiling? You just happy to be in my company? I wanna know because I wanna smile like you." Will is primary, instinct is secondary, intellect is after that. Talent is somewhere below that. My sabbatical has made me rusty but day after day of eating the dirt has pushed my will further, and that is more than a sum gain, far more. Linus quits at eleven minutes.

After the dog has tripped us during sprints, Hargraves blows his whistle. "Goddamnit, all of you make me sick! I want someone to show me something. I want two of you space monkeys right here, in this circle." On the opposite side of the crowd from me is Linus. He's looking at me. "Right now!" Hargraves says. And what is in the look is a challenge, it's without a doubt an invitation to get in there with him so we can see who's better. I start to step forward.

"I'll do it," says Kryger, and then, right after, Ucher says, "I'll go." Hargraves looks disappointed, you could see his disappointment from space, but he puts his whistle in his mouth, and we all stand there and watch some mediocre wrestling.

"Now buddy carries," Hargraves says.

Kryger, who is my weight, jumps on my back. I carry him up the bleacher steps. I'm expecting him to pinch my ears or utter a streak of curses, but he's entirely silent, as if I'm carrying an animal. I've been around Kryger for a while now, and though he'll never beat me, he'll never work as hard as I do or want it as bad, I don't not respect him. I don't dwell and he's never been much to me, but he's probably the third-best wrestler on the team and I probably have him to thank a little for pushing me.

But I'm not sorry I extinguished his career, I'm not sorry about anything.

Ahead of me, Linus carries Slim John Carpenter. I can smell him. Whenever the two of us walked on campus and passed school security, every single time and for no reason, Linus would lean over and mutter, "Be cool, just fucking be cool, all right?" and would look at his fingernails and do that thing where you buff them on your shirt. Linus climbs the bleachers quickly and lets out a quivering fart.

After practice, in the locker room, Hargraves delivers a second speech, which is on hardship and is somewhat a continuation of the first speech, and which ends with a description of Jupiter's Great Red Spot.

After Hargraves leaves, dragging the dog out by the leash, Slim John Carpenter waits a few seconds and then says to everyone, "Is it just me, or is Coach's personal life a dumpster fire?"

But then Farrow, who maybe we forgot was still in the room, says, "Hey, cool it."

A few of them, Whitey and Young William and Jerry, realize Elder William is taking a really long time in the shower and ransack his locker and hide all his clothes. When Elder William walks out dripping in a towel, he stops in front of his empty locker and says, "Now, what the fuck is this?" Then Jerry runs by behind him and smacks a palmful of newly shaven hair bits onto Elder William's wet shoulder, where they stick. "Elder, you got your merkin all wrong!" Whitey says, but Elder William tiredly sits down, his tiredness comes from a deep, old place. "I'm going to beat the bottoms of your feet," he says. And Whitey says, "What's that? You don't get dressed, you're gonna be late for parliament, you old fag!"

As I'm putting my shoes in my bag, Linus says, "Did you write that poetry?" He's standing at my locker with his coat on.

"No, it wasn't me."

"It was good, I thought."

"Robert Frost is who wrote it."

"Well, are you trying to seduce me with his poetry? If you're trying to show me you've changed, you're doing a good job, I'm ready to take my underwear off for you, I'm ready to marry you, if only you'd ask."

"If only."

A few months ago, around Halloween, he asked, "What percentage of the world do you think limps?" Students were already walking around in their costumes and we were running to the goiter tree.

"Fifteen percent."

"I was exactly going to say fifteen percent."

It had never occurred to me that someone could be selfish about certain things and not about others.

✦

A few hours later, another lesson happens when I open my door and find the muddy gorilla mask slid inside, the one I wore to the Carver farm, the one the goat kicked off, with a paper note jammed in it that says *Do you think I forgot.* The lesson is that this is a part of my life now, that it won't ever really go away, that it just drifts into the background temporarily. I incorporate the fright into my life, just like everything else. I leave the mask on the floor because it's another symbol and as much a part of my life as the crutches under my bed and the green notebook hidden in my desk, I can't get rid of them. I just lock the door and don't sleep, though how much of it is because of Garnes and how much is because of the mask on the carpet is unclear.

✦

On Sunday morning, while I'm washing my hands in the bathroom, I notice my fingernail's fallen off.

✦

When you try to talk to God you don't get him, instead you just get a sniveling little assistant who says he'll relay your question and who goes around the corner for thirty seconds and reports back what he says God whispered in his ear, but you know that's not what he's done, there's no one around the corner, he just stood there and counted off a reasonable time. As you know, that's what religion is.

✦

In the afternoon, when I'm folding my underwear in the laundry room, I spot the crossword book facedown by the trash can. Flipping through it, in a variety of red and blue and black inks, all five hundred puzzles, which get steadily more difficult, are completed. The last puzzle, which looks like it has a coffee stain on it, has the clue "Thoreau's Germanic ideal." In the puzzle, the person filled in *Waldeinsamkeit.*

✦

After it gets dark, I take my flashlight and stagger out onto Egg Lake. I'm a coward again because I have something to lose. That's my policy. I'm a coward again and I'm practical. I locate the hole the pistol went down, which luckily someone's been reusing. I take the mask out of my sweatshirt pocket and shove it in. It doesn't want to sink at first, and I have a panic moment watching it float, but then when it finally does, I immediately think of Mary Beth, and the feeling is maybe astonishment, or between that and the nameless feeling that inspires you to crawl along the floor, grasping for the unutterable. I think what no one else can: that Mary Beth is the one thing beyond wrestling that hasn't toppled over, that I keep going back to her in my mind and it never once disappoints or reflects false light, that I lose my grip on everything else, but not her.

✦

A few hours before the Jan Gehring match, I walk to the gym and search the training room until I find the athletic directory. I call the phone number for Roland Fink, and Mrs. Fink answers.

"Hello?" The baby is crying in the background. "Sorry, can you call right back?"

The line goes dead. I listen to the dial tone, find out what comes after the dial tone. I keep getting my ethics policy and moral policy mixed up. I dial the numbers again.

"Hello. Sorry about that. How can I help you?"

"Is this Mrs. Fink I'm speaking to?"

"Yes?"

"Mrs. Fink, I'm with the Oregsburg College Administrations Department. I was just calling to confirm you and your husband's address? Can you confirm it?"

"Is something the matter?"

"Nothing at all, ma'am! Just keeping the records current. Can you confirm your address?"

"Seventy-seven Maytime Drive."

"Thank you, and this would be the Aiken zip code?"

"Correct." The baby suddenly starts crying again.

"Thank you, that's the address we have on file. Have a great day, Mrs. Fink."

"You, too. Good-bye."

I put the green notebook in an envelope with a bunch of stamps and mail it.

✦

Pretty soon they start coming in. I can hear the Garnes people outside the locker room. They have a chant about falcons that's probably meant to stir up intimidation. The big hullabaloo in here is that Hargraves wants Ucher at 149 because Elder William is home with a tension headache. So he drags Ucher around like a rag doll from the stationary bike to the showers and back again, weighing him between to gauge the progress. Ucher has less than thirty minutes to cut 2.6 pounds. Seeing that they're not going to make it, they bring the bike into the shower room. Hargraves takes off his clothes down to his briefs and goes in there with him. He has Whiting put up a plywood board and block in the shower entrance, and then he turns all the showers on full heat. On the other side of the board, through the whishing water sounds you can hear Hargraves screaming at Ucher. "You made a deal, son. You made a deal. What can I do to get through to you, son?"

I put my singlet on. Jesus Christ. I welcome the nausea and finger the curled Friedrich card before placing it back in my shoe. When they all file out to the gym, I go into the bathroom and slam the stall door behind me and slap my face until I'm satisfied. I head out with no warm-ups on. As soon as I enter the gym, I feel all the eyes in the stands on my knee, the special type of judgment-based attention, a feeling of being watched that I haven't felt to this degree since high school, when I got over the exhibition of my bulge to the spectators, when I finally stopped thinking about my body.

I have an early draw. Linus gets the one before me. I pace around the fringe of the mats. Anyone who tells you wrestling is a team sport is telling you a lie. Anyone who tells you you tried your best after you lose is telling you a lie.

Linus and the kid he's facing line up for the match. Just before it starts, Linus does something strange. Jumping up and down, standing on the edge of the circle, he raises his hand and puts his middle finger and pointer to his temple and flicks his thumb, as if firing a trigger. Sweat pours down his face like water, dangling from his eyelashes, and he is looking right at me. Then the match starts and he pins the Garnes 125 in under two minutes. Watching what he does to him is like watching a ritual sacrifice. It's so quiet it's uncomfortable. At the end, after the pin is called but before he lets go, he says something distasteful into the kid's ear and the kid tries to take a swing at him, but Linus is already walking off the mat, and when he passes by he smacks my butt.

When I walk onto the mat, I tug my straps and set my headgear, bend my head back. Though she does not want to be seen, though she's sitting in the back corner of the gym's bleachers with a Twins hat and sunglasses on, I recognize Mrs. Fink, and I feel a flickering strangeness in my body, something similar to what the voice of Aunt Lorraine or Topaz caused.

I'm ready to face Gehring because I've been under the assumption that I would face him the whole time. I stare at his face across the mat. I find plenty of flaws in Jan Gehring, know exactly what to do. I don't need to rehearse. I'm ready to go.

They give me Jan Gehring and this is what they get. You give me a fragile toy and I'm going to break that bitch.

The moment I put my hands on him, it all comes back. My injury leaves like the red curse. It's like how you forget what the zoo smell is, that all zoos smell the same, but then you walk past the ape enclosure. As the scouting report said, he tries to hand fight, but I slap him away and shoot low four seconds in and hook and drop to the outside of his left leg and as he's falling forward, I step over to his right leg from behind and drive, and we fight for who knows how long, him trying to push me off like I have raging lupus and he's disgusted. I've had to get used to the sourness of losing but goddamnit I'll never get tired of winning. He gets his right leg out, and I make note to attack his left from now on, and he wiggles out and his knee catches my chin and closes my mouth like a cupboard, but we're not going to be patient because that's what he wants, so I duck under his graspings, going again for his left leg, getting his right, too, despite him wishing I wouldn't, he's right back where he was before, and this time he's pushing at the cups of my headgear with more desperation and worrying, which is good, and I climb up his body like a beetle, I pin his sides like I'm packing him up for the coffin, I pressure his head and force it to the mat, and beyond him the referee squats to watch the angles, I push his far shoulder like I'm crowbarring open Tut's tomb or I'm Lazarus moving aside the rock for the big reunion, but it still won't touch the mat, then Gehring makes a sound like something's about to happen he doesn't want to, and so I push until his shoulder sinks, brushes the mat, and then the ref calls it. The display clock has the pin at 2:46.

I get my hand raised and start toward the exit. In the direction of the Garnes section, I yell, "I waited months for this and this boner is the best you can do?"

When you get older, I guess you learn the importance of flowers and good food and old friends. That's called settling down. But I don't need to be old to know that to look back and realize you didn't push yourself for something you loved is the greatest regret you can have. I can already sense what that'd feel like. I suppose I would marry her, and we would be honored to be the other's widow. Someday she will help slip on my socks while I sit on the edge of the bed with calcified hips. A lifetime and at the end, guaranteed silent trips to hospitals, hoping for the best over and over. I try to get a reaction out of Mrs. Fink so I blow a kiss in her direction, but she's very far away and she has her hand over her mouth, like something's upset her. "Louise! I put your murderous husband in jail!" I yell, but the buzzer screams over the entire gymnasium, inciting the next match.

Just this once it'll be something great, something that starts to be remembered right after it happens.

There is no real Stephen Florida. I am only a giant collection of gas and light and will.

AT THE LAST MINUTE, because I want it to go well, or maybe because I know it won't, I stop in the bathroom in the middle of the hall and put a red flower-print Kleenex in my nice shirt pocket, a makeshift pocket square. Tidying up my outfit. I've never had a pocket square before! I dab my face with some cold water. I don't want to be here, but I walked all the way over. Then I go into the office of Dr. Cynthia Barnes for our appointed meeting, much of which I forget as soon as it happens.

"I'm not taking any drugs. Just so we're clear."

"It's not within my bounds to prescribe you any. I've been looking forward to our conversation. I think we can help each other out."

"I'm not sure I like this. This is a very nice office."

"That's O.K., that's not uncommon. You're a wrestler?" She gently touches her own pristine, delicate ear, which is like a seashell. The kind the crab picks first.

"I mean, that's not super hard to figure that out. Sorry, that was rude. So you know all about me?"

"I know what you chose to put on the diagnostic paperwork."

"I don't even remember what I wrote on that thing."

"First, can you put your suicide in perspective for me? How strong is your urge?"

"I'm not sure I understand."

"In your paperwork you indicated suicidal thoughts. As in,

would you carry a metal pole in a lightning storm? Ride in a shaky prop plane? Minor cutting?"

As though on a postcard, I can picture the pistol in the silt and marl at the bottom of Egg. "You don't sound like a psychiatrist."

"I'm not, I'm a psychologist."

One could conclude from her alternatingly receptive and poking demeanor that she gets pleasure from controlling the tone and direction of her conversations in this room, and probably also outside it. If she weren't so smart and pretty and perceptive, I'd say she was a cactus of a woman.

"Fine. What are your thoughts on Wilhelm Fliess?"

"Do you feel angry at other people?"

"I don't feel much for most people. What are your thoughts on Wilhelm Fliess?"

"Why not?"

"Don't get me wrong, I don't believe I'm one of those bored psychopaths. I just don't feel like I have much in common with other people."

"Why not?"

"Most people, I think, don't work hard enough." I work harder for this one thing than almost anyone works in their life. I work harder than a therapist, and almost say so, but my manners are improving. "I have little pity for anyone. Actually, I have pity for the poets. The poets have it rough."

"Is wrestling your only outlet?"

I picture *outlet* as a tremendous gutter pipe at the back of a nuclear plant, dumping out gallons of waste every minute. "No."

"What's the worst thing you can think of?"

I think about it for a second. "Alzheimer's."

"And is suicide something you think about because it would prevent Alzheimer's from ever happening to you?"

"Well, I'd rather be dead than not be able to remember things, if that's what you mean. If you forget everything, you're not really you, are you?"

"I want you to do me a favor and take this. I prepared it for our meeting today. It's a case study of someone who showed similar tendencies as you. I want you to read it and tell me if you see yourself in it. Here."

"The last thing I want to do right now is read this stupid paper."

"Why did you say earlier that you wouldn't take any medicine?"

"Taking medicine is like lying."

"Why?"

"It tricks you into thinking things are fine, when you can see with your own eyes when you're off the medicine that things aren't fine."

"Have you been getting enough magnesium in your diet?"

"Why does everyone keep asking me that!"

"All right, no need to make this a shouting match. That's it, please sit back down. Are you calm?"

"Yes."

"Let's try a game. Close your eyes."

"O.K."

"How many buttons are on my jacket?"

"One hundred and fourteen."

"I can see you're not taking this very seriously."

"What?"

She looks right at my pocket square. "You know what I'm talking about, this mocking attitude. There's a napkin in your shirt."

"But I'm not mocking! I dressed up!"

"I'm not upset. Don't worry about hurting my feelings. You could never do that. I think what this is, it comes from the same place that enjoys being challenged. Maybe you don't find this challenging. You like to be challenged?"

"Well—"

"When an obvious obstacle is not in your way, you go find one and put it there."

"Well—"

"I've seen this before. Some people need to be challenged. It's not a bad thing."

"O.K. But I'm not retarded, I've read about psychology. I know I, sort of, need competition because it's a way to disprove my lack of selfness."

"In the end, what it breeds is a life of expectation. Yes?"

"Man, you are really giving me the fifth degree."

"Yes?"

"Yes."

"Mm. What are you going to do after you graduate?"

"I don't know."

"Have you been to the career center?"

"I'm going tomorrow."

"That's great, but I'm going to go ahead and make an appointment at the career center for you for later today. You need to get your life going. I think it will help you to get going right away. Right now."

"Oh, I don't know—"

"I've seen your kind before, if you'd take a look at this case study, you'd see that your problems are not once-in-a-lifetime, that you're not alone, that many people before you have fixed exactly what you're struggling with. Take this paper with you. I want you to go home and read it, then I want you to look at yourself in the mirror. Then I want you to read it again, and then look at yourself in the mirror a second time."

Her jacket has six buttons. "You know, you really are a wet blanket." I take the paper.

She looks into my face, as if deciding whether to let this go a certain direction. "Someone called me that once before."

"Oh yeah? What happened?"

"It was the only time I threw a drink in someone's face."

In the time it takes me to walk down the long hallway, she's apparently buzzed in ahead of me, because as I pass by, her assistant at the front desk says, "Mr. Florida, I've just spoken with the career center. I have the following time arranged for you there." He hands me a slip of paper. "In the meantime, Dr. Barnes would very much like to make a second appointment, she feels strongly you have more to discuss." But I'm already at the door, and he's repeating my name over my shoulder.

SAME SHIRT, SAME TIE for the career center meeting. A middle-aged woman lets me into her office. I sit down and smile with all my teeth out because they keep putting me in front of witnesses to assess me, keep telling me to play a record, but they only want to hear one record and so I put that on for them.

"I hope first names are good for you. Gina," she says.

She pops open a can of Fresca (it's nine thirty in the morning). A scuba noise as she drinks from it. There's a picture on her desk, facing the invisible line between us, of her and her man indoors on a couch in identical white hats with a little blue button on top.

"I like your tie."

Her office is decorated more or less with the same uniqueness that actually amounts to blandness. I stare into the open mouth of the soda can. We will now have a sustained discourse.

"So, what can I do for you?"

"Well, I was hoping you could help me."

"With what, exactly?"

"Um . . ."

"Say no more, the deluxe package. I've seen your type before, it's O.K. Is that your transcript?"

I hand it over. She tilts her head back, pouring the Fresca in, the whole time looking down her nose and reading my report. She finishes both at the same time. "I see you're on track with a liberal arts degree. That's good. Lots of options. What do you think you might like to do?"

"I'm not really sure."

"No problem." She drops the can in the garbage and then leans over and goes through a drawer on her side of the desk. "What we like to do in this situation is show this sheet. It's a list of potential career tracks. The whole initial appeal of liberal arts is it gives you all these choices." She slides a piece of paper across the desk. "What I want you to do is put a mark next to all the professions you find interesting."

I do. When I'm done, the paper looks like this:

REAL ESTATE
X TRAINING SPECIALIST
LEGISLATIVE ASSISTANT
PUBLIC RELATIONS
JOURNALISM
NONPROFIT ORGANIZATIONAL DIRECTOR
ENTRY-LEVEL MANAGEMENT PERSONNEL
RECRUITER
HUMAN RELATIONS OFFICER
MINISTER
POLICY ANALYST
GENEALOGY STUDIES
POLITICIAN
RECEPTION
ADVERTISING ACCOUNT EXECUTIVE
MEDICAL COMMUNICATIONS TRAINER
URBAN PLANNER
LOBBYIST
GRANT WRITER
SPEECH WRITER
POLICY ANALYST

ANCHORPERSON

X HOTEL MANAGEMENT

X MUSEUM MANAGEMENT

X ARCHIVIST

"Policy analyst is on here twice," I say.

"I know," she says, snatching the paper. "Let's see what we've got. Why don't you tell me about why you marked the ones you did."

"Can I see?"

"Sure."

"Well, in terms of training specialist, I feel like I am a good leader at things. I have been a wrestler here at Oregsburg for four years now and believe I lead with my examples. I am good with details because I pay attention to them. I think I would be an asset to any company in keeping their own employees in line, and making sure it's a tight ship."

"O.K., and what about these other ones?"

"Hotel management and museum management, I just like hotels and museums. I have been to the Petrusse Art Museum numerous times. I recognize the value of art and would be interested in preserving it."

"And this last one, archivist?"

"Isn't that just like a librarian? I have spent a lot of time in the library here, furthering my studies. But I've also been in there even when I had no assignments! As with art, I believe books are to be preserved."

"I'm glad you have a positive forward outlook on possible careers, Stephen, it's very good. I can put some feelers out for you. But I'm going to be honest. Your grades are not going to be of real help to you. I've been doing this for twenty-four years and believe me, I've seen your type before. It's nothing to be worried about. I'll tell you what I'm going to do. My nephew Shane works up in the oil fields, have you thought about that for a career? I can give him a call and he can show you around. We could start there. You have some options, I just want you to explore and find the best one for you."

"Thank you."

"Look, I know being a roughneck probably isn't—"

"No, it sounds nice, thank you."

"There are a hell of a lot of positives."

"O.K., thank you."

NEPHEW SHANE DRIVES VERY FAST. While he diddles with the stick, I mentally fill out the North Regional 133 bracket, which I copied down before leaving and stuck in my non–Mary Beth shoe. He lights a cigarette and tosses the pack onto the dash, next to a green glove and two socks. For most of the three-hour drive, we've been under a silence he insisted on. He turned the radio to the country station and the whole time, his hand has either been down his pants or holding a cigarette. Somewhere west of Stanley on Route 2, I stopped recognizing what I saw out the window.

"The foremost thing I want to stress to you has real importance. You can make a lot of money."

"How much?" The fields here are not like regular Oregsburg fields, they don't appear to have a function. Some are full of gravel. But then I see: a sign for residential development in one plot, and then another, and then in the next one what looks like a house for phantoms. A grand building uterus, rectangle holes for future windows, blowing Tyvek.

"You work twelve-hour shifts. Two weeks on, one week off. Plus you get a daily living allowance if you're living in a Junette camp, which I am. I could buy anything I wanted. I'll put it this way: I could buy antiques. I could buy a Japanese sword. The work's not going to slow down for a long time, either. You know that much about oil?"

"I saw the James Dean movie as a kid."

"You have a lot of testosterone running around here, a lot of competition. You find your friends, you know, but there's not so much compassion. Lots of weapons. If it's late and you're in a bar, you can expect a fight, cops are already waiting outside for it to get going." Shane turns down the radio, which is playing Dolly Parton. We pass through a town far larger than Aiken, with restaurants and bars, lights, general stores, and three different car dealerships. "Lots of strippers. Guys show up to work with red eyes from when they got pepper-sprayed the night before. They deserved it. You have people sleeping in their cars, people not careful with exhaust fumes and closed spaces, it was twenty-four below the other night, if you're, you know, doing the trick where you turn the heat on and off to save it up, you can fall asleep and forget to turn it off again. A lot of greedy people, bad things are going to happen. People are bad at giving up. A lot of the time they don't do it early enough. But a lot of the guys come up here for three, four, five months, trying to save some money up, get back on their feet. Then there are guys who are up here for good. People end up in a new situation, they don't act like themselves. People are animals. Men, really, is who I mean."

Then the derricks appear. Dozens of them. Across the white fields the heads of the pump jacks nod slowly, the cranes rotate. Stacks of steel pipe. Perpetual gas flares.

I can't wait to get to Kenosha. I've never met a real genius before, that's where I'll get a chance to wrestle at least a few of them. That's a gift and I'm lucky.

I have wondered dozens of times whether I have a special skill at turning the people I come across in my life into ghosts, into glass, temporary figures. I wonder sometimes if that's my backup talent. Maybe someday one of them will look me up.

"We're close," he assures me, and we stop at a gas station.

While he fills the tank, I stretch my legs. I walk to the edge of the pavement and stare off at the neighboring field, four rigs in scattered positions, termite mud tunnels below. Two white trucks pass each other on the road. Snow keeps coming down on my head. Behind the rigs and their holes, I see the willful, inarticulate loneliness. It leans its head around the edge to see if you've spotted it. Every time you turn to face an oil field, you feel something was just there a moment ago but has evaporated.

Where the pavement becomes snow, there's a Honda parked with a dog, a German shepherd, leashed around the door handle. The dog picks his head off the ground, snow and dirt on his chin, and sits up but doesn't bark as I approach the fender. The backseat is cluttered all the way to the roof with junk, bits of a life or two, things you'd find at a garage sale, boxes. Both of the front seats are reclined all the way back. On the driver's side is a man and next to him is a pregnant woman, and both of them are asleep.

"You ready?" I turn around. Shane's carrying two huge bags, walking from the station store. "Toilet paper's on sale, ninety-six rolls." He jams them between us inside the truck. "This much, even if it's on sale you can't help looking like a cretin. Hey, can I ask you a question? How do you feel about your ears? Like is that something you're self-conscious about or is it dust in the wind?"

I look over the top of the toilet paper at Shane. "Dust in the wind," I say. He nods, turns, and stares straight ahead, and when he blinks, his eyes stay shut for long periods of time.

"Your aunt was a big help to me. At the college."

"Oh yeah? What's your major?"

"Liberal arts."

"That's the one with all the choices?"

"Yeah. She helped me narrow it down."

I want to get the whole story out of him, about how often she sends lost students to spend time with her nephew, the one who's straightened his life out, who's saving up thousands of dollars for no clear reason in exchange for being alone.

"Have you spoken with her about other students?"

"I don't talk to Aunt Gina too much anymore."

And then he turns off the road. We drive on a dirt track toward a towering gray derrick. Every single rig looks exactly the same. Like the head of Vladimir Lenin put up at the Pole of Inaccessibility.

He parks next to a few other trucks. I look at the various-height platforms, yellow railings, a windsock, a crane, floodlights facing every direction. He emits a theatrical sigh and takes the green glove from the dash, slipping it onto his right hand. "You are supposed to have two of these," he says. "Don't tell nobody. O.K., turn around while I get into character."

While facing away from him, looking at a shipping container with the Junette logo on it, a red elephant's head, a question arrives: Is this a lonelier person than me? Or is he simply someone who has taken loneliness to heart in a more painstaking manner? I stand there and for a moment fantasize about making up with Linus. I spit into the snow.

Shane emerges in red coveralls and a red hardhat. We walk over to stores where he rustles up the same outfit for me, handing it to me in a folded military-style stack, with a little baggie of earplugs on top. He gets a new package of gloves. "Everyone's already here. Hurry up, we're late."

The rig has more men in red suits. "There are three main rules: don't drop anything in the hole, don't put anyone else in danger, don't put yourself in danger."

"Hurry the fuck up, Shane, you prickhole!" someone yells from somewhere above, and then I realize I'm walking under a ten-thousand-pound machine and it's emitting an enormous, spaceless insect drone. I get a glimpse of one of them on what appears to be the central platform, where the good stuff happens, twenty or thirty feet up, but Shane leads us the other way, farther under.

"What's he doing up there? Those people?"

He looks at me as though I've asked what a dog looks like. "They're drilling."

"What are we doing down here?"

"My job is leasehand. There's six people per rig, all of them have different jobs. My job is to keep the rig clean and clear. We don't just all crowd around the hole. The work is hard."

In an effort to connect with him, I say, "My therapist tells me I make obstacles where there aren't any."

He coughs and says, "Put your earplugs in."

For the next three hours, we move heavy chemical bags from one side of the site to the other side, closer to the center hole. Potassium chloride, fly ash, bentonite, calcium carbonate, guar gum powder. Shane never explains why we're moving them to the new place.

"What's this do?" I say while we're carrying sacks of barite.

"It increases density, adds weight to the drilling fluid." It's obvious things will only be explained when I directly ask, but his answers are so pissy that I shut my dirty mouth.

Our meal break lasts thirty minutes. Shane eats an orange and leaves one earplug in. By the time it's over, it's already getting dark.

We clean walkways and stairways, then we clean tools to a military shine in the tool den. We move more chemical bags. While Shane poops in the portable bathroom, I eat an orange. I let the peels fall in tatters on the snow and when it's all gone I smell my fingers, which are full of perfume. We "keep an eye on things," which I take to mean the rows of motors and generators and pump displays all over the site. I enter a place of boredom and serenity, I have a hard time believing any of this. All of it seems like the vast dream of a colossus. I have a hard time believing that Nephew Shane makes his living on a rig and lives alone and just works, perpetuating a savings account for an unclear reason. The rigs look like huge props in a huge stage play with no theme and a plot where faceless people just enter an empty field and pull levers over a deep hole, and then send what they find to other faceless people who really, really want it.

They don't pay any attention to the loneliness because they feel lucky, they've been caught up in feeling lucky since they got here and they are loyal to the feeling. The premise is recent but that's what they settled on. That's that. Oregsburg is a place where it's understood a jazz teacher possibly killed his wife and a wrestling coach is in jail for what he did to the youngest and smallest person on the team, and the custodial staff is willing to engage in physical activity with students late at night. That's that. It's the same here as it is anywhere else, they accepted it immediately and have never once thought of going back on their acceptance.

We drag hoses out from under tall red tanks on the perimeter for two hours. I try to figure out what I've learned.

During the night meal break, one of them comes over and says something quietly to Shane. Shane nods, looks at me, and asks, "Are you doing all right?"

When everyone's done eating, we walk back out into the night and Shane says, "This is a light day relative because we're drilling. They've been drilling all day, up on the floor. We're going to go up there now with them. There's a problem down-hole, probably the drill bit is worn out. We have to trip pipe. That means we have to pull out all the pipe from the well and replace the bit. This could take a while. Do you understand?"

"Yes."

"This will be a lesson for you."

I lose track of time watching them under the floodlights, hearing the drone in my ears closer than ever before, the floor moving through my shoes, they do the same thing over and over, pulling segments of the pipe and disconnecting them as they emerge from the center hole and attaching them to a descending arm that pulls the pipe away. At first I'm reminded of hospitals putting those worm cameras in people's butts to check things out, but after a while (I'm not allowed to participate or even get close), I'm not reminded of anything, watching the routine repeat itself countless times turns it into something different, the purpose dissolves, the act becomes the representation of itself, the same way reading a whole book in Sanskrit if you're not Sanskrit has nothing behind it, the way you stare at a shut curtain and imagine the actors getting into place on the other side. When they finally reach the end of the line, they inspect the drill bit, which looks like a deep-sea-life cluster, three huge oysters stuck together. A few of them shake their heads. I look at Shane for a reaction, but I can tell from his still face that he's in a glazed state of mind.

Someone touches my shoulder. I turn around, and there's three or four other men in red Junette suits. The new shift crew.

He tells me to go wait in the truck while he changes out of the dirty coveralls. A few minutes later he comes jogging up without a coat on, only a white T-shirt with black splotches on his neck and wrists. In the truck, he immediately lights a cigarette, then he says, "Before we go, there's porno in one of the lockers in the stores if you want."

"No, I'm O.K."

"Don't be embarrassed. All of those guys in there? They want you to think they're really great fathers but they're all just furiously jacking off all the time."

"I'm not embarrassed."

The drive is very short. He only says one thing the whole way: "Do you consider yourself a spiritual person?"

Though I don't want to answer, I feel like I don't have a choice. "I'm not opposed to the idea, but in my life I've had zero mystical awakenings."

It's dark and there are few lights, but soon there's a pattern of repeating trailers alongside the unplowed road, which we bump over slowly. The same square cell of a house, a number in red next to the front door. There are so many houses, they're divided into blocks and the numbers reset after twenty. Shane turns the truck onto one of the dirt roads. In one out of every seven or eight houses, lights are on. Shane's window is part of the way down for his cigarette but there's no noise, no overloud TVs or other motors. It had never crossed my mind that most of the units could be unoccupied. Shane says, "This is it," and points the nose of the truck at the wood steps to his door. His house is the same as the ones on either side, except those are empty.

He pulls out a rifle from under his seat. "If you want to wait inside the key's under the mat."

"What's that for?"

"I've had some coyotes coming around. I just want to check around back."

I don't move, because I don't want to go into his weird house by myself, so I sit in the passenger seat with the toilet paper leaning on me and watch out the windshield as he creeps around the side of the house. I look down the empty road, listening for the gunshot I'm fifty percent sure is coming. I tell myself that I'm not being led through the steps of this experience, but that I'm a living person who chose this and who's been around for two decades and that this is just something new and that it will, like everything else, have little effect on what comes after for the rest of my life, until I'm dead. I try not to be edgy about why I can't picture what's inside the house or how he's moving around in the dark with a rifle. Then he reappears and opens the door and puts the rifle back in its place. "Come on, it's cold as shit. Leave your shoes on the mat."

Shane's place is mostly one large main room. I eyeball the dimensions, and my first thought, though it's unintended and sudden, is, could this place support my family? Would I even have a family if I ended up in a place like this?

I hesitate at the doorway. He laughs. "Your Excellency is troubled?"

There are stacks of newspapers all over the floor. The one nearest me has a paper from last October on top. A mainly empty bookshelf, except for a row of books by R. Austin Freeman, wedged into one corner. A television that looks like it could never possibly work. Two pieces of furniture: a couch and a recliner. There's an unmarked, rumpled paper bag on the ground between the couch and the wall. Something smells like moist cook stink. The stains all over the thin beige carpet look like clouds or footprints. He turns a light on next to the couch, which is dark purple leather, and carries the toilet paper into the kitchen.

"Couch is where you'll be. Over there's the bathroom. I got extra covers in the closet, that's the door next to the bathroom. Here. And on this side is the kitchen and my room. Self-explanatory." On the largest wall is the kind of art you see in a nameless hotel where crime drifts through on a regular basis. It's a panoramic watercolor of a woodsy lake at dawn, but it's enormous, maybe twenty feet long. It's very cold in the house.

"Do you feel tired?"

"Yes."

"Good. That means you did it right. Mostly, I come home and take the edge off, then sleep. Take a seat, make yourself at home." He walks into the kitchen.

I do what people do in the movies, which is study the spines of the books. Aside from the Freeman batch, there's nothing, except three shelves lower, by itself, an extremely thick book with a white spine called *The Original of Man*. I slide it out. On the cover is a photograph of an ape looking out from behind a thick tree branch. I can't find an author name anywhere. The back of the book says: "The diary of the prophet Mels through the greatest events of the premodern world. Now with expanded events surrounding the prehuman existence of Jesus Christ."

I turn to the back: it's 1,344 pages. Then I flip to somewhere in the middle, to a random page.

> *Under the warm yellow glow of the lamp, two butch queers were taking turns sodomizing each other on the far side of the room. Another hairless man masturbated while watching them. This was alongside the eunuch he had stabbed, over and over. The candlelight licked their luminous skins. Everything smelled of turmeric. He took his eyes away from all of them and gazed down at the slave mistress. In his ears he thought he could still hear the dripping from the cut pig, the fat one the kohanim wouldn't touch. Over the sounds of the pained moaning in the room he could also hear the Hivite crowd outside. The city was full of pregnant whores. "Perhaps I shall destroy the Pharisees with my semen," he said to the girl, inspired by how enthusiastically she lapped up every drop of his semen while passionately sucking his penis with her mouth. "It would be a curse on them,*

would it not? I am a pagan." And then the slave bitch tried to say something but he ejaculated hard into her mouth. He laughed at her while she continued to play with herself rabidly between her legs. He looked around to make sure the other slave whores were watching for what he was about to do next, and then he took from under

I slam the book shut and jam it back on the shelf. He comes out of the kitchen with two cups. He walks up to me and hands me one. There's something brown and brown-smelling in it.

"In a man camp, mainly the rules are no alcohol, no women, no drugs, no visitors. At least that's in principle." He puts his mouth on his cup and swallows.

"I was just looking at that book you have over there."

"I've never read anything like it," he says. "I'll have to let you borrow it sometime."

"I don't mean to be uncourteous. Don't take this the wrong way. I don't drink any of that stuff."

"All right," he says, grabbing the cup from me, then he walks back into the kitchen with both of them. I hear something bang, he slams something. When he comes back out, his hands are empty.

"Do you want to shower first or should I?"

He sits on the couch with his cup. "You go first, there's towels and soap and shit in there."

I take clean clothes from my bag and go into the bathroom. It's exactly the size of two coffins. It's cleaner than expected. I sit on the toilet but only pee. Then I stare at myself in the mirror for two or three minutes. I don't open the medicine cabinet. Then I pull open the shower curtain and on a hook in the tiles, there's a gorilla mask, the hook curving through the left eye hole.

I walk out of the bathroom. "What is that? Why do you have that in there?"

"What?"

"That mask in there."

"What's wrong? It was my roommate's kid's. His kid was a little gorilla for Halloween and he kept it around here. Don't ask me why, he was weird and I didn't know him."

I shower. All the grit and stick from the rig comes off. The hot water runs out quickly, but even after it's done, I stand under the water in order to shorten the amount of time I have to spend with him. I do not let my thoughts address why I'm uncomfortable. I swallow cold water from the shower head until I'm not thirsty anymore.

When I exit the bathroom, the first thing I notice is my bag's moved closer to him on the couch. "I just left the towel on the floor in there, is that O.K.?"

"Yeah, no problem, I'm just getting the edge off."

I'm standing behind him and can only see the back of his head.

"Can I have a thing of water?"

He goes into the kitchen and comes back with one cup, clearly the same one he handed me before.

"Thank you."

There are black specks suspended in the water. He goes to his bedroom and turns the light on, gets something, and closes the bathroom door behind him.

I go over to the recliner. I can hear the shower water. I become nervous about what's in the paper bag between the couch and the wall. Standing up, I nudge it with my foot. It slumps over. Then I open it up. Inside, there's a pile of old hamburgers.

While he's in the bathroom, I do sit-ups and push-ups alternating until I'm spent. Then, breathing hard, I sit in the recliner and take out the regional bracket. I'm in the top half of the bracket with a mid-seed, the lowest-ranked seed to get a bye in the first round. On the other side of the bracket is Joseph Carver and Jan Gehring. I'm going to have to wrestle Marty Marion in my second match, the one-seed, a pasty, volatile junior from Standberg who's finished fifth and fourth the last two years at 133.

When I hear a car approaching, I sit up straight and listen, I wait for it to pass by.

He comes out of the bathroom in only underwear. Down the middle of his torso, there's a vertical line of black letters. He turns off the brightest lamp in the room, so the only light is a reading lamp between the couch and the recliner.

"What's it say?"

He sits down on the couch, on the end close to me. "Latin. 'Let not your heart be troubled.'"

But it doesn't say that. I look up into the stucco ceiling, try to take comfort in the bumps and dots, but find none. He's made it darker in the room. I can hear his breathing. It's very cold in the house, I have the feeling he messed with the thermostat when I wasn't paying attention. I try to put out of mind that I don't know him very well and that I've never taken Latin before but I know "cor" is the word for "heart" and that's not anywhere in the letters on his chest.

"Do you have a girlfriend?" I ask.

"There's not a lot of girls out here. Some drivers, some work on the rigs. I don't know how they do it, it's hard enough if you're not white, imagine being a woman. They don't go out after dark. There was a teacher here, the other week she went jogging, they found her sneaker in a ditch. It's a real problem."

My attempt to keep focused on the ceiling ends, I bring my head down and my eye catches something in the corner: a huge waterless fish tank. The car outside goes by again, and I'm sure it's the same one.

"What's that for?"

"I'm saving up for an octopus. I read a thing in a magazine. It said they're cannibals. I read about a female that after mating wrapped her arms around the male and closed off his mantle, where he takes in his oxygen, and then carried him back to her den."

"I didn't know you could have one here."

"It's allowed. You need a one-hundred-eighty-gallon. I'm going to get two for the tank there."

I realize Shane might be a more disturbed person than I thought. And gradually, a thought comes over me that turns my stomach: there hasn't been a long line of lost students invited up here, that I'm the first, that I'm the only student he's brought back to his house.

Just then, over his shoulder in his bedroom, the lights shut off.

"The lights just went off in your room."

"I have them on a timer."

I think how many thoughts I've had in the past month that've turned out to be incorrect. I discard the image that's forming of Shane in his house reading *The Original of Man* while an octopus silently floats around the fish tank in his living room.

"You're by yourself?"

"Yeah, most everyone comes out here by themself. I had a roommate, he was here until about a week ago, his name was Hector, he would travel during his week off, go see his kid. I guess he couldn't do it anymore, I don't know." That's when I hear the thump, coming from his bedroom, but I pretend I don't, pretend I'm relaxing and not paying attention. I can feel him looking at me, and I try to forget that he's not wearing a shirt and it keeps getting colder.

"Are you sure we're alone?"

"I already said it to you. It's odd. I don't know, sometimes you get to wondering."

"Wondering about what?"

"About what happens to you when you get left alone for so long. As a person, you begin to change. Sometimes I've been so angry I thought I couldn't go to work. I don't feel like myself sometimes."

"You mean like thoughts?" There's something behind the back of my chair with its jaw hanging open.

"Yeah, I've had some thoughts, bad ones. I've had . . . once or twice . . ."

There should be at least the sound of traffic or the wind, but there's nothing, and suddenly it's very dark and I sit still and don't move, hoping what's at the end of the sentence is not what I think it is.

He is looking right at me.

"Once or twice what?" I say quietly.

His chest fills with air and he sighs. "Just a few times," he says, breathing faster. "It gets . . . bad."

I don't move my eyes or make any noise, but what seems to have bobbed up near the surface has gone back down again. I dance around it and take delicate steps.

"I understand this is very hard."

"It is, very hard."

"I can see it."

He stands up and rubs his face. "I think we should go to bed, O.K.?"

"O.K.," I say. We both stand up. "In one of my classes we talked about how octopuses will do self-cannibalism."

He goes over into his room and slams the door.

I walk outside, down to the end of the unfinished block. Either something's moving around the settlement or it's completely empty. I can't tell. I can't make anyone feel better. I can't make myself better or any of them. I forget the name of the town I'm in. I forget where I am geographically in relation to anything I've encountered before. Then I remember.

In the dark, straight past the gravel road and the huge plot of grass under snow, is a potato field, and standing in the middle of it is a giant.

Then when it gets too cold, I walk back and lie down on the couch, and probably would've been too frightened to sleep if I wasn't so tired or if I was afraid that kind of thing could ever really happen to me.

THE TRUTH IS I've barely come up for air. I got my teeth fixed at the dentist. I sat through the lectures and took down some notes. It wasn't anything. What is life but one prolonged, serious push? I read the papers. I read about the bizarre weather that's coming, clouds and fronts meshing strangely above Alberta, and then I read about the Junette disaster that killed five of six on one of the rigs. It happened because they got ahead of themselves. I didn't read the follow-up stories, I didn't want to find out if Shane was one of them. When I was a dumb little child I didn't think anything cost more than one hundred dollars. My mom bought me a thick, expensive winter coat and I couldn't believe it. I remembered that a week ago, that feeling, so I bought a new coat in New Rockford, I went there just because I had time on my hands, I took the bus an hour and got off and bought the most expensive coat they had in the store, a black coat with a fur collar, and I feel like a million dollars when I wear it. I wore it into the regionals gym outside Minneapolis with the hood up, I didn't listen to anyone, didn't listen to what Hargraves or Linus talked about on the drive here while I sat in the backseat and hummed Dolly Parton until I ran out of gas. Rudy sent me a letter about the coat but I didn't open it. The coat is the nicest thing I've ever had. Sometimes I put it onto my visage and just smell the fur. I've been thinking about my mom a lot lately. Then they call me up for my first regionals match. They run me out there for a second-rounder against a junior from Wheaton named Marv Garber, and I do away with him halfway through the second period. I've been practicing on him in my head for weeks. He's won a lot of matches, but I do away with him like a scarecrow. I wish this emptied me out better. Or that it didn't refill as quickly. There's barely time to clap before I'm off the mat and they bring up the next two, and I'm sitting back where I was before, under the bleachers, where I've been all day. I eat half a banana and scream. Two making-out teenagers are scared away down at the other end. I reach up and grab a beam and hang and pull. I can see up the ladies' skirts who choose to wear skirts in February. I do not touch their dumplings but am close enough to smell the verbena fragrance, then I drop back down and rub my front against the wall. Frottage. No one sees. When I hear them announce the Marion-Worthington match, I emerge like some kind of woods troll and stand off to the side. I watch Marion build up a 7–2 lead on Worthington through a period and a half, but Worthington blows forward for Marion's leg and in the process Marion's shin gets caught under and bends the wrong way to the side, the leg going from an *I* to a crooked *L*. It's how it goes. I watch him try to cover it up, I watch them stop the match and give Worthington the win and haul Marion out of the gym crying. Then I return under the bleachers. I pass time by eating small nibbles and making myself sweat. I think of my dad, who could get angry very easily, who picked objects when there were no people around, and the one Sunday my mom and me came home and found the vacuum dismantled in the backyard and my dad, in a sweaty shirt, said, "Sorry." Joseph Carver wins to go to the semis, Jan Gehring has already lost. On the bleachers I spot a sack of Cheerios and steal it from the child, and then I write my name out with them on the hardwood. All the art I made as a kid looked like a retard did it. I don't mind, I got good at other things. I fired up a small sea monster in a kiln and painted it red and green and gave it to my mom, but how, when I gave it to her, could she not be disappointed that it was so poor? She put it on the window ledge above the kitchen sink and the paint faded in the sunshine, and as I got older I was embarrassed that it was so terrible, that it only had value to her as a representation of me, of me trying hard at something, I was embarrassed that I could only make art that was sloppy and ugly. I wish she was sitting in the bleachers, I would trade the whole crowd for an empty gym if it meant she and my dad could watch. Linus wins his semifinal, then they call me out again. I go where they tell me to, I sit through the movies they want me to watch, I learn the courses, I sleep in their hotels, and when they call me out I do my business. The strategy I go out with is what I stick to and it's two parts. The first part is to go right at him, nine times out of ten what gets you beat is you hesitate on a shot, but I go right toward him and discard the flutters of the brain, I keep shooting at him and I get his leg and then his other and he's not talking to me during, that's how I know I'm pushing him, two, then three takedowns, and one time he's too fast but so am I and I escape, but the important thing is to just keep pushing, I go high and left and right, more points, I go so fast and I look for such small signs like the transference of his weight and go after it without control, and at some point Hargraves is yelling instructions between the periods but I don't hear, I get another two points and go through him, and when he begins leading with his hands I know he's going to start trying to get back the points I've racked up by shooting, and this is when I switch to the second part of the strategy and sit back and wait for his shots, and if he gets me down I tell myself I will get out, he reaches for my leg and I don't give it to him, he dances me around the mat, and they call it for the third period and he wants top, of course he does, because I'm up so much that he needs a home run, but forcing it from top is the worst thing you can do, it's like driving under the influence, you lose sight of what you're doing because you're scared and it leads to easy escapes, and then after he knows it's all over, he just keeps trying to clutch me and I let him and this is how the match ends, 13–7. What I say to Worthington is: "My body is not to be touched by you or anyone else." I walk off the mat and stand at the edge of it while Joseph Carver wrestles the second-highest wrestler named Jim McBride and loses. I have no opinion about this. When Joseph Carver walks off past the mat, where I've stationed myself to be sure this exchange happens, he hardly looks up and doesn't recognize me, and I content myself with the washed-up fate that keeps messing up its only job, and before I go back under the bleachers I watch the 125 final, where Linus goes right at Daryl or Darren Johnston, puts him wherever he wants to put him, as though he's a piece of a tea set. He wins 14–2. When Linus finally loses, it will be to someone as aggressive as he is, who pushes directly forward, pushing aside Linus's forcefulness with his own forcefulness. I sit and wait my turn while crunching the Cheerios to wet powder. McBride is too good a wrestler to set out a trap for, so I just stare into the void. Linus comes through the beams and sits down next to me and he says, "I know what's going on. I've seen you around her place. I followed you. I think you should fess up." My head sails away. How could he have known anything? I was so careful, I thought I found Anna Michaels's apartment building without anyone noticing me, I told myself no one would catch me at Louise's manless house, studying the different wallpapers in each room, looking at the child's crib. I waited until night every time. Abruptly, Linus stands up and walks away and so it's someone else who asks me, have you ever believed you were going crazy? and I respond: Craziness is not having anything to put your behavior into. Craziness is when your behavior drops off a ledge into a canyon. I'm putting mine toward a service. I'm winning. How can I be going crazy if I'm winning? My glory flaps in the gusts like an old windsock. A few people stand up and applaud the two of us for getting all the way to the regional 133 final, and I in turn start up a clap directed toward McBride until the referee gives me a warning. We start and I put my hand on his lips. This is the only time I'm allowed to show myself, display the limit of my capability. I get five more opportunities and then no more. How many times total did Bach or even Monert get to sit down at the piano to show what he could do? Two or three hundred? It doesn't matter who you are, you only get a few chances to display yourself. I make the best of all the opportunities I'm given. McBride has a green singlet and I watch for his tries left. I know he got lucky but not against me. I strip his headgear strap down so it's slung across his eye like an eyepatch. When he tries to shoot I fend it off, and when he gets high enough for me to do it I give him a head snap because I can see it annoys him. He calls me mayonnaise boy. The whole first period passes this way and I let it, because each time he returns to a stand, I give him a head snap and he opens up so that by the time the first is over I can see he's agitated, and I smile. I start the second on bottom, and I wait to see which way he goes and when the whistle blows he tries to go under but I'm faster and I sit down on his hand and I hear him yelp because

I bend a finger or two with my tush and I squirm out for one point, but none of this looks like how I'm explaining it, trust me, it's little shivering steps fitted together like violence, which is so abstract as to be the departed past, an ambulance full of context-free furniture pieces. There's a force working in me that's stronger than I am. He's shaking his hand and mad now and coming right back after me and he goes high because I've trained him to do so, but it's like I'm thinking the same thing and can see what he's going to do before he does it, so I go just a level below him for a high crotch and his legs are apart and I get to the gold mine and lift and throw and hold him there for the rest of the period because he's not being cooperative, already down 3–0. Then they put us back together for the end, for the third, and I put my ear to his back, like I've done my whole life, and I wait for it to start and when it does, it's not like anything I've ever seen before, it moves like the pages in a book, in one direction that I follow, I latch on to him as though a part of himself he dislikes, he first gets ambitious with an attempt at a switch and then grows less ambitious and tries a sit out, and I will give him credit because he does not get tired but I've done this before, I'm in control, I have his flank and when he tips over onto his face, I hook my hands together where the authorities can't see and he screams about it but they don't catch me. Deep down, I have the sense that I was once the strangest man in Europe. My life is full of exceeding strangeness but very little nuance, as if a child could grasp it. He's good enough that he gets out eventually, but not before he's cut his own legs out from under him, so that when he tries to shoot for the last fifteen seconds his heart's gone, and when the whistle blows he perhaps doesn't hear, because he keeps trying and I tell him that it's over and he squeezes my ribs and his head drops to my shoulder, he collapses and sighs, and then the referee inserts his hands between us.

I'm going to go sit down inside my coat for a while.

I walk off the mat, look up at the bleachers. Jan Gehring and Joseph Carver are sitting next to each other like friends.

MARY BETH SENDS ME A PHOTO OF HERSELF. She's in a room with her hair up and a bunch of dolls behind her. She's wearing her mackinaw and is not smiling, and for at least five minutes I sit down and look at the picture. There's a note with it that says:

> *I looked up the qualifiers and saw your name, s. florida, it was like that, and so congratulations. It feels good to get what you always wanted. I got another job offer, manager. I'm not going to bore you with the details. I'm too sensitive to boredom. Pictured is me at the Nun Doll Museum. I couldn't think of anything else so here's this picture and congratulations.*

✦

A week of warm weather comes through, and when the snow melts, three months of trash and dog poop are exposed. The warmth fools everyone, including the bugs. I walk around at night, thinking about the bracket. Joseph Carver lost the third-place match to a senior named Pat Fisher, and they announced that Fisher, McBride, and me were named to the championship, but they don't announce the matchups until four days before. I think about how they put me on top of the red pedestal at regionals and the little metal wrestling trophy they gave me, shaped like a man.

At first the world was inauthentic, but then I became the inauthentic one, I think. Something is going to happen when the season is over, but I don't know what it is.

✦

I run into Perry in the hallway, outside the bathroom. He has a coffee can with the lid on in his hands. "What's in there?" I say, and he says he has the flu and breathed into it, canned his flu, and he's going to dump it on his ex-girlfriend.

✦

On Wednesday, they suspend all classes in Opal Hall because of a gas leak. You can smell it standing outside, moving in a playful way through the air around the building.

✦

Another fatal accident happens involving students leaving the Honky Tonky.

✦

Tired of trying to figure Silas's secret out, I skip a Jazz class and walk around school while the rain keeps stopping and starting. I pass by Petrusse and look through the glass doors. Inside, lying down on one of the benches with his legs spread and his fly flamboyantly open, is Pervis.

✦

The man in the trophy is the size that I can close my mouth around almost all of him. He's in a stagger stance with his hands raised.

✦

On Thursday, a tornado comes through and rips apart the retirement home and the houses south of school, lifts rocks from the quarry and tosses them all over the area. The power takes a week to come back. Gardner, the southernmost dorm, gets a chunk taken out of it and they announce a lottery to temporarily reassign the students who lived there for the rest of the semester. There are two days between when the lottery is devised and when the new assignments are released, and the whole time I go back and forth about whether I want a roommate, whether I'd want someone to be forced to live with me for the next few months. But then they announce it and I don't get selected, but Linus does. Tornadoes don't get names like hurricanes. They're too insignificant.

✦

Two rapes happen in the chaos immediately following the tornado.

✦

During the blackout, someone breaks into Mooney. He steals a stereo and two watches. The next night he breaks into Leon. In the second room he enters, a student is home so he runs away.

They find out who did it by seeing that the same fingerprints were on seven straight doors on the east side of the hall. He had tried doors until he found one that would let him in. It was a white man in his fifties named Cider or Cyper.

✦

The cold comes back. The snow does, too. It drops forty degrees in five hours.

✦

Sometimes I listen through the door to Linus and his new roommate talk. His name is Zachary and they stay up late talking.

✦

Silas tells us the midterm is coming up. It's half fill-in-the-blank, half listening. "If any of you need to listen to the music again to study, just come ask me and I'll let you borrow any of the records. If you don't have a player, there's one in the music studios down the hall." After class, I go up to his desk and ask for Duke Ellington's "Concerto for Cootie." He turns his back to check his bag for the record. On his desk, under some papers, I spot his keys. There are two and they're attached to a little plastic trumpet key chain. I snatch them and shove them in my pocket just before he turns and says, "You're in luck, thought I'd left it at home."

✦

A few times, I go out to Silas's house and lie down on the hill watching it. After I get over the sad rush of lying in the same spot where I was with Mary Beth, I think about going inside. If I can just get in his bathroom, I can tell her the answer. The key's in my pocket. One time, when he comes home, I happen to sneeze right as he's in his driveway and he turns and suddenly begins walking fast, coming right toward me through his field. I get up. "I see you!" he yells. "I see you!"

✦

I listen to "So What" so many times in my room that Perry marches down to my door and begins kicking it.

✦

I remember a time, back in November and December, which is no longer the case, when I only didn't miss Linus when I was with Mary Beth and vice versa. This is no longer the case, as I said.

✦

Hargraves drills me and Linus every day. He tells both of us we are Oregsburg's only hope.

✦

One time, months ago, I found *winsome* in the *Barron's* and I saved it for Mary Beth to call her it.

✦

Is Stephen Florida fatuous or just glib?

✦

Silas's backup key is under his welcome mat. I've seen him get into his house that way. So one time, I went out to his house early and took the key out from under the mat and went back to the hill. When he came home a little while later and found the key missing, he went around the far side of the house and didn't come back around. I guess he climbed through a window.

✦

During the midterm Pervis sits in the seat right next to me and copies everything I write. So this is what it feels like to be desired for your brains. During the listening section I know all the songs' names, I've listened to all of them over and over in the music department, listening for codes.

✦

One night, Zachary (who I've never seen) tells Linus about his brother, because they've gotten to that point already. I can listen by approaching in my socks from the side and keeping my feet outside the frame so they can't see my shadow. Then I can lean over and hear all I want. Zachary's brother, as I hear it, worked in a city doing construction on tall buildings until one day a steel beam went into his head. They thought he was dead, but he wasn't. They fixed him in the hospital, but when he woke up he had a different personality. "Different how?" Linus asks sensitively. Different like he was mean now, and aggressive, and generally didn't give a fuck about anything. He whipped his privates out and would slap strangers over nothing because you have no inhibitions after something lances your head. And then the most horrible thing happened: he got Cushing syndrome, his face and body started to change. "And I thought the sickest thing, I thought, 'My brother's starting to look like the horrible new person he's turned into.' Here's a picture of him," Zachary says, and I listen to the span of time in which Linus looks. The brother broke up with his girlfriend, he moved away to Utah, he told everyone he didn't want anything to be how it was before the accident. I listen to Zachary sniffle and Linus give him solace and peace.

✦

I go back to my room and decide to write a threatening note to Silas. But first I fall asleep for a few hours and have a nightmare I can't remember, one that doesn't last long but rips me out of sleep convinced that Fink is in my room, and so I quickly turn on the light and check the corners. "Where are you, little shitman?" I check the lock on the door, even under the bed and inside the closet, separating the shirts, already not believing in my fear anymore. I don't bother to look at the clock, dismayed at myself, and fall immediately back asleep like I have the vapors.

✦

I walk across the school to Opal in the dark, trying to whistle, with images of Zachary's moon-faced brother haunting me like a gutted building. Then I think back to how I was in August when I told Linus about my parents. I couldn't have been as pathetic as that cheesecake Zachary, could I? I get to the Jazz classroom and slide the homicidal Silas note under the door. All the lights behind the doors are out, I put my hood up to shelter my head from the snow. It's when I'm in the staircase back at McCloskey, on the other side of campus, thinking about a hot shower that I realize I've made a mistake. I run back to Opal, cursing myself for thinking I'm invincible. I sneak my fingers into the door crack, but it's only wide enough for a sheet of paper. I walk to the side of the building and look toward the center of school. The clock tower says a little bit after six. Because of everything that's been happening, they've started a new policy where all the classrooms are locked until the professors, the only ones with the keys, show up and open the rooms. I wait until it gets to be a believable time for a request like this, and then go to campus security.

"I need a room in Opal unlocked."

The security guard, who looks up from four or five black-and-white televisions, says, "We can't unlock doors except during emergencies."

"This is an emergency, goddamnit. I left my pet turtle under my desk and he's going to freeze to death."

"It's not our policy."

"Your policy has a big gaping hole in it, right there in the fucking middle."

I skip Geography to hover near the door. Well, that's it, my goose is cooked! A few times, teachers walk by and I think they're going to unlock it but they go to different rooms. A few minutes before class, two of the females in the class wait by the door with me.

"What did you think about the test?" one with brown hair says.

"I don't know."

When I spot Silas, my stomach tightens. He reaches into his pocket and takes some keys out. I position myself right where the door will open.

"Good morning," he says.

"Good morning," I say.

I take my coat off and he opens the door. I push forward immediately and take a step into the doorframe and pretend to drop my coat, drop it right on top of the paper. "Sorry." I pick my coat up and scoop the paper into it. Everyone takes their seats. Pervis, the greatest eccentric I've ever known, doesn't show up.

The class is about Ella Fitzgerald. I barely hear any of it. Half an hour in, he tells us he's going to let us go early. The female who talked to me outside asks him about the midterm, and he says he's still grading. He puts a record on the player and right before it starts playing he says, "Stephen Florida, can you stay after, please?" The song is Ella Fitzgerald scatting for six and a half minutes. Silas stares right at me while the nonsense sounds of the woman bang off the walls. "Feel free to go whenever," Silas yells above the music, and it sounds threatening, so pretty soon people sheepishly leave. When the song's done, I'm the only one in the room. In my extravagant coat, I walk down to his desk and he lifts the needle.

I say, "You know Pervis is cheating off me, right?"

He's in his chair with his head down, ruffling through his bag.

He fingers through some papers, and his delayed response almost causes me to demand just what the fuck is going on, but then I remember that I've nearly been caught a number of times recently, and so remain quiet.

He pulls out my midterm, which has at the top *100* written in red pen. I haven't gotten a hundred since a ninth-grade vocab test.

"How do I know you're not the one cheating off Pervis?" he says, glaring at me.

I take the test in my hand and look at my handwriting in all the question blanks. One hundred percent free of error! When it's sunk in that the document is real, I stare back. I have new teeth and I give him my Sunday smile. "Do you truly believe it is I who's been the cheater?"

He undoes his ponytail so it flops out like a horse mane and then puts it all back in. "No, I don't think that."

"I'm very interested in jazz," I say unhelpfully.

"Do you play?"

"Play what?"

"Music. An instrument."

"No. I wrestle."

"Why's that?"

"What?"

"Why wrestling?"

"I don't know. I guess because sailboating and horse jumping, kite contests, golf, those aren't sports. Anything that needs an object or water or an animal is not a sport. Wrestling is genuine and true and real."

"How old are you?"

"Twenty-two."

"Have a drink with me."

"O.K."

"I'm busy until Friday."

"O.K."

"Honky Tonky all right with you?"

"Yes."

✦

The television in the student union reports that a suspect is being held for one of the rapes that took place during the tornado. The news anchor says the rape happened outside "a local bar," but then the television cuts to the road between Oregsburg and the Honky Tonky. The news anchor goes on to say that the victim will remain anonymous, but that she is an Oregsburg student. Over the next few days, with nothing new to report, they just reiterate the same information. But then a few days later they have a new development: the suspect, Frank Florence, forty-four, two-time convicted sex offender, first turned himself in to the Aiken Police Department at two o'clock in the morning a few days prior, seriously bleeding. He was suffering from a groin injury and had to be rushed to the hospital. Authorities released part of his statement, which claims he was the recipient of a "ritual castration" as "punishment for what [I] did to those girls" and that "now [I] have the courage to turn [myself] in for what [I've] done."

✦

Hargraves says: "We're gonna use these two weeks to tighten up the little stuff, eliminate the little mistakes that can cost you a title. You're the first ones in history from Oregsburg to go to Kenosha. You're the only hope. I want you to think about that. I want you to feel like the explorers you are, you're going into uncharted territory as far as we're concerned."

"If we are both Oregsburg's only hope," Linus says to me later in the locker room, "doesn't that mean we're Oregsburg's last two hopes? Meaning neither of us is the last at all."

✦

One night, I hear Linus like a forty-one-year-old man telling Zachary about a service he uses. It's a student on campus, a philosophy major who's a junior, who writes papers for you. "He wrote all my history papers, and he's got two of my sociology ones right now." Zachary gets the student's name and location, which I also take note of.

✦

It is psychologically healthy every now and then to experience something you don't tell anyone, that you don't let out for any reason, that's only yours. But perhaps I'm doing this too often. The thought arrives sometime after midnight in the bathroom while spiders crawl around me in the stall. The way to tell if you're dreaming is to look down at your feet. Linus and Zachary are laughing about something behind their door.

✦

When they search Frank Florence's trailer, they don't find anything directly related to the crimes, but they find a large number of knives.

✦

Sometimes, once or twice, I've gone away from school and found a disused track of the Soo Line, it ends out in some weeds, the ties just stop. They remind me of my stitches.

✦

Mrs. Willard drags her desk chair to the front of the room, sits down, and tells us about the Mad Gasser of Mattoon, which happened in Illinois during the war, when people kept waking up and smelling gas and throwing up because of it. Next to me, a girl begins drawing a full-page chart of the incidents, and there are a lot to keep track of. Footprints were found beneath windows, window screens were found torn. There were so many reports of people smelling gas in their houses that anyone who made a report but wouldn't submit to a medical exam would be arrested. A woman named Bertha Burch described a figure as a woman dressed as a man. "Women's footprints" were found at the scene. Mattoon had a diesel engine manufacturing plant. A lot of the authorities chalked it up to "female hysteria."

And then she says that a whole similar set of circumstances had happened ten years earlier, in the county of Botetourt, Virginia.

At the end she asks all twenty of us in the class what we thought was wrong, what was going on in these two towns separated by hundreds of miles. No one answers and she says, "That's too bad." And then the class is over.

◆

It is an altogether funny feeling to hear about faraway events in the world and realize you had nothing to do with them, like voices outside your window. All the time these days, I'm reminded of what Mary Beth said about serious things: in the long run they usually only seem serious to a small number of people in one place.

◆

More and more things keep happening to me. Insignificant things and significant things and boring things and sacred things and terrible things and nice things and strange things. They disguise themselves as new events but really I know what they are, they're ancient events that have happened before and they've just run to the back of the line to wait their turn again.

✦

Without enough evidence to go on, they let Florence go.

✦

I pay a visit to the philosophy student. He lives in Leon and trustingly lets me up to his room.

He's bigger than me but has a jaw that's never been knocked around. I like a challenge.

"Can I help you with something?"

"You do papers for people?"

"Sometimes."

"You any good at it?"

"Do you want to come in?"

"Of course not. What do you charge?"

"Fifteen per page. If you get less than an A-minus, I discount to ten, but I've never had to discount."

"Do you by chance have a paper or papers from Linus Arrington?"

"Yeah, he gives me his papers."

"Maybe I would like to come in."

His room is basically the same as mine, except with blackout curtains and a lot of personal photographs of himself with people taped on the concrete walls. It becomes clear he is a sort of man about town. There's a big bong on the floor, next to a paper titled "Pythagoras Was Not Real, He Was a Group of Men."

"Is that *true?*" I say, pointing at it.

"Yes."

"You do philosophy?"

"Yeah."

"In my experience, philosophy is just like the parabola and the axis, always approaching the axis, closer and closer, like that, see my hands like that? Closing the gap but not ever closing it."

"What you're describing is an asymptote."

"What do you think of Wilhelm Fliess?"

"He's not my favorite."

"Goddamnit! Is that the papers you're working on?" I point to his desk, at an overstuffed manila folder labeled *paper business* in red pen.

"That's it, yeah."

Quickly, I reach over and grab a bunch of papers from it, and shove them down the back of my pants and snatch the bong and wave it at his head. Water flies out the end and douses him. "Hey, what the fuck?" The rest of the papers flutter to the floor.

He takes a step toward me but I swing wildly and he ducks away. I lick my knuckles.

"Listen to me. I would recommend you write them bad. Badly. Linus's papers only. I know you've got two sociologies. I don't care about the rest of these. I admire your hard work a little bit. But if I find out he gets anything higher than a D on the ones you have, I'm going to the provost or whoever with this."

"Jesus Christ, man. I don't care, just put my shit down and leave."

"All right." I set the bong on the carpet. "Which philosopher would you recommend if you like Wilhelm Fliess?"

✦

I'm running out of things to say, though I never had much to say to begin with.

✦

I wait a few nights outside Linus's door to hear the results of my visit, but they don't ever talk about it. I get so frustrated about this, it drives me so crazy that I take the hairs from my shave and fling them on their threshold to find.

✦

I wonder. If at the end. Life is a very bright light. That you just wanted turned out.

✦

An anagram is an ingenious rearrangement.
Daphne Floister.

✦

Levi Silas and Roland Fink are not anagrams but it doesn't matter, does it?

✦

And I guess I never should've been surprised Fink turned out to be a temporary problem, an inconvenience. He rolls to the left side of my skull when I tilt my skull to the left. An inconvenience was never going to realistically threaten me, Kryger and the rest of them were never really going to threaten me. They're all just like the skeletons on springs around the funhouse corners, they're all thin dreams and smoke and fake threats, I can wake myself up from all of them.

✦

When I open my eyes, it's sometime in the night and my mom is sitting in the desk chair.

"Hi, honey."

"Hi. What time is it?"

"It's pretty late." There's an unlit cigarette in her hand. "How are you doing?"

"I'm O.K. Where's Dad?"

"Oh, he's somewhere around here."

I hear footsteps in the hallway. It smells like smoke.

"I saw all the bad things. It's all very sad. I'm worried about you."

"What are you worried about?"

"Your father had tendencies. He could be a real knucklehead. Did I tell you about his urination charge?"

"Yeah."

"There were times I thought the M'Naghten rule should've been renamed the Gerry rule!"

"What are you worried about?"

"Did I tell you about one-trial learning?"

"Mom, you sound like the therapist."

"Don't say that. I don't like her. I don't sound like her."

"You're right."

"Is your finger O.K.?"

"Yeah."

"Let me see it." She gets up and places the cigarette in her mouth. She holds my hand in both of hers, turns it gently, and warmth goes everywhere at once. "You need to stop biting your nails."

"I know."

She puts her hand on my forehead. The cigarette wobbles when she talks. "Please take care of yourself."

A door opens in the hallway.

"I have to go now. I miss you very much."

"I miss you, too."

✦

On Friday, I wait outside the Honky Tonky in the dark for twenty minutes. In order to keep warm and pull down my anxiety, I take a lap around the parking lot where, close by, the rape happened. In the inside pocket of my coat, there's a pair of scissors I bought from Pharmart for the occasion. It's what I did to be conscientious. I keep putting myself in these situations, I keep asking for it. I tell myself if he's not here in thirty seconds, I'm going home. The only thing that stops me is my vivid hope of defrocking another evil Oregsburg educator. I walk back to the door and look inside.

Silas is sitting at the bar with his back to me. The whole place is a lot smaller than I thought. I approach quietly, trying to see if his posture indicates threat, but then I realize there's a huge mirror behind the bar, and he's using it to stare right at me. He puts his head back and drinks, like one of those people who look up their skull and flutter their eyelids, challenging the dead.

"I've been waiting for a half hour," he says as I walk up.

"Sorry."

He pats the stool next to him, and after I sit down, he sniffles and burps. "I'm on top of the world!" he shouts. Everything about him is in bad taste, but he's got a black talent for burying it. The bar's lit mostly by tons of red Christmas lights slathered over the wood panel walls. The only other light is from the lamp over the mirror, and the cigarette machine and pinball machine in the corner, near the hallway for the bathrooms. He asks me what I want. I don't answer. Silas has the bartender give me what he's having, whatever that is. Everything is red.

"Drink it," he says.

I put the tiny glass up to my mouth and swallow and exhale loudly.

"Like a Gila monster, whoo-ee!" he says, laughing, putting a cigarette into the lowest hole of his face and lighting it. "Tell me something, were you late because you were wrestling?"

"No."

"Well, I'm glad you came, even if you're not so punctual. I'm glad we're here together."

In the mirror, he squints while he sucks the cigarette, and puts the ashes in an empty glass next to his drink. There are nine or ten other people in the bar, some in the booths over my shoulder. No women.

"Do you bring other students here?"

"A few. Fewer and fewer people are taking my class every year, so I have fewer to pick from. Let me get you another."

"I don't want another."

"Either you loosen up or I'm liable to have no fun," he says, threat sticking up like wire in his voice.

"Fine with me."

I make eye contact with him in the mirror, where I have the sinking feeling he's been waiting to see me look. "You chew your fingernails, yeah?"

"What's going to happen to Pervis?"

"Well, I'm going to fail him. I haven't decided what else." He abruptly stumps out his cigarette with half the tobacco left in the paper. "Do you know why fewer people are taking my class?"

"Jazz is a dying art form," I say, also trying out: "people appreciate fewer things."

"That might be right. But I don't think it's the reason." The glass in front of me is refilled. I swallow it to keep him talking. "You don't have to drink the whole thing like that."

"Muh."

"Language is so interesting. It's like the mouth. The mouth is what you learn to lie from. Do you know, it had to be six or seven years ago. A person was going around pretending to be a medical examiner for insurance companies to get into people's homes. He would show up on their doorstep and just guess an insurance company, if he got it wrong he would just mumble something and leave." He drinks the remainder and his glass is refilled. "But if he guessed right, and he got a trusting person, he'd get into their house. It happened four times. He took out fake forms, sat at their kitchen table with them and asked them questions about their medical history, but this is all leading up to the real reason he's lied. They'd get to the part of the exam where he said he needed a blood sample, and he used the same unsterile needle on each of the four people (two women and two men) he fooled, and then he had them urinate in a cup. He took the blood and urine with him and then left. I'm not even talking about music. It's just so interesting. Do you like the music we've listened to this semester?"

"Yes."

"Why? Tell me why you like jazz."

"I like it because you have to pay attention to figure out if it's good or not. I like concentrating."

"Which was your favorite?"

"Miles Davis."

"That's a little bit disappointing. But. I guess no. It's not. Everyone's favorite is Miles Davis. It's like saying Shakespeare is your favorite. Miles Davis beat up women pretty bad. Do you hear that when you wrestle?"

"I don't hear anything when I wrestle."

He puts his arm around my shoulders, and I become more nervous. "I like you, there's something about you." My glass gets refilled. I have a flash memory of them showing us *Fail Safe* as third graders, and half the kids who weren't asleep crying in fear at the ending.

A song ends and another one starts. "This is the Small Faces. It's 'Green Circles,' is the name of it." Whenever the conversation momentarily sags, I start to bring up Mary Beth, but he won't let me, or I'm not ready to bring her out between us, I'm nervously protecting her. He dumps the rest of his alcohol into his body, then puts his coat on. "I have to make a phone call."

I watch him go past the pinball machine, around the corner. Immediately, I snap my finger at the bartender a few times until he notices.

"Hey," I say, "listen to me. Does that guy, does he bring students in here?"

"You're a student? You're trying to give me trouble?"

"No."

"Then shut the fuck up."

I begin to reach for my scissors but realize I can't do that, I can't do any of that, and so I make it look like I'm reaching for the nearby cigarette pack the whole time. The bartender leaves me alone. I get nauseous, not just because of the alcohol, but because I'm tired and sick of the way everything keeps failing to add up. Silas has no bag. He wore his coat to make a phone call. There is no evidence. I go after him, but when I turn the corner into the little hallway, the pay phone is vacant. I walk into the bathroom, which is half the size of my room in McCloskey, one urinal and one stall. The stall is shut, I can see black shoes on the yellow tile. At the urinal, I fake it. I don't go, I'm too scared, so I just stand there and listen. On the ceiling, a big animal is stretched over the whole room. The bathroom is quiet except for the Small Faces coming through the door, they say "green circles" over and over while I wait for what's going to happen, but there's not even a shifting on the toilet or a rustle of fabric. And so I flush the empty trough and pretend to wash my hands and leave. At the bar, I get a water and drink it. I pay taxes, a fractional speck of a cent, to feed Fink now. I pull a splinter out of the wood. I think about walking my empty glass into the bathroom and kicking the stall door open and hitting him in the head and face with the glass until he admits he killed his wife. I think about using the scissors after the glass is broken into pieces too small to continue using. But then the song stops and another one comes on and I don't know what it is. And what always stops me stops me.

"Etta James," Silas says, approaching and zipping his fly. "Do you do inquisitive things like bend over while urinating to study the stuff coming right from the spigot?"

"How was your phone call?"

"Let's get out of here. Why don't you come over, I have something to show you." He puts his cigarettes in his coat.

"O.K."

In the parking lot, he leads me to his truck. During the ride, he turns on the radio so we don't have to talk. His driving is normal considering how much he's had to drink.

As we near the driveway, I say, "Is that your house?"

Like in Shane's truck, I experience the feeling of approaching something unaccountably large. A reality stands just beyond the skin of my eyelids, and another reality lives inside. Somewhere between is the truth, on a vast, invisible plane of banshees. When we get to the side door, he says, "I've been having a problem lately with lost keys." He grunts as he bends down and pushes aside a rock and takes a key from underneath.

The door leads into a living room. Two recliners and a couch, a small television in the corner. The rug is a thick Oriental. I glance through the entryway, on the other side is the kitchen. "There's a thing in here," I say.

"Litter box, it's over there."

"Where's the cat?"

"She doesn't like visitors."

"This is a nice house."

He waves the compliment away and sits down in one of the chairs. There's a black case on the floor. He bends down and unclasps it and removes a gleaming trumpet.

"Sit down," he says.

I sit in the other chair. He's between me and the door. I'm not to see the back half of the house, the more personal rooms, but I scan the walls for an oil painting that could have eye holes in it.

"Take off your coat if you want."

"I'm O.K., I get cold easily."

"Are you from someplace warm?"

"Idaho."

"Aren't you used to it?" His menace casually dallies around the room. It's quite evasive and I can't decide whether he goes at the top of the psychopath ladder, also containing Fink, possibly Nephew Shane, who also might be dead, and Frank Florence, or somewhere near the bottom, with the idiot Kryger. When he puts the blowhole of the trumpet to his face, I distinctly see his tongue circle it in a wriggling fashion. He starts playing something that's very good and also sad, and I take it I'm not supposed to ask questions. A songbird is born with defective vocal cords and so cannot sing and so dies without a mate, unsuccessfully.

"Come here," he says.

I don't move. He gets up. My back is pressed into the chair. He gets right on top of me, his hand touching my neck, and he puts the trumpet in front of me. "Do you know what my favorite note is? E. When you hear it, you can sense the other notes on each side. It's like a note of omission. A ghost note. Play it." And then the hole is in my mouth. "Press your lips medium hard." I try to pull my head back but it hits the headrest. His fingers press down on the first two plungers and lift on the third. "Medium hard." A line of his leftover saliva runs inside my lips. I push and experience what must be the lowest grade of feeling, because it's nameless. A note comes out, it falls out into the house and over the entire deprived countryside. "Keep pushing, just like that," he says, and moves his fingers around, and through my pushing and his fingering, he plays a dancing series of notes, his hands in front of my face. I close my eyes and find them wet.

"There, you just played an arpeggio."

He goes back to his chair and sits down. "Can I offer you a glass of water?"

I wipe my eyes and say, "Does it smell like smoke to you?"

"I know what you're doing. I'm not stupid."

"Why did you invite me here?"

"I've watched you in class. During the listening you have this . . . impenetrable concentration."

"That's all? That's *all?*"

"Because you seem like someone who treats things seriously. You seem to me . . . to be an ideologically greedy person."

I can picture a sentence I underlined in the homework reading that applies to this situation, but I can't quite remember it so I say, "I'm just trying to get the truth."

He rolls his malignantly beautiful green eyes. "What's the truth? What's that in your pocket?"

"To get you to admit that you killed your wife."

"I'm under no obligation to answer that."

"I'm not like everyone else. Who wants to know the answer."

"Why are you trying to get me to admit that?"

The answer is for Mary Beth, she's the entire reason I've crawled into this hellhole, but am I in love with Mary Beth or am I just using her as an excuse? The milk's slopped all over my fucking skull, and what I say is at least mostly a lie, which is, "Justice. Law and order. What's right and all that shit."

"Well, now you're getting into theory and—"

"Oh! I don't give a shit!"

He mime-plays some notes on his trumpet, I can hear them clicking. "Let me ask you something. Say I did kill my wife and then say I admitted to it, you get me right now to admit to it, but also say that I tell you, and you are somehow blessed with the divine knowledge to know it is true, that I will never ever for the rest of my life, not once, commit a bad deed, that in fact I will commit more common good deeds on a day-to-day normal basis for the rest of my life, however many more years that is. I live quietly in this house, I teach my class, and I don't bother anyone. Is it still 'what is right' if all that you're really doing by getting me to admit to murder and locking me up forever is preventing me from living another few years that no one's really going to notice? Doesn't that seem like a waste of time? What's the point? What you're changing is so minor that it doesn't even register. All this effort, and for what?"

"Shut the fuck up! Answer the fucking question." I put my hand in my coat on the scissors.

"I didn't kill my wife. O.K.? I didn't do anything. Anything. It was an accident."

The end is coming. Here it comes.

"Do you remember a student named Mary Beth? A girl in your class named Mary Beth?"

This is the part where I feel myself ready to make the final push, to rush at him and stab him in the body and skin with the scissors, the moment he remembers her and I can intuit the wrongdoing in relation to her, Mary Beth, and to the dead wife, whose name no one's even mentioned. I can take the plunge. Kill him in his house as divine sarcasm, a feat so troubling they wouldn't even find me before I at least finished up in Kenosha. Then they probably would. I promise I am not unhinged, this is a clear-eyed assessment of the situation. The cusp of a murder is not widely divergent from the cusp of anything else, but I can only speak for my own experience. And it prances along my mind's sorry, no-good terrain that my time with Silas is not so widely divergent from my time with Shane, but if those both ended in murder, the first would be for passion and vengeance and the second would be for self-defense. Either way, nobody's taking me down the goddamn rabbit hole. My fingers go around the handle of the scissors in my pocket.

He sighs and rubs his eye. "Doesn't ring any bells."

"She took your class last semester, you bozo."

His eyeballs shift to the top left corner, the coordinates of recall. "Yes, maybe. Pretty?"

"Well, she's also smart, and—"

"I wouldn't know anything about that. My class doesn't test brains." He looks right into my face, blinks, then says, "But I can see you're very loyal to this person. This wasn't even your idea, was it?"

"Listen—"

"Maybe I was off about the ideological greed. But in any case, can I tell you a story about loyalty?"

"Lis—"

"Can I tell you a story?" When I don't answer, he reaches down into his trumpet case and pulls out a flask, which he finishes. "One time, a long time ago, a man knitted my wife some socks and sent them to her. He was a boy she had grown up with. It struck me as so obscene, so obscenely intimate, and I lost it watching her unwrap it and how she lit up, I was sick over it, but I did not let her know what I was feeling. They were fuzzy green. She grew up with him in Canada. The lure of the neighbor boy next door. She was Canadian. I'm very drunk, but I'm not sorry. Are you listening? I drive up there, drove. I went to his house. Took hours. He never sent my wife anything again. Not a letter. She never found out, she thought she'd done something wrong. And I said, 'Honey, that is just the way some people are. You have done nothing wrong.'" A little bit of drool tips out of his mouth's corner, which he wipes away. "The lesson is, you have to learn how to keep quiet about the things that are most important to you."

It boggles the mind to see someone who's never wanted anyone else's forgiveness. It's thoroughly unbelievable but it's true, it's a self-protecting flaw that he can sense sitting in his chair, fingering his cranium where the tissue should be but isn't. I say, "Can I use your bathroom?" and look at him hard, but he's not even slightly rattled by encroachments into this territory.

"It's right down there."

I go into the bathroom and lock the door. I turn the lights on and run the water and rub my eyes and very carefully look for any signs or evidence, for what I can report back to Mary Beth. I inspect the wallpaper, the toilet, the mirror, the sink and counter, under the sink and counter, the floor, I climb on top of the toilet and look at the ceiling, then I pull back the shower curtain, I finger the tiles and the bow of the tub, and I find nothing. Nothing at all. I step over the rim of the tub and get on my hands and knees with my face at the drain, and when I pull up on the little silver disc it rattles. I can see maybe three inches inside. In the brown rusting pipe is a wet old nickel. I toss the drain top against the tub and it bangs loudly. I go over to the toilet and unzip my pants. I don't lift the lid, I just piss all over the toilet and the floor and the wall.

I take out the scissors and hold them in my hand for my walk out. I open the door and go quickly around the corner with them ready, but he's not in his chair. There's a dragging sound around the corner, in the kitchen. I open the front door and leave.

I walk fast up the driveway of the either sad widower or wife murderer, to the road, which isn't lit at all. I'm not sure whether I trust anything he's said.

I get home mainly by feel.

IN MY ROOM, I turn the desk lamp on and take out four pieces of paper and begin writing all I know, and I do not stop until I've filled all of them front and back. It comes easily, and thankfully I forget everything else outside, outside of letters on blue lines. The words and sentences fall out of me so that only afterwards am I aware of the actual writing, the process of mind to hand to pen to paper, it seems like the thoughts travel directly to the page from my head, as if I'm inventing a new way of expression on the fly, something no one's ever seen before, as though I could be writing with my toes or by putting the pen in my mouth and bobbing and articulating all over the page.

I finish at dawn. I paperclip the pages, then I go to the closet and start putting the nice clothes on. I pick the blue tie.

I'm the only one waiting when they open the cafeteria. I sit at a table by the window with a bowl of oatmeal. Expecting to be fully moved, I read what I've written. But instead of returning me to the feeling I had when I wrote it, the paper is immature and overly sensitive, trying too hard. I rip it ceremoniously, down the middle, but just after I've split the first page, I realize I have nothing else and nothing better. After I bus my tray, I walk over to the career center, go up to the second floor of the building where the offices are. The secretary lets me into the waiting area and has me take a seat. She goes over to her desk and unwraps some foil, and quickly the room fills with the scent of eggs. I fall asleep.

Something bumps me awake, a woman's leg, a girl's. I turn my head and she's pretending to study her notes, but looks up right away, too fast, so I know she's intentionally awoken me.

"Hello," I say.

"Hi."

This is one of those conversations I'm meant to push forward. She notices my torn opening page.

"I had an accident," I say. "What's your presentation on?"

"First, ask me what my roommate's doing."

"O.K." I rub my eyes and she tells me about her roommate's plan, her presentation, which is to photograph every winner of the Michaelis Medal, a photography prize that's given once per year by a foundation in Germany to the taker "of a single distinguished photograph representing man's consciousness and/or ontology, and/or the line between." Her project will take her all over the world, and she'll have to photograph forty-three people, including sixteen gravestones, since the recipients have an eerily high mortality rate.

"Your roommate, she's a photography student?"

"Yes, she's already filed some grant applications."

"Grants, wow."

"Mine's a few experimental models predicting famine. I've been working on them for a few months." She angles her paper over and I make out this equation:

$$EL_m = \frac{I \times COE}{NRI[P_g + (P_v \times VGR)/1{,}000] \times (1 - T)}$$

"This one I used the abandonment formula for oil fields as a starting point, and I plugged in new pieces and basically just tinkered with it like crazy, and got some interesting results." She has on a red headband I'd like to tug. "What's yours on?"

A wave of foreign dust comes over me. Unconsciously, I lift both arms and begin the process of unscrewing my head. It's time to reveal it to her. But then I quit, seeing her face, which is not Mary Beth's, to whom I'd silently promised the privilege of being my widow, her face is not even close. One of the mollusk's sixteen tentacles squirms beneath my tie, having had such a close call.

She leans over and reads out loud the first sentence of my paper, which is the homework quote I'd wanted to shove down Silas's throat. "'Among the possible groups of truth-conditions there are two extreme cases,'" she says. "That's good. What's it mean?"

"Mr. Florida?" the receptionist says. I smile at her and she yawns.

The door I'm sent through leads into a room that's much smaller than expected. A single man is sitting at a desk. "Hi, Mr. Florida. Please take a seat, my name's Graham Danbury and I'm temporarily taking over the Howard presentations."

"Where's Mrs. Howard?" I'm suddenly afraid to look around the office, as if she's hiding in one of the corners.

"Sorry to say she passed away in December."

"But I have her real signature. It was a letter addressed to me last month."

"Yes, well, Mrs. Howard was in the habit of signing a lot of her correspondence ahead of time." A signature from the hand of a dead woman, a thing of weird and terrible power. "Do you have any questions before we begin?"

"So am I the last round of the scholarship now?"

"Not at all. Mrs. Howard had a lot of money—waste engineering—so the scholarship will keep going. But there will be some changes. We'll now hear presentations the whole academic year instead of just in March, which was the only time she visited Oregsburg. The rest of the year she lived on Baffin Island."

"Baffin. Well, O.K."

"The scholarship was very important to her, and she spent a lot of time, almost an entire month, deciding the recipients. She picked you out of everyone. There's a reason for it."

"Thank you."

"Would you like something to drink?"

"No, let's get on with it."

"O.K.," he says, leaning back in his chair. "Whenever you're ready."

"I'd be amiss if I didn't first point out that the content of my presentation includes real things. In that light, I've changed the names in order to freely talk."

"All right."

"The name of my speech, I wrote it out here, is 'The Inextricable Connection Between Jazz and Murder, A Case Study.'"

HARGRAVES DRIVES ME and Linus to Kenosha five days early. We stay in a tall hotel. Hargraves finds a middle school that lets us use the gym during the afternoons, and we practice over and over. He drills us on different scenarios, I'm the aggressor, then Linus plays someone who likes to shoot left, I practice sit outs for an hour, then we switch.

They give us the brackets. 133 looks like this:

(1) Bodner
Hahn

Heckelman
(8) Luecke

(5) Gerber
Jones / Borden

Northrup
(4) Florida

(3) Skouras
Cooke

Zasadzinski
Fisher / (6) Chanatry

(7) Taube
McBride

Iralu
(2) Veith

Hargraves gets off the phone with Farrow and tells me about Aldo Northrup. He got third in the West Regional. The strategy for Northrup is he likes to shoot from the outside, and so it's very simple: tie him up and get in his face. We drive back to the gym. We stretch and pull, warming up like always, and Linus pretends to be Northrup for the morning, and I pretend to be his first-rounder in the afternoon. Over the years I've wrestled and sparred thousands of times and sometimes, not often, when you're continually close against the other person, the roughhousing can turn in a different, deeper direction, a sexual direction, where you feel their skin as distinctly not yours. I've felt it when I've touched Linus's acne scars, seen his tongue come out of his mouth when he's hand fighting me. You feel them being brought nearer and nearer to you. The whole thing just happens. There's not really another way to put it. It hasn't happened in a while but it's happening with Linus. Every time it does, there's no chance the other person doesn't feel it, too, and after the first time with someone, it only returns stronger the next time. Toward the end of the day, Hargraves has Linus try to stalemate me. He tells Linus (and this is true) that he needs to work on developing out of an inferior position because he hasn't had the practice of being behind yet. I go in on a high crotch and he falls over, and I know what he's trying to do, he's trying to get my ankle, so I pull my leg away and he only gets my calf. "Basic defense!" Hargraves screams. I spin over on top of him, his clenched teeth, looking down at his face, the whole history of ours is there, the sloppy container of all I have for him, and he's not anyone else's. I find myself pressing my hand against his face, mashing it to the mat, squeezing, his visage squirming out of my palm and trying to get up, but I can tell we're not practicing anymore so I don't let him. "Hey!" Hargraves yells, but he gets ahold of my knee and pulls it, the bad one, and I feel something inside there just as I drive my other knee, the good one, into his ribs twice and he grabs anything he can to get me off his back and what he gets is the waist of my shorts and pulls them down to my compressions, so I gather his facial features in my hand and squeeze again like it's a bike horn, everything is sooner than expected, I'm ramming my knee into his ribs, the same place, harder and harder, and he tries to turn over like a fish and I give him credit because he's good so he's able to, he's very small and slippery, and what happens is because I put my face right up against his elbow where the skin is smudged darker than the rest of him he cracks me right above my eye socket, the eyebrow, and he again shakes his face out of my hand, but I immediately slam it down onto the mat and when I see his face again it's got jam coming out of the middle.

"Fucking shit, goddamnit!" Hargraves screams, wedging between us. When Linus finally rights himself, the blood goes down his mouth and blobs on his shirt. Hargraves has to lie down on top of him. I stand up and shrug my shoulders, walking out, not letting them see what's happened in my knee, and so I deal with the pain and don't limp. Practice is over for the day.

We go to a family restaurant (Hargraves sits between us) and eat in silence until the waiter drops three plates of steaks on the ground. After we've finished laughing at him, we are again able to pretend like nothing's happened. Linus has gauze in his nostrils.

During the few nights in the hotel, I shut myself in my room as soon as we get there and leave the television on until morning. I stare for hours at my kneecap and the curved, grinning scar. The wall the television's on is the wall I share with Linus, and I keep it very loud. I think about Linus's tendinitis, Linus's face. The same way a word loses its meaning if you say it over and over, a human face ceases being a face if you look at it long enough. It's hard to elect to join the human race, I mean fully, when they all just appear to be a collection of moving blood tubes and protein. The television talking is still going when I float up from sleep, news going into sports going into news again, a cycle that shifts words every four hours as new things happen. I do sit-ups and bounce on the bed. I open the window and bend over the balcony. I can't believe my luck, I've got enough for two people! I stand in the shower, set the television loud enough so I can hear it over the water. Though his room is right next to mine, Linus never once knocks on my door, and I don't knock on his.

That's not true. The night before it starts, Thursday, I'm cleaning up after a shower when I hear a series of doors slamming or just one door slamming a few times. There are three or four voices in the hall. I put my clothes on, and after standing with my forehead pressed against my door, breathing in and out, I open it and knock on Linus's door. I stand there for sixty seconds. I count it out. And then I realize that he's left to be with his family, that they've driven here from Nebraska to be with him and that he's gone and I've knocked on a door to an empty room, which is just as well because all I've got left are cheap, discounted feelings.

No one ever called me a monstrous talent in the newspaper. I was always in love with the unfaithful thing. But look where I am anyway, on top of a hotel in a faraway city that I was invited to, alone, all this room. Watch.

I have a dream that a Stasi agent named Carl is very sorry about it, but he creeps into Linus's room late at night when he's sleeping and sprays radiation on him. He is so quiet and good at his job that he doesn't even disturb Linus's tycoonish dreams. After, as part of the assignment, Carl follows him around at a distance pointing a Geiger counter at him, to keep track of the demise. He was told in a letter, which also included all Linus's information, that Linus was an enemy of the state, but Carl didn't care about the state, he had two daughters and needed to work. And then the dream ended with me at Linus's funeral, outside the church, pacing in front of the door like a father outside the delivery room, unable to work up the nerve to go inside. He died of a vague, unplaceable cancer and was buried with his lacrosse ball.

On Friday, I wake up and turn the television off. I've been sleeping naked. The knee is quiet but I'm always aware of it. My singlet is hung up in the closet. I sit on the toilet and void everything, then I go to the sink and run cold water into my cupped hands and dump five handfuls over my head. Then I step into my singlet, and put the rest of my equipment in the bag. I'm not expecting Mary Beth but I've brought her earrings. I lug the worms around. Their nest is inside my knee. I wait downstairs in the lobby for the car.

On the drive over, it's just me and Hargraves. I have four matches left. I start laughing.

Linus meets us in the parking lot by the main doors. We walk through the general entrance with the rest of the crowd. Linus and Hargraves and me are stuck behind a menopausal woman, one that has an enormous, grotesque tush, the kind where it's a gland thing, where she has to buy the special wide-seat pants all the time, the kind where she relies on vehicles and elevators because her body is malfunctional, she's very short and her whole self looks like a garlic bulb. We're stuck behind her, and so we enter slowly.

The cavern of the gym is already filled up. Linus leans over to me. "Jesus Christ, we are so talented!" He gently touches my ear, squeezes the thick parts. His are starting to flower, as he hasn't requested a drain since Fink got locked away. He lets go and walks away before I can speak.

They weigh us.

Hargraves leads us through a bunch of tunnels, passing groups of wrestlers everywhere, huddled together and sparring at half speed or jumping rope, or jumping in place, shaking their heads like water's in their ears. We take a bunch of turns. When there's an empty hallway, he stops. Shouting echoes off the walls. He puts his arms around us, leans us over so we're huddled with our heads together.

"I don't know what's left to say. You guys are here. You're really here. Stephen, you got your knee busted up but you worked your way back. Linus, you came in and right from the get-go you dominated, you lost your grandma and you kept dominating. I can't fucking believe it's going to be over so fast and you're going to get on that pedestal with your trophies. I'm going to leave you two be. Linus, you come up and meet me when you're ready, you're almost up."

And then Hargraves leaves us alone.

We stretch each other in silence. I tell him vaguely to stay away from my left leg, and after, he practices stagger stance and shooting on an invisible opponent. Then we stretch again.

I try my best.

"I know you put the notebook there for me to find it."

He doesn't say anything.

I say, "In the training room, you put it there. Were you afraid to admit anything out loud?"

I'm holding on to his arm, bending it back to ready the muscle and keep it loose. "Stephen, I don't know what you're talking about. What notebook?"

If he's not going to be truthful I can wait until he's ready. He's mine and I guess I'm still somehow his.

"I'm sorry this happened to you but it's over now."

"Yes, I know."

Then he leaves, jogging around the corner. He's the 125 one-seed and he doesn't need me to be there to watch him pin his opponent. I'm alone in the hallway. Months ago, on one of those nights after practice when he'd sit in my chair and read, he said, "Do you think we'd still be friends if neither of us wrestled?"

I attach my headgear. The debris spins around my kneecap like an agitated snow globe. I start writing in my head the biography of Aldo Northrup. It's a lie, it's a game I play with myself, but I won't have to do it much longer. I lace my shoes all the way down to the foot of the tongue, then go all the way up, rolling the knot at the top. I'm sweating through my singlet. Life and the human condition are the exact same thing and it makes no difference, the design is sadness, gravitational and old, except the few times it hiccups and it's not. I come out one tunnel after another. I wear my coat until the last hallway mouths up against the full arena, the blue seats barely visible under all the flesh, and then I take my coat off.

Linus and two fat people are next to me.

"Stephen, these are my parents."

They're standing behind him, as though afraid.

"Hello, I'm Stephen."

The father is the first to step forward to shake my hand, then the mother. She says, "I'm so glad we got to meet you finally. Linus has told us so much."

"Thank you for the deodorant."

"You're welcome."

"Is this a bad time?" the father says.

"Yes, it is."

I walk around the sides of the mats. There are six of them: two red, two blue, and two black. I'm in front of thousands of people. I turn my back to them. The noises they make smash into one sound that rushes in a wave past my body onto the mats. The end is the point of wanting something in the first place, isn't it? I good-luck tug my straps and square my bulge.

The successful mentality I've been going into every match with is this: if you're lower-rated than me, I've been insulted and have to make a show of how much better I am, if you're higher-rated than me, I'm being insulted because they think you're better than me, and I make a show to prove they're wrong. Either way, I hand the insult back.

I walk past Hargraves, who says something.

My designated mat is one of the red ones. Aldo Northrup is in a white singlet with a blue stripe. I put the red anklet on and then the official puts us in the center of the circle. All of the cement and bone and sticks of wood crowd up against my sides but stay out of the circle, an effect of heat, a halo of heat and closeness gathers, and I never look at Aldo Northrup's face. But I do hear the whistle. I get very close to him in a defensive stance with my legs out to the sides, I creep toward him with my elbows to my chest. He tries shooting, he's very fast, fast enough to shoot from that distance. I knock him away, my knee stinging every time. He tries high and low, both sides. We go around the circle. I finally get him to tie up with me. At first he doesn't want to, but he runs out of space to back up and so I finally get my forehead against his. I keep close, I'm trying to wrestle him in the phone booth. He tries to get below my hands but he can't, so our wrists and forearms keep tangling, which is what I want and what he doesn't want, we're rotating but he's too frustrated to notice he can back up and he finally reaches, which is what I want, and I get him in an overhook. I'm lower than him. I step forward, between his legs. I body lock, driving him all the way across the mat until his feet catch and he goes flat on his back, and though I can't get the pin, I hold him to the mat for the rest of the period, and I know I'm going to win. He picks bottom for the second, which is foolish. I think he's just a sophomore. I ride him the whole second, conserving my knee. He gets out at some point toward the end, but I get the point back at the beginning of the third, and the rest of the time, he can't decide if he wants to shoot from far, which I won't let, or close, which he can't. And so I roll up like an armadillo and store my energy. The whistle blows.

Hargraves puts his hands on my shoulders. "You got Gerber next. I watched him. He's defensive, a real turtler. He's going to wait for your shots. It's going to be hard to get in on his legs."

Like I'm following a trail of pebbles, I retrace all the hallways to the empty one. Every few turns, there are doors to the basement, where losers are already crying their eyes out. One comes out and holds the door for another going down, both red faced. I turn the last corner and am relieved to find Linus isn't back there, so I test how bad my knee is. There's a door to a stairway up at the end of the hallway. I walk up and down some stairs, over and over, until my head gets light, trying to keep loose, trying to forget everything, but what I keep thinking is this: that I beat a wrestler named Garber and now I'm wrestling someone named Gerber.

In his second round, Linus executes one of the most beautiful pins I've ever seen, collar tie to high crotch to double leg to pin. While it's happening, gravity seems to get sucked out of the building, and he puts the kid through the paces like diagrams in a textbook, one, then the other, then the other. And then it's done.

I retreat down a hallway and get my heart up. Then I go back out.

My match is on the same mat as the first. Gerber gets there after me. He also wears a white singlet. I don't look at his face. I put on the red anklet. I tap my toes. I get ready and the whistle goes.

I search for a direct line of sight between my eyes and his legs. He immediately crabs up and gets his head and arms in the way. I take a testing shot at his left leg and his forehead bangs against mine, and suddenly his hands are grabbing all over, and I barely have time to get my hands in the way and step back before he gets ahold of me. We fuck around. He gets a stalling warning and becomes a little bit more aggressive, and in my attempt to unturtle him, I get a stalling warning. We stroll around the middle of the circle, I'm trying to follow him. But I didn't get here by bullheadedly sticking to any system, I got here by adapting to what they gave me, and so I cross off the legs, everything below the waist I scribble out, because he's not going to give them up. Anything I do he's going to try to sprawl on me. So I look upper body. I get close. I get nearly on top of him. I knock him out of his stance. He backs up and then when he can't do that anymore, he goes to the side. I keep pushing on his stance, breaking his base, ignoring my knee. I feel his legs lift and immediately I grab and get double underhooks on him, I choke down on him and after he briefly tries to clear his arm in response, I snap and almost right away he falls forward, as if he doesn't want to put up with it at all, and I fall with him. But before I can even begin to try to flip him, he's got my hook separated from my body, he breaks it like a string and I'm grabbing at his scrabbling feet. And this is the way the period ends: with Gerber back in his turtle stance.

I get bottom first. Eventually, I get the sit out, but he racks up more than half a minute of riding time. Down 3–1, I know he's going to be more aggressive, to get a takedown and try to run up the riding time, but it's like a switch flips, he's coming at me faster than I expected, and I'm not ready for it, his hands are a mess of slaps and he's got my left leg and I'm on my back before I know what's happened, landing so the knee is braced and putting me in a worse position, and he's trying for the near fall or pin but by now I'm caught up, I reach down into the woods of myself and I look into his face for the first time. He has green eyes. I turn my head and swim and he's holding my flank instead of my chest, and at that point it's a matter of steps, piece by piece of my body unlatching from his, less and less leverage, until I break his hands. The period ends with me up a point, but Hargraves tells me he's got a minute and twenty of riding time, which effectively means we're even. "I guess I'm just going to have to ride him under a minute, then," I tell him.

I crouch behind him and right before the whistle goes, he starts. He gets a caution. We reset. The whistle goes and I hold on for the sedation, but the mistake a lot of people make on top is that they try to ride instead of trying to pin, and that's how you get in trouble, so before Gerber throws all manners of sit outs and turns and roll attempts, tugging my singing knee and all its tendons around with him like a caught fish, I make myself as heavy as possible on his back and try to get my arm up around his head for a half nelson, but he won't let me pin him, he won't get flat. He keeps kicking and turning and I crawl around with him for what feels like nothing, but then Hargraves's voice gets out of the thatch: "A minute!" I'm not just going to ride him under a minute, I'm going to ride him until the very end, which becomes an increasingly proximate thing while I have a seizure of absence, a particularly good one, aided by the harp music of my knee, or the stuttering piano of "Clair de Lune," or both, because in the seizure all music is an abstract, academic concept. "Twenty seconds!" It's difficult to ascertain whether I've ridden down better wrestlers than this or I've gotten heavier on top, a dichotomy worth ruminating on while I keep pushing, attempting a tilt and holding his arms, he's in my control and my mind whites out like I'm filling out my taxes. He neither budges nor pushes out, it's like he's distracted by trying to stop me from turning him, which is enough when the whistle blows.

I fall back and lie down and close my eyes. Inside my knee, it feels like someone's reached up my leg from behind and is tuning the wires. I roll up to my feet, get my hand raised with little air inside my head.

Hargraves takes me back to the same family restaurant. Linus is somewhere with his parents. He talks to me about his brother's family, his two nieces. I don't say anything. It's not lost on me that Bodner, the one-seed, lost right after my match to the eight-seed, Luecke. None of that is lost on me, but what can I do about it until tomorrow? I eat the chicken dinner and blank out my entire life history.

That night, I stand by the loop driveway and watch the cars pull up to the hotel. I have part of my hood's fur rammed into my mouth. I wasn't told exactly what animal went into the collar because the sales associate was unsure, but I have a suspicion that it was a beaver. When I've been out there for thirty minutes or so, a car pulls up and Linus opens the door. I'm off to the side and he doesn't see me as Hargraves walks up. They have a conversation I can't hear, with Linus standing at the passenger door. They talk for three or four minutes, and Hargraves walks back into the hotel. Then Linus sees me. He turns to his car and I hear him say, "Go around," then he shuts his door and starts walking toward me. Behind him, his car begins to make a loop.

"Hi there."

Erstwhile. *Erstwhile* is a word in the *Barron's*.

"You know," he says. "I know that's the same Robert Frost poem everyone uses." I don't answer. What do you say to that? He says, "Have you heard the one about the overconfident boy?"

I shake my head.

"Lemonade was his favorite drink. He drank lemonade every day. But only yellow lemonade, he hated pink lemonade. He told everyone that he could taste the difference between pink and yellow, and that pink was horrible. One day the boy was sitting in the hall after school waiting for his mother to pick him up. She was late and he was very thirsty. A man came down the hallway. He noticed the boy. The man said, 'Where's your mother?' and the boy said, 'She's late.' The man said, 'You look very thirsty, can I get you a drink from the vending machine around the corner?' The boy didn't know exactly what vending machine he was talking about, but he was really thirsty and he said, 'Yes, a lemonade, please,' and the man said, 'One lemonade, coming up. Oh wait, pink or yellow?' And the boy made a face and said, 'Yellow, please, pink is horrible,' and the man said, 'It is? Are you saying you can tell the difference?' The boy assured him he could. Then the man said, 'Want to make a wager? I have a blindfold here in my pocket. I put this on you and get you a lemonade and you take a sip and tell me what kind it is, pink or yellow. If you guess right, you get something, if you guess wrong, I get something.' The boy thought it would be fun and he agreed. 'Put this on,' the man said, and the boy put the blindfold on. He heard the man walk down the hall, heard his footsteps go around the corner at the end of the hall. Then he heard nothing else for a few moments, and when the quiet kept going, he started to become scared. But then he heard footsteps coming from around the corner, heard them coming closer, until they were right in front of him and they stopped. 'Here,' the man's voice said. The boy blindly reached out and took a bottle, and he began to feel uneasy. 'Take a drink,' the man's voice said, and the boy put the bottle up to his lips and drank. He swallowed. The boy said, 'That's pink. It's definitely pink.' And the man didn't say anything. The boy was suddenly afraid to take the blindfold off. He said, 'Well, am I right?' And then the man's voice said, 'It's not either. And now for you to give me what I get.'"

Linus's car pulls back into the driveway. He turns, and as I'm watching him leave, suddenly I'm struck with the thought that the Frogman is only waiting around until after the season. I go upstairs. I didn't get this far without being able to repress my fear, and though the fear of the inevitable is the deepest and coldest yet, I can focus on what I want, I just need to sit on them all for one more day, and it works, because what I dream about is a city full of alleys, thousands and thousands of alleys.

This is the part with only one interpretation.

On the drive over, I roll down my window and breathe Kenosha's empty air. The collective unconscious of the nation is a wedge or pool of buzzing flies and it won't get out of my head. The collective unconscious is killing me. Hargraves parks in the same spot as yesterday.

I have two matches left in my entire life. I warm up with my coat on in the empty hallway. My bad kneecap is noticeably larger than the other. The nest of worms wriggle around inside.

It used to be that if I didn't feel worked up enough I'd just pull up the face of Ben Davis, or Patrick Young, or John Henry Rees, or Fred Husbands, or Patrick Seber, or Lewiss Tong. But now I realize that whenever I imagined them, their faces were made up, I couldn't actually remember what they looked like when I'd lost to them, they wore out so long ago.

I do no scouting on Luecke, there's no point. All I need to know about him is that he beat the best 133 in the country because he is aggressive. I have maintained close and careful control of the proceedings. They'll never slip through my fingers again. I head through the hallways to the arena, and when I get there, the most astounding thing happens.

It seems to occur in one prolonged moment, as though the period had no stoppages, but it happens with forty-five seconds left in the second. Linus pushes on the kid, he keeps setting up his shots, breaking the kid down, but the kid keeps breaking Linus's momentum every time he's about to strike. There's some connection between Linus's move, the move he wants to make, and the kid's response, every reaction is timed perfectly, as if they were responding to the same signal. But by the end of the first, and when the kid gets out from bottom to start the second, it's clear that Linus is agitated. They break apart and size each other up, he's agitated after every reset after a failed shot. And with every failed shot, shots to the kid's legs and body become less attentive, and the kid's rebuffals become more forceful. With a minute left in the second, Linus shoots messily, which is the same as lazily, and I guess it might as well have happened this way. It might as well be the kid hitting Linus with a Russian and pulling Linus's arm forward, might as well be Linus taking a step forward to catch himself, putting all his weight on the foot that gets kicked out from under him, the whole thing takes a little more than two seconds, and when it's over, Linus is flat and frozen-up under the kid, and in the instant it takes for the match to end, while Linus is folded up like a cheap party chair, I distinctly hear, over all the others, Hargraves let out an agonized bellow.

I watch Linus. Something upsetting happens: he doesn't dwell on the mat, he gets up and without heartbreak or defeat, he walks straight off like he's walking home from the bank. He makes a line straight for me. I have a few seconds to ready my sympathy, which is there, but I've never had the practice of comforting him after a loss because I never thought it'd happen, and anyway, he speaks first. "I think I saw Mary Beth."

When it's a few minutes before my turn, and I'm waiting on the sideline while Hargraves rubs my shoulders, I spot Luecke walking through the crowd on the other side of the mat. No one's talking to him. When they call us up for the semifinal, he pushes forward through the bystanders, straight for the mat. Instead of meeting me in the center, he walks around the circumference of the circle, but not as though he's afraid to go inside it, more like he's confirming where it is, like a dog pacing outside the last door he saw his owner go through. Luecke does this until the referee yells at him, and then he comes into the circle. He has scratches and red cuts all over his arms. There's something wrong with his lip. He won't look at me. He quickly tilts his neck to the side, trying to crack it.

I have good news and bad news! The bad news is that the abyss and the void are all the same thing and it is monumental and everywhere. The good news is you can lie still in your bed while the cursed and the unskinned walk around in it and not feel a thing.

"I want a good match, you two. Good luck." And just like that, he steps back and we head into the fuckery.

He comes right after me. He wrestles like he wants to hurt me, a sensation I recognize from high school when I couldn't redirect the madness in my brain. The ideal is to approach this sensation, to feel it coming closer and closer, and hold it until it stops struggling and helps you. The asymptote of harm. He tries double leg, high crotch, single leg, he goes for the body and the legs, but I keep getting my arms and head in the way, at one point he drives so hard with his head at my legs that his forehead crashes into mine and an inner cymbal clangs. He steps back and blinks. I can taste my knee in my mouth. He comes right back, so I engage his hands, waiting for him to reach but he doesn't, he gets his head in the place on my shoulder sentimentally reserved for loved ones, and tries to drive, but I shrug and get him in a Russian, but he won't open up. He tries a level change but I have his arm locked so he can't, but then he pushes into me with a violence I haven't felt before, and as he snaps my head down and locks it, I see the whole history of Luecke, a wrestler who's maybe undergone more shit than me and found a way to process it into a force of frustration, and up against something I can't control, I'm looking straight down at the white line on the mat and can't move when suddenly I hear the whistle. "Illegal hold, green, one point, red." I'm bailed out by him, by how bad he wants it. I suck the snot back into my nose and we reset, and he comes right after me again, with the same violence as before and this time I can't stop it, maybe he's an all-time sufferer because he gets both legs and the wind goes right out of me when he puts me to the ground and tries to roll my leg to my chest. Finally the whistle goes, and when it does, the violence immediately leaves Luecke's body, it goes lax.

How the fuck am I going to solve this one?

I get bottom for the second. When we start, the wild, reckless energy, the one I can't stop, seems to have gone away, but because he's good, I can't get out. I can't get out. Getting out's like trying to write a note while someone's rattling your desk under you. He seems less concerned with turning me than choking out my air. Every few seconds, I feel a nudge from a different place and I push it away. Time passes. For the first time in what feels like forever, the sound of the crowd gets into my ears, and his hand moves up my neck and I feel like I've eaten a group of old pills, the referee mutters for him to watch it, and the only way to get rid of the feeling in my throat is to turn so I'm on my side, which is exactly what he wants, he's putting me through the stages. It starts to get really bad. From behind me I can feel him bend me over and I can't help it, I'm straining so hard against it my nose runs, something bends in my neck, between my neck and shoulder, but I keep pushing against it, everything is collecting into one shape and colors fill my eyeballs, he's going to get a near fall on me, or worse. He has my arm behind me and the feeling drops out and something's about to pop in my neck when the whistle blows.

He lets go of me and I flop forward onto a spot of my own fluid, sucking for breath. My first thought is to buy time. I hadn't realized how close to losing consciousness I was, the pain is in at least three places and it's worse than what Carver did to my knee. I step up to my feet and stay still to gather myself. Blood comes back into my head and I shake my left arm. The feeling is like crackles of light and that's the best I can get out of it.

"Red, let's get it going here."

I take my spot on top, going into it the way I always do, with my left around the waist, but I realize it's weaker. I flip and put my right around his waist. He has a full two minutes of riding, a full period of it. I put all of it into one idea. It only takes him a few seconds to get his knees out but I'm right behind him like the devoted husband for the water birth. Both of my hands are on his left arm, gripping it to his chest. I put everything into it. I do a two-on-one, I rip and plant, plant with my knee and pay for it, but I rip him back into my lap as hard as I can and he rolls with me, it's like magic, like the trick working for the first time, you only need the trick to work once. I plant my left leg under him,

I've never felt any pain like this, and he tries to jump through but he can't do it, I have my left arm under his face-up body and my right arm on top, latching his arm to his hip, he can't do it, his stubbornness works against him now, he keeps trying to roll toward me. By the time he realizes he needs to go the other way, that's all it takes, I get my two-count, but because he's so stubborn it turns into a five-count, and I get my three points put on the board. Finally he turns, but I go with him because it's like he's doing exactly what I've whispered in his ear, and we're back to where we started the period, me on top. I was correct in assuming he'd be easier to handle on the ground, but now I feel the violence rise up, I can feel it start to move out from his center. I have just enough time to turn my head so I get smashed in the cheekbone, and all I can do is hold on to him for a few more seconds before he's out, and then he comes at me harder than ever. He changes levels right away and I barely get my head in front of his, but he keeps pushing, he pushes me back like I'm nothing, and his hand hits my shoulder, close enough to the spot that's pulled in my neck, and I just try to keep close to him though he's trying to keep me off, and when he tries to pull away to reset for another shot, I hear something rip. The whistle blows. Luecke steps back, looks at me in shock. It's my knee. It's my knee again. But I look down, and there's a tear in the strap of my singlet. "Grasping the singlet, green, one point, red." I look over at the clock. Twelve seconds left. I just have to hold on. The brain in its seat way up above the duodenum is instructing: Finish Finish Finish Finish. When I tilt my head to the side, a shingly shower of pesetas shifts to the tilt and we reset and I look at him and know he's coming after me with everything he has, I just have to hold him off for twelve seconds. The whistle goes and he almost dives forward, but I don't engage, I circle, I intentionally move away, and it takes six seconds out of the twelve for the referee to call me for stalling, to give me the warning. He comes at me one last time, but I get as low as I can and dive back, and we're standing each other up when the whistle ends the match.

When I leave the mat, after Hargraves hugs me, I go and stand at the bottom of one of the stairs that leads up to the top of the arena. I look over the entire crowd because superstition is the belief in the causal nexus. I wait for her, or whoever it decides to be, to stand up.

A little girl leaves her row and starts walking down the stairs toward me. She wears pink Velcro shoes and a pink coat, and I watch her walk all the way down. When she gets to the bottom, she looks up at me and for a moment, only one moment, I promise, I believe she's going to ask me for my shoes, but what she says is, "Excuse me." I limp out of her way and as she walks past it all pours over my head like a pot of tar or honey, coating all my face's front-facing holes and there is a time of no air, and I let it, because it'll slide off eventually, it always does.

On my last day I don't feel fevered or keyed up, I feel resigned to whatever decides to happen. It's not that I don't feel in control of myself, it's that I don't feel in control of anything else. That's all done. I have the earrings, just in case. I could work the rigs, I could go to Japan, I could rush home to the lake before the ice melts and slip under the covers for good. It was not so long ago that I was a lost and distracted person, it took me so long to pull myself out of all that. I sit back, put my spine against the stairs. I could do any of it.

In the stairway where I'm sitting, Hargraves brings me Linus's singlet. Mine is hanging by one strap like Tarzan.

"Did he win?"

"Third, yeah. See you out there, Florida."

I take it off and put his on in the stairway. I cup my kneecap like a warm, filled mug.

A long time ago, I read about the subway in New York, which if I remember correctly lets you ride as far as you want on one fare. Think of that: taking the steps down to the underground tunnel below, riding trains forward and backwards again, transferring all over New York City, the greatest city in the world, hundreds of platforms and stations, thousands of people, seeing everything, for the price of one fare. Why would you ever get off?

I wish I could say I prepare for Veith, but I don't. Guilt is just as valid an incentive as anger, or stubbornness, or delusion and stupidity, and they're all my energy from time to time, coming and going as they see fit, letting themselves in and seeing themselves out. When I blink my eye, just the one Luecke elbowed, it's like I can feel the stem back there throbbing, and all my thoughts vanish or disappear or go up in smoke or evaporate. Identity is curious and always getting misplaced, sometimes you have to hold it pretty hard to keep it from getting away. I was never once the most talented, not even close, but I always had my single-mindedness, foolish greedy dodo single-mindedness.

With my coat on, I gimp out into the arena. I walk like the old days, like the lovely old days in winter when I'd just shed my crutches and was feeling grateful and horny. I wear my coat as far as they let me, which is the edge of the mat. I like the mat and the circle, which is the defined space I can make perfect. I've spent all these years only trying to make the sport perfect for myself. I wanted the pressure. All I ever wanted was the chance and now that I have it I forget my knee, when you finally have the chance nothing's surprising anymore and everything turns blank. I give my coat to Hargraves. Thousands of people I don't know and will never meet are creating sound, and my desire is bigger than anyone else's in the entire building.

And if they had taken me to the movie, sitting in the backseat, instead of leaving me at home to watch television and fall asleep on the couch? I've always wondered what would've changed, and now I know. It would've stopped any of this from happening. That's all. And when you think about it like that, it's not really very much, is it?

I bend back my head and look up. In the rafters, between the lights, I look for a black creature, an animal waiting to descend. But there is nothing. It has stopped following me. The truth is that enormous. There is either no menace left in Kenosha or it is coming from me, it's coming from *my mouth*.

They've removed five of the mats so there's only one black one in the middle. I spit on the outside of the circle.

Immediately the referee blows his whistle. He walks over to me. "Red, what the hell was that? You going to be trouble?"

"No, I'm all done, I just had something inside."

An attendant boy is already at my feet disinfecting the spot and wiping it clean with a ragged old towel.

I'm brought into the center of the circle. That's it. The whistle blows.

Bang-collars, changing levels, Russian ties, every time one of us moves, the other moves, too, and nothing happens, no one takes any offensive chances. The first period ends 0–0, and while we're resetting, I hear a few boos. I get bottom for the second and after some back pressure, escape. Back steps, footwork, hand fighting, cautions, arm drags, starts and stops. At some point, I've lost my ideas and am just reacting automatically. Array, Array, Array, Array, Array, Array. I have too much respect for all this to throw it away on one cheap shot. The second period ends, and when I start the third on top, he gets out easily, just as I did last period. Hand control, head snapping, stalling warnings. The boos get louder. With twenty seconds left, he pulls hard on my neck but I slip it, and no one gets any closer than that. They start us in neutral for overtime, and more of the same happens. Halfway through the overtime, when we break for one moment and I back up far enough to see his face, I know he's resigned himself to the second overtime, for what happens with the fucking disc. It might as well be a fifty-fifty flip that determines everything. It's both the shit and the stars. We keep locking up and hand fighting only for the sake of doing it, alternating between who's slightly more aggressive, but whenever one tries to push the other, it's clear that the wall of strength you brush up against is too much, there is no more strategy.

They blow the whistle and more boos come out. The referee returns us to center.

"O.K., you both know how this works. I'm going to flip it. Whoever gets the up side gets to pick position."

He has the disc in his hand. He flips it.

Red.

"Bottom," I say.

"This period's thirty seconds."

I get down on my hands and knees. I feel him lean on my back. When I sense the start, I take in a very deep breath.

I push and turn. And as I'm breaking his hold, there's one last moment where he tries to slip his arm under mine, but I slide away from it and push back to my knees, facing him, his hands free of me. The whistle blows.

I stand up and shut my eyes. A hand lifts my arm. I open my eyes and walk out. I find a door to the basement. The stairs are dark and the basement is full of intention and blankness, my head leans against a concrete wall and the mechanical drone that energizes the whole building blurs out everything. Winning is timeless, I never got tired of winning. How glad I am to be tired. This is real life. This is real. This is real. This is real. This is real.

I walk up to the stairs and head back to the arena. Hargraves hands me my coat. I zip it up all the way. I try to put the hood up but they take it off and lead me over to the pedestal. I climb to the highest spot and stand there. "That's some limp there," they say to me, handing me a big cardboard with the completed 133 bracket on it.

The chairman is not smiling, it seems to me he's making a real effort to frown.

"Congratulations, Stephen."

"You all act like you've never seen a champion before."

"Well."

"You've got to reach up a bit, I'm all the way on top here."

I put my head down like the first step of a Victorian courtship ritual, and he hands me my trophy.

A few photos are taken. I'm paraphrasing.

Mr. and Mrs. Fink are gone, Aunt Lorraine is gone, Linus is gone, Mary Beth is gone, Mom and Dad are gone, Silas is gone, Shane is gone, Bird is gone. There's only this.

Once again, from the pedestal, I look up at the rafters. The shadow has spread to the size of the building.

And would you believe it? I sleep the whole drive back.

I get out of the van and walk on the main path, across the school.

I've waited most of my life to find out what this feeling is like. I knew it wouldn't feel like winning any of those other matches, but I thought it might feel like the opposite of losing. But it's not personal, I do not take this inside myself the way that I took years and years of falling short into myself, it does not untie those knots the way losing tied them. It's only relief. It is absence. It's pressure being taken away. The noise has stopped. It's relief.

There are not many people out. It's ten in the morning on a Sunday. Under the clock tower, there's that situational atmosphere sound, which is particular to a place, which in Oregsburg is similar to the air just beginning to turn up the spiral of a large seashell. Or the sound of a heavy object, an immense object, dropping down the ocean and finally landing on the floor, and the final reverberations in the sand and rocks nearby that take minutes to quiet down before the object rests there for good and begins its erosion. But then again I've never been to the ocean.

Inside my bag, wrapped up in the singlet like a surprise parcel, is the trophy, a nice desk-clock size. I walk through the snow, between the posting board and the benches, think to maybe sit down and kill some time. Memories always appear as unfinished circles. I had never guessed that wanting one thing for so long, wanting it at the cost of everything else, I never would've guessed that finally getting my hands on it could not feel really any different than how it felt all along, how it didn't push out the boredom and the terror in the rooms, in every room I've ever spent time in.

I think about going to the cafeteria or the student union, to wait until Petrusse opens up. My heart is going uncomfortably fast now, and I'm not sure why. Maybe there's something on television. I think about walking around the library until I find something new to read, and sitting at one of the wood tables in the basement until I've finished the whole thing, in one sitting.

Closure and reason are impossible. Understanding, on the other hand, is the best you can hope for.

When I go back to McCloskey, there's no one at the front desk. I walk through the lobby and take the stairs. When I get to my floor, I take my keys out but stop when I see my door's open. There are wet footprints on the floor leading to my room. Then I go down the hallway, up to the doorway, and look inside.

In my room with the lights off and sitting on the bed there's someone. Who stands up.

"Oh, there you are."

ACKNOWLEDGMENTS

Thank you, PJ Mark, for your brilliance, gutsiness, and thoughtfulness.

Thank you, Chris Fischbach, for seeing something when no one else did.

Thank you, Caroline Casey, for your toughness and heart.

Thank you, Lizzie Davis, for your sharp insight.

Thank you, Marya Spence, for your perceptiveness.

Thank you, Ian Bonaparte, for keeping track of all the pieces.

Thank you, Mandy Medley, Carla Valadez, Nica Carrillo, Kellie Hultgren, Sheila Bayle, Timothy Otte, and Rob Keefe, for giving me a home and giving life to literature.

Thank you, Trevor Goodman, Jane Alison, Seth Satterlee, Lindsay Hill, George Boorujy, Ian McCutcheon, Jason Guder, and Mike Harvkey, for your friendship, teaching, and inspiration.

Thank you, Hanya Yanagihara, Garth Greenwell, and Dan Chaon, for being life-changing writers and generous readers.

Thank you, Mom and Dad, for everything.

This book would not exist without you, Julie. So thank you for taking me with you, for making it all worth it, and for being the best surprise of my life.